Marion F. H. Harmon

One Woman Wandering

Europe on Limited Means

Marion F. H. Harmon

One Woman Wandering
Europe on Limited Means

ISBN/EAN: 9783337194123

Printed in Europe, USA, Canada, Australia, Japan

Cover: Foto ©Andreas Hilbeck / pixelio.de

More available books at **www.hansebooks.com**

ONE WOMAN  WANDERING.

OR

EUROPE ON LIMITED MEANS.

BY

MARION FLOWER HICKS HARMON.

CINCINNATI
THE EDITOR PUBLISHING COMPANY
1899

TO THE LONE ONES IN THE LAND,
ESPECIALLY TO THE
SOLITARY SISTERS,
IS THIS
VOLUME
CORDIALLY DEDICATED.

CONTENTS.

ONE WOMAN WANDERING

CHAPTER I.

Not because I was especially fitted either by nature, education or habit, to paddle my own canoe, not because I had no desire for, or any objection to, a *compagnon du voyage*, did I suddenly determine last year to venture forth alone into the rushing tide of foreign travel that has of late periods set so strongly toward the Old World. But like many another woman I had been bereft of all that life and love hold dear, and at a mature age was left stranded solitary, with a slender though assured provision for that future which now stretched blankly before me. What could so completely occupy my attention and employ my energies as a trip abroad?

But was this among the possibilities? No ties had I to bind me here or elsewhere; no household to maintain in my absence; no reason why the modest sum necessary for my personal expenses should not be expended abroad instead of in my native land. Would this be sufficient? I began to investigate.

My first step was to write to various Tourist Agencies, whose name is legion, requesting such information as each could furnish concerning routes, rates, outfits, and the like. I may say in passing that I ever received most courteous attention to my inquiries. I thus accumulated a mass of material much of which was valuable, and my vague design began to take form and substance before me. My little fund would take me across, provide for my return in case of emergency, and keep me in unpretending comfort until I could receive supplies from home. But— I must go alone; I could pay no companion or guide. True, there were several excursions advertised to which my available cash would admit me as a member, but these were of but two or three months' duration and seemed to consist of one grand scramble from beginning to end, in making trains and taking wildly hurried glimpses of a few noted scenes and masterpieces. So I came to the conclusion that one could see and learn most by traveling independently, thus being hampered by no contracts or limits as to time and place. Could I do this all by myself, in a foreign land amid a foreign tongue, I who had lived all my life in the seclusion and protection of the home-circle? But the dear home-circle was forever vanished. Life was ended along that line. Wherever I might be I was alone and must live inexpensively; I was already fairly familiar with my own land. In Europe even commonplace environments would be new and interesting to me. I would go.

I did go and for many months wandered alone but safely through storied scenes and classic shades of varied beauty and interest, returning at last with a host of delightful recollections to beguile many an otherwise weary day, and with the resolve to promulgate as far as possible among the "lone sisters" in my own country, such practical knowledge of ways and means as I acquired myself in my journeyings, so that any one of them, finding through untoward events that the "days are dark and dreary," might feel it possible to take her courage in her hands and go and do likewise. And so I begin my record.

In almost any town of a few thousand inhabitants one may purchase a through ticket of the principal Steamship Companies, to almost any point abroad. I, however, took my ticket from one of the Tourist Agencies in order that I might feel at liberty to call upon the local office wherever I might be, for protection or advice, have the benefit of its banking facilities, bureaus of information and the like. This idea proved all right in the main, but at first, as I shall explain later, I had reason to believe that all my provisions in these respects were as unsubstantial as the baseless fabric of a dream. I did not take a passport as there are few European countries where they are essential, but in the light of my later experience, I should take one if going again, on account of the convenience as a means of identification when such becomes necessary. The cost, I believe is two dollars.

The Agency of which I finally bought my tickets, as an inducement for me to do so, promised to have a man meet me in Chicago to give me all necessary aid in transfer,—my starting point was about seven hours distant,—and another man at the New York terminus to take charge of myself and luggage, and to see that it and I were safely placed on board the steamship in good order and at no extra charge unless in the way of monetary exchange. These promises gave me great satisfaction, and it was well that they did, for it was all I had; inasmuch as, so far as attendance was concerned, this Agency, —I will not, as I might, take so cruel a revenge upon it as to publish its name abroad,—almost entirely failed to make good its engagements.

I descended from the train in Chicago, bag in hand, refusing offered attendance as I supposed I was provided for; but, trudging along over the long platform to the transfer 'buses, no sign of a tourist agent did I see. Inquiries right and left were of no avail. There was only one hour and three quarters between trains, but, though my ticket included transfer through Chicago I could not go directly on, because my money had not yet been converted into foreign funds, and I had still much promised instruction to receive. After a moment of indecision I took a 'bus to the Agency.

Perhaps my inexperienced countrywoman would like to learn that in Chicago all authorized transference facilities are in the hands of one organization, the Parmelee Line. In purchasing tickets that necessitate a change in Chicago, one should stipulate for a transfer coupon. Then, on presenting the same to any of Parmelee's men, who are always on hand, one has no difficulty in finding one's proper conveyance. On my doing this and stating that I wished to interview my tourist agent before going to the other station, the attendant kindly informed me that he would drop me at the right place *en route*. This he did, but by stopping I was of course obliged to lose the benefit of my coupon, besides having all the bother and uncertainty of looking up the agent.

But I found and sternly confronted him with my demand for advice and exchange. The official had the grace to seem surprised at my appearing there alone, and tried to explain that a man had been sent to meet me but "probably had got a little behind time."

Minutes were precious and I wasted none in reproaches but proceeded to business. The agent recommended putting the most of my funds in circular notes of English money, as available to be cashed in any foreign currency on presenting a letter of identification which he also gave me, at any place where I should be likely to go.

Reserving enough of the balance to provide for my expenditures to and in New York City, he put the remainder into French money as I was sailing on a French ship to a French port. At this date, an American, or rather, a United States' dollar was worth a little more than five French *francs*, four German *marken*, or four English shillings. Here let me warn my unsophisticated sister against ever confusing the English shilling with the value recognized under that name in the United States. The United States shilling is simply unheard of and unknown abroad, (as it ought to be at home for it does not exist in our money table) and wherever the term shilling is used it always, without exception, signifies the English shilling of twelve pence or twenty-four United States cents. I mention this because I saw so many cases where unfortunate Americans were hopelessly confused on account of persisting in using the term shilling to represent twelve and a half cents, to the great mystification of their foreign hearers.

Regarding exchange and letters of credit, any banker would do the service quite as well as a Tourist Agency, and in many cases it might be preferable to have it done at home by one's acquaintances; but, going alone as I was, I deemed it better, as I mentioned before, to have as much claim as possible on the attention of some well-known corporation as easily accessible abroad as at home. But all this is a matter of expediency.

I made particular inquiries of the agent, as to how to escape in New York the difficulties that had presented themselves in Chicago, as in New York I should be more helpless, never having embarked for a foreign tour and not knowing just what to do, nor even whether a woman alone would be capable of doing everything. But I was assured there was no possibility of my missing their man there, that the Company had men in uniform with the name of the Agency in large letters, to meet all trains, that I could not fail to see them, that everybody knew the agency-men, and moreover they had been advised to look out for me, and so on. So I departed comforted, with a man,—in this instance a nice, friendly lad,—detailed to put me on the New York train, see to my sleeper and so forth, all of which he did politely and efficiently, and I was soon rolling away toward New York.

The hours went on; night came and went and the darkness of the second evening closed in upon us, for not until eight P. M., were we within the confines of "the great city." A baggage-man appeared—as on all through trains nearing a terminus, to whom one may give one's checks with perfect safety, receiving a claim-ticket in return—and soon my luggage would be on its way to the steamer-docks where I would find it in the morning.

At eight forty-five, we stopped in the Grand Central Station of New York City. I walked out confidently expecting to be accosted at once by my promised messenger but, alas, he did not materialize. I looked about here and there, backward and forward, right and left, in fact in every direction except heavenward,—which last, in consideration of the nature of my past experiences, seemed futile to do,—but no one did I see who had apparently the least concern as to my welfare. No uniformed men except the trainmen and the red-capped porters, all of whom declared total ignorance concerning the agency-men, did not even know their uniform; such also was the result of my inquiries in the waiting rooms and at the Bureau of Information. The fact was that I had simply been allowed to arrive with no attention provided whatever. I dwell upon this point because the Agency had been so lavish in its proffers and promises both verbal and written, that I had had no anxiety whatever on leaving home, and had I not been warned by my experience in Chicago, should have relied on them implicitly. And I feel moved to declare that I consider the Agency's course as a culpable breach of confidence, from which the consequences in the case of an unaccustomed traveler, a lady, arriving alone at night in this great, modern Babel, might have been deplorable in nervous strain if nothing more. I will say that, some months later, I received a most polite letter of regret and apology from the Agency, but this, though gratifying, hardly served to atone for the neglect. Fortunately for me, I was in a measure familiar with the place, so I picked up my satchel and went across the street to a well-known hotel where I obtained a comfortable room on the parlor floor at one dollar a day without meals. In the restaurant attached, one may consider one's purse in ordering from the *menu*. The rates seem high to a resident of a town of thirty thousand inhabitants, and if one is desirous of keeping expenses down still farther, one may go out across the street to a most attractively bright and clean eating-house, where wholesome and appetizing food is served

at surprisingly moderate charges. All this for
the benefit of that "lone sister" whom I have
in my mind's eye in writing these lines.

At the hotel I tried to telephone the Tourist
Agency. "Office closed for the night," was
the report, so I betook me to my couch thinking
I should certainly get word in the morning· Of
course city offices are rarely open before nine,
A. M., but as the next was a "sailing morning"
the hotel manager thought I would find the
agency men on hand early. So I tried at seven,
A. M. "Closed." The steamer was to sail at
ten and I was I knew not how far away. At
any rate all the way from Forty-second street
zigzaggedly across the city to Morton's Pier.
No use to go personally to the office as it was
closed. The hotel manager was kind and interested and gave me as good advice as he possessed, but of course he could not speak with
authority. Finally, partly because time was
slipping away and partly because, in classic
phrase, "my spunk was up," I decided that if
worst had come to worst, I was equal to the
emergency of getting off for Europe alone, or
anywhere else, and that no effete tourist agent
should, by his indifference or inefficiency, com-
pel me to lose my passage, nor entail upon me
unneccessary additional expense. So, as economy was the order of the day, I did not even call
a cab but boarded a Fourth Avenue car. I knew
my way pretty well and was burdened only with
my handbag.

At Fourteenth Street I took a transfer to the
pier. When I presented my ticket to the trans-
fer-man he vociferated violently and offensively,
as if I were offering him a personal insult, "That
hain't no good! Yer gotto pay another fare!" I
was not at all appalled at his demeanor nor did

I "lose my head" or temper, though it certainly was not my fault that I had a wrong transfer nor had I objected to paying a second fare though entitled to transfer. I do not understand why these street-car employès are so ready to deem that a gentlewoman in appearance and speech deserves brow beating and crushing when she is merely trying to follow the routine of the road so far as she comprehends it; but such is too frequently the case and I only mention it here and my reception of the same, as a possible aid to the "solitary sister" when she "will a-wandering go." I let the fellow expend his rudeness without remonstrance and when he had quite ceased speaking I civilly asked him to kindly show me which car to take; he had evidently keyed himself up to receive a torrent of expostulation on my part, and when none came he seemed dazed for a moment, then acceded to my request in a manner comparatively calm, and I went on slowly but surely toward Morton Pier. I was the sole passenger when the car reached the end of the route and here it was my good fortune to encounter so kind and gentlemanly a young man, albeit in the guise of a conductor, that I almost felt like forgiving the before-mentioned surly brute in consideration of his being a co-employè of this young man. Of course he could not leave his car but he pointed out where I must go and told me just what to do and was so interesting and painstaking that if we had been, as I was later, in a foreign land, I should have "tipped" him well for his civility; as it was, I would not insult his manhood by offering to pay him for being polite to a woman.

It was now nine o'clock. Steamer to sail at ten. I rushed across the tracks, before and behind cars, carts and quadrupeds, ignoring the surprised glances of everybody at seeing a wandering woman dashing about utterly unattended in that busy and hubbubby place. I felt a sort of unholy glee in getting on so independently of that faithless agency man, who was probably at this moment reading his morning paper and toasting his toes at ease before his fire, imagining that I must await his pleasure. I made my way into the great building placarded, *Compagnie Général Atlantique*, where my smattering of French enabled me to read the signs and labels about, and I was able with few questions to get my luggage, send it aboard by means of three men whom I paid twenty-five cents each, (which payment I afterward learned was entirely unexpected and unnecessary,) and finally I walked up the gang-plank myself and stood upon the deck of *La Champagne*.

I have thus detailed these trivial incidents, not because of their interest but to give the "inexperienced sister" some idea of transportation at small expense. I rather enjoyed it on the whole, but if the "sister" is timid or nervous, she would better take a cab for the pier, at her hotel door. Rates are high and though the hotel manager will procure for one a trusty driver, it is quite necessary to have an explicit understanding as to terms, before one starts.

I will not deny that emotions of new and varied sorts filled my breast as I looked down from the deck upon the swaying crowds, the infinite diversity of faces and figures, the cabs coming and going, the incessant stream of ladies, gentlemen, porters, seamen, children, dogs and so forth, passing and repassing up and down the plank, and heard the continually repeated screeching of whistles and jangling of bells mingled with shouts and cries, with the rush and roll of carriage and cart, of barrel and cask, the dumping and thud of box and bale and chest and all the innumerable stock and store of a ship's cargo, and reflected that I had succeeded in "getting there" all on my own responsibility. And I began to felicitate myself that I alone had attended to everything and still had plenty of time. Then I noticed a party coming up with bags and bundles and steamer chairs.

Scissors and teapots! I had forgotten my steamer-chair! A glance at my watch,—nine twenty-five,—steamer sails at ten! Back again down the plank—a mad rush for the *bureau*—a wild demand in impossible French for the desired article. Rent, a United States "dollaire" for the round trip. No money but French—offer a five *franc* piece supposing it an equivalent— rejected as not enough—nothing else but gold— frantically hold out a handful, whereupon the *commissionaire* takes pity on me and pushes it back, accepting my silver piece and kindly saying in broken English: "Teez owanlee troah sonts, navaire mynde." Whereby I learn that the current value of a five *franc* piece at the *Bureau Transatlantique*, is ninety-seven cents; though if you offer a dollar for something valued at five *francs*, you get no change in return.

I hurriedly gave the man my name and sped back. Again looked at my watch; nine fifty. Plenty of time and everything really ready at last. Later on I find myself transformed by the label on my chair, into "Madame Heexheimer."

I may as well say here that this expense of a chair was in my case entirely unnecessary. It being winter, there was no especial temptation to sit on deck, as if one wished to be outside it was much pleasanter to move about. Moreover there were plenty of benches on deck if one chose to sit. I used my chair but twice, and then only because I thought it the regulation thing to do. As I had not decided to return by this line, I lost the benefit of my round trip payment and by engaging a chair I became liable to the deck-steward for a fee, whether service were rendered or not.

In summer, when there are many passengers and the weather is fine, a chair may be most desirable, but in this instance I might have made a clear saving of at least two dollars had I been familiar with the situation. I may note here also that since my outward bound passage, there has been a change in the method of renting these chairs and one now must pay a dollar a voyage instead of for round trip, as before. All of which I commend to the consideration of my imaginary "lone woman."

And now it is ten o'clock and the great steamer begins to quiver. We all know the couplet:

> "She moves, she stirs, she seems to feel
> A thrill of life along her keel!"

and a dozen other lines as apropos will spring to mind. The little tug was noisily doing its duty. The pier was a sea of upturned faces and waving handkerchiefs.

"Good-bye!"

"*Adieu!*"

"*Lebewohl!*"

"Good luck to you!"

"*Bon voyage!*"

"*Glueckliche Reise!*"

Some were laughing, some were in tears, all were excited, and a responsive throng on deck gave back farewell, smile and tear.

I stood apart. I was alone. The good-byes and good wishes were not for me. No one there knew of me. It was rather a melancholy thought; and yet there was a bright gleam of satisfaction in the reflection that, being there thus alone and by my own unaided efforts, I was under no sort of an obligation to waft even the most formal of farewells to that inert and ever elusive tourist agent.

CHAPTER II

At last we were abroad upon the mighty deep. Gradually we had made our way out from the slips, piers and docks and from the crowds of shipping of every description and nationality. Out away from the marvelous span of Brooklyn Bridge and from the majestic statue towering above the busy harbor and forever lifting toward high heaven the deathless torch of liberty. Out away between shores wharf-lined and covered as far as eye could reach with street on street of structure, lofty and low, proud and plebeian, rich and wretched, and permeated everywhere by seemingly the same restless, rushing, hurrying throng, until by and by the fields and hedgerows began to appear, pervaded even now with a faint, subtile shade of green; soon we passed the various isles that dot the harbor, the old fort on Staten Island standing out phenomenally distinct, and then suddenly the fog closes in and shuts out all the world. Reluctantly we abandon our posts of outlook and pass inside to make acquaintance with that interior where we shall eat, drink and sleep for so many days.

Surprising indeed is the spectacle we behold. All is bewilderment and confusion. Everybody seems to be in every other body's way. The poor people in the steerage, of whom we get occasional glimpses in our present futile attempts to find out "where we are at," are huddled together amid their forlorn "bits of things," like a flock of frightened sheep and look sad and pitiable. The second-cabiners are as yet unseparated from the first; everyone is more or less unsettled, even the old stagers,—or should I say "shippers?"—to whom a sea voyage is but the veriest episode. Shouts and commands in a foreign tongue and the inability of the ship's company to understand our American French, add to the general distraction. We find later that most of the crew speak good English, but this fact has not as yet dawned upon our perturbed brains. Bags and bundles of all sorts are heaped in apparently inextricable disorder, laying traps for unwary feet. Dogs and children are trotting about astray and lifting their several voices in howls in various keys and of varying intensity. Birds, large and small, are shrieking in dismay from divers and sundry cages, and amid all is heard the thud. thud of the steamer's machinery as it steadily beats out the revolutions that, God guiding, shall pause not nor delay till we reach the strange shores so far distant.

As a temporary diversion the cabin passengers are very soon summoned to an informal luncheon while the ship's force indefatigably toils to bring order out of chaos. And here may I caution my unsophisticated "solitary sister," as a possible preventive of sea-sickness, to partake sparingly through the first day at least, of the abundant and tempting fare provided on the great ocean-liners?

The striking of "deep water" is usually the crucial test of one's powers as a "good sailor," and one who escapes this ordeal will probably pass along almost unaffected to the other side.

The work goes untiringly on; wandering mortals find their cabins; weeping women are consoled and irate men pacified; timid passengers are encouraged, while stray children and pets reach their proper owners, and at last, by the time the electric lights leap forth and we are bidden to our evening meal, a semblance at least of order and regularity reigns in the brilliant dining-room, or *salle-à-manger*, as we are taught to consider it. The western continent has dropped below the horizon and we begin really and truly to be rocked in the cradle of the deep.

The first day out, as customary, we were each assigned a seat at table, and given a sailing list. Here I found I had undergone another transformation and was now figuring as "Mr. Hanson." Others, however, had similar surprises and it was like solving a puzzle to find out which name belonged to whom, and what it really should be instead of what it was. Different ships have different methods of arranging the sittings at table. On *La Champagne*, a very polite steward called at each stateroom door and asked if the occupants thereof had any choice as to seats; if so, they were gratified if possible, and to each person was handed a card with a number corresponding to that on his chair at table.

At my table are a *Mlle.*H.,of New York City, whose name is not on the list at all, a Mr. and Mrs. M.,of Berkeley, California, and a *Senor* U., of *Le Havre*. *Mlle.* H. and Mr. M. speak both French and English; Mrs. M., only English; Senor U., Spanish and French, so when we are all there we manage to keep up quite a continuous conversation, the learned ones interpreting for the less so. Scarcely anyone on a French steamer appears before *dejéuner*(pronounced "deh-zhoon-eh," with no accent,)a sort of heavy luncheon about eleven o'clock. The first repast is truly a "break-fast," being but a roll without butter, and a cup of "coffee with milk," served usually in one's cabin before one rises. There is, I understand, a meal called the "American breakfast," provided for such incorrigible natives as are unable to fall into foreign ways, but this is alien to the general atmosphere; individually, I took very kindly to the custom of keeping my berth until the first warning bell sounded half an hour before *déjeuner*.

It so chanced that *Senor* U. and myself usually appeared first at our table and frequently finished our meal before any of our table-mates came in. As he spoke neither English nor German and I had no Spanish and but a smattering of French, and as the politeness of his nationality, I suppose, would not permit him to sit in a lady's presence with no effort to entertain her, many desperate attempts were made by us to evolve some method of communication; but it all resolved mainly into an assiduous offering of each to the other of whatever was within our reach, accompanied by a series of "nods and becks and wreathéd smiles" whenever one caught the other's eyes. I shall always remember him as a most *painfully* courteous man, and I dare say he will long recollect his arduous endeavors in my behalf.

The table was excellent, served carefully in French *table d' hôte* style, that is, only one thing at a time, which I do not like, as I prefer my meat with my vegetables. Also I like butter on my bread and cream in my tea and coffee, which preferences astonish the French caterer. If he serves you with butter at all it is unsalted and given you upon a plate the size of the ordinary dinner-plate. If you insist on cream with your coffee, he brings you a concoction which he calls "*café-au-lait*" wherein the milk which does duty as cream, is boiled with the coffee, and with it he brings a tablespoon; I verily believe the French consider it a sort of soup. And as to tea, the drinking of it at all seems to be conceived as springing from a mild aberration of the English and the American mind, and one is looked upon with surprise, not to say suspicion, if one declines the *cognac* that is always brought on with it and the tiny cup of "black coffee" served at the close of dinner. Then again, I do not like wine of any sort as a beverage, especially the thin, sour *vin ordinaire* that is so universal and tastes very like poor vinegar. Nor am I especially fond of the cheeses and sauces which are served so abundantly, but of course all this soon becomes a matter of custom.

It seemed odd to have knife, fork and plate removed with each article of food. I will not deny having been accustomed to the ordinary changes between courses, but the fashion of having as many plates, knives and forks as there are articles on the bill of fare, was new to me. Nor did I ever before see ice-cream made into a large roll, like butter, and passed about on a platter, each person helping himself and being provided with a desert spoon for consuming it. I do not remember ever before having seen snails on a *menu*, so I thought I would try some. The *garçon* brought me a plateful apparently *au naturel* in their shells and looking "quite too awfully" snaily. He brought with them an implement suggestive of Hamlet's bare bodkin, with which one is supposed to manipulate the shells to get at their contents. I made one or two attempts, then finally begged the waiter to prepare them for me, which he deftly did, bringing them back *sans* shells and looking exactly like a tiny "mess o' greens." I tasted them and found them delicious in spite of preconceived prejudices.

Our dinners are quite long in course and served about seven in the evening. Lights are generally extinguished in the *salon* about eleven; in our staterooms we have the privilege, not always granted on ship-board, of turning the electricity off and on to suit our convenience, but a placard most politely worded requests us to use our illumination as sparingly as possible.

So hour after hour goes on monotonously enough, and day after day finds us, our little community of some four or five hundred souls, struggling onward in this wide waste of waters where for days and nights we are encompassed by the same unchanging, impenetrable, white mist. The great fog horn sounds at intervals of one minute, night and day. Once forth from out the darkness comes a response, but where away in that vast, outstretching region of cloud and mist there rides another vessel.we have no means of knowing. Strong head-winds that yet have no perceptible effect on the density of the fog, make our progress difficult and slow.

The huge waves roar and rave and thunder around, below and above us and beat at our ship's sides, but she is staunch and they do not enter. At last, one night we hear an unusual shock, the vessel shakes and shivers, settles herself again, then quivers laterally and from end to end. I feel sure that we have run down something and, lying there in my snug cabin, I try to picture the scene without on the dark, tossing ocean. But though there is some increase of hoarse commands and heavy, hurried footsteps above, I hear no alarm and address myself again to sleep. In the morning we learn that we have lost a part of our screw and from

that time on, we have a sort of compound wiggle
and jiggle and jerk added to the ordinary roll and
tumble of a steamer in difficult seas, which is
rather too much for the equanimity of many of
our company. Our ship labors bravely on however and all is well save the inevitable cases
of *mal-de-mer* which one, of course, expects.
Our *salle-à-manger* is mostly deserted, by the
ladies especially,

Personally I escape all illness, which is a matter of surprise and congratulation. Even while
the steamer rises to meet the oncoming wave, or
pitches downward into the trough of the bil-
lows, or rolls from side to side, am I able to
stand either above on deck or below at the port-
holes which are continually first plunged into
the depths and then lifted dizzily aloft, and to
gaze out on the "multitudinous seas" as they
swell and sweep and wrestle and leap and break
into feathery spray far heavenward, and to enjoy the spectacle and marvel over its beauty.

At length one evening we note that the
"dead-lights" are down and at dinner the tables are a network of racks and bars to keep the
dishes in place, which all betokens heavier
weather. We make inquiries and find we are
about to enter the "Devil's Hole," which is always, as they term it, "a nasty place." All
this time we have scarcely seen the sun. Ever
the same white, cottony fog, with the green
waves breaking through to grin at us. I begin
to realize what it must have been when the
"earth was without form and void." We are
told that the voyage is always tiresome and difficult at this time of the year until we get away
from the "Banks of Newfoundland,"—not meaning the shores of that country but certain areas
of the ocean.—after which we shall probably

have smoother seas and fairer skies: and if we can only escape the clutches of His Satanic Majesty while invading his "Hole" to night, to-morrow we may hope for better things. So we go on and on and on.

Day comes again and we find we have left the Devil behind us and by the next day the fog lifts and the sun appears. Not long does he bless us, however, for it comes on to rain, and thus almost continually under cloud and storm do we make our passage. We see a steamer on a distant track and exchange salutes. We learn many days later that shortly after leaving us she encountered a waterspout which we barely escaped. We have no excitement. We see no whales nor icebergs. There is little or nothing to distinguish one point of time from another except the daily posting of the ship's progress in the main companion-way, and the setting forward of our watches forty minutes each noontide.

Very strange it seemed day after day to see only the same persons, to do only the same things and to move about only in the same places. *La Champagne* is a very comfortable, somewhat luxurious, but not very modern vessel. To my surprise there is neither reading-room nor library. I am told there is none on any of the French liners though a little cupboard on *La Champagne*, containing perhaps fifty volumes of French and English novels which one may purchase at fifty cents each, is dignified by that name. We are, of course, cut off from newspapers and it really becomes a matter of charity in one possessed of any sort of literature, to circulate it among his or her needy neighbors.

Judging from my own experience and the difficulty I had in obtaining really suitable and practical suggestions regarding an outfit that

should be sufficient but not superfluous, I fancy
my imaginary "woman and sister" may desire
to know something about what is necessary
for such a journey as mine. Let her bear in
mind that a ship is the merest atom of light and
warmth upon the awful ocean, and that the
ocean is always cold. Moreover, there forever
do "the winds their revels keep." I found, as
nearly every inexperienced ocean-traveler does
find, that I took much more than I needed.
One's traveling garb should be as heavy as one
can wear without weariness. One will need in
winter, leggins and 'overshoes and close, warm
underclothing. Tights are almost indispensable.
A hot-water-bag is also very desirable. A long,
loose outer garment with hood attached and fur-
lined, is most convenient, as is also a similar
garment or "domino" of light weight, likewise
with hood, which one can wear about if one is
ill, without troubling with hair-dressing. One
needs a warm steamer-rug and one or two private cushions are very comfortable. The rug
may be represented perfectly by a large blanket-
shawl. Of course if one could count on never
being ill, many of these provisions would be
superfluous; but on this point one can never be
assured and must prepare accordingly. If one
is ill, the quickest and usually the only way to
recover is to be out on deck regardless of
weather or inclination. Frequently one must
be carried above by stewards and placed comfortably and safely in a sheltered nook to let the
cold, pure sea-winds do their reviving work.

The cabins at best are but stuffy places.
There are none with but one berth and to one's
own distresses may be added the moving spectacle of a room-mate in serious case. So I consider full equipment for warmth and comfort on

deck, to be a necessity, though thus far I have not needed it myself. My cabin held two berths, but on account of the season of the year, I was able to occupy it alone, to my never-ceasing thankfulness. I took my steamer-trunk, my two grips and my roll of wraps into the cabin with me but I should never do so again. If I had had a room-mate, I do not know where her things could have rested. I find that one gets out of one's cabin as soon as possible after rising, and elaborate toilets are uncalled for.

Perhaps it is as well to have a light waist or two accessible in case of an evening concert or other entertainment, such as are frequently gotten up if the voyage is reasonably pleasant. But the woman to whom I am specially addressing myself is not going abroad to display her wardrobe, or as a little friend of mine once remarked, to "cut a gash," and I think she will be relieved to take as little as possible. I have known ladies going abroad for a summer vacation to take only a bicycle dress and a traveling gown. The woman traveling with an escort, or a young girl properly chaperoned, might find it no trouble to have a little more variety, but it is not necessary and some question whether it be good taste. I learned the lesson to send in future everything unessential, to the hold.

Baths, of course, may be had on application to the steward. While these are not extra in themselves, a tip is due to the attendant at the end of the voyage. One may patronize the steamer hair-dresser or do one's locks one's self; but let me warn my sister with a "bang," that no hair-curling appliances are allowed in the cabins, and when we consider what an unspeakable horror is a fire at sea, I know that none of us will question the wisdom of this regulation.

Besides the bath-room steward and the hair-dresser, the other attendants on the usual ocean-liner are the stewardess—who will wait upon you if you desire but who does not attend to your cabin—the bedroom steward, the deck steward and the dining-room steward, that is your special waiter at meals.   A steamship is usually divided into sections, each of which has its own retinue of servants.   In *La Champagne*, a vessel of eight thousand tons, there were two sections. Of course a passenger is under no obligations as to tips to those serving in any section but his own.   If one requires much service, one is supposed to tip more liberally than otherwise, but what has become an established custom so far as I could learn, is to present one's stewardess, one's table steward and the deck steward each with about two dollars and a half on leaving the ship.

In my case on *La Champagne*, the stewardess had no occasion to perform any service whatsoever for me, but she received my tip on the morning of debarkation with all the serenity of long-tried and deserving merit.

And again in regard to one's outfit, let the "lone female" also remember that in France and other "warm countries," the houses are cold and damp though the outer air may be soft and mild, so that it becomes more essential than with us, to dress warmly within doors, particularly at night. A warm bedroom-gown and slippers are really a necessity the greater part of the year.

Of course I do not learn all these items at once, but as I go along; if they lighten up the matter for any who may come after me, I shall be well pleased.

But we were getting on, and lo! one evening,

. away off over the heavy expanse of waters could be seen a tiny gleam of light that alternately shone and disappeared. Yes, there was the long looked-for beacon, there were the Scilly Isles, there was solid land after these many days.

That last evening, according to a time-honored custom, was served what is called "the Captain's dinner," though in reality given by the transportation company, at which unusual delicacies are spread, with unlimited champagne. Mirth and good-fellowship abound, and with the dessert on the present occasion was served an assortment of fancy "pop-crackers" which, on being pulled out, developed into a collection of fantastic head-riggings, high and low caps of all varieties, sombreros, capotes, helmets, and the heads of all sorts of animals. Each person donned his own, and we all marched about the *salon* in majestic style at the close of the feast.

The next morning the shores of France, snow-covered and looking in the distance much like the southern shores of Lake Superior, were distinctly visible on the right, and a few hours later, on the left, also. The bold outlines of *Le Havre* soon rose to view and we entered the wide harbor with its great solid piers and massive masonry.

To our intense disappointment the tide was out and it became necessary to land us in a tender. We watched it putting out from the pier, dancing up and down through the waves and seeming indeed like the veriest toy in comparison with the huge steamer on which we stood.

The transference was a long and most tedious process. First came the steerage passengers from below. Such a "motley crew," with bundles of clothes and bedding and household effects. Poor things, they looked pale and ill; no doubt

our rough voyage which had so tried even us who
were more comfortably lodged and fed, had
caused them to suffer severely.   Then the occupants of the second cabin, who were most respectable in appearance.   Last, the "first classers"
were called upon to "walk the plank."

It was not the pleasantest thing imaginable,
either, to step out upon the swaying, bobbing
concern that hung from our deck down to that
of the little steamer below us, rising and falling
with her as she courtesied to the motion of the
waves which rolled all too apparently beneath,
while a bitter wind tugged wildly at us as if to
tear us from our slender support. But we all did
it somehow, and were stowed away more or less
comfortably on camp-chairs or benches or rolls
of luggage, as the case might be.   .

Now, we supposed, we should soon be on
shore, but to our inexpressible disgust, we were
taken around to the other side of our ship, and
there we had to wait, shivering and sneezing, until the whole amount of luggage from hold and
cabins was transferred to the tender.   Why this
could not have been done first and the passengers taken on afterward, no one deigned to explain.

But now at last we are really in motion once
more, and dance along over the choppy waves
toward the wharves of *Le Havre*.

High and picturesque the city lies back from the
sea, with long lines of streets handsomely built
after an old-world fashion, stretching away over
the heights.   Upon these heights, we are told,
are the residences of the aristocracy, and the
home of the president of the republic is pointed
out to us.   One of my co-voyagers, a young lady,
exclaims: "Oh, do see the cute little French soldiers."

Surely enough, there they go marching down past the pier in their gay red and blue uniforms. Like boys they look, and boys, I presume, most of them are.

Our steamer is behind time and there is not much bustle over our arrival. We reach the pier, we mount the landing, and at last, after nine long days, once more we

> ———"take our stand
> On land, on solid land,"

albeit it is here covered with a moist unpleasant slush.

The claiming of luggage now takes place, a proceeding tiresome and, to the United States mind accustomed to checks, entirely unnecessary. They who, like myself, have through tickets to Paris, are saved this trouble as our packages went on in the special train which met us here. It was now about four o'clock and we could not reach Paris before midnight, so Mr. and Mrs. M. and myself decided to stay in *Le Havre*. Accordingly we filed through one door into a waiting room which is indeed fitly named, as here we were obliged to wait a long time for our turn to have our hand-bags examined and to declare that we had no tobacco or silver; whereupon an attendant, in my case a fat, old woman, marked each piece with a chalk design, and we filed out again at an opposite door and into the street, where we stood for a few moments taking in our first impressions of an alien climate and a foreign shore.

CHAPTER III.

It was, on the whole, difficult to realize that
we were really in France. In the first place,
everything was heavily covered with snow, and
this, I think, does not accord with one's mental
pictures of France, *la belle*, the land of vintage
and perfume. To be sure, we were in the far
north; to the south might smile verdant slopes
and sunny skies. Then again, the throng of
"raggedy men" and boys about the landing
seemed much the same as at home; although
they spoke excitedly in a foreign tongue and
gesticulated in a foreign manner, the general
effect was very similar. Our boat having been
late, there were no vehicles awaiting us, and for
the novelty of it we decided to walk on to seek
a hotel, a small boy offering to carry our bags,
pressing into service another little lad who
"wanted to go along because he was his brother."

Off we went through the slush, the narrow
streets reminding one of Old Boston; but the
stalls of flowers here and there amid the snow,
and the bareheaded women running about everywhere with, at most, but a muslin cap upon the
head, did not seem at all familiar. Girls, men
and boys were laughingly pelting each other
with snow-balls in an eagerness and enjoyment
that betokened an infrequent pastime.

Far to the left, overlooking the harbor and
the open sea, is the great Hotel Frascati, famous
for its baths and general festivities, and a favorite resort for both French and foreign in the
season. We crossed a great stone bridge, skirted

around queer and angling corners, and soon came to a fine street with buildings of quaint but good architecture. We learn afterward that it is the *Rue de Paris* and that it stretches straight on, a beautiful avenue, to that city.

Following it we came to a little park; trees, statues, fountain and flower-stalls all looking out from the snow. This is the *Place Gambetta* fronting which stands our hotel.

It was dark when we reached it. Bare and chill enough seemed the tile-paved little rotunda in which was the *bureau*, or office, poorly lighted and with no perceptible heat. We were shown directly to our rooms, being preceded up the long, twisty, cold staircase, by a maid bearing, to my amazement, a solitary candle.

Mr. M., who had been abroad before and was familiar with foreign "tricks and manners," was much amused at the horrified expression of his wife and myself. There was no elevator, they being only in the new and modernized places that are largely patronized by Americans. The house itself was stately and imposing, but sadly deficient, to the modern idea, in convenience and comfort. The hostess—it is always a hostess in the true foreign hostelry,—told us the building was an old mansion of a noble family and built in the early part of the century, but had been used as a public house for about forty years. While the ceilings were exceedingly high and the walls adorned with frieze and arabesque in classic style, yet the passages—they could not be called halls,—were narrow and crooked and floor-clothed with something that looked like heavy, brown wrapping-paper. We noted a curious arrangement of folding panels in several of the rooms and were told that many of them were originally one, and had been, in the course of events, made so that they might be shut off or thrown again into one, at will. For a generation perhaps, however, they had not been disturbed.

There was no light above the ground-floor,—which, by the way, is never the "first floor," as with us,—except by candles, (and these an "extra") and no heat unless specially ordered.

There happening to be but two chambers vacant on what we would call the second floor. the larger was given to my companions, and truly, it was a spacious apartment, I should think about twenty by thirty feet. The glittering white walls were chastely and beautifully ornamented in high relief; two great windows overlooking the park in front were composed of tiny panes and opened outward down the middle, as most foreign windows do. The wide mantle was of the whitest of marble tastefully sculptured, and all this space and grandeur was illuminated(!) by one little candle.

Mr. M. quickly perpetrated the great extravagance of ordering in two more, and a fire to be lighted in the tiny fireplace beneath the grand mantel, and we really felt quite festive. We were pleased to learn that these candles were the "very latest improved" and considered most superior in that they had each three holes down the center, "which obviated the dripping of the wax and secured a perfect draught." The idea of improving candles in this day and generation, tickled alike the fancies of Wisconsinite and Californians.

I now retired to my chamber across the passage. I had not so much magnificence as my neighbors and I had but one candle. I did not believe that any number of "improved" candles could give as much light as one good lamp, so I inquired if I might have one.

"Ah! no. Madame, the hostess, was desolated, but there were none in the house; they were so very dangerous!" Then I resolved, as an experiment, to find out how much one really could see with one candle as our forefathers and mothers must often have done in the "good old days." So by its flickering flame I essayed to take a survey of my apartment.

The floor was dark, bare with the exception of a heavy, soft rug before the bed, and polished to a perilous degree. My feeble luminary did not penetrate to the ceiling above. I groped my way to a kind of oblong structure with a marble slab on top, which stood at one side. Its use I could not conjecture but it suggested nothing so much as one of the old tombs around Trinity Church in New York City. Next came a quaint, narrow little table with spindly legs and a drawer. In this drawer were writing materials and a printed form in which "*M. M., les voyageurs*" were prayed "to have the goodness to be willing to fill up the blanks with names, surnames, ages, professions, birthplaces, habitual residences," and so forth and so forth. It was farther explained that this was "for the benefit of the police."

This made me feel "sort o' creepy," and as if some "Old Sleuth" might be upon my guilty track. Conquering my quakings, however, I proceeded. Next was an odd sort of toilette-table, marble-topped and with a folding lid, mirror-lined, which might be shut down over the top of the concern. In the morning I discovered another mirror on the wall but this was now lost in the gloom. There was the tiniest ewer and basin imaginable for their purpose, towels the same, soap-dish but no soap, (there never is any) and a bottle of drinking water; no ice to be seen and none to be had on demand.

Close to the bed was a queer little piece of furniture, solid, square and also marble-topped, which I afterward learned was styled a *table de nuit*, though it looked nothing like a table; this, of course, was for one's candle.

And then came the bed itself. It was a peculiar looking affair. High above it, showing faintly out from the obscurity, was a round canopy from which depended long, full curtains of a dusky red looped away in front. The bedstead was heavy and solid, and resembled a huge box on casters, though not wide enough for two occupants. It was built up with a sort of upholstered mattress and bolster, to a height nearly equal to my own. These were covered in a kind of gray damask linen and over this were linen sheets resembling homespun. Then blankets and spread as customary but over all this an immense cushion, in fact what the small boy might term "a young bed," of feathers or down, covered in red. As there was no way of heating my chamber, this cushion looked very comfortable to me, though extremely odd. A chair or two completed the furnishings so far as I was able to discern, and everything was most daintily fresh and clean. I then tried first to read, next to write by the candle but failed utterly. I will add here from after experience, that before my return a year later, I acquired the power to do both with perfect ease, and frequently used a candle in preference to gas. So much for one's environment. But now, as I had been kindly invited by my neighbors to sit at their fire, I took my candle and bore it in to swell their state, and in the light of the four, and the glow of the coals we sat in a semi-circle about the hearth stone and talked of our native land.

CHAPTER IV.

Next morning about eleven, we met at *dé-jeuner* which, as I noted before, is the first regular meal a Frenchman takes, having his *café-au lait* and *petit pain*, or roll, in his chamber at whatever hour he desires. At meals he drinks nothing but wine. But Mrs. M. and I could not accustom ourselves to the wine, so she ordered tea and I coffee. In paying our bill, we were surprised to find these charged as "extras." As the price of the wine was reckoned in with that of the meal, we had the privilege of paying for all these beverages. The charges at the hotel seemed light, but when in addition to the cost of my room, (eighty cents,) I had paid for service, twenty cents; candle, twenty cents; given a tip to maid and man, and still had had no fire nor serviceable light, I concluded I would rather pay United States prices and enjoy United States comforts. I was reminded of James de Mille's laughable exposition in his *The Dodge Club*, of the foreign system of charges and the schemes by which his characters protected their purses; one of which consisted in carrying off on their departure all the candle-ends in their rooms. I had not come to this as yet, however, so I left my pieces of improved illuminator to be charged up again to the next traveler.

Going out into the pleasant street, we were soon taking a drive in a comfortable carriage in which three, its full capacity, were allowed to ride as cheaply as one. Our coachman proved sociable and we picked up some bits of informa-tion, not all new, but yet interesting.

Havre, or *Le Havre*, as the French call it, is a large and flourishing city of about one hundred and seventeen thousand inhabitants and, next to Marseilles, the most important town in France. It has extensive ship-building yards and sugar-refineries. It was formerly called *Havre de Grâce*, from a chapel of *Notre Dame de Grâce* founded by Francis I., in 1516, which is still to be seen in the *Rue de Paris*. The city has be-come much modernized of late, and has many fine edifices and wide, beautiful boulevards.

Bernardin St. Pierre, the author of *Paul and Virginia*, was a native of Havre and an artistic monument to his memory stands in the *Rue de Paris*.

Some very handsome official buildings stand upon the *Rue de Strasbourg*, which stretches from the railway station on the east to the sea on the west.

The harbors and docks of this port are espec-ially fine. At the principal dock, the *Bassin de l'Eure*, the huge transatlantic steamers lie at ease within its fifty acres area. This was ten years in construction and finished in 1856. The *Bas-sin du Roi* was excavated in 1669. The *Canal de Tancarville* was opened in 1887 and connects the Seine directly with this harbor and enables ships to escape the tidal wave in the estuary.

There are two cable railways and three elec-tric tramways running out to points of interest, and little steamers ply three or four times daily to watering-places near by; all seem to be well patronized.

On reaching the station we were permitted, on account of holding through tickets, to pass through and to enter our train without delay.

Funny little coaches we saw, of first, second and third class. In France, we learn, no one rides third class who can in any way acquire the price of the higher grade.

We were about to take an ordinary first-class carriage when we were told that by paying one *franc* extra, (everywhere an extra!) we might occupy a coach with a toilette-room. So to avail ourselves of this great privilege,—free to the poorest who rides in the United States,— we each disbursed our *franc* and stepped into the carriage designated, which stood at a level with the platform; and conveyances of this sort are fitly named "carriages."

It may chance that the "sister" for whom these lines are written has no clearer idea than I had myself, of the continental car, so I will describe this one which seemed to be regarded as the acme of convenience.

We first note how small all the carriages are. Those with toilette-room are a trifle larger. A door on each side with window in upper half gives entrance and we find at the rear end two double seats like the usual horse-carriage seat, nicely upholstered in smooth, gray cloth, as are the walls of the vehicle itself.

Opposite the further seat and separated from it by the width of the door, is another double seat, and by the side of this a single one resembling a comfortable easy-chair. The occupants of these three places must ride backward. On each side of the door-windows is another of like size and all are lifted or lowered as the ordinary carriage-window may be, that is, by straps, and there are also straps as in carriages, by which to hold on. Curtains of soft blue cloth are looped back from the windows. In the center of the carriage-roof is a small, red lamp of about two-candle power, which is all the light to be had in the darkest night. Around this another blue curtain is arranged to be drawn in case the traveler finds this illumination too brilliant for his comfort! Heat to a moderate degree, is supplied from below through a perforated strip of metal on which we rest our feet.

The compartment contained but seven places. Immediately at the left of the entrance on the right was a narrow lane leading forward, passing the wonderful toilette room, which, by the way, was of the most primitive kind, though containing a good but small mirror,—and along by a sort of inner compartment shut off by itself, which I presume corresponds to the "stateroom" in our sleepers at home. I caught a glimpse of the four occupants, all it would accommodate, as I glanced down the lane, and they did look funny enough shut up there in a box within a box. But I dare say they were quite content, inasmuch as they were thus divided from the "vulgar herd" as represented by four ladies and three gentlemen in the rear section.

Smoking, it seems, is allowed in any of these carriages except a few reserved for ladies alone. Indeed I do not know but that it would be allowed there should any of the "lone females" desire the solace of the weed, but I presume in fact, that excluding men virtually excludes smokers. By the way, I have heard that there is a mild prejudice prevailing against these carriages, ladies seeming to feel that there is a suspicion of "old-maidism" attached to the occupants thereof, and often declining to enter the same for fear of falling under the ban. All these different styles of compartment are to be found usually in one train, so, reversing the old adage, "you takes your choice and you pays your money."

But now we are off and we speed away with a gentle motion, very comfortable. We see no conductor nor news-boy and are absolutely undisturbed. All the excitement we have is occasioned by a violent altercation that takes place between three of our fellow-passengers. One, a stout, ruddy gentleman whom we English-Americans would unhesitatingly dub a German, but who was a citizen of the United States and deemed himself an "American" to the core, had been a passenger with us on our voyage. He also had stopped at the same hotel and was proceeding to Paris. The two others were a French lady and gentleman, probably residents in the vicinity. The stout man in conversing with Mr. M., dwelt forcibly and at length on the superiority of everything American, and evidently his remarks were understood and resented by the French couple, for suddenly, without warning and with the greatest vehemence, they burst into the conversation, but in French, and presumably threw down the gauntlet of all France before the champion of America.

He apparently with alacrity picked up the same, and then they had it back and forth, "hot and heavy," shouting, gesticulating, hurling at one another scathing glances of ineffable defiance and disdain, and seemingly on the point of coming to blows then and there. We watched them amazed, while Mrs. M. and I consulted as to the expedience of trying to interfere, when quite as suddenly their fury moderated, their voices modulated, and soon they were smiling blandly upon one another, exchanging gracious bows and probably also the most elaborate of compliments.

We are fairly under way and have gotten out

of the suburbs. How strange it seems, looking out at our first stop, to see the historic and poetic name of Harfleur above the station door! But its glories are departed and little is left of interest except a fine Gothic church attributed to Henry V., of England. Thirty-one miles from Havre we come to Yvetot, recalling that "King of Yvetot little known to fame," who "slept exceeding well without glory."

We find less snow as we ride eastward, the country appearing much like the less mountainous portions of our eastern states. It looks somber and sere, but as we go farther inland the landscape brightens and the trees lose their shivery air. Picturesque homesteads with farm-buildings clustered closely about, mostly of neat, red brick nicely painted and picked out in contrasting colors, are seen on every hand, and occasionally an ancient, stone windmill comes into view, of the type familiar in their geographies to school-children, and totally unlike the modern water-pumping variety. These mills are round at base and conical in shape and have four great wings extending in as many directions. A Frenchman who has recently entered,—for our warlike couple has departed, —tells us that the mills are relics of the old-time, Holland occupation of this region, and are used even yet to grind grain.

The country looks more and more prosperous and picture-like as we go on. Trim hedges and tidy fields, everything cared for in the highest degree; no waste nor débris anywhere, all things betokening the small and careful land-holder.

Soon a hateful tunnel shuts off the scene, but as we emerge and near Rouen, the valley of the Seine with the great river winding along through the midst of it, lies about us in unspeakable loveliness. We seem to be in a sort of gigantic basin, the rim of which is the low, circling hills not thickly covered with trees.

How silvery and serene the river looks as we gaze out and see it stretched away for miles in the distance. How gently it flows between its fertile shores and the quaint hamlets clustered here and there in cozy nooks along its banks.

Now rise into view the spires and domes of a great city. We come nearer and nearer. 'Tis Rouen, with its wealth of medieval architecture and its grand, Gothic cathedral, some parts of which date back to 1207. There is a singular incongruity, unsymmetrical in plan yet beautiful as a whole, about the various portions of this famous edifice. One lofty and graceful pinnacle, we are amused to learn, is called the Tower of Butter, from having been erected with the money paid for indulgences to eat butter in Lent.

This is the old town that bade defiance to Henry V., of England, and Henry IV., of France, "centuries ago." All this is too much for Mr. and Mrs. M. to resist; they are fascinated and leave the train to go on later. I, however, prefer to journey to Paris by daylight, so I do not stop.

At first I do not seem to have gained much for we almost immediately plunge into a series of tunnels; but on reaching daylight once more, we have yet another surprisingly beautiful view of Rouen and the shining river. Then we cross and re-cross the Seine and rush again through tunnel after tunnel to my great chagrin, for I do not like to lose a bit of the charming landscape.

But we come out again and once more skirt the Seine. Yonder on the hills rising from the river may be seen the old church of *Bon Secours*. All along here are interesting reminders of the ancient, close intermingling of the French and the English. Only ten miles away, at Les Andelys, are the ruins of Castle Gaillard, erected by Richard Lion-Heart. It afterward became a state-prison and in 1314 Margaret of Burgundy, wife of Louis X., was murdered there. It was destroyed in 1663 by Henri IV.

At Vernon is a conspicuous tower built by Henry I. of England. We pass through Mantes where, by falling off his horse, William the Conqueror received the injuries from which he died at Rouen in 1087.

We continue to skirt the river with ever changing, ever delightful views. We come to Poissy, the birthplace of Louis IX., "St. Louis," whose memory is held so sacred in parts of our own country to-day. At Poissy was held the great conference in 1561, between the Roman Catholics and the Protestants, from which was hoped so much but realized so little.

Still we cross and re-cross the river, for the last time however at Asinières, one of the environs of Paris and a favorite resort for boating, and the like, in the season. Next comes Clichy, another suburb though containing more than thirty-one thousand inhabitants. Now we pass through the fortifications, for Paris is a walled city; then through the last tunnel, under the *Place de l' Europe*, and enter the station St. Lazare.

Here stepping from the train we give up our tickets at the gate, foreign fashion, and at last, after twelve days' pilgrimage, do I reach the end of my long journey and find myself in Peerless Paris.

CHAPTER V.

And now what shall I say of Paris? Paris, so
storied and sung from time immemorial. So
exalted and so abased, so joyous and so dis-
tressed, so brilliantly prosperous and so crush-
ingly ruined, by turns, throughout its whole
marvelous existence since first the Roman con-
querors set foot within its borders.

Not for me has been left the part to recount
its mutations, nor to depict its glories and dis-
asters, either past or present.

Travelers of to-day, even as did the adventur-
ous wanderer of the dim past, seek Paris as the
needle seeks the pole, while readers of to-day
have spread before them an embarrassment of
literary riches from which to select at will.
Enough be it for me to relate how it befell one
wandering woman within the confines of this
wondrous city.

My first glimpse of Paris was from the third
floor of the great caravansary that almost surrounds the *Gare St. Lazare.* One leaves the
train, goes through a gateway, and instead of
passing into the open street, comes directly into
this mammoth edifice.

It was nearly dark when I arrived and by the
time I had taken some refreshment and been assigned a room, the day was done. I could not
as yet realize that I was in Paris any more than
in any other large city. The huge hotel with
its spacious *salons,* electric service, lifts and
English-speaking servants, seemed familiar
enough. True, neither the queer, high, French

bed with its close curtains, its bolster and great feather cushion, nor the candles on the mantel (to supplement the electricity!) are, so far as my observation goes, to be seen in the United States. Neither are we obliged there to pass an examination in our personal history, on registering; nor are we, after paying for service and attendance specially itemized in our bills, expected to present the servants continually with small coin, unless indeed we choose to ape foreign customs; but otherwise the "altogether," as Trilby might say, differed little from like hotels at home.

On reaching my chamber I hastened to part the window-curtains and gaze down upon the great thoroughfare below. The impression of vast space was astonishing. The wide area beneath stretched out and away, leading off in all directions into broad, bright avenues through all of which multitudes of persons riding, driving, wheeling, walking, were passing to and fro with celerity and ease, yet with no crowding nor jostling. It was raining gently and the army of umbrellas moving swiftly along in the brilliantly illuminated expanse, viewed from above at that height, produced a peculiar effect, as of a remarkably lively company of ebony-hued mushrooms out for a promenade. The intense radiance of innumerable lights reflected back from the smooth, wet, glistening pavement, and the buoyant mien of the quickly shifting throngs in no wise depressed by the falling drops, gave an air of animation and festivity to the spectacle that was striking.

The current of my cogitations had been continually interrupted by an annoying "click-click," and I now turned to investigate the cause. Following the sound, I discovered an upright object perhaps fifteen inches high upon the mantel. It possessed a glass face and two short metal bars that jumped forward about an inch at every click, seemingly causing the same. I tried to open the face and arrest the motion, but in vain. Then it occurred to me that I might tilt the concern up sidewise and thus by throwing its machinery out of balance, perhaps stop the clicking.

It was very heavy but after many struggles I succeeded in moving it a couple of inches when, to my dismay, I found it to be attached in some way to small, colored worsted ropes that disappeared mysteriously into the wall behind. I began to think that it must be some sort of a secret registering-machine ''for the benefit of the . police,'' and almost expected that my unwarranted interference with the affair, would bring down vengeance in some unforseen manner upon my unprotected head.

But nothing worse ensued than the continued persistence of the maddening ''click-click,'' which all night long resounded in my ears and did most effectually ''murder sleep.'' The next morning, being still alive and uninjured, I hastened to the hotel-office to ascertain the nature of this ''infernal machine.'' I was relieved to learn that it was ''only an electric clock,'' and would be stopped if I desired; so after that I slept in peace.

The modest tourist with limited means will not stay very long in quarters so public and expensive as the great hotels; though I will say that, all things considered, the prices range from a surprisingly low figure. For instance, one may get a room in most of them for four *francs* a day, or a little less than eighty cents, but one must pay from one to two and one half *francs* a day for light. In the present case, I paid five *francs* for my chamber which though small was very comfortable, even luxurious. It is not necessary to take any meals in the house, but the ordinary charges at the *table d' hôte* for the first meal or "little breakfast,"—to translate literally,—consisting of coffee or tea with bread and butter, is from twenty to fifty cents; *déjeuner*, about ninety-seven cents, and dinner, from one dollar and a quarter to a dollar and sixty cents. Of course by ordering extras, one may swell the amount unlimitedly.

All these hotels also have restaurants attached where one may be served very well indeed, by the card, and where one's meal may be more specially adapted to one's purse; but the prudent traveler will seek out some less pretentious place to regale the inner individual and it is surprising how satisfactorily one may be served for a small sum even in the great city of Paris.

The most continuous drainage upon one s purse in these large hotels, and the most annoying because of one's inability to average it in any way, is the great number of servitors who are to be tipped every day for incidental services, which indeed are divided up amongst as many attendants as possible, so that each may have a claim for *"pour boire,"* as they term it. This practice James de Mille has also amusingly set forth by describing the train of servants which followed him from his carriage into the hotel, one bearing a tooth-brush, another his cane, still another an umbrella and so on with each separate article of his outfit, every one of the force expecting a special tip.

Besides the charge each day from one to two and a half *francs*, (about twenty to fifty cents,) for attendance, one must tip the "chambermaid," (who is a man,) the porter, the servant who opens the door for one, gives one any information or any sort of service, such as calling a cab, fetching a newspaper and so forth, so that one's *francs* and *centimes* melt away unceasingly without any very perceptible return for one's outlay. This complication is avoided in a degree at the smaller places where the servants are less numerous and where the size of the tip expected is much less.

The *Restaurants Duval* which are found scattered about in all parts of Paris, are particularly desirable for wandering women, though also patronized by men; the places are neat, attractive, comparatively inexpensive and thoroughly respectable.

The waiters here are women in a decorous uniform of black gowns, white caps and aprons. A peculiarity of these places is that every identical item has a separate charge, but so comparatively trifling that the sum is not exorbitant. For example: napkin, table-cloth, each one cent; half bottle of ærated water or wine, three to ten cents; bread, two cents; soup, five cents, and the like.

Butter is always expensive. Tea costs more than *café-au-lait*, but the latter is only served in the morning. If one takes cream or milk in one's tea or "black coffee," that is "extra." One's attendant here will be satisfied with a tip of three cents, though of course more is graciously accepted.

For a person meaning to remain some little time in one place, and this is really the cheapest way to establish one's self as reductions are given for prolonged residence, the best plan is to seek some recommended boarding-house or "pension" as we soon learn to call it. A good

way to get on the track of such, if one has no
personal acquaintances, is to ask advice of some
Tourist Office, and here is where one benefit of
having bought tickets of such an organization, becomes apparent. By the terms of one's contract
one is entitled to attention and advice and feels
that one has some sort of backing, which lifts a
part of one's burden of responsibility from one's
own shoulders.

Before I get too far away from the huge hotels, I will say that although almost all places
of lodgment in Europe are conducted on what
is very properly known as the "European Plan,"
yet I did find houses in Germany and Switzerland where a higher charge was made for lodg-
ing if no meals whatever were taken at the place
of sleeping, but as a rule there is no objection
to renting beds without board.

Here, perhaps, is a good point to answer the
question so often asked by persons contemplating
foreign travel, namely: "Is it of any advantage
to have the superficial knowledge of foreign
languages that one acquires from books and in
a class under a Professor, without opportunity
of hearing it in general conversation?"

I think it is; to be sure one will not be able to
understand the foreigners at first, no matter
how glibly one may read or pronounce the
alien tongue. But it will take less time to ed-
ucate one's ear to the spoken language and in
the meantime one is able to read signs, placards,
circulars and newspapers, from which one may
glean very many desirable hints and much information on almost any department of everyday
life; often, on account of such proficiency, being
able to dispense with guides, thus lessening
one's expense. The guide books gotten out by
many Tourist Firms are cheap and reliable; but

for an utter stranger, particularly my "lone
sister," I think one more voluminous and giving
special hints as to prices and routine of tiavel,
also addresses of inexpensive, respectable stop-
ping-places, is by far more serviceable though
considerable more costly.

But there is one thing especially noticeable in
foreign lands, even in the grand, opulent city
of Paris, and that is the universal recognition
of, not only the necessity, but the commendable-
ness of suiting one's expenditure to one's means.
There seems to be no odium attached, as too frequently with us, to the attempt to live as cheaply
as possible, if one's finances are slender, in order
to put by even from such, some sort of a provision for the "rainy day," and there are always arrangements of a desirable and even attractive kind though of course extremely simple,
made for persons so situated. Indeed it is
considered most blameworthy not to exercise a
reasonable prudence and economy, though naturally they who have ample means find no difficulty in being relieved of any surplus. But let
my "solitary woman" take note of the fact that
it is absolutely necessary to have a clear and
specified understanding in any bargain whatsoever, or one will be likely to find one's self
charged more than one has supposed would be
the sum total. Let her remember that in France
a week is reckoned at eight days and in taking a
receipt to see that the revenue stamp required
is not omitted. And I would strongly advise her
to familiarize herself as much as possible with
the currencies of the countries she means to
visit, thus lessening her chances of being imposed upon.

Cab-hire is so inexpensive that one at first
fritters away a considerable amount in the ag-

gregate upon it, which afterward, when one has
learned the routine of the very comfortable and
convenient trams and 'buses, one is quite likely
to regret.   There are numerous lines of these and
two or three lines of steam-trams into certain
suburbs, and one cable; they traverse the city
and environs everywhere, with no confusion and
with unusual safety to pedestrians.

Vehicles and equestrians, however, here as in
Germany, have the right of way, and if you are
run down you must "pay for it," which perhaps
may be the secret of so comparatively few accidents.

Most of the trams and 'buses have an "upper-
deck" reached by a narrow stairway and this
upper portion is truly the pleasanter place in
good weather, though the fare, three cents, is
but one half that in the lower part. On these
high, open tops may be seen widely contrasting
groups. Bareheaded women riding on undisturbed by chance wind or rain, closely contiguous to handsomely garbed ladies; student and
laborer, artist and shop boy, priest and washerwoman, side by side. One need never fear
crowding and jamming in such conveyances in
Paris, or almost any other foreign city, as no
passenger may enter a vehicle unless there is a
definite place for him.

The sooner one gets so one can go about independently and understandingly, the sooner one's
expenses may begin to lessen. It is often said,
"You find English-speaking people everywhere;"
while this is true, generally speaking, it is also
true that to find them you must frequent those
lines of travel and entertainment where there is
so much English and American business that it is
an object to provide especially for it, but it must
be paid for and the tourist must pay it in the

long run, so that it is is more expensive than if
he were not thus hampered; moreover, one does
not then get outside of the beaten track and certainly does not get down into the real, native
manners and styles of living, as one does to
wander where one listeth. The country people
are usually friendly and disposed to assist a
stranger.

If I might add a word as to one's mental attitude when traveling, I would say do not go
about in a critical or carping mood; look for
pleasant things instead of disagreeable, both of
which are to be found everywhere at home or
abroad; and above all, do not be aggressively
American, though by no means concealing or
apologizing for one's nativity of our own broad
and magnificent land that, in a paltry three or
four centuries, has, in so many respects, so far
outranked the degree of progress attained in the
old world through thousands of years.

Following the method of procedure recommended in the foregoing chapter, I was soon domiciled in a delightful family at Neuilly, a suburb of Paris. The proprietor of this home is an actor at the *Théatre du Palais-Royal*, where his wife also played until her marriage. Cultivated, refined, and also delightful musicians, they are indeed charming in their French fashion, for they speak no English.

There home is described as a *hôtel particulier*, which being interpreted, means simply "a private house;" the word "hotel" not meaning necessarily, as with us, a place of public entertainment, but signifies specifically a gentleman's house, or a mansion of some sort for special occupation. This one has the rare appurtenance of what we should term a "yard," but called here a "garden."

It is inclosed by a heavy wall some ten feet high in front, and at the sides and back by the neighboring walls of the high, adjacent houses. An iron gate closely locked and having a bell, defends us from all intruders.

All through the house are found the slippery, waxed floors so smooth and fair to look upon, but so tiring to feet and ankles. The place is fitted up in exquisite taste, with much beautiful woodwork and fine china; everything glistens with polished cleanliness; the ceilings are very high and the house is "as cold as a barn." Yet it is supposed to be heated because in the basement there is some sort of an arrangement whereby a tiny wave of warm air is sent through exceedingly small apertures into the *salon* on the ground floor; that is, when there is any fire, which is by no means continually, even in winter.

Lights and fires are "extra" in France, but this establishment is considered to make great concessions because lights are "thrown in" and only fires in one's own rooms are extra.

If my fancied "sister" has not traveled much in her own country, she may not know that in parts of our own land, as in the south and in California, similar conditions exist; and I must own that the French landlord is in this respect more reasonable than the American; for the former charges usually so moderate a price for his rooms that the extras are not very burdensome, whereas the American, particularly the Californian, exacts a most exorbitant remuneration for his accommodations, and then calmly informs you that you can furnish your own heat, "as they do abroad."

In this dwelling, the great, high, bare halls were a grand coursing-place for drafts, and the stone stairs and polished balustrades seemed chill enough. My room was so cold that I sat in street-garb much of the time, even to over-shoes and gloves, and for real warmth and comfort I went to bed.

Speaking of beds, imagine my horror on first beginning to reside *en pension* in France, to find that bed-linen is expected to do duty for three French weeks, twenty-four days, without change. I could not believe it when so informed on requesting the maid to bring fresh linen. I thought that I was being "victimized' as a foreigner; but on making inquiries among persons who had been longer in residence than myself, I found that this circumstance is as true as it is awful. Two towels are supposed to be plenty for the eight days' use. Usually American travelers if stopping long at one *pension* are impelled by a sense of the proprieties, to supply themselves with an extra change or so and to provide for the laundering of the same.

The French wash-stand-ewer holds about a quart of water, with bowl to match, and a bathroom is indeed a rarity. Of course the foregoing observations do not apply to the great hotels that are chiefly calculated for, and supported by foreign travel.

There being a fireplace in my chamber, I at first committed the ruinous extravagance of ordering a fire; but finding that the capacity of my fireplace was utterly disproportioned to the amount of space it should, but did not warm, I at last abandoned the measure; having then the partially consoling reflection that at least I was no longer sending up my moderate provision of *francs* through my chimney to no avail.

How do these people endure this discomfort? The houses though carefully and solidly built as regards permanence, are yet so badly constructed in regard to the conservation of heat, that even if fires were constant, which they never are, the slight degree of warmth from the tiny fireplaces would be entirely inadequate to counteract the blasts sweeping in around windows and doors, and the dampness inherent in the cold, stone walls. But I found that one gets acclimated in a measure, after a while, though it was sometime before I reached that desired consummation.

The interior of the average French home, though usually tasteful and perhaps artistic, is rarely cheerful and gay. These attributes are found outside in the boulevards and gardens. On the chilliest and dampest days of winter I would go back to my *pension* tired, wet and cold, to find no fire in any part of the house unless perchance it was near a meal-time, when there would be some heat in the kitchen.

"Where is Madame, the mistress?" I would inquire? "Can I not go to her for fire a little?"

"Alas! Madame is out."

"But Madamoiselle, has she no fire?"

"Ah! Ma'm'sel' also promenades herself."

In fact there would seldom anyone ever be *chez lui* except the unfortunate servants who must keep the household going. So I would have to wait with benumbed fingers and toes and chattering teeth till a handful of fire could be put into the small grate in my apartment, so small that it was utterly unequal to heating the room ; but as many rooms had none at all, I endeavored to be content, though vigorous drafts continually rushed in through the high ventilator which there were no means of closing, and the fire being as I have said, literally "a handful," genera ly went out with much greater celerity than it had been kindled.

I was continually reminded of an elderly gentleman whom I met one season in Southern California. He had just arrived from Boston to spend the winter in a "warm country." Like all new-comers, he was going about heavily wrapped, wearing overcoat and overshoes, and almost blue with chill. True, the sun without was shining gloriously, the heavens were a radiant azure, while blossom and verdure ran riot everywhere; a state of things very different from that in France at the same season for, though it is not really cold out of doors and the grass and shrubs in the parks are green, yet the

skies are gray and the trees bare. But to return to
my old gentleman. Some one said to him one day:
"Well, Mr. K., how do you like Southern
California?"

"Oh," he replied, "if I could just go back to
Boston and get warmed up once, I believe I
should like California first rate."

Thus with me; if I could only go back to
Wisconsin and "get warmed up once," I should
like Paris "first rate."

Neuilly, though a part of Paris, is in itself a
city of twenty nine thousand inhabitants. The
old *Château Neuilly*, once the favorite residence
of Louis Philippe, was totally destroyed by a
mob in 1848.

Near my stopping place here is a beautiful
little chapel, St Ferdinand, erected on the spot
where Louis Philippe's oldest son died in 1842,
in consequence of a fall from his carriage. It
was in Neuilly that Parmentier made his first
experiment in the culture of the potato. A
bronze monument near the chapel represents him
as investigating the properties of this vegetable.

My quarters at this time were about fifty
steps from the *Avenue de la Grande Armée*,
across from which the short *Boulevard des
Sablons* leads into the lovely *Bois de Boulogne*.
Being then unfamiliar with Paris, I did not
know at first how far I was from the heart of
the city nor that I was "without the walls." I
came to a realizing sense of this, however, one
day on going home in a cab, for I found I had
not only to pay extra for the short distance beyond "the gates" to my place, but was also
actually obliged to give the driver an extra *franc*
for himself and vehicle "to return." I felt a
strong desire to tell the man in forcible "United
States," that I did not care in the least whether

he ever "returned" or not, but being a stranger in a strange land and limited to a small assortment of phrases in a foreign tongue, I contented myself with a feminine version of the thought attributed to the "Dutchman's son,"—("Hans, I know vat you tinks. you tinks 'dam'!")—and wisely held my peace.

After wandering about to my heart's content in this neighborhood, I decided to change my quarters. I next took up my abode in a "cute" little family hotel just around the corner from the Madeleine and near the Tuileries. Everything here was on such a diminutive scale that it seemed almost like a toy establishment.

I was taken past a pretty, little *salon* and a neat little dining-room to an upper story where, passing through a doorway about two feet wide, invisible when closed, I was conducted down a narrow, dark, quaint, "corkscrewy" little passage most delightfully "Dickensy," into a tiny, semi-circular chamber that took my fancy at once. To my surprise, considering the tortuous and inconvenient method of approach, the room turned out to be in front overlooking the avenue; it was most beautifully light and shiningly clean.

Wonder of wonders,—for they are so rare here,—this house possesses an elevator, or *ascenseur*. It is an automatic affair, circular, and on crowding might hold four persons. When I desired to go to my room that evening, I was inducted into this machine, a bit of candle in a glittering brass holder was given me, a lever was moved and I began to ascend. Comical enough I felt to be rising thus by some unseen agency, slowly and steadily, candle in hand, all alone, straight up through the center of this unfamiliar edifice.

But I arrived safely at my floor, when the machine, giving a jerk and a mysterious grunt, stopped short and I let myself out upon the landing. I found out afterward that it was a sort of an unwritten law of the house, that persons should go down by staircase instead of elevator, it being I suppose, only an "elevator" pure and simple, and not a "depressor" as well.

At this place, for the first time since my arrival in France, the rather odd but very comfortable feather cushion for the outside of the bed was missing; also the bed-curtains, which I never can see without being reminded of Mr. Pickwick's adventure with "the lady in the yellow curl-papers." My floor was bare, painted in a set figure mainly dark blue, and varnished till it resembled enamel. A soft, large rug covered the center. On one side, or rather, in the middle of the semi-circle, was a recess, and in this was an affair new to me but which I judged to be some sort of heater. It looked like a little temple with flat top of dark marble from which a large pipe led into the wall. Otherwise the apartment had no special peculiarities.

Settling myself here, I should have been very comfortable, had not light and heat been considered such luxuries.

It may be of interest to mention that this house advertises no charge for light and attendance. This, however, does not preclude the necessity of giving tips. It only does away with the fixed charge in one's bill of a certain amount every day under that head.

The light, to my amusement, I found was half a candle *per diem*; if this would not serve, guests had the privilege of paying for more candles or a lamp or electricity. But I will add that the charges here were not at all exorbitant, especially in consideration of the very desirable location.

CHAPTER VII.

And now I devote myself to exploring Paris.
Strolling along through the wide, wonderful
boulevards, gazing into the bewilderingly beautiful shop-windows, dropping here and there
into the convenient restaurants always filled
with a tidy, happy, prosperous-seeming throng,
and prowling about in the queer little streets
that lead from the great avenues, one notes such
peculiar customs, such strange and motley garbs,
such a variety of persons.

A large number are in conventual or clerical
attire of some sort or other, that of the women
not being specially unusual, but that of the men
sometimes unique enough. I met a sturdy young
fellow the other day arrayed in what might, in
a "Ladies' Magazine," be described as a "very
genteel walking-costume."

He wore a kind of *princesse* robe with full
skirt just clearing the ground. A wide sash
encircled his rather robust waist. was knotted
behind and floated downward to the edge of his
gown. A pretty shoulder cape and a modest
hat looped up at the side with a chaste cord and
tassel, black like the rest of his costume, completed his very feminine dress, if I may except
his stout, serviceable boots of unmistakable mas-
culinity, which looked odd enough appearing
below his otherwise womanly array.

I see every day any number of plump old
gentlemen walking about in little be-ruffled and
be-laced white muslin "breakfast jackets" supplemented by neat, black skirts which they

deftly hold up from the pavement in the most ladylike manner; also others in comfortable though not very becoming mantillas and flowing robes of black, brown or white, and with wide-rimmed walking-hats that appertain quite as much to the female as the male human being, so that it really sometimes seems that, in Paris, a state of affairs exists contrary to that alleged of the United States, and that men are appropriating the garb of women instead of women adopting that of men.

Then there are the soldiers with their gay-colored uniforms, some red and blue, others blue and yellow, red and yellow, blue and white and gold, silver-trimmed, gold-trimmed, lace-trimmed, braid-trimmed, infinitely varied in style and combination; some in the old Zouave dress familiar in the United States in the sixties; some in more modern "bloomer" costume; still others with great knee-boots and glittering helmets and floating plumes, riding, driving, walking, marching by squads, standing guard at all public buildings, and so forth and so forth.

To one soldier, however, I am indebted for an amusing spectacle. He came rushing down the street in full uniform on a bicycle. He wore a shining metal helmet, heavy and hot, trousers of a brilliant red and fashioned in expansive bloomer style, polished high boots of cumbrous make, and a great blue cape that floated out from his shoulders like huge wings, giving him the appearance of some unwieldy, tropical bird that might have swooped down upon the wheel and was struggling to rise again with it in his talons.

Walking one day down the *Boulevard des Capucines*, I was suddenly surrounded by an eager and animated crowd which looked and pointed excitedly up the street. The roadway was quickly cleared and on came a dazzling cavalcade in full military array, horses prancing, accoutrements jangling, every appointment in immaculate order, as it swept by us in hot haste, escorting a rapidly-rolling close carriage which was followed by a second detachment of finely caparisoned cavalry.

"What is it all?" I hastily inquired of a bystander.

"Oh, Madame!" was the reply, "it is the President who passes!"

The President! Ah, yes. They have no monarch here! *Vive la Republique!*

All this parade and display of armed men seems very strange to a resident of a republic that rarely has occasion to demand military service, though never finding it deficient when required. I suppose it is impossible for us in our great, free country, with wide oceans between us and our most powerful neighbors, to realize what it must be to live constantly on guard against foreign invasion. Let us remember and be thankful.

Not that the President of France invariably goes about in this ostentatious manner. I am told that he sometimes is seen proceeding alone like any unimportant individual. But since the assassination of the preceding President and the present disturbed state of affairs on the frontiers, there has been manifest even more than usual of the pomp and circumstance of military authority.

The streets of Paris at present do not show as many cyclers in proportion to the passers, as are to be noted in our cities when the roads are in good condition, as they are here at all times. The *Bois de Boulogne* is said to be a favorite wheeling-ground but even there cyclers are now comparatively few; all of which leads me to conjecture that perhaps cycling in Paris is less a matter of business than with us, and is therefore practiced principally when most likely to be pleasurable as well as speedy. The pavements are in excellent shape and the temperature generally not colder than with us in the middle of October, and at the present writing, (March) becoming steadily warmer, in fact, in the country peach and almond trees in bloom; still on many days I see no bicycles at all and as yet have encountered but one female rider.

This was on the *Boulevard Hausmann*, in the very heart of one of the busiest quarters. She presented rather a startling appearance, being clad in a bright pink shirt-waist, white hat, veil, gloves and shoes, with hose and accordeon-pleated bloomers of a soft dove-color. She seemed not a whit abashed by her overwhelming minority but crossed the street just ahead of me, trundling her wheel with the utmost nonchalance.

I had been in Paris nearly two months before I discovered an electric car and my discovery was accidental, all persons of whom I had inquired never having seen any in the city and being unaware that the cars had been introduced here at all. One day, however, I was journeying out in the suburbs, and after proceeding a part of the way by horse-tram, I was informed that I must at a certain point, exchange into a *tram électrique*; then I ascertained that there are three such lines, though none of them cross the heart of the city, but proceed outward respectively from the Madeleine, the Opera and the *Place de la Republique*. These cars are two-storied like most of the trams and 'buses of Paris, but unlike them, have a canopy over the upper story that shields from sun or rain. The only other time that I ever met with this style was in our own country at Coronado Beach, Southern California. While I was in Paris, a great agitation was going on in the newspapers concerning the feasibility of an electric route across the *Place de la Concorde*. The project was most violently opposed by a large number, but I think it will be put through in time.

One of these electric lines leads to *St. Denis*, a city of about sixty thousand inhabitants and a prosperous industrial-center. Both the route thereto and the city itself are very unattractive; there is nothing whatever to please the eye, and there would, I presume, be few visitors in this direction were it not for the antique cathedral or *Basilique*, which is interesting as being the burial place of the ancient kings.

The monuments that mark these royal resting-places, (though in some cases the bodies have been removed,) are within the cathedral and, in many instances, of rare and exquisite design and execution; others are more curious and interesting than beautiful, while most of them are more or less imposing.

A very singular feature is noticeable in one or two of the larger and more elaborate tombs; this is the representation,—in addition to life-sized figures of the commemorated majesties in full coronation-robes,—of a second set of life-sized figures of the same personages in recumbent posture and, in fact, at the moment of death. These last are intensely realistic, nearly nude, with convulsed limbs and distorted countenances, and present a grewsome and ghastly spectacle.

This cathedral is one of the few places either in or about Paris, where visitors are not permitted to go about without a guide. It seems a pity to have it so anywhere, because the professional guide always hurries one on so, in order, I suppose, to receive the gratuities of one party and be ready for the next. Then if you happen to ask him an unexpected question, he is all put out and has to go back and begin over again.

The *Basilique* of St. Denis occupies the traditional site of a chapel erected about the year 275 above the grave of St. Dionysius or Denis, the first bishop of Paris, who suffered martyrdom in 270 on a hill famous in the annals of Paris, now known as *Butte Montmartre,* but formerly *Mons Martyrum* or *Mons Martis.*

St. Denis may also be reached by railway if one prefers, as may almost any of the suburbs. The tramway is cheaper but takes more time. I, myself, usually choose the latter mode of transportation because it leads more directly among the people, winding in and around through the busy streets and stopping wherever one may suddenly wish to pursue some side line of exploration.

To St. Cloud, Versailles and Sèvres, I went by steam-tram; this is a very pleasant route, taking one through charming little suburban centers and affording a lovely prospect of semi-rural scenes. One may also go by boat on the Seine, a most inexpensive method and delightful in the season; I, however, found it too chilly for this during my stay in Paris.

Serves is a charming village, picturesque in itself and specially interesting as being the place where the lovely Sèvres porcelain is made. The manufactory has been the property of the government since 1756. The exhibition-rooms contain exquisite and priceless specimens of this lovely ware, but the work-shops are not fully thrown open to the public, the most interesting processes being kept secret. The present building is compartively modern; the old manufactory, at a little distance, is now refitted and used as a normal-school for young women.

St. Germain, St. Cloud, Fontainebleau, Versailles and the Trianons; what a flood of recollections rushes through the mind of the lover of history and romance at the very names. It seemed so wonderful to think I was actually there; I, who first saw the light thousands of leagues away across mountain, moor and main, long, long years after the startling events, thrilling spectacles and brilliant pageants that followed in such swift succession within the boundaries of these royal residences, had wrought their destined effect in the history of mankind and, with all their actors, had vanished forever into the impenetrable past.

Births, marriages, revolutions, bloodshed, death, all have had their turn in these spacious areas lying here now so peacefully silent, and still the sun shines down and the leaves rustle and the fountains play unaltered.

What a long line of ghostly footsteps go stealing down the quiet avenues. They do not disturb the gay and thoughtless, modern pleasure-seekers who scarce remember, if they ever knew, the noted names, famous and infamous, once so familiar throughout all the length and breadth of the known world.

Louises VII., XIII., XIV., XV., and XVI., Francis I., Henrys III. and IV., Charles V., Napoleons I. and III., Louis Philippe, Pius VII., Queen Christine, Marshall Biron, the Grande Condè, Voltaire, Pompadour, Du Barri, Charles X., Marie Antoinette, Bluecher, Josephine,—how vain to try to complete the roll, to recall the innumerable multitude,—but all are gone.

Yet the influence of their lives and fortunes goes on for good or evil, and the world can never be as if they had not been

In those days more or less ancient, these lovely pleasure-grounds and elegant *châteaus* were far removed from the bustle and turmoil of what was even then called the great and wonderful city, but to-day we scarcely know when we have left the city proper behind us and entered into the environs. Everywhere are similar, beautiful and interesting scenes; everywhere the busy streets and the thronging people.

I have seen no baby-cabs as yet in the streets of Paris. Babies there are in hosts, and the parks, or "gardens" as they are termed, are swarming with children of all sizes and conditions in all weathers. Perhaps the baby-cabs and the bicycles are waiting for the summer, though I should think these lovely spring days might bring them out. The babies are borne in the arms of a *bonne*, usually a gayly arrayed female in a long, full cloak of soft, bright cloth, no bonnet, but a snowy muslin or lace cap handsomely fluted and decorated with very broad, brilliant ribbons that stream downward over the back of her attire. The babies themselves are all in white; white, close bonnets with funny little white pompons standing up stiff and defiant, white cloaks, white veils and white mittens; they cuddle down comfortably in the arms of the *bonne* as she strides along, and view the world with complacent eyes. Imagine the disgusted dismay of the average United States "nurse-girl," were it even suggested that she perform like service.

The cats of Paris seem to be a favored set of felines; fat and frisky, saucy and sleek, of uncommon size and possessing unusually long,

thick fur, they challenge admiration in restau-
ant, shop, and even in the parks, by their majestic presence and condescendingly sociable ways.
One magnificent, great, brindled fellow took it
upon himself to superintend my breakfasts at a
delightful little *crèmèrie* to which he was attached. Seated upon a chair near by, and singing charmingly the while, he gravely inspected
my operations as I disposed of my coffee and
roll. He would accept proffered morsels most
politely, but evidently only to avoid mortifying
me by a refusal, for he never ate them but
deposited them at his feet where he gazed upon
them pensively from time to time. When I later
went to another part of the city, I much re-
gretted severing my connection with his catship,
but had the satisfaction of knowing he was well
cared for. Indeed these animals seem everywhere to be treated with the utmost deference.
I did not see a starved or frightened looking cat
while I was in the city. Even the dogs seem to
regard them with profound respect.

But the horses, the poor horses! How they
are whacked and lashed both with whip and
tongue; how weighed down and overtasked
with impossible loads on these stony, slippery
streets where there is no foothold for them. I
have seen them fall again and again only to be
kicked and pounded and cursed until they
should struggle up from their poor, broken
knees. It makes one's heart ache.

I have seen only five colored persons during
my sojourn here amidst this vast multitude of
people. This seems strange to a resident of
even the northern United States, and compared
with my experience last winter in the region of
orange and palm, in our southern section, where
the very atmosphere seems darkened by their

omnipresence, their absence here is conspicuous. By the way it is rather amusing to note how foreigners universally confuse our northern and southern states with North and South America. One can scarcely bring them to comprehend that a resident of a southern state is not a South American.

Then others, on learning that I am an American, have been quite astonished to find that I have no extensive personal acquaintance with the "red Indian." I have met, however, with this latter species of astonishment at home in our own New England, where surely it is inexcusable, and one would suppose impossible to persons of the intelligence and general information of the average New Englander. But it is a fact that he, and I do not know but that I may also without error include the Middle Statesian, often looks upon his compatriot outside these specified localities, as being but little, if at all, removed from barbarism. I do not think such a state of opinion concerning their fellow-countrymen prevails among inhabitants of different sections of other countries,—but this is a digression.

CHAPTER VIII.

The season of the carnival is celebrated with much vigor in Paris. All sorts of practical jokes seem to be in order, and the throwing of *confetti*,—minute disks of thin, bright-colored paper,— into unexpecting faces never fails to produce convulsive merriment in the beholders. while the recipients take it, according to their temperaments, with smiles or wrath.

The streets looked very festive with the vari-colored showers everywhere pervading and the gay streamers of tinted paper twined and inter-twined and floating from every possible niche, nook, angle and projection of column, gable and tree.

It seemed to be a point of honor for everybody to seize any such floating streamer within his reach and carry it onward with him until it should snap from the strain, when it would be wound around the neck or wrist of the captor, adding to the jubilant appearance of the throng.

A year before, I was in New Orleans during the carnival-time and, though Parisians have the name of being the gayest people in the world, still it has seemed to me that here they did not appear so joyous and light-hearted as the merry crowds in that southern city. In fact, much of the Parisian fun seemed to be largely of a lower grade and there was much intoxication observ-able both in men and women.

The street-parades in New Orleans too, were more beautiful, strange though this may seem, for of course, taste, ingenuity and expense to the wildest extravagance, are by no means deficient here in Paris. I fancy climate has something to do with the character of the festival; here the skies were of a chilly blue and the wind was too strong for comfort, while there the genial sun was shining prodigally, the air was soft and balmy, and inanimate nature as well as man himself seemed to rejoice.

Of course all sorts of gay parties, *bal masques* and extravagancies wax fast and furious in these the closing days of the *carnivale,* or "farewell to the flesh." I did not see or hear of anything in Paris corresponding to the beautiful pageant at this season in New Orleans, when Rex and his royal retinue approach the city in a fine ship and are welcomed with pomp and splendor as the keys of the city are presented to him.

In New Orleans the queen of the carnival is chosen from the ranks of refined society, as a few years ago when the daughter of Jefferson Davis figured in that role; but I was surprised to learn that here in Paris the choice is made from the *blanchisseuses,* or in plain English, the washerwomen. In the middle of Lent in this part of the world, there is a relaxation period which, I think, does not obtain widely, if at all, in the United States, and this is called *Mi-Careme.* Then come more parades, more *confetti,* another washerwoman is chosen queen and the community is given over again to the "world, the flesh and the de—" lights of feasting and revelry for a few hours, when sackcloth and ashes are supposed to prevail once more until Easter Sunday.

Sunday as we understand it at home does not exist in Paris. That the day has come is manifested by an increased jubilance and hilarity throughout the boulevards and avenues. True there are services in the churches, but so there are on so many other days that this is no distinction. Most places of business are open if not in active operation and many reserve their most brilliant displays for this day. There are a few exceptions, however, chiefly among American and English houses.

Failing one Sunday to secure a copy of the *New York Herald* at the news-stands, I thought I would step into the office on the *Avenue de l' Opéra* to get one. Arriving there, though the place did not seem to be formally closed, I yet found myself unable to open the door for the simple reason that the outside part of the handle was missing. This had exactly the same effect as might be in case of the traditional "latch-string" when pulled in; there was nothing on which one could lay hold to raise the latch. This was so very peculiar a situation that I was undecided as to whether it might not be accidental, instead of being meant to keep out visitors.

A number of gentlemen were standing outside, reading through the windows the news-sheets that are always displayed close to the glass and, after much cogitation as to the form of my phrase, I finally mustered courage to address one of them for information, so in my very best French I asked him if he could tell me whether the office were really closed. To my surprise he turned red, looked embarrassed and at last said in broken French, "I do not understand."

"Oh," said I in my native tongue, "you are English."

"No," he replied, "American, from Michigan."

I then told him I was his "neighbor" from Wisconsin, and we both, strangers though we were, indulged in a little laugh over our painful and needless struggles to communicate in French. But I did not get into the *Herald* office.

One unique characteristic in public worship here fills the average American mind with amazement and, I fear, amusement. This is the employment of beadles, or *Suisses*, who are a regular feature in all the great churches of Paris. They are usually very large, finely-built men and are most gorgeously attired. They serve in pairs as nearly matched as possible in height and size, and it is a sight to be remembered to behold them stepping out in their rich velvet, gold-trimmed dress-coats, their marvelous, long waist-coats and superb "continuations,"—as Dickens has it,—their delicate stockings, wonderful cocked-hats and buckled shoes.

Each wears a lengthy gold chain and bears a heavy, glittering *baton* of office, about five feet long, and at certain points in the service, such as conducting the celebrant to and from the altar, or taking the collections, they precede the line of attendants and at each step, bring down their heavy rods to the floor with a grand thud that is most impressive. Their office seems to be purely ornamental as, except to head and escort these various personages and processions about the church, they perform no service whatever. They deign not themselves to handle the little velvet bags into which are dropped the contributions of the congregation. No, indeed! This inferior duty is performed by what, I presume, they consider inferior creatures, that is, by women, who meekly trot about after "their high-mightinesses"and deprecatingly present the bags to each of the spectators.

The theaters and all places of entertainment are in full blast on Sunday, both *matinées* and evening performances being given at most of them. During the week they are open nightly and, in a few instances, for a Thursday *matinée* and are always crowded.

At the Opera House are the grandest and most imposing spectacles; the *Odéon* is devoted principally to the classic drama, while the *Théatre Français* is noted for the elegance and purity of its diction. The *Vaudevilles, Théatres des Variétés* and *des Gaité*, the music-halls and the *Cafés-Concerts* are of course, without end.

It looked very odd to me to see men sitting during the play with their hats on, and also to see both men and women leave their places between acts and pass into the halls and *foyers* for promenading and refreshment. No orchestra is visible at any theater that I have visited, though audible from behind the scenes. In some parts of the theater, ladies are obliged to remove their hats; in others, one must appear in full dress or be refused admittance; there are women in attendance to take charge of one's wraps for a small fee, which however is not a definite charge, but regulated by the patron's means or generosity. I had a somewhat mortifying and yet amusing experience at one of my visits to the theater. I had gone in haste and omitted to ascertain as usual the contents of my purse before starting out. Not until I went to claim my wraps after the performance, and had opened my pocket-book to tip the attendant, did I become aware that I had nothing whatever therein, over and above my fare home, but two insignificant bronze coins equal to about a cent and a half of United States money.

In vain I held my empty purse open deprecatingly before the eyes of the lofty and important functionary who, in all her dignity of bestarched and be-frilled cap and apron, was waiting my favors while I eagerly sought to explain in my halting French, how I had neglected to provide myself with money, and how annoyed and sorry I was to be unable to recompense her in a fitting manner; she would have none of my explanations; she only conceived that I was offering her that insultingly trifling sum, and she brushed aside all my apologies with the freezingly sarcastic words: "Since you are *so poor*, Madame,"—what a scathing emphasis there was on those two words as she measured me from head to foot taking in my somewhat festal attire!—"I will take pity on you; you may keep your seven *centimes*!" Humbled and abashed, I crept away but my keen enjoyment of the utter absurdity of the situation was a most happy mitigation of the crushing effects of the dame's disdainful irony.

In some of the theaters one must pay extra for a program, but at the Opera and the *Français* at least, these are furnished free of charge.

The feature in Paris theaters the hardest, I think, for Americans to understand, is the *claque*, or company of paid applauders.

They usually sit, I am told, in the center of the house, underneath the great chandelier. They lead off at intervals with vigorous rounds of applause, most vigorous if failing to elicit addd applause from the general audience. I understand that many attempts have been made to abolish this singular custom, all of which have thus far failed.

CHAPTER IX

Funerals here are dismally pompous affairs and yet they do not seem solemn. The ceremonies are so overdone and the mechanism so apparent that the force of the pageant is lost.

Going to the Madeleine one Sunday, I found the whole imposing front of that classic edifice covered by two great black curtains looped back in the center. These were edged with white fringe and had a wide border in Grecian key pattern.

On the broad, colonnaded portico stood a large table with like covering, and here sat a being in an immense black cocked-hat trimmed to match, as were his long waistcoat, knee-breeches and swallow-tailed coat. His gloves were white, his long hose were black and he wore low, black shoes with frosted buckles. He seemed to be the master of ceremonies. Fancy our decorous and unassuming funeral directors in the United States, tricked out in this manner.

Inside the building were two grand and awful personages in the same depressing garb, each bearing a huge staff with black streamers. The demeanor of these mighty-seeming ones, however, did not comport with their majestic appearance. for they ambled about hither and yon and seemed,—to use a plebeian but forcible expression,—to be "sticking their noses into everything."

A number of persons were standing about here and there, others walking around, still others sitting; (by the way, if you take a seat

in any of these churches, you must pay three
cents, which is collected during service whenever one sits down;) all were staring.

In the center of the church stood a high bier
heavily draped, as was the interior of the building everywhere, in the black, white-fringed and
bordered trappings of woe. Innumerable candles in tall, massive holders faintly illuminated
this bier and the high altar.

With the melancholy reflections naturally
suggested by these symbols of mortality, I gazed
upon the bier, supposing of course that upon its
top and draped by that heavy pall, rested the
pulseless form of one who would tread life's
paths no more. There was some music to be
heard at intervals but no one paid any attention
to it. There were no mourners visible, no one
seeming to have any closer connection with the
deceased than the hired functionaries and the
careless spectators.

All this time, men, evidently workmen, were
running to and fro in the church and continually
breaking in upon what should have been the sol-
emnity of the occasion. After some time two
of these men, going up to the catafalque, as I
supposed to lift from off it the casket, stooped
down instead, flung up the drapery, revealing
a flimsy, cheap, unpainted framework, and there
underneath upon the bare floor stood a plain
wooden coffin. This they shoved out by means
of feet and hands into the aisle, where some more
men got hold of it and began to carry it out.

At the same time other men commenced pulling down the bier, piling up its light timbers
and rolling up the drapery; others extinguished
the tapers, disclosing thereby that they were
but candle-ends stuck into long tubes simulat-
ing candles; others still grabbed up the heavy

candle-sticks, whereby I saw that they were only wood silvered over, and others again appeared in the upper galleries and, running along on the wide cornices, began to rip off the heavy curtains with all possible speed, throwing them to the floor, thus dislodging much dust and mustiness and evoking consequent numberless sneezes through the sacred edifice as the men devoted themselves to bundling up everything pertaining to the occasion, getting it outside with great celerity. All this while the body was yet on its way to the door and the congregation still standing about within the church.

With the current of my thoughts effectually changed I went outside, narrowly escaping being knocked over by the hurrying workmen with their heavy loads. Finding a safe spot I looked down from the imposing colonnade upon the broad, bright avenues below.

A long line of mourning-coaches was drawn up in waiting, each almost hidden beneath black, white-edged draperies, and provided with horses also nearly concealed under similar funereal housings; while, attired like the beadles in cocked hats, knee-breeches and all the appurtenances, the coachmen sat upon their boxes gloomily monumental. A few men clad in the same style walked at each side near the head of the cortège; immediately following the huge, grewsomely decorated hearse was a long double row of men and women on foot; after these came other heavily and lugubriously draped carriages.

Thus was this solemn ceremony conducted at the Madeleine, that classically beautiful and historically interesting pile, one of the finest and most important of the sacred temples of Paris.

Since then I have seen many another Parisian funeral where there was not even the imposing effect of a large scale of operations, yet they were all carried on in the same ponderous and artificial manner, the grandeur and extent of the display being, I suppose, regulated by the purse of the afflicted family.

We talk of funeral reform at home, but after witnessing such a mechanical and cumbersomely dreadful pageant, our most elaborate method seems simplicity itself; and at any rate with us there is a gravity and a quietude of procedure that causes no jar to the tenderest sensibilities by its too obvious machinery.

The Madeline is not an ancient edifice as antiquity is reckoned abroad. Founded but little over a century ago in 1764, its construction continued until 1842. I lingered within the stately portico through which already have passed such innumerable multitudes, the distinguished, the renowned, the insignificant, to mingle with the ceaseless stream below in activity, or to be borne on, silent and passive, never to return.

The soft spring sunshine fell peacefully down, lighting up roof and pavement, pillar, façade and people with a faint glow. The long funeral train moved off in its progress toward the distant cemetery. As it wound along the brilliant boulevards a strange quiet fell upon the hubbub and unrest of the changeful scene. Men bared their heads; men, women and children crossed themselves and stood silent. Such is the custom here. It has a singular effect sometimes in the midst of the gay, busy, hurrying throng.

The principal cemeteries of Paris perhaps, are those of *Père Lachaise*, *Montmartre*, *Montparnasse* and *Picpus*, of which the first is easily the leader. There are in all, I understand, about twenty-two or three.

The space parceled out as one lot in these cemeteries is limited in the extreme, and the large and imposing memorials huddled together in consequence, present a disorderly and uncomfortable spectacle to one accustomed to the usual spacious areas and almost boundless vistas of America's broad acres. There is, I am told, an average of nearly one hundred graves required daily in Paris, so that the above burial spots would be greatly inadequate, were it not that the poor are committed to the *Fosses Communes*, or Public Trenches, large pits each containing from forty to fifty coffins.

. Bædeker informs us that burials in such "common graves" now take place outside the precincts of the city only.

Burial-places for the individual are secured in a variety of ways, of which outright purchase, the ordinary method among us, is rare and difficult. A *Concession a perpétuité*, or perpetual privilege, granting a very small, private burial-place of twenty-two and one-half square feet, may be obtained for about two hundred dollars, the price of each additional square meter (about eleven and one-third square feet), beyond six, is six hundred dollars. A *Concession Trentenaire* providing that a grave shall remain undisturbed for thirty years, may be had for sixty dollars; a *Concession Temporaire* for five years, ten dollars. After the time of each limited concession has expired, unless it is renewed, the bones must be removed to the *Fosses Communes* to make place for more recent interments for which those interested will pay the price.

So the majority of graves are practically only rented and, as in life, if the rent is unpaid, out you go. This, I dare say, seems as shocking to my "suppositious sister" as it did to me when I first learned it; if so, she will be surprised to hear that I did not come upon this state of things first abroad, but in our own city of New Orleans, which has so many truly French customs. I believe like arrangements prevail to more or less extent, in most crowded cities abroad.

All this has given rise to a number of burial associations, the members of which contribute to a fund for the purchase of a plot of ground in a cemetery, whereon is erected a general tomb provided with receptacles for a certain number of bodies. This arrangement like many other wholesale dealings, comes much cheaper than the individual purchase singly, and assures each member of an undisturbed place of repose after "life's fitful fever."

To quote a popular hand-book, all burials within the Department of the Seine are conducted by a certain Funeral Organization whose charges are regulated by tariff varying from sixty cents to nearly fifteen hundred dollars, exclusive of the price of the coffin and the officiating clergyman's fee. Two chaplains are attached to each cemetery for the gratuitous performance of the burial rites of the poor.

Père Lachaise, or the *Cimetiere de l' Est*, is the largest and most interesting of Paris cemeteries. It is named after Father Lachaise, the Jesuit confessor of Louis XIV., and occupies the site of that prelate's country-seat. It lies on a low, undulating hill at the extreme east end of the city, within the walls. It has an area of one hundred and ten acres and contains more than twenty thousand monuments, many of which "are deeply interesting as memorials of great personages, while others are noteworthy on account of artistic excellence."

How touching here as everywhere, the vain attempt to keep in the memory of man, that existence which, however dear and necessary to its own bereaved circle, has yet left no other influence to impress the world at large. Others there are whose lives shall never be forgotten, and large indeed is the number of these who here rest from their labors. How startling the wondrous array of illustrious names that gleams forth at every turn.

Singer, soldier, scholar and statesman; poet, philosopher, priest and painter; actor, artist, author and ambassador; astronomer and archæologist; composer and consul; who could recount them all? To think that this dust beneath our feet enshrines the mortal housings of every phase of divine genius, of dauntless bravery, of exalted excellence, that the world has ever known. All at the same level now and whirled around resistless from sun to sun, "with rocks, and stones, and trees." "But thanks be to God Who giveth us the victory through our Lord Jesus Christ."

It is in this cemetery that are interred the bodies of Abelard and Heloise who, in spite of their varying fortunes and their phenomenal gifts and learning, are remembered chiefly by mankind in general, through the piteous tale of their most woeful love. Their recumbent statues lie upon a sarcophagus beneath a Gothic canopy, all of dark marble, and re-constructed by Lenoir from fragments of an old monument.

Upon the tomb of Alfred de Musset are inscribed his own beautiful lines which may be freely translated as follows:

> "Dear friends, I pray, when I shall die
>   Plant near my grave a willow tree;
> I love its rustle sweetly sad,
>   Its leafage pale is dear to me.
> Its shadows soft shall lightly rest
> Upon the earth above my breast."

His wish is gratified for a willow gently murmurs above his dust.

Over the grave of Paul Baudry is a bronze bust and statue with the following brief but touching inscription upon the pedestal;

"Glory hath crowned thee, and I,—I mourn thee, alas! a widow alone with my babes."

An attempt to depict the wonderful beauties and artistic perfections so lavishly displayed here as elsewhere, does not come within the province of this unpretending manual; and small need is there that it should, in view of the gifted and exhaustive works already published along these lines. Sometimes, as one wanders on in a scene which, though in itself unfamiliar, may yet be a type of others better known, and with the mind prepared for a certain sameness and routine in objects and occurrences, there will occasionally start forth something a little different, thus specially attracting one's attention, though in detail it may be nothing particularly noteworthy. To r·cord such intelligibly and possibly with some interest to another as they strike me, is all that I can hope to achieve.

A very odd and conspicuous monument is to be seen at the western end of the *Avenue Transversale*, No. 1, and is visible so far away as the *Arc d' Etoile* in the *Champs Elysées*. It consists of a huge pyramid one hundred and five feet high, and was erected to himself at a cost of twenty thousand dollars, by Felix de Beaujour, formerly a consul. Strange to say, this work is popularly known as the "sugar-bread."

There is a Jewish cemetery included within the boundaries of *Père Lachaise* and in this portion is the family tomb of the noted Rothschilds. Madame Rachel, the great *tragedienne*, is also buried here.

At the extreme north end of *Père Lachaise* is situated a Crematory which though unfinished, has been in use since 1889. I am told that the process of cremation lasts one hour and is accomplished by means of refracted heat from a fire of eight hundred degrees.

The flames do not touch the corpse. The ashes left weigh about one twelfth of the original weight of the body. The cost, including the right to a niche for five years, is from ten to fifty dollars.

The Cemetery of *Montmartre*, or *Cimetière du Nord*, lies above the city upon the hill of that name so famous in the annals of Paris. It is much smaller than *Lachaise*, but has many interesting features. Just aside from the main entrance are four tombs containing the remains of seventy Polish refugees, the first tomb bearing the inscription in Latin, "May an avenger one day spring from our ashes." Horace Vernet and Paul Delaroche are buried here, also Ary Scheffer, Renan, Heinrich Heine, Carlotta Patti, Samson, the actor, Theophile Gautier, and many others of fame. One of the inscriptions on the latter's tomb, runs something after this fashion:

> "The bird departs, the leaflet falls,
>   And Love has fled before the chill;
> Thou little bird, when trees bud new,
>   Above my grave, Oh! warble still."

The Cemetery of *Montparnasse*, or the *Cimetière du Sud*, is much less beautiful and romantic in location than the two preceding. Here are buried the sculptor Rude and Henri Martin, the historian; also Henri Gregoire, afterward Bishop of Blois, one of the first of the clergy to swear fealty to the new constitution in 1790.

Not far from the entrance, behind a small pyramid, is an enclosed space devoted to the graves of Sisters of Charity. Among these rests Sister Rosalie Rendu who was decorated by the Legion of Honor, in recognition of her devoted services in the Crimea.

There is a curious old structure at a considerable distance toward the right of the principal avenue; it is the tower of an old mill belonging to a convent of *Frères de St. Jean-de-Dieu.* For some reason not ascertained by me, it has always been allowed to remain here in spite of incongruity.

Two large monuments stand opposite each other in the newer part of the cemetery, one commemorating all soldiers who have died in defence of France, the other, all firemen who have perished in execution of their duties.

In the little cemetery of Picpus are interred many of the oldest families of France. Here sleeps Lafayette, so dear to American hearts. At one end of the inclosure, are buried thirteen hundred victims of the Revolution who perished by the guillotine. Among these are the poet André Chénier, the chemist Lavoisier, General Beauharnais, and many others long known to fame.

The Cemetery of Passy, situated in the lofty and beautiful suburb of that name, is quite peculiar in location. One reaches it by means of a long flight of solid stone steps, broken into short lengths. Arriving at the top, one does not come directly into the cemetery but seems to have entered a different world, so sharp is the contrast between the little streets of tiny, picturesque homes upon the hill, and the broad, imposing avenues of stately mansions one has just left below. One soon turns in at the right and enters the quiet and lovely little city of the dead, where are many fine monuments.

Here just beyond the entrance, is the mausoleum of the gifted and erratic Marie Bashkirtseff, which was designed by Emile Bastien-Lepage. An exterior of pale marble is covered with florid ornamentation of various sorts, scattered flowers, wreaths, butterflies, draperies and so forth. Upon one façade are graven two stanzas, one from André Theuriet, the other from E. Ducross. The interior is a pleasant chamber perhaps twelve feet square, illuminated by large stained-glass windows and a glass door covered with metal grill-work through which one can see distinctly all within. Here in the tempered light may be seen a life-sized bust of this young genius whose earthly course was so brief. It stands upon a sort of altar whereon also rest her palette, her manuscript diary, a laurel wreath and other relics. One or two graceful chairs stand about and a cushion or so disposed here and there, with a guitar carelessly resting at one side, give an attractive, occupied seeming to the place and one almost looks to see the young girl enter to resume some one of the varied pursuits of her many-sided character. The structure is finished with a graceful dome, minarets rise from the four corners and a glittering metal cross surmounts the whole.

In all the cemeteries that I have visited, I have noticed another marked difference in the way of decoration, between foreign taste and our own. Even in *Père Lachaise*, so renowned for its sculptured marvels, where monuments of rare beauty testify to cultured taste as well as loving hearts, are to be seen hanging upon the sepulchers, huge garlands and wreaths of tin and iron beads fashioned and colored into a remote semblance of natural flowers. They fairly set one's teeth on edge. But there are others still more dreadful, of crockery, also intended to simulate floral offerings.

The most appalling of all are great, solid circles, or rather, rings, their surfaces variegated with a faint suggestion of closely set petals, colored yellow, and perhaps supposed to represent *immortelles*; as if they were not frightful enough of themselves, they are frequently converted into a veritable nightmare by being wrapped in some coarse, thin, black stuff that probably does duty as crape.

If these barbarous mementoes were to be seen only on humble graves, one might fancy that limited means had occasioned the use of a durable substitute for the perishable beauty of naural leaf and bloom, but as a matter of fact, I believe these set pieces are not inexpensive, and as before stated, they may be seen upon the most costly tombs. I must s'y, however, that I saw this same incomprehensible style of decoration in the old cemeteries at New Orleans upon French tombs. How is it that the French, who have such a world-wide reputation for exquisite taste, should be able to find satisfaction in the use of these hideous objects?

I notice in each of the different cemeteries here, at some prominent part of the grounds, a simple but beautiful monument reared "to the memory of all those who have no other monument." This seems to me a tender and touching tribute, the like of which I have not observed at home.

CHAPTER X.

Go where one will, one seems ever to be in the
great central midst of things.   Everywhere one
finds wide avenues and grand boulevards converging into spacious and beautiful *Places* or
Rond-Ponts and filled with great throngs coming and going, and yet somehow there does not
appear to be that everlasting rush and jostle
that we notice in our own large cities.

There are many beggars with their professional
whine, and yet few compared to the population.
Upon the steps and within the porticoes of the
churches, particularly the antique and venerable
ones, do the beggars specially congregate, often
even within the edifice itself, having acquired a
sort of right of old and established usage from
time immemorial, to display there their infirmities and deformities to the worshiping and sight-
seeing multitudes.

Some, perhaps, of those who desire alms ought
not to be called beggars, as they profess to give
something for one's money. It is somewhat
surprising to see a man or woman, or both, suddenly step out into the middle of a street and
all at once lift up voice or voices in stentorian
song, after which contributions are solicited.

The most annoying class are the street peddlers; they follow one for blocks, persisting in
their importunities. It will not do to notice
them by glance or word, even of courteous refusal, as they will then dog one indefinitely, "ar-
guing the case,'' hoping, I suppose, to weary
one into purchasing. One may rid one's self of

them, I believe, by speaking to a *gardien de la paix*, but this seems rather heavy artillery to bring against the poor wretches, so one usually endures in silence.

There is another sort of street-vender who is not to be classed with the peddlers for he is an institution by himself. He may have garden produce for sale, he may be an "old-clothes-man" or a dog-barber, but whatever he is, he does not pester one unnecessarily; he,—or she, for perhaps it is a woman, and if so, bare-headed— betakes him down through the center of the street, pushing before him his goods or his tools, while ever and again he gives vent to a most peculiar refrain consisting of a few set notes that ring out high and strident, yet not without a certain melody, above the conglomerated noises of the busy thoroughfare. It is impossible to know what he says; he has a *patois* of his own. If, from the looks of his wares, you desire his attention, he serves you at once politely, but he importunes nobody and goes on his way still warbling.

One is constantly meeting in the streets, long lines of boys and girls of all ages, being escorted to and from their respective schools by their teachers. I am told that during the first few years of childhood, the sexes are educated together in governmental schools. A little later a division is effected and women are appointed to teach the girls while the boys are put under the charge of men, always, I believe of some clerical order. Still later the girls finish their education in the convents while the boys are sent to the universities. It looks odd to see these processions of tall youths filing by, carefully conducted and watched over by half a dozen or so priestly attendants, as if the lads were incapa-

ble of walking unharmed abont the streets alone.
In their times of play, unless in the public gardens, both lads and lassies are hidden by the
high, opaque walls of their respective schools
or homes, such a thing as a "door-yard" open to
the public gaze, being unknown in Paris.

Shop-boys have a fashion of bearing surprising burdens on their heads, like our southern
negroes. At a corner of two principal boulevards, amid all the elbowing and confusion of a
densely packed crowd that had gathered to watch
a carnival parade, I saw a baker's boy making his
way unconcernedly across the street, hands
thrust in pockets and upon his head a basket of
delicate pastries about which he seemed to have
no consciousness whatever. When he came to a
more than usually impenetrable part, he would
calmly demand : "Is it that I may pass?" and
somehow pass he did with his burden unharmed.
Sometimes you may see one with perhaps a load
of eggs or fresh butter upon his cranium, yet
walking on and reading a newspaper with sublime indifference as to the perishable nature of
his burden. Or, maybe one with basket of
snowy linen will stop to watch a game or possibly indulge in a few rounds himself, without in-
jury to himself or his charge.

Bread seems sometimes regarded as a literal as
well as metaphorical "staff of life." Often you
may see a young fellow going along with a yard
or two of this comestible in his hand, swinging
it like a cane ; or a woman will be coming down
the street with a like thin, long roll clasped in
her arms ; or you may see it leaning against a
doorway waiting to be taken in ; or two little
children will be skipping along, each bearing
one end of it, like a stick of wood.

Another thing that has surprised me somewhat, is the size of the average French woman's foot. There is no difficulty in getting a knowledge of it, for the ladies of Paris hold their skirts at a remarkable elevation from the pavement, and the fact is thereby revealed that instead of posessing, as I had fancied from reading, tiny, dainty pedal extremities, they as a rule have noticeably generous, substantial "understandings." American shoes are considered far superior to all others and are advertised accordingly.

Ladies and gentlemen walking together usually lock arms even by day, reminding one of pictures in old editions of Dickens and Thackeray. I am told that this is generally customary on this side of the water. Very often, too, both ladies and gentlemen, forsaking the foot-pavements, betake themselves to the middle of the street, down which they walk nonchalantly, evidently deeming their right of way equal to that of horsemen and vehicles.

Just now the shop-windows are full of curious cartoons anent the first of April, though instead of stigmatizing a gullible idiot, as we do, an "April Fool," they here depict him or her as imposed upon by a fish. I have wondered whether our term "fish story", might trace its origin to this custom.

The large *magasins*, or department stores, of Paris are interesting institutions. Besides their wondrous displays of art and fashion in infinite variety, many things in their arrangement and management are peculiar. The *Bon Marché* —pronounced "Baw Marshy" with a strong nasal twang,—in the Rue de Bac, covers a large square and is, perhaps, a model of its kind. Its employés are boarded at the place, with which are connected dining room, kitchen and other domestic offices. Four repasts, I understand, are served each day, of excellent quality. A fine and spacious reading-room made beautiful by artistic decoration, painting, plants and bric-a-brac, is provided with stationery, current journals and periodicals for the benefit of shoppers.

There are no fixed seats at the counters, as with us; if a customer is given a chair it is either as a special courtesy or on a special occasion. There are no cash-carriers of any kind, animate or automatic; each purchaser must accompany the clerk who has served one to the *bureau* of that special department, where one pays for and receives one's goods. This entails considerable extra walking and every step counts on the extremely slippery, hard-wood floors, but the custom does away in a great degree with the long waits necessary in our stores, during which, as the jokers have it, one grows gray and tottering before receiving one's change.

There is always at least one functionary in these great emporiums who "spiks Ingliss," though it may be fearfully and wonderfully made.

The demeanor of the employés in general is an improvement on that of many of our "sales-ladies and gentlemen" at home. One is not petrified by a stony stare if one desires merely to look at a display of the wares without immediate purchase, nor is one annihilated by glances of ineffable disdain if one ventures to ask for a less expensive article than that shown; on the contrary one is treated with much deference and the right to inspect freely and to suit one's purse in buying, is conceded as a matter of course.

I notice in Paris an odd method of street-watering, calculated however for limited areas, the like of which I have never seen in America. The apparatus consists of several lengths of iron pipe, each of about ten feet and mounted at each end on little cross-pieces that in turn have at each end a small iron ball revolving in a socket and resting on the pavement; the pipes are connected by very short lengths of flexible, rubber hose.

A man in charge rolls this apparatus into the street, fits one end to an aperture in the pavement communicating with the water-supply, puts a nozzle on the other end and straightway he is enabled to wet down a considerable space with very little trouble. There are watering carts too, of course; queer looking affairs like boxes, about three feet high and four long, mounted on two great wheels like a dumping-cart.

A large number of horseless carriages of various styles and sizes, and calculated to carry from one to half a dozen persons, may be seen running all about through the streets of Paris. I have also seen a three-wheeled affair resembling a bicycle. The rider of this machine does no pedaling and seemingly has no care whatever except to direct his course by means of the handle-bars. I have never seen these elsewhere and they are more terrifying to me than all the 'buses and trams together, for one never knows when they may whizz across one's path, as they are confined to no set tracks, like the trams and are heralded by no beat of horses' feet, like the 'buses. They speed over the pavements, swift and silent, the only warning one has of their approach being a shrill, little "toot" which one thinks, if one notes it at all, is produced by some small boy's tin trumpet. I believe the motive power is petroleum.

It strikes me that the Parisians are great
sleepers. It may be because they live so fast
that they are obliged to take "forty winks"
whenever they can; at any rate they seem to
sleep everywhere. On the benches, in the gardens, in the galleries, the museum, the omnibuses, even in the cafés with their glasses before
them, you may see men and women too, sitting
bolt upright and wrapped in placid slumber.
The news-dealer slumbers at his stand; the boot-
cleaner slumbers at his post; the cabman slumbers on his seat; if you wish the latter's services
you must waken him; if you make a round of
calls you will find him relapsed into slumber
between each one and you will probably have to
poke him up every time, before you resume your
drive.

One can apparently never exhaust the odd
spectacles one is continually meeting in a promenade. Fancy defunct porkers and lifeless
mutton-legs gayly garnished with artificial
flowers; or a plucked fowl tricked out with
strings of red berries around its neck and "drum-
sticks;" or a salt cod-fish tastefully decorated
with sprays of green. There is a great display
in the open street of all sorts of wares, from
eggs to engravings; many things to the United
States mind, calling imperatively for an An-
thony Comstock to rise up in righteous wrath
and sweep them from off the face of the globe.
There is always an interested and critical throng
about these varied exhibitions and I believe the
art of window-dressing reaches its height in
Paris.

Many of the streets have most absurd names.
Here are a few jotted down in my meanderings:
"The Cat that Fishes," "September Fourth,"
"July Twenty Ninth," "Good Children,"

"White Mantles," "The Step of a Mule," "White Horse," "Five Diamonds," "Scissors," "Comet,""Equality,""White Doctor,""Hell," —for a fact, both a boulevard and a passage are called by this name usually unmentionable to ears polite,—"High Pound,""Iron Pot,""White Queen," Poor St. Julien," "Old Pigeon-House," and others quite as queer. But these are relics of olden times, whereof the precise significance has been forgotten.

Equally singular and sometimes, to the Anglo-Saxon idea, verging on the profane, are the titles of some of the shops, such as,—all translated, of course,—"The Mother of a Family," "The Good Devil," "God the Father," "The Chicken in the Pot," "The Devil's Four Quarters," "The Grace of God." This last is a dye-shop and were it in England or the United States one might try to evolve some connection between the "grace of God" and "dying" in one sense and so, by transference, to "dyeing" in another; but being in France, even this labored explanation is impossible.

Though I gaze with admiration on the great, wide, modern thoroughfares with their marvelous display of architectural beauties, and rare as well as costly wares, yet I am really most fascinated by these same quaint, old streets and localities that are in the midst of, yet so far removed from, all our conceptions of life as we know it now.

Imagine the state of society and of traffic that could exist among these narrow ways, little more than lanes, in many of which it would be impossible for one vehicle to pass another. Naturally we infer that there were no vehicles to pass; upon the backs of men and horses were transported through the towns all the necessities of life. But can we go so far as to imagine all the carts, carriages and conveyances banished from the streets to-day, and the consequent hush and general stagnation that such a condition of things would imply? Would life be worth living? And yet they lived, those people of the olden time, and did good deeds and brave and passed on that we might come after.

I say little about the magnificent palaces, cathedrals, art-collections and other places of note in Paris, although there is scarcely a day in which I do not visit some of them. They are all well-known to fame and stand solidly on their own merits to which, or from which, I could add, or detract, nothing, even were it incumbent on me to try. But impressions of sights and sounds that attract the attention of a stranger in novel environment must be tinged more or less in every instance with his own individuality and thus in a measure unlike all others, which is my excuse for rambling on.

Many a day have I spent in the Palaces of the Louvre and the Luxembourg and numberless others, amid their wonderful treasures of marble and canvas; many an hour amid the cool, secluded shades of Notre Dame, St. Sulpice, St. Germain-des-Près, the Madeleine, the Pantheon and others too numerous to name.

Ah! to think of the quiet feet which once passed restlessly in and out of these vaulted aisles; the silent voices once lifted here in earnest prayer and praise. All gone, but their places are not vacant. Still rush and throb the feet and hearts of surging humanity, ever coming, ever going; still rise anew its vibrant voices in song and supplication.

There is an antique, crumbling and moss-grown edifice standing in its own grounds at a corner of the bustling, modern boulevards, St. Michael and St. Germain. It is called *Hôtel de Cluny,* (*Hôtel* meaning private mansion,) and occupies the site of a Roman palace founded between the years 292 and 306, A. D.

Here in 360, Julian was proclaimed emperor. The old palace has long gone to ruin and the only part left to-day is the ancient *Thermes* or baths connected with it. The fact that the *Frigidarium* or cold-bath chamber, is sixty-five by thirty-seven and one half feet in area, and fifty-nine in height, indicates something of what must have been the imposing dimensions of the ancient structure.

Above this chamber lay for many years, until 1810, I believe, a garden, yet its weight and moisture did not affect the stone roof of the apartment lying below,—then all unsuspected,—so substantial is its masonry. Many antique pieces of sculpture more or less defaced are found here, one of Greek marble representing the Emperor Julian himself, and a battered and disreputable old creature does he appear now, whatever he may have been in his prime.

In 1340 the ruins came into the possession of the wealthy Benedictine Abbey of Cluny, the abbots of which caused to be erected in the fifteenth and sixteenth centuries, the present *Hôtel de Cluny.*

This edifice, a remarkably fine specimen of late Gothic combined with Renaissance features, still exists and quaint enough it looks amid the surroundings of modern civilization. The estate became national property during the Revolution and in 1839 the *Hôtel de Cluny* came into the possession of M. Alexander du Sommerard, a learned antiquarian. He died in 1842 and the property, together with the *Thermes,* was purchased by the government and thrown open to the public free of charge. By the way, Paris is remarkable for the numerous means of recreation, instruction and culture which it furnishes gratuitously to both residents and strangers; and it is rare if even a nominal fee is asked for the care of one's umbrellas or canes when left, as they must be, with the door-keepers.

The *Hôtel de Cluny* contains a most valuable collection of mediæval objects of art and industrial products to the number of more than eleven thousand.

But what renders it supremely interesting to me is the fact that the somber old rooms with their low, timbered ceilings, black with time, their ponderous but pricelessly beautiful furnishings, their deep, wide-mouthed fire-places mutely testifying of an epoch when France had logs to burn, and having classically ornate mantels, their quaint windows set high from the floors and their dark antique decorations of a by-gone age, are left intact; and again I fall to wondering what s)rt of persons trod these floors, looked from these windows, loved and hoped and wept and died within these walls and whether they too mused upon the old fashions and queer customs of their predecessors.

But the "silence" is "unbroken" and the "stillness" gives "no token," for there are none left to answer, so I turn my thoughts from the things that were to the things that are.

Among the many wonderful and quaintly interesting institutions of Paris, and yet one that is not always visited by the hasty tourist, is the *Gobelins*, the state-manufactory of that famous tapestry. The foundation of this manufactory, it is said, dates back as far as the time of Francis J., but the product did not receive its present name until 1662, when the brothers *Gobelin* began its manufacture and produced not only tapestry but all sorts of royal furniture. "From this period,"says one authority, ' dates the celebrity of the *Gobelin* tapestries, which are veritable works of art."

They are now reserved entirely for the government, for the draping of public buildings or as presents from the state to foreign courts, to persons of exalted rank and the like, and are entirely withheld from the general market.

It is amazing to watch the busy weavers, for they work from the wrong side and the beautiful, finished portions are turned toward the visitor as he passes along in front. A large copy of the design in progress hangs at one side out of the workman's sight, but the small part on which he is actually engaged is drawn in crayon on the stretched threads. Behind him is a full sized copy of the finished design, and a basket in front of him holds his wools, fourteen thousand hues in all,each having twenty-four different shades.

Copies of famous paintings are reproduced not only with faultless accuracy as to details, but are actually more beautiful than the originals, on account of a softness and delicacy of tone wherein the colors blend with an imperceptibility of shading that is truly surprising, while there is no glitter or hardness of varnish to offend the eye.

I was struck with the smallness and delicacy of the workmen's hands; at first as I saw them weaving in and out, the owners themselves being invisible, I supposed them the hands of women, but learned later that no women are employed.

An area of six square inches is the average

daily task of each man. The loom does not especially differ from the ordinary machine. It is impossible for the casual observer to estimate the degree of patience, skill and exactitude, required in this work. Day after day these toilers sit here behind their looms, in silence and unceasing application, isolated from all visitors and almost from their kind, as the looms in front shut them off in a measure from their companions as well as from the public.

The *Gobelins* also include the *Savonnerie*, a carpet-factory started in 1604, by Marie de Medicis, in what was originally a soap-factory, hence the name, and which was united to the *Gobelins* in 1826.

The main building of the *Gobelins*, which is very quaint and old, is situated in the *Avenue des Gobelins*, and is surrounded by a high wall. A large gate at one side, near which stands a uniformed attendant, is opened to the public on Wednesday and Saturday afternoons.

We enter an ancient little court with a tree or so at one side, and turning to the left come into the first of the exhibition rooms of which there are four, exclusive of the two work-shops, the staircases, the long corridor and the workshop of the *Savonnerie*. On leaving this building, we step out into a quaint winding way between low, ancient, whitewashed structures, all within the inclosure, until we come again into the little court, at the farther end of which we find the chapel attached to the place.

This is indeed queer and old-timey. Its principal decorations are seventeenth century tapestries after paintings by Raphael. A portrait above the entrance is striking in its vivid lifelikeness.

I saw here something not included in any

guide-book or list of remarkable objects, but which, while astonishing and unique, left in me no desire to ever again behold the like. I had noticed a figure in the ordinary garb of a lady, standing with back toward me before the mediæval altar, evidently consulting a hand-book. As I approached, this figure turned and addressed to me a civil inquiry, and I earnestly hope that the amazement and horror that I felt while endeavoring to reply, were not depicted on my countenance, for the "lady" had a well-trimmed and luxuriant moustache, which curled gracefully about her mouth in the most approved fashion. Her manner did not betoken the least consciousness of anything unusual in her appearance and, thanking me politely, she glided quietly away.

Everywhere one goes one sees a continual washing and polishing of counter, window, floor and pavement. Men are scrubbing down the seats placed at intervals along the grand boulevards, also giving the railings and arbors in the gardens a thorough rinsing. Even in the cemeteries is seen on every hand the vigorous application of soap and water to both outside and inside of tombs. This sounds strange, but the tombs here are almost invariably temples of greater or lesser size, entered with as little difficulty as an ordinary dwelling. A tomb will contain probably one or more windows of stained glass, an altar of some description, a painting or piece of sculpture, perhaps a seat or two; in fact, there is almost as much variety in their interiors as in those of homes in general; but I must confess it has a singular effect as one is passing along the quiet though not deserted avenues, to hear voices from within these tombs, no occupant being visible. One involuntarily recalls that dismal old hymn beginning:

"Hark! from the tombs a doleful sound,
Mine ears attend the cry,"

though the "sound" is more practical and energetic than "doleful," while the swish of brush and splash of water instantly banish all reflections of a supernatural tenor.

CHAPTER XI.

About this time I again change my quarters
and I now find myself in a typical French met-
ropolitan dwelling-house. The average citizen
of Paris is housed in this fashion with accessories more or less elegant, as his purse may war-
rant.

There are few streets in Paris in which the
lower floors are not occupied by shops of
some kind, but this where I now reside is one of
the few that is given over to dwellings simply.

About two blocks from my habitation the
street converges into the beautiful *Avenue de l'
Observatoire* taken from the ancient palace-
garden of the Luxembourg, a side entrance to the remaining area of which, lies just
around the corner from my present abode; while
the spacious and busy boulevard of St. Michael
runs along the other side of the garden and also
converges into the *Avenue de l'Observatoire* at
the point mentioned above.

There is no tram nor omnibus line on my
street and, as one stands at the end and looks
along its length, it has an appearance of quietude almost deathly. But this quiet street has
had some famous residents and stirring scenes
in its time. Here Emile Littré compiled his
great work, the *Dictionary of the French Language*, while living at No. 108; it was then
called No. 48, *Rue de l'Ouest*. Littré himself
has described the house as one from which the
Communists fired upon the Versailles troops during three days. Littré died at No. 44. No. 76

has a tablet inscribed: Here lived Jules Michelet, the historian, born at Paris, August 22, 1798, died at Hyòres (Var) February 9, 1874.   No. 14 was long the residence of Pierre Jean David, the sculptor, called David of Angers, to distinguish him from Louis David the painter.   At No 84 lived the painter Jerome Marie Langlois, a pupil of David the painter.

The buildings in this street look more like warehouses, factories, or even prisons than homes, for they stand flush with the pavements, having no areas, railings or outside steps, as with us, and across the lower windows is usually some kind of an iron grating.

The houses are all of a smooth, cream-colored stone and are commonly faced up two or three feet with another stone of dark gray, rather somber in effect.   A large double-do'r like a warehouse-entrance, on a level with the street, gives ingress to each; and whatever of loveliness or luxury there may appertain to these homes, is hidden from public view behind these doors.

Leaving the general for the particular, I ring the street-bell of my present domicile, whereupon I am admitted by the *concierge*.   I cross the threshold and find myself in a lofty passage or vestibule, perhaps twenty feet broad, neatly paved, and having smooth stone walls finished off in pure white.   The ceiling is ornamented with panels in low relief and supported by eight, symmetrical, snowy pillars.   The cream-colored stone floor is cut in a decorative pattern and on each side run four wide, shallow, stone steps extending the whole length of the passage.   On the left side are two double-doors with upper halves of plate-glass; the first opens into the quarters of the *concierge*, for no French family ever lives on the ground floor of such a building,

unless attached to its service. The other door
has upon it in gilt letters the name of an Agency,
and I presume leads to an office. These doors
are joined to each other and to the two end walls
by large windows, also of plate-glass. On the
right hand is but one door also double and
glassed, on each side of which is a handsome
pedestal about three feet high, upon which
stands a beautiful, large porcelain lamp of exquisite design, looking like some rare vase.
Spread along the steps at each side, are soft,
bright rugs, very clean. Within the right hand
door one sees a fine mosaic pavement and a light,
ornamental staircase seemingly constructed
chiefly of glittering brass; this winds up and
away into regions unknown to me, as my way
lies farther on; I may say, however, that each
floor is a separate flat.

I imagine that the lot of a Paris postman "is
not a happy one." True he does not have to
mount all these stairs and visit all these flats,
for the outer *concierge* takes charge of all the
mail or parcels coming into the building, which
by the way has but one number for all its many
divisions; as for instance in this place we are
all "No. 70," though there must be as many as
a dozen families in the house. But though the
concierge thus far relieves the postman, the latter must still be on the alert, for mails are de-
livered here not only in the daytime on week-
days, but also in the evenings and on Sunday.
The postman wears a dark blue uniform and his
mail is carried in a shallow, square box of many
compartments and is suspended horizontally in
front of the man by means of straps from
the shoulders. Stamps, aside from at the post-
offices, may be purchased of the tobacconists.
Tobacco being a governmental product and un-

der its protection, a license is necessary for the sale of the weed, and with this is given the right to sell stamps.

But I have not yet reached my apartment. At the farther end of the vestibule is another large double-door, of stained glass. This has no bell nor lock, so I turn the handle and step into a large, open court perhaps fifty feet square. I use the term, open, in the sense of having no roof; it is, however, fully inclosed otherwise by the four inner walls of the building, six stories high besides the attic. The edifice is, in fact, built around this court, so that the latter is shut off from the street and all other outside communication, by, in effect, a lofty barrier two rooms deep on all sides.

The court is paved with ornamentally cut stone; in the center, elevated by one or two very broad shallow steps, is a curbing of fanciful design perhaps twenty by twenty-five feet in dimensions, which is fill·d with ear h and set out in flowers and shrubs. This plot, by the way, is called a "garden."

The main apartments of the structure face this court, and six rows of windows, besides the dormer windows of the attic, look down upon it and receive no more air and light than may enter from above. In this respect the higher flats are the more favor(d; residing in the lower ones is something like living within a deep well.

Across the court from the entrance is still another double-door, half glass like the others, before which are more wide, light-stone steps and more bright clean rugs. Pulling another bell, I evoke another *concierge* who admits me into a hall about twelve feet wide. Another floor cut out in patterns, this time of marble, and covered with a soft rug through the center, leads

to another staircase opposite. This stairway is
of polished hardwood, but mercifully to the ankles, a carpet is laid in the middle.

Each landing is lighted by a large window of
stained glass. Through these when open, may
be seen the tiniest imaginable space of greenery,
a shrub or two, and a high, iron fence, immediately on the other side of which rise the grim-
looking walls of a great convent which, facing
the other way, shuts us off from the street behind us.

I walk up the last mentioned stairs, turning
at the half-way landing, and find myself on the
first floor, (foreign reckoning,) where I am admitted by the *bonne* and go down the hall to my
room, for I have at last reached the particular
flat in which, for the time being, I dwell When
ensconced here, there are betweem me and the
public street. three solid walls, (for my room
faces the court on the further side,) one single
and four double-doors. It is quite a proceeding
to really get outside, and in the case of those who
dwell in the upper stories, it becomes a pilgrimage, as elevators are unconceived of. I wonder
if all this difficulty of access, all this getting
away as far as possible from the public gaze,
arose from the necessity in ancient, rude and
war like times, of placing the family, usually
tender and helpless, as distant as possible from
outside attacks.

It is diffi·ult in viewing the Paris of to-day,
to realize its tumultuous and terrible past. The
scenes of violence, bloodshed and destruction
have, almost without exception, been so completely transformed and beautified that one
must turn to the pages of history to find evidence that affairs have ever been other than as
now.

But there is one stately ruin standing to-day in what is known as the Aristocratic Quarter that testifies silently yet powerfully to a season of terror not very far removed from the present time.

This is the *Palais d'Orsay*, built in 1810-35 and latterly used by the *Conseil d'Etat* and the *Cour des Comptes*.

In the dark days of '71, this palace was fired by the Communards, and to-day the lofty exterior walls, still standing in spite of their terrible ordeal, are all that is left to witness to the grandeur and dignity of the once magnificent structure. It is an imposing edifice even now, covering the area bounded by the *Quay d' Orsay*, and the streets of Lille, Poitiers and Bellechasse, but the interior is completely gutted; chaotic heaps of broken masonry here and there, while suggesting something of the outline and dimensions of grand *salon* and gallery, yet preserve no indication of the former elegance and beauty of design and decoration. All is silence now within its roofless chambers into which the sunshine and the rain of heaven alike fall pitilessly, while vines and shrubs look out of the empty window-spaces.

The public gardens of Paris are beginning to appear very lovely now with wealth of leaf and bud. Not a great profusion as yet but enough to brighten and ornament the scene.

In all these numberless beautiful gardens belonging to the municipality, laid out with skill and art and embellished with statues, ponds, fountains, and flowers, the children have full sway and are allowed to run, romp, roll and disport themselves altogether as they see fit. Some of the gardens are of modern origin; others date back several hundred years and have seen dynasties rise and fall; but whatever they are, they are open from morning until night, for the special benefit of the rising generation.

It gives much food for meditation to stroll through the ancient palace-gardens such as those of the Louvre, the Tuileries, the *Palais Royale* the Luxumbourg, Versailles and the like, all planned and perfected by a corrupt and selfish royalty for its own exclusive enjoyment, and to mark the freedom with which all classes of people (except indeed the very class of those ancient aristocrats themselves) now pervade for rest or recreation these once sacredly guarded precincts: while their children, shouting from terrace or leafy nook, wake echoes once answering only to the stir of a royal retinue; or, racing down the winding avenues and around the marble margins of plashing waters, do tread all unabashed and unrebuked in the footsteps of ancient kings.

CHAPTER XII.

I left Paris one mild morning in a drizzling rain, so that my last view of her avenues and vistas was as through a mist of tears.

Not at all, however, did I regret leaving this wondrous city, the magnificence and beauty of which are so indescribable, but whose spacious areas and splendid structures seem somehow designed merely for external display, with little thought throughout those broad stretches, of the inner domesticity and cosy hominess so dear to less excitable if also less brilliant peoples.

Parisians as a rule seem to live in public and to seek home only for reasons somewhat similar to that influencing the too convivial gentleman who went home at four o'clock in the morning, "because all the other places were shut up."

I shall not soon forget the extreme surprise and volubly expressed amazement of both mistress and maids at my *pension*, when occasionally, wearied out by incessant promenading and sight-seeing, I elected to pass the day quietly in my own room.

"What! Madame has not gone out? But surely, Madame goes out presently? Madame does not stay with herself all the day. That understands itself without saying!"

Thus the women of the household; and no one of them, mistress or servant, seemed to be able to approach that point of view wherefrom it might appear reasonable or satisfactory to refrain from making a *sortie* into the outer world.

This seems the prevailing state of opinion; and perhaps it is not inexplicable why the seclusion of the domestic hearth is not so prized by this light-hearted, emotional folk, as by some other nationalities.

In the first place, the "domestic hearth" scarcely exists even as a figure of speech. The homes in general, as noted before, are damp and, to the American, dark and somewhat dismal. Fuel is expensive and brought in only in small quantities. Such a thing as keeping up a continual fire for general warmth is almost unknown.

As soon as a meal is prepared, the cooking fire is extinguished, while the small fire lit in the dining-room just before each meal, is carefully raked out as soon as the meal is over. But the most surprising feature of it all is that the "native" does not seem chilly and, even while the American is shivering, opens doors and windows for fresh air.

In a land of continual sunshine, like Italy or California, I can understand how persons get into a habit of going out of doors to keep warm; but in Paris where there is so much chill rain and often quite protracted spells of really cold weather, it is incomprehensible to me that they should not, unless in poverty, strive to be a little cosier at home.

Of course sun and light are not so easily obtained as artificial warmth might be. The living-rooms, looking out as they usually do upon high, closed courts that shut off much of what sunlight might otherwise shine directly in at the windows, are often in the shadow all day long, which does not add to their cheeriness, nor can their occupants command any view of what is going on in the outside world.

Then the French custom of breaking fast in the morning with a bit of bread and a draught of coffee taken alone, either in bed or during the toilet, does away with the pleasant and hospitable reunion around the breakfast table, which our own countrymen so highly prize; and the average Frenchman hurries out into the street as soon as may be, for warmth and society. What wonder then that the brilliantly lighted restaurants and the wide, clean avenues with their constantly shifting throngs of gay comers and goers, should seem most attractive to these volatile people, especially here where they have made their city with very little exception, the most splendid and beautiful in the world.

But now it was behind me and I was soon speeding over a green and fertile country and through thrifty, picturesque towns.

I could not but note the difference between the United States and France, in the degree of care taken to reduce to a minimum the danger of railway accidents. Everywhere was the approach to a station most carefully guarded. Nowhere did a railway and a country-road cross at the same level; either by a strong bridge or a well-walled excavation did the train pass over or under the wagon ways; and throughout the whole course, the tracks were laid between earth trenches well protected by thickly growing hedge or solid mason-work, so that by no possibility could any creature, biped or quadruped, find itself upon the rails unguarded. Recalling the manner in which our trains at home dash through crowded cities and out across the open, utterly unprotected country, I could not but feel that we might learn much in regard to the proper care and preservation of life, even from these same ''volatile'' Frenchmen.

There is not much in the scenery along this "Road of Iron of the East," to keep one's attention as we journey on hour after hour with the rain still gently falling. We pass through an undulating country well watered with noble streams and fair with verdant fields. There is little to remind an American that one is in a foreign land, except perhaps the sight of peasant women of all ages toiling on the *fermes* at the most menial of out-door tasks, the extreme tidiness and "finish" of homes and gardens, and the dramatic vivacity of the alien tongue at the stations.

I soon turned my attention to the interior of my carriage. For the first time I now found myself in a second-class compartment and I looked curiously about to see what manner of place it might be. It certainly was not luxurious but was very comfortable. As in most continental carriages, it opened at each side by a door into a narrow lane running between two rows of seats facing each other, each row accommodating five passengers with barely room for opposing knees and feet. Light was admitted by small windows at each end of the two rows of seats and through the glass upper half of the two doors. Window-curtains of some coarse, dark-blue worsted stuff; walls and ceilings being covered with the same; the former being padded up three or four feet to form backs for the seats, which were cushioned in the same dark-blue.

There were no means of heating the place nor any provision for artificial light; no opportunity for moving about nor, if the compartment were filled, of changing one's position; no toilet conveniences of the simplest description and no way of getting out until released by the *garde*.

For several hours I traveled on alone and undisturbed. I had paid a man an extra *franc* to put me into a carriage but had not thought to stipulate for a "non-smoker;" in compartments not labeled thus, smoking is permitted if no occupant objects, with the exception of the places reserved for ladies alone; there are also still other compartments labeled "Smokers," where one must not demur at smoking if one takes a place there. During the course of the day, ladies and children came and went, but no one wished to smoke until late in the afternoon when my solitude was invaded by eight men, evidently commercial travelers, one of whom politely inquired if his smoking would be offensive to me; I replied literally that it would not, but when, without further inquiry, the remaining seven also produced cigars and began vigorously puffing the same, I did feel that I had fallen a victim to my good-nature. But after an hour or two, these gentlemen departed as they had come, in a body, and I was left again in solitude.

And what a solitude it is. Not a sound but the steadily rolling wheels and the occasional high, thin "toot" of the whistle, which is something entirely different from the ear-splitting shriek of our engines in America. No possible way of communicating with any human beings between stations. In fact, a prisoner in solitary confinement am I, only to be let out at the discretion of the guard. I cannot call him "conductor," he is so utterly unlike anyone we recognize under that title. He seems to have the vaguest idea of anything one would suppose to belong properly to his province; exhibits the greatest indifference as to one's tickets; indeed, on mine is a printed request that the "*voya-*

geur" will see personally that "the right coupon is detached at the right place!" He never gives any information as to necessary change of trains or other details, unless specially importuned, and even then his replies are unreliable and persons are left to find their way about as their intuition suggests. All this is rather hard on strangers in a strange land and of a strange tongue.

However I cannot help feeling sorry for the guard, he looks so forlorn, as he runs along in the rain outside the carriages, first on one side and then on the other, now and then casually mentioning the name of the station as he trots down the line. He does not look in at the windows and one would not suppose from his demeanor, that the travelers had the least interest in the matter. Then he disappears. I have yet to learn what becomes of him between stations.

What a contrast to our brazen-lunged train-men of stentorian tones. Can my "lone sister" imagine anyhow, a train with no brakemen, no pop-corn and gum fiend, no time-card, no literature, no ice-water, "no nothing," so to speak?

About this time, I gather from sights and sounds at a station we approach, that there is some refreshment to be had. The guard re-appears and unlocks my door; I question him and find that I am not in error. I step out, (the carriages abroad are almost invariably on a level with the platforms, so there is no climbing up and down) and follow the crowd into a long room filled with small tables. I have a cup of coffee with milk and sugar and a roll with butter,—I mention items because each is charged for separately, butter, milk and sugar not being matters of course, as with us,—for which I pay

about ten cents, United States, and start to go
back, but now to my astonishment I find I cannot get out.   I naturally had returned to the
door by which I entered, but find that locked
and exit cut off.   Then on diligent inquiry, I
am directed hither and thither, through narrow
passages, in at this door and out at that, until
finally after a tortuous way, I emerge with bewildered brain, at a totally different point from
that at which I had entered the building.

Two or three ladies now join me in my compartment and from their conversation, (which I
must of necessity hear, there being no privacy
in these carriages,) I learn that at the next station we reach the Belgian frontier, where our
luggage must be examined.

I am very glad to be thus forewarned, otherwise I should have been sorely dismayed at the
sudden invasion of our carriage as it comes to a
halt, by two or three excited men who seize our
hand-luggage and rush off with it. We follow,
though the men have vanished; we make our
way into a large room where everyone must
claim his or her possessions, produce keys and
submit to the inspection.

There are two points to be considered ; dutiable articles and overweight of permissible com-
modities.   It is a little odd that one may have
as much hand-luggage as one can get into
his compartment, with no extra charge, but on
all that goes into the luggage-van, one must
pay extra in France for anything over sixty
pounds, in Germany all over fifty-five pounds,
and in Belgium for every pound. These regu-
lations and the usually short distances from
one frontier to another, necessitate a continual
opening, weighing and re-weighing of trunks,
baskets and boxes, most tedious to experience,

as everybody must go personally to attend to
the matter. But there is no hurry. Everyone seems to have plenty of time and at last it is
over once more. Here again we find ourselves
locked in: after many efforts I discover that
the exit is at the opposite side from the entrance, and as before, in an entirely different
part of the building, but after turning here and
there through more doors, we come into a large
waiting-room which we are directed to cross
and finally are permitted to come into the open
air, when we all trail back again to our places,
fee our porters and set off once more.

And now we enter Belgium. No beauty is
there to be seen here along the line of the
railway. Occasionally a few grim, sterile looking hills and now and then a fine river, but the
country is mostly flat and uninteresting and
black with its numerous coal and iron works
with all their unlovely products. We roll along
with little variety until we have traversed the
tiny country and reach the German outposts. It
seems strange to reflect that I have crossed two
countries and entered a third in a little more
than half a day, when at home I have traveled
day after day and night after night without
ever getting outside the boundaries of the grand
and glorious United States. A little "spread-
eagle-ism" may perhaps be pardoned in one who,
having been for several months remote from
"Columbia, the gem of the ocean," begins to
yearn for the freedom and progress of that
"happy land."

But here we are in Germany, another custom-
house must be gone through, with another
weighing of luggage, another set of porters to
fee and another settling down to our places.

I was startled at the sudden contrast of the

North German physique to that of the lean, wiry, little Frenchmen among whom I had been so long. The officials here were a wonderfully fine looking set of men with brilliant and handsome uniforms. The station-masters, I learn, always wear a bright orange cap, so they are easily identified. One lordly creature in splendid cap and bright green, braided costume condescended to inspect my trunk.

He stood on one side and I on the other of the long, low barrier that runs across all these baggage-rooms. He undid one strap and ordered, not requested me to undo the other; astonished, I complied. He then took hold of one end of the tray and ordered me to lift the other. Speechless with amazement, I obeyed. He then deigned to proceed without further mandates. I wondered afterward what would have happened had I refused to obey his commands, probably something equal to "battle, murder and sudden death," for in Germany man is indeed, "lord supreme," and unless yielding homage to rank and position, absolutely lacking, as a rule, in any of that deference that the genuine American, whatever his station. always pays to women, young or old, lovely or otherwise. I almost wished I had told the official to "do it himself." However, I was too much startled to "let my angry passions rise" and did not, in fact, fully take in the extent of the man's—perhaps I should say "the gentleman-and-officer's—"rudeness until I was once more in my little compartment.

I may add here for the benefit of my "solitary woman" the sum of information gleaned later by me on this point. The usage is that any woman, gentle or simple, unless having a servant of some kind, must wait upon herself the same as a man does; though should it get whispered about that she is of high rank, she would receive servile attention. If one travels without a maid or man-servant, one may fee a porter to undo straps and other little jobs difficult for a woman to manage, but no service will be volunteered *gratis* nor should one ask it. One pays the porter what one pleases, from about two cents up; one would wish to be just and certainly not mean, but the veteran traveler never gives inordinate fees.

Our progress was soon again interrupted, for at the next station we had to change trains with yet again the bother of claiming boxes, bags and bundles and feeing porters. But our change was a vast improvement on our situation. We were now on the governmental railway of Prussia and found that second-class cars in Germany are as good as, and more convenient than, first-class in France.

This compartment held places for six; the customary lane ran from side to side connecting opposite doors; the long, back seat was divided by movable arms into two of two places each; opposite was another double-seat facing, the occupants of which must ride backward.

In the space usually devoted to a continuation of this short seat, was a door leading into one of the tiniest lavatories, having the scantiest of furnishings. This opened also into the next compartment, one lavatory thus serving for two compartments.

In each compartment a "Danger Brake" was fixed on one wall with a placard stating how and when it might be used and the penalties for misuse. Another complicated arrangement was also provided, with directions for summoning help in the case of illness or aggression on the part of any of the passengers. There was an electric bell "for the use of ladies." There was an apparatus by which, through moving a lever, the temperature could be changed from "cold" to "medium" or to "hot", though I am sure I should never dare to meddle with this or the others. As a farther provision for safety, the walls of the compartment failed by a few inches to reach the ceiling, thus making it possible for anyone, by standing upon a seat, to survey the interior of the next compartment and thus, I suppose, to cause any chance villain who might desire to injure his fellow-travelers, to realize that he was, theoretically, under surveillance, though I fear that, pract'cally, the arrangement would be of little avail.

The seats were upholstered in corded velvet of a grayish brown, very soft and comfortable; foot-rug and curtains of the same hue; ceiling and walls decorated with a neat, cheerful paper; while a small lamp fixed in the center of the roof would provide enough light in an emergency "to make the darkness visible."

One lady accompanied me in the change but after a few miles she also vanished and I was left journeying onward alone.

The sun had now come out and the country looked very pleasing; not unlike the region of the United States through Wisconsin and Minnesota; not quite so well-watered perhaps, but the aspect of things in general made it seem not at all incomprehensible that our North-German immigrants are able to settle down so contentedly among us in that section.

The fir-t stage of my journey ends at Cologne and I step out toward evening at this city of fragrant associations. After many formalities, (which, however, need not disconcert the "lone female,'' even though she does not understand German, if she will keep calm and hold her ticket plainly visible,) I am safely inducted into a cab and soon am driving forth with wonder and interest through the streets of this historic town.

CHAPTER XIII.

I can hardly describe, much less account for, the comfortable feeling that took possession of me as soon as I began to mingle in German scenes and to come in contact with the German people.

Somehow a sensation of confidence and "at-home-a-tive-ness" pervaded my mental being at once, of which I had not the slightest experience during all my sojourn in France.

Possibly it may be attributed to the fact that a resident of Wisconsin must necessarily be somewhat familiar with the German type, with its method of thought and with the sound of its language, and though both type and tongue are markedly modified with us, by the influence of American environment, yet there is enough similarity in countenance and cadence here to make me feel that I am not among utter strangers. The rosy, rotund, blonde and beaming gentlemen and the fair, friendly and amiable ladies whom I see all about, may be met in counterpart any day at home, while the familiar names I note everywhere intensify the home feeling.

Then, as a general thing, the German is a well-balanced being. He does not fly off in a tangent of wild excitement on the slightest or no provocation. Neither does he seem to have a deep-rooted suspicion of all foreigners nor lay himself out at once to get the better of all such by sharp practices. He seems to assume that strangers mean to be fair and honorable in dealing with him, and he is willing to give them the benefit of a doubt in all that he may not understand.

Again, his, or perhaps I should say her, housekeeping is very like our own. The country is full of homes and restful places for the weary. Their couches and chairs are made for rest, their rooms are light and warm, (though they do not overheat them as the Americans do,) and their "front apartments" are not at the back, but survey the pleasant avenues and the tasteful gardens so arranged that their beauty may be enjoyed by passers-by.

As with us, the family gathers at the breakfast table, though one does not find the variety at this meal that Americans expect; this however can generally be obtained by ordering an "American breakfast," and paying extra for the added dishes. Two is the usual hour for dinner, seven for supper; breakfast is a more movable feast ranging from half past seven to nine. As a result of this routine, I presume, banking hours are from nine to two and from five to seven. Tea and coffee are served at these meals much more commonly than in France, and without extra charge, though beer-drinking is universal and that of wine almost as much so; but our United States habit of ice-water drinking is incomprehensible to the German as well as most other foreigners; in consequence, the average United Statesian meets with considerable ridicule, generally good-natured, for his aqua-imbibing propensities; but usually unless very young or foreignized by long residence, he maintains his abstemiousness in this respect. This practice is a scource of surprise and even dismay to the friendly foreigners one meets, and often, some kind-hearted persons would take an opportunity to remonstrate with

me on account of what they deemed my pernicious habit.   "Why, you will certainly be ill,"
they would exclaim, "it is impossible to drink
water habitually, without getting one's system
out of order." "But I do it at home," I would
reply.

"Oh!" they would cry, "but you Americans
have more typhoid fever than any other nation
in the world."

"But I never had typhoid fever in my life,"
I would rejoin. Still they would not leave me
to my fate. "Mark my words," they would
add impressively, "you cannot do it here. Be
warned in time."

But I persisted in imbibing the crystal fluid,
though I will confess that at first, supposing
some subtle danger might lurk therein, I strove
to satisfy my thirst with wine and beer; but very
shortly decided that I would suffer illness if so
it must be, rather than swallow the sour and
bitter stuff that I saw consumed all about me
with such relish. Then as I remained provok-
ingly healthy, my companions would regard me
with amazement; no doubt exclaiming, like the
old-school physician whose fever patient recov-
ered after swallowing a strenuously forbidden
pitcherful of ice-water:

"Great Heavens, what a constitution!"

But I was proud to find that with most foreigners, the name of American, especially from
the United States, was synonomous with tem-
perance, if not total abstinence; and by the way,
I was amused to note that "American" means a
United States citizen, with the average native of
the Old World. "Is so-and-so an American?"
I would ask.

"Oh, no! He is a Canadian," would be the
reply, or a Mexican, or whatever the case
might be.

"But Canada is in America," I would remark.

"Oh! is it?" many would rejoin; while others, especially among the English, might say: "Oh, well! We never think of *them* as Americans."

In Germany, coffee with light wafers or *kucken* is usually served at four o'clock and sometimes tea also, though the fashion of drinking the latter in the middle of the afternoon, is an exotic from England, as it is in France and America. There is always a hearty welcome for a friend or stranger and the "house-mother" is seldom absent from her post, where she provides for the comfort of all. One peculiarity at least, of social etiquette in Germany surprises the foreigner, that is the requirement that the stranger shall make the advances toward acquaintance with residents, calling upon them for purposes of introduction.

On my arrival in Cologne my first act was to refresh the inner woman, which I did with, among other things, the first cup of really good coffee that I had found since I left home, and the first butter that did not taste like whipped cream.

My room was light, airy, clean and well-furnished, at a moderate charge; seventy-five cents a day, I believe, with fifteen cents additional for service, but no extra charge for heat and light; tips *ad libitum*; there was an exceedingly comfortable bed, though this is no rarity as I found excellent beds everywhere. One never sees the large English double-bed in France or Germany, always single; if the bed-room is intended for two persons, there are two beds.

Of course in the hotels, linen is changed daily, as with us; but I was glad to find later in the *pensions,*—for the Germans have adopted the French term,—that more liberal ideas are prevalent than in France, bed-linen being changed once in a fortnight, "Just as they do in England," to quote my German hostess; and as a week is only seven days as with us, there is consequently a difference of ten days in the time one is expected to use one's slips and sheets.

The Germans also have more advanced views in regard to towels, though bath-rooms are almost as rare as in France. But I will say for the *pensions* of both countries, that the linen and bedding furnished are of excellent quality, soft, fairly fine, ample and sweet smelling, and the room-fittings as a rule far surpass in quality and comfort, those provided at greater cost in our own country. This last clause applies also to the table, where usually much care is shown to appointments and serving though the list of dishes is much shorter. The housekeeping I find immaculate everywhere. But this is a digression. I return to my hotel.

Wonder of wonders, there is here an elevator. As we use that term, while the English say "lift" and the French "ascender," (translated,) I was curious to know the German designation, so asked the lad at hand; to my amusement he replied "riding-chair," (also translated.)

The next morning I began my exploration of Cologne. It is a fine city and, as we all know, full of special interest. The "sweet waters" that have made its name a household word everywhere, are to be seen on sale on every side, in gayly decorated flasks more or less elegant.

The great cathedral attracts one's attention at once. Would that I could fully express the singular impression of extreme airiness, delicacy and elegance, conveyed by this wondrous structure, which is at the same time so grand and imposing. Inapplicable as the word may seem to such a pile of stone, the epithet "lovely" immediately rises to one's lips.

The two twin towers reaching up so far away into the vault of heaven are a landmark for many and many a mile both up and down the Rhine, and far off over the hills and plains out from the city.

Though the tallest towers in Europe, in fact, I believe the tallest of any structure in the world, they soar aloft with a marvelous grace which is exquisitely blended with an impressive majesty.

One should ascend these towers not only for the far-sweeping view, but to look upon the great bells and to read the inscription upon the huge *Kaiserglocke*, which some one has translated thus:

> "I am the Emperor's bell;
> The Emperor's praise I tell;
> On holy guard I stand,
> And for the German land
> Beseech that God may please
> To grant it peace and ease."

The bells in the southern tower were hung about the middle of fourteen hundred, and the enormous crane that did the work remained undisturbed until 1868.

Strange that the name of the original architect of this marvelous creation, should be lost in the mists of obscurity. It is ascribed by many, though, I believe, without sufficient corroboration, to Albertus Magnus; and even he is supposed to have been assisted by supernatural agents, the Virgin appearing to him in a dream with four canonized masons, Severus, Severinus, Carpophorus, and Victorinus, who sketched the plans in lines of fire. Awaking, Albertus hastened to reproduce them, but refused to call them his own, ascribing them to the hand of God.

Another legend, however, imputes this supernatural interference to a directly opposite power, and declares that the devil appeared to Gerhard, an ambitious young architect, and dared him to originate something more splendid than had yet been achieved; after attempting this in vain, unintentionally producing only copies of famous plans, he shouted angrily, "Do it yourself, then!" Whereat His Satanic Majesty did it, but at the price of Gerhard's soul; but just as he was about to sign the contract, he bethought himself of a holy silver cross which he wore and, having the plans safe, he drew the cross forth and dared the devil to "come on."

The baffled devil retired breathing fire and vengeance and vowing, "You will find, presumptuous one, that it is unwise to be dishonest even with the devil Though you build the cathedral with my plans, your own name shall be forgotten forever."

The earthly fate of this daring young architect was peculiar; for "while he did direct those that toiled," there opened "suddenly a great pit whereout came a great and loathly worm" which seized the poor man and. cracking his neck, drew him into the pit which then closed up and he was seen no more. In the south tower, upon two pillars of the west side, may be seen two ancient gargoyles said to be a "true likeness" of Gerhard and his faithful dog; the animal catching hold of his master's gown, strives to draw him back from the pit, but is engulfed with him.

The moral of this legend is dubious, seeming to imply that it would have been better not to outwit the devil but to acquiesce in his schemes.

The only definite fact connected with the name of Gerhard is that he was the first superintendent of the building of the edifice.

The history of this cathedral from the first inception of the sacred edifice in the mind of Hildebold in the beginning of the ninth century, down to the placing of the final copestone by Emperor William I., in 1880, is most varied and exciting.

Bombardment, conflagration, spoilation, destruction and even murder are associated with the gradual, often intermitted, progress of this great and noble work, until now it stands proclaiming,—to quote a royal patron and promoter of the sublime undertaking,—"to yet unborn generations, a Germany which, owing to the unity of its princes and people, is great and powerful, and bloodlessly compels peace among the nations of the world."

Entering the magnificent structure at the main portal, I found another variety of the genus *Suisse* or beadle. This one wore a long, flowing robe of scarlet, finely ornamented in black, and on his head was a high cap or turban of black velvet. He carried a long rod of office and stood guard in the center of the great nave. He was, however, not so gloomily dignified as his French brother, strange to say, but seemed of an affable disposition and kindly whispered to us to "please keep still until mass was over."

I had not known till then that a service was in progress, as the worshippers were in a far-off angle not readily visible from where we stood. They soon quietly dispersed and the visitors wandered about here and there, admiring and marveling.

All the proportions and decorations throughout are, of course, beautiful and magnificent to

an unspeakable degree, but here, as in other
instances,—though it goes to my heart to pass
on without my best tribute to the ineffable
loveliness and majestic sublimity that almost
moves one to tears from very excess of emotion,—
I only pause to mention something unusually
quaint or antique which might possibly escape
notice by one who were properly describing, as
many have described already, the glory and
grandeur of this and other famous wonders of
art.

To get at once a comprehensive view of the
whole magnificent interior, one may ascend to a
gallery in the eastern pillar of the south portal.
In the north wall are some very odd, ancient,
stained windows dating from the sixteenth century. In one of these appears the figure of the
founder of Cologne, holding the standard of the
city, while underneath is the inscription (freely
translated) in that rhyming-couplet so dear to
the German mind of the middle ages:

> "Marcus Agrippa, a Roman man,
> The Agrippa Colony first began."

Opposite him is Marsilius with his little
rhyme:

> "Marsylis proud, a heathen's son,
> Held Cologne and triumphs won."

Queer neighbors they, these rude and warlike
men, for the Holy Family, the Magi, the Saints
George, Maurice and others who occupy the rest
of the window.

Below the organ is a wooden urn dating back
to 1063, containing the remains of Queen Rich-
eza of Poland. St. Peter's staff is one of the
curiosities here; also an image of the Virgin,
"which," as an inscription testifies, "has worked

many miracles:'' here too are ''the relics of the Magi,'' received in 1164 from the abbess of a Milan convent, and which rest beneath a marble monument of rare beauty in the Chapel of the Magi, the fourth chapel of the choir.

The beautiful windows of the choir are the oldest in the cathedral, being of the twelfth century. Others equally beautiful are placed on the left of the nave and date from the fifteenth.

The right of the nave, however, has been fitted up with hideous specimens of modern achievement. They were probably expensive, as they were the gift of William of Prussia and Ludwig of Bavaria, but they compare with the others somewhat as a cheap chromo might with an ancient masterpiece of oil.

The choir itself, so grandly and somberly magnificent, has seen many mutations during its completion. At one time houses were built all around it and where the nave should have been, and during the occupation of Napoleon First, the French used it as a forage storehouse.

Opposite the Chapel of the Magi is a monument in memory of Archbishop Dietrich von Moers, 1860, excessively ornate and consisting of several figures of most sacred personages, such as the Virgin, the Infant Jesus, St. Peter and others, who are represented as associating in the most intimate and friendly manner with the aforesaid bishop. There is an epitaph of the most fulsome praise, extoling Dietrich to a superlative degree, but unfortunately an unappreciative and skeptical posterity unkindly declares that the bishop not only ordered the monument, but actually wrote the eulogy himself.

The seven chapels about the choir are filled

with curious and costly objects of historic and artistic interest, but I must not stop for details. Archbishop Philip von Heinsburg lies in a huge, battlemented tomb, thus signifying that he first fortified Cologne.

A mighty figure in solid brass lying upon his tomb under a Gothic arch, represents the great Konrad.

The greatest art-treasure in Cologne is the famous *Dombild*, or Cathredal-Picture, a triptych of Meister Wilhelm's, representing the Adoration of the Magi, and to the uninitiated, it would seem that it should be in the chapel of that name, but for reasons wise, no doubt, we find it in that of St. Michael, though formerly in St. Agnes' shrine. The central panel shows the Magi offering presents to the Child; their followers throng the background on the wings, St. Ursula and her maidens on the left, St. Gercon with warriors on the right; on the outside of the wings, the Annunciation.

The city of Cologne, as perhaps some "lone sister" may have forgotten, had its origin in a military colony (whence the name) placed here by Marcus Agrippa fifty years before Christ, so it really was old before the first conception of even the predecessors of the cathedral was realized. Intensely interesting as is the narrative of the city's rise, progress, decline and later return to importance, or "boom," as we of the later day might term it, yet it is but one of the innumerable, fascinating spots of this wondrous "Old World," to which no manner of justice can be done by the casual tourist.

A weird reminiscence of former trying times is observed at St. Ursula, where are exhibited in glass cases what are said to be the skulls and bones of eleven thousand virgins who came with the holy Ursula, a British princess, to Cologne, where they suffered death as martyrs. St. Ursula's bones are deposited in a shrine in the sacristy which is also said to contain a curiosity catalogued as "one of the wine-jugs used at the marriage of Cana." These various bones are exhibited for a consideration and are truly a revolting and piteous spectacle.

Most of the streets of Cologne are narrow, with queer-looking houses, also narrow and of peculiar architecture.

At a corner of Neu-Markt and Richmodis streets, may be seen a building from the attic of which two wooden horses are looking out. Concerning these the legend runs thus:

In fourteen hundred, when Cologne was terribly devastated by the plague, Richmodis, wife of knight Menges von Aduct, was one of the victims and was buried in the Apostles Church. Her wedding-ring was left upon her finger and the grave-diggers noticing the same, went the next night to steal it.

They opened the grave and the coffin, but their rough attempts to remove the ring, roused her from the trance into which she had fallen; she started up, frightening away the thieves, and ran back to her home where she knocked for admittance.

The servants alarmed ran to their master. He went to the door and demanded who was there.

"Your wife," was the answer.

"Ah!" he exclaimed in sorrow, "my wife Richmodis is dead, and my horses would sooner ascend to the loft of my house and look.out of the window, than she would be asking to come in."

Scarcely were the words uttered when the

horses were heard going upstairs, and in commemoration these wooden heads were affixed to the windows. One can only say to the sceptic, "If you don't believe it, I can show you the windows."

In Sternengasse, No. 10, stands a house on which are placed two memorial tablets, one declaring that Marie de Medicis died, the other that Reubens was born here. I believe the former statement is not contradicted, but the latter is false, though it is true that he passed a part of his early childhood in this dwelling.

Aside from these and like relics of an olden time, there are in Cologne, numerous charming modern avenues containing magnificent buildings of varied and beautiful designs, as well as shady promenades and handsome squares. A series of elegantly planned boulevards, denominated *Ringstrassen*, extend around the whole town.

I took a leisurely survey of these from the window of a horse-tram one lovely day. A very friendly conductor added much to my pleasure and stock of information, by his cheerful conversation.

A cheery, gentlemanly sort of a young fellow he was; he left his car and took the utmost pains in piloting me safely to another when I left his line. It did seem odd to have him accept with a "*danke sehr*" and without indignation, a coin or two of trifling value when we parted, and I have learned since that I gave twice what might have been expected.

I should have become accustomed to the "tip" system by this time, but it still gives me a shock every now and then when some well-appearing, courteous person betrays his or her inferior origin by the placid acceptance of one's small change.

Usually at first the American mind, in chatting with a sociable stranger, considers it only a case of mutual information and interest; but gradually one awakens to a realizing sense that the affable individual is only lying in wait for one's loose silver. Sometimes it is hard to know just what to do. I have often spent a miserable half hour when visiting some famous gallery or palace, in trying to decide whether the splendid creature in immaculate and decorated "get-up" who has shown me so much polite attention, is really an official to whom it would be wildly insulting to offer recompense, or just a common person who is confidently calculating on what he may receive. But I have generally found it to be the latter. Often too, it has seemed to me the height of impertinence to proffer fifteen or twenty-five cents to the important and responsible head-clerk or manager of my hostelry, though, to be sure, he is not so imposing a being as his prototype in America. I find, however, that he is always willing to accept the slightest favor in this line.

I saw no electric trams in Cologne. In fact, electricity is little used abroad in comparison to America; foreigners usually consider it far too dangerous for familiar use. The German management of the street-car system, as noted here and confirmed by later observation, struck me as very sensible. In the first place, one pays according to the distance one rides, all the way from five *pfenniges* (about a cent and a quarter,) up to twenty-five or thirty *pfenniges*; I have never found it higher. Then one receives a ticket showing how much money has been paid. The cars are neat and well-kept, with a definite number of seats as in Paris, so that there is very little crowding. Expectoration is most strictly prohibited. There are many points in our foreign cousins' ordering of the transportation business in general, that we might copy with great benefit to our own methods.

Later on I took a stroll out through an old arched gateway, along a delightful road skirted on one side by beautiful gardens, both public and private, and on the other by the silver, flowing waters of the romantic river Rhine.

How fair it all was, glowing in the "evening sunset-shine" till one could almost seem to see the "Niebelungen's ruddy gold" reflected from the depths of the clear waters, back upon the pleasant paths and parterres above. It is not hard in Germany to muse and dream.

My next stopping-place was Duesseldorf, an hour or so from Cologne. Again I was locked in all by myself and so continued in solitary state absolutely uninterrupted, until I reached my destination.

There were no halts, the train being express, so there was nothing to occupy one's attention except the fair, green, smiling landscape with its fine streams and splendid trees.

I do not like this way of traveling. When one is alone it is so "awfully" lonely, and when others are in the compartment, one is brought so disagreeably near them; one must either sit opposite, staring and stared at, or side by side, as one might say "cheek by jowl." If one happens to be in the middle, one has no access to the two windows, and at best one has little opportunity to change one's position. Yet foreigners dislike the American railway car because it is "so public." I consider it much more exclusive. In the latter one has one's own section where no other person can "molest or make afraid," yet one has the advantage of the space and light of a roomy car, with one's fellow-travelers at a proper distance and with no occasion to face them or to ride backward unless from choice.

I do not note quite the same caution in Germany that I observed in France regarding the safety of life. While the roads are well and solidly constructed, yet they usually run across the open country with very little, although somewhat, more protection for man and beast than with us. There is usually a low hedge along the line on either side, but it could be easily overstepped by men or animals. Every wagon-road, however, is provided at every point of crossing a railroad, with strong gates on each side of the track, and a gateman—who is sometimes a woman—stands on duty as we dash by; while in the towns there is simply no getting upon the track without permission, the rails everywhere within town-limits being either between walls or elevated on massive masonry.

My journey this time was short and we soon entered the fine, roomy station of Duesseldorf.

This is a pretty town with wide streets and very spacious, ornamental avenues called *Allées*, which latter have magnificent trees in double rows down their centers. One of these *Allées* is especially fine. A broad canal faced up with solid mason-work and bordered by these beautiful trees, extends its length through the thoroughfare, which is double the width of the other boulevards. Graceful, decorative bridges span the waters, and light, ornamental railings insure safety; while frequent seats along under the trees provide delightful resting-places for the pedestrian.

There is a beautifully "rural" park lying almost in the center of the little city, where the grand old trees and bowery shrubbery, interspersed with frequent natural pools, and threaded by delightful paths all carefully ordered and kept, give all the charm of nature with the added adornments of art. Here, in a secluded dell and yet close to the busy street, standing upon a thick carpet of living green and embowered in overhanging branches and clustering vines, stands Duesseldorf's monument to her slain in battle.

The creation is of pure white marble. Two or three broad, shallow steps lead up to a spacious, semi-circular court or platform of this material, encircled by a low railing of the same. Upon this foundation is placed the oblong base of the memorial, which is classic in conception. Rising from this base is a pedestal supporting the full-length figure in heroic proportions, of a dying warrior in half-recumbent position, while at his side the lion of Germany, pitying and powerful to avenge, holds beneath his mighty paw, the broken spear that has made the deadly wound. Upon the front of the pedestal are graven the following lines from a German poet:—

"Fame have our heroes enough, and triumphs and
        ever green laurels;
Tears from poor mother-hearts wrung, builded this
        symbol of stone."

On the back is the inscription:

"Grateful Duesseldorf to Her Fallen Sons."

The snowy whiteness of the marble, the deep, restful green of the foliage, the quiet nook wherein the monument stands, the majestic simplicity yet marvelous effectiveness of design and execution, all combine to make the memorial an object of most impressive beauty.

There are a number of interesting old edifices in Duesseldorf and many beautiful modern ones. The style of architecture is mainly on broad, severe lines, with decorations of an elevated type. Kunst Halle is one of the prominent new structures and was built to properly house and display the art treasures of Duesseldorf, which has a rather peculiar school of its own.

I had a somewhat odd experience while mak-

ing my way thither one morning. I had been
to visit an ancient church and was inquiring
my way along, when I met an old lady of whom
I asked directions. I repeated my question two
or three times as she informed me that she was
a little deaf, when suddenly she grasped my
meaning and ejaculated, "*Ja, ja, ja!* I am
going there myself; come along with me."

I did so and found I had struck a living fount
and endless torrent of information. The old
lady walked, as she talked, very rapidly, and I
could with difficulty keep pace with her, while
the rattle of carts and wagons over the stone
pavements made it almost impossible for me to
understand her quick utterances in a, to me,
foreign tongue.

However, I learned that she was the "widow
of an artist, the mother of an artist and the sister of an artist;" that she "had a complimentary
membership-ticket to the exhibitions," but that
I would "have to pay;" and then she went on
and gave me a hasty yet comprehensive sketch
of the beginning, progress and completion of
the new gallery: the condition and contents of
the old; the history of the removal of the collection, the later additions, and kindred topics too
many to recall; while all I contributed to the
interview was a look of interest, an occasional
smile and an interjectory "*so!*" "*ja, ja!*" or
"*gewiss!*", wherever they seemed best to fit in.

She conducted me safely to the building,
piloted me in, led me around through the different rooms and gave me an account of everything she deemed worthy of notice.

She, it appeared was, or else her brother, son
or husband was, or had been, personally
acquainted with nearly every contemporary
artist of note, and really her knowledge, range

and interest were amazing. She insisted on my
"doing" everything thoroughly, and I certainly
made a much more exhaustive survey of this
collection than I had any idea of making when
I set out. It struck me as quite amusing that
a casual inquiry of a chance stranger in a
by street of a foreign town, should open
to me such a store of what might be termed
"compulsory education." But I finally was
allowed to bid the old lady farewell, whereupon
I returned to my hotel whence I soon resumed
my journey, setting out for Hanover.

On this stretch I made my first acquaintance
with what the Germans call a "Day-tsoog,"
(spelled *D. Zug*,) which name I was quite at a
loss to understand. I knew that "D." was
"D.", and "*Zug*" was "train," but the combination suggested nothing to me, unless something akin to the "big, big D." of the Captain
of the Pinafore.

Later I was told that it was a contraction for
Durch-Zug, and as that translates "through
train," I concluded I had solved the puzzle.
But soon after I learned that *Fern-Zug* was the
term for what we understand by a through
train, so I was nonplussed again.

Finally after a long time and much question-
ing, for the dictionaries were silent on the matter and most persons didn't know and few
seemed to care, I met a friendly inn-keeper who
kindly made it all plain to me.

It seems that *Fern-Zug* is really the through
train, that is, a train made up for travel without
change between two distant points, the termini
of the line; and though *D. Zug* is truly a contraction of *Durch-Zug*, yet that expression is itself a contraction for *Durch-Gang-Zug* or "corridor train," which gives a very different aspect
to the meaning.

It was easy to understand why this train that
I now entered should be called a corridor train,
for a corridor, or passage, extends from one end
of the car to the other, not through the center,
however, but on one side and across the two ends.
In some respects the cars are like ours in America. First; they are set up higher than the
ordinary continental coach and are entered by
means of two or three steps; but these are not
at each end leading up to a platform as with us;
instead they run along on each side like those
on an open street-car, and the doors, of which
there are four, open opposite each other, from the
sides into the end passages. Second; the train
is vestibuled, so one can pass, as in ours, from
one end of the train to the other without ex-
posure.

Into the side corridor the compartments open;
eight or ten in all, perhaps, of both first and
second class, in each carriage, or *Wagen*, as the
Germans call it. There is very little difference
in the two classes in Germany, in fact I could
see none in point of comfort; the upholstering
in the first class may be of finer material, and
perhaps a little gilding or two or three small
mirrors not larger than a dining-plate, may be
"thrown in," where the second class has none;
one cannot speak with certainty in such
points; sometimes there are none at all
anywhere, and at others both classes will
have them. In each compartment are six
places, three opposing three, and divided by
adjustable arms. The seats are roomy and easy,
but the fine finish and skilled handiwork seen
in our cars, are entirely lacking.

The corridor taking up one entire side of the
carriage, there are but two places in each compartment next to windows, so the first two arrivals

are the lucky ones. If one comes after these, one has no chance to view the scenery except across one's neighbor's corporosity. The neighbor will probably entirely control the curtain and keep it drawn or not as he prefers, while the remaining occupants may be, at his pleasure, deprived of light or dazzled with too much. Then very likely some one of the six will be mortally afraid of the "publicity" of the corridor along which an occasional traveler or train-man may pass, and so insist on having the door into the same tightly closed, and there you are shut up in the stuffy little place with four or five other hot, dusty, irritated mortals.

But there are electric bells in each compartment and a small, meagerly equipped toilet-room in each car; also a buffet somewhere in the train where beverages may be procured, so the train is more American-like than the usual style here, though far less comfortable than our ordinary day-coaches. On these trains there are women employed, one or two to each carriage, who wear white badges upon their left arms, labeled *Dienst-Frau*. I hardly know what they do, unless it is to scrub and wash dishes, for they do not answer the bells; if you ring, a man appears.

Meals may be had *en route*, by telegraphing ahead through a porter who takes your order. The repast is brought into the compartment, and is sometimes odiously obvious to other occupants who, not being hungry themselves, do not enjoy seeing and smelling eatables at such close quarters. The food, however, is very good and not at all expensive to our United States ideas of train prices. Drinking-water must be ordered and paid for at so much a bottle, but it is a great convenience to be able to get it even this way, for on the ordinary train one must go without, unless one carries it with one or can hail a station-porter during a halt and send him for a bottle, which he fetches without ice.

On this special "*D. Zug*," the seats were extra, though I have found them so but once since; about two marks, (nearly fifty cents) between Duesseldorf and Hanover, one hundred and seventy-eight miles. It was really a much appreciated privilege to rise occasionally and walk up and down the corridor. I was amused to note that the conductor and other trainsmen did not seem to realize that they could go through it in announcing stations, but ran up and down on the platforms outside as before. Such a strange custom for the persons inside who are anxious to know, cannot hear, while those outside who can hear, know already. Perhaps though, the men are forbidden to pass through the train unless absolutely necessary. There are a great many "don'ts" and "mustn'ts" in *Deutschland*. But I should think the train men would be glad that they are not obliged to pass along the steps at the sides, clinging to the iron hand-rail while the train is in motion, which is the only way to go from one compartment to another in the ordinary train, rain or shine.

Not far from Duesseldorf is the ancient city of Duisberg, a manufacturing place and largely interested in coal traffic, but noteworthy as being the burial-place of Mercator, the geographer.

It struck me strangely to see a monument to him, for he had never seemed a real being to me; though I confess he has never occupied my thoughts to any great extent since my early childhood, when I used to ponder over the very odd maps that appeared on the first pages of my

primary "geography-book,"—as the English say,
—and were labeled "Mercator's Projection." I
recalled a little friend who once, on hearing a
Mr. Spalding mentioned, exclaimed:

"Why! Is Spaldin' a man? I fawt 'e was
a glue!"

Likewise my youthful mind had never "fawt"
of Mercator as "a man," but merely as a Projection.

At this place our train crosses the Ruhr and five
miles farther on we come to Oberhausen which
has the rare distinction in this old country, of
being a "new place." It is of about twenty-five
thousand inhabitants and has extensive iron-
works.

The region roundabout is very level and not
specially interesting, though the verdant fields
and abundant water-courses have a pleasant
look in the sunshine.

As we approach Dortmund, however, the
face of the country changes and, to the left,
breaks up into ranges of picturesque hills. Dortmund is ancient and venerable, as well as
important and progressive. It is mentioned in
history as early as 927; in 1387-8 it successively
resisted a siege of nearly two years, by the
Archbishop of Cologne and forty other princes.

The old walls have been leveled and fine
promenades laid out along their foundations. It
has numerous old churches and many "up-to-
date" foundries, being the seat of the mining
authorities of Westphalia.

It was in this locality that the ancient, secret
and terrible tribunal, the *Vehmgericht*, origin-
ated, which exerted such a fearful and powerful
sway over the whole empire. Dortmund was
the seat of its supreme court and here in the
"Court-Yard under the Lindens" the Emperor

Sigismund himself was initiated in 1429. One of these lindens is still standing and must be considerably more then four hundred years old. The last meeting was convened here in 1803.

Distant ten miles is Hamm (suggestive name!) which is quite noted for its warm baths. It is not here, however, as would seem fit and proper, that is located the great depot of Westphalia hams and sausages so well known to fame, but in the little village of Goetersloh, thirty-three miles on, across the Lippe and the Ems.

Here also are the head-quarters of the far renowned *Pumpernickel*, a dark-brown bread or cake considered very nutritious. It is made of unsifted rye flour, sometimes iced, and is dear to the German palate but not to mine.

The country grows more hilly and is interspersed with many busy and flourishing towns rich in historic interest and containing innumerable fine relics of "ye olden tyme," in the way of cathedral, castle, wood-carving, painting and stained glass.

Bielefeld is the center of the Westphalian linen trade. Herford possesses many cotton and flax mills. At Enger, a small town five miles aside from the railway, was the seat of that stubborn opponent of Charlemagne, namely the Saxon duke, Wittekind, who figures so extensively in the semi-historic, semi-traditional lore of Germany. His bones are still preserved in the abbey church here, which was built in the twelfth century.

At Lemgo, a quaint and handsome place of seven thousand inhabitants, is an extensive factory of meerschaum pipes.

About three miles from Detmold, (where Freiligrath was born,) rises, in the valley of the Werra, the Grotenburg, eleven hundred and sixty feet above the the sea, one of the highest points of the Teutoburgian forest. Upon its summit, plainly visible for miles around, the celebrated *Hermann's Denknal*, or Monument of Arminius, rears itself. Upon an arched substructure one hundred feet in height, stands the colossal figure of the prince, fifty-six feet high, with raised sword the point of which is thirty feet above the helmet. This is the work of Ernst von Baudel, who devoted most of his life to its execution. The cost of the monument, which is of copper and iron, was about two hundred and seventy thousand marks, equivalent at the present rate of exchange to about sixty-six thousand dollars. An admirable prospect is visible from the gallery of this monument.

In ascending the hill some very ancient German fortifications known as the *Kleine Hoenenring* are passed. Going on to Horn and Paderborn by *Diligence*, one comes upon the *Externsteine*, an odd group of five rocks over one hundred feet high, protruding from the earth like gigantic teeth.

In one of these rocks is a grotto that leads to a cave. According to an inscription dated 1195, in the grotto, it was fitted up by Bishop Henry of Paderborn, in imitation of the Holy Sepulcher. Some very curious reliefs hewn from the rock, represent a Descent from the Cross, in two sections. In the upper part colossal figures show the removal of the body by Joseph of Arimethea; above hovers God the Father carrying a banner and a little child.

The lower portion shows Adam and Eve entwined by a serpent and waiting for redemption.

At Oeynhausen are warm saline springs considered especially efficacious in paralysis.

Now we cross the Weser and presently notice
to the left, on the Wittekindsburg eight hundred and twenty feet above sea-level, a monument recently erected to Emperor William I.
Next comes Minden, an ancient cathedral town,
the fortifications of which were leveled in 1842,
and which contains many handsome modern
edifices.

Still we go on and on, passing many a relic
of bygone eras in *château* or tower or crumbling
wall and finally, after speeding some time over
another long, level and fertile stretch, we see
the winding, yellow waters of the Leine and roll
into the handsome and imposing station of the
flourishing city of Hanover.

CHAPTER XV.

Hanover has about two hundred thousand inhabitants and is situated in a fertile, somewhat rolling plain, well watered, principally by the navigable river Leine, and its tributary, the Ihme. I was much pleased with the clean, airy and generally ornamental appearance of the place and remained here several weeks.

I was most fortunate in my location, having been referred to a family of ex-governesses, four maiden ladies of middle age, who, in addition to being excellent hostesses, were also refined and cultivated ladies, not only educated, but exceedingly skilled in music, drawing, painting, Latin and modern languages.

The eldest was a "plump and pleasing person," and a most painstaking and indefatigable housekeeper, though highly accomplished as well.

The second sister had just returned from "finishing" the daughter of the deposed King of Hanover, having been a member of this royal household many years, traveling and residing with her patrons in almost every part of Europe. Her reminiscences of the familiar daily "walk and conversation" of the august and titled persons with whom she had come into contact, were most interesting, including personal recollections of the Queen of England, the Emperors of Germany and Russia, and nearly all of their numerous distinguished connection, the House of Hanover being, as we know, the source of the present English line.

The third sister was also a traveler, having
spent in discharge of her duties, two years in
America and some time in France, Switzerland
and Holland. In France she had charge of the
children of our own ex-vice-president Morton.

Neither was the fourth, whom we used to
call "the little one," a "stay at home." She
had spent eighteen years in England and was
familiar with France and Italy.

Naturally their information and experience
were extensive and the ladies were really almost
walking encyclopedias. But this very fund of
knowledge and the having been for so many continuous years in positions of authority over
pupils to whom the governess's dictum on all
points was final and decisive, had given them
each somewhat of an arbitrary tendency, causing them sometimes to forget that the transitory
members of their household were not of undis-
ciplined minds to which the governess's opinion
or decision must be conclusive and without
appeal.

This trait was especially noticeable in "the
little one," and many were the good-natured
tilts engaged in between herself and the various
nationalities around the "festal board." Her
information was usually extremely correct but
she could with difficulty admit any point of
view other than her own, of a subject, and
rarely knew "when she was beaten," for like
the "man convinced against his will," she
would be "of the same opinion still." This, of
course, was her privilege and was of no very
great consequence, though forcibly illustrating
the conservative tendency of old-world education; and sometimes, even when we were quite
willing to accept her conclusions, she had a way
of stating them with such a superior air, as if

she had settled the question forever, that it was
a trifle irritating. The little lady could not
yield readily to the idea that perhaps some of
these "dreadful Americans," being fully her
own age and often with wider experience, might
possibly be able to judge fairly well as to the
elegance and propriety in diction and pronunciation of their native tongue; like many other
foreigners, she had judged a whole nation by the
worst specimens that she had seen, failing to
reflect that if we of America should do the
same by our immigrants from their shores, we
should have indeed little conception of the
learning and culture of the old world.

One special "passage-at arms" interested us
all and, as America proved itself well supported
by standard authorities, it may not be out of
place to relate it here. The word "menace"
was used by an American, with the accent on
the first syllable as customary.

"Oh!" said the "little one," "You mean
'men-*ace*,' I presume."

"Do you find it so?" inquired the American
who was, in fact, from the United States; "I
have never known of its being pronounced other
than *men*-ace, though of course there may be
more than one pronunciation." This, by the
way, is almost unheard of in correct German
pronunciation, so it is hard for a German to
realize that it may be different in English.

The possibility of two pronunciations, however, the little Fraulein would not admit; men-
ace it was and men-*ace* it must be uncondi-
tionally.

"But what is your authority?" some one
asked.

"I lived in England eighteen years," replied
the little governess with dignity, "and I always
heard it so."

"But you must be aware," remarked another, "how inattentive many persons, even of culture and position, are to points in pronunciation, and I should not think that decisive."

"Well," she returned somewhat warmly, "I should think the English ought to know how to speak their own language."

"Certainly they ought;" assented the American, "but whether each individual does, is a question, as it is in any nation. But as I feel sure you did not hear all the English people speak and as English is also my own language, I am confident in assuming that I am not in error; though, as I said, it is possible it may also be correct to say men-*ace*, so I suggest we leave it to any undeniable authority."

"I know I am right;" she replied; "of course, I do not know what you Americans call it, for really,"—with a superior air,—"the two (!) languages are quite different."

"What do you say, Mrs. A.?" inquired the American turning to an English lady at the table. She was a relative of Baroness Burdett-Coutts, by the way, and the daughter of a baronet, so should be a representative of a fairly cultured class.

"Oh! don't consider me authority," she replied, "I seldom look up words; but I always call it as you do, *men*-ace."

This was rather a "staggerer" for the little governess, but rallying she said: "Webster gives men-*ace*."

"Well, I never have noticed it," said the American, "though I know he gives *men*-ace, but where is your Webster? Let's look."

So Webster was brought and consulted but, alas for the "little one," there it stood *men*-ace, as the American had said, and nothing else.

But the small one was not yet vanquished.

"Oh, well!" she returned, "of course, he's an American; he isn't a proper judge of pronunciation."

Notwithstanding this rather rude thrust, the representative of America preserved an equable front and replied that he could not recognize any such distinction, that he considered good English was also good American, and *vice-versa*: and that unless indisputable reference to the contrary was produced, he could see no reason for changing his pronunciation.

"Well," said Mrs. A., "I have an English standard dictionary in my room, let us look at that."

It was soon brought, and the word found; here also but one pronunciation was given, and that was as before, *men*-ace.

The "little one" saw it but said nothing, though we felt from the expression of her face, that it would always be men-*ace* with her, "though the heavens should fall." But, in spite of this "fixidity" of idea, she was a most interesting and engaging little woman.

Afterward when any question of this sort arose, Mrs. A's standard English dictionary compiled by an Englishman and published by an Englishman in England, was consulted and found to agree with the best American usage always. For instance; such words as "incomparable," "Tuesday," "jewel," "immediately," "invalid," and the like, which are so often mispronounced with us as well as among the English, are given exactly the same in both English and American lexicons; so that, in most cases, the peculiar "chewing" of their words by the English, is as indefensible by their own authorities, as the flat, strongly nasal intonation

of many Americans, is unsupported by our stan-
dards, though all these defects are wide-spread
on the respective sides of the water.   Of course,
that the English speak well down in their
throats while we use more head-tones, may be
probably accounted for by difference in climate;
and equally of course, there are ignorant and
careless Americans and English in all parts of
the world.   Later, on visiting England, I was
able to verify these observations.

I was really quite elated to find our usages so
well authorized, for indeed "American English"'
is quite generally regarded abroad, something
as the barbaric utterances of a Fiji Islander
might be in the world at large: it being taken
for granted that any variation in an American,
from an accent or diction familiar to a foreigner,
must be, of necesssity, an exhibition of deficient
culture, and the former is calmly put in the
wrong without appeal and without a suspicion
on the latter's part, that the "dreadful American" may possibly have had access to quite as
many pure "wells of English undefiled" and
have quaffed therefrom with quite as much judg-
ment as the critics themselves; and though I
must sadly own that many of us have room for
great improvement in speaking, I will not grant
that we have more than the average Englishman.   .

There are three words, however, "mamma,"
"papa," and "were," which I am forced to admit are almost universally mispronounced even
by cultured Americans, though I am glad to
say that these did not happen to be instanced in
any of our little lingual skirmishes.

Foreigners declare that we say "mommer,"
"popper," and "wur," and alas! I cannot deny
that many of us do, and though I do not know

but these are quite as correct as our English friends' ''mammaw,'' ''papaw,'' and ''wear,'' yet I could wish a little more attention might be given these words by some of us.

CHAPTER XVI.

The handsome and prosperous city of Hanover, now the capital of the Prussian province of this name, possesses unusual advantages for the student desiring to acquire the best German accent, while its friendly, hospitable citizens make the sojourn of a stranger in the midst of them, very comfortable and delightful.

It was formerly the capital of the kingdom of Hanover, but in 1866 the Prussian William made war upon all neighboring small kingdoms that would not vow fealty to him, and though the Hanoverians resisted nobly, they were comparatively few in forces and were vanquished, while their king was banished.

The older generation can not forget the sufferings and indignities entailed on their royal family, and, though the province is Prussian by name, this portion is loyal at heart to the deposed line; but such sympathizers have to be extremely careful about expressing themselves, for the stringent and powerful police system is ready to make an example of any reported disloyalty.

The royal palace of Hanover from which the unhappy reigning family was driven, now stands vacant though kept up in good order for the occasional visits of Emperor William II. Many of its choicest treasures have been taken to Berlin but the beautiful floors are undisturbed and are said to be the finest in Europe. They are of rare woods and inlaid in the most elaborate and intricate fashion.

From another quarter of the city, a magnificent avenue of lime, or linden trees, one and one quarter miles long and one hundred and twenty feet wide, leads out to charming *Schloss Herrenhausen*, which was the favorite residence of Georges I., II., and V.

This estate is the private property of the deposed king; for this reason, I understand, escaping confiscation, though he is never allowed to reside or, in fact, to come here at all. For the benefit of his beloved Hanoverians, however, he keeps the grounds open to the public, who are, by the payment of a small fee to the custodian, also admitted inside the palace, the palm-house and the mausoleum.

The garden comprises one hundred and twenty acres and is laid out in old French style with clipped shrubs, antique statues, allegorical fountains and an open air theater; the waters of the great fountain rise to the unusual height of two hundred and twenty-two feet; I was told here that this fountain plays higher than any in Europe, but am unable myself either to deny or confirm the statement. A colossal sitting figure of the Electress Sophia stands on the spot where she expired of heart disease in 1714.

The mausoleum, containing monuments to King Ernst August and Queen Frederika by Rauch, is thought by many to equal the famous one at Charlottenburg.

The royal stables have recently been removed from Hanover. In them are kept the famous Hanoverian, or "Isabella," horses. We have all heard of the Queen Isabella who vowed never to change her linen until certain troops should be victorious, and as a consequence was obliged to wear it until it assumed a decidedly saffron-like hue. This tint, however objection-

able in linen, is rather handsome in horses, and
is the color of the favored equines who are the
bearers of the royal line; no others are allowed
to use them; the animals, with their deep canary
tint and white manes and tails, are beautiful
creatures.

The imposing *Welfenschloss*, or Palace of the
Guelphs, stands in the avenue of limes. The
edifice is of Romanesque style, having five towers;
since 1878 it has been used as a Polytechnic
School. A colossal figure of the Saxon Horse
stands in the great square in front of the palace.

Hanover has a fine system of electric trams
moved by the underground system; that is, the
force is conducted beneath the surface. I never
realized before what a desirable thing it might
be, to be rid of the trolley poles and lines. There
are also many horse-cars and funny little
omnibuses in which latter one may ride about a
mile and a half for about a cent and a quarter.

According to Bædeker, the "guide, philosopher and friend" of the general tourist, the central railway station of Hanover, is one of "the
most imposing erections of its kind in Germany."
It faces the *Ernst August Platz* and is embellished by beautiful surroundings of fountains,
foliage and flowers. Immediately in front rises
a huge statue on horseback, of Ernst August,
"The Father of His People," done in bronze.
The rails themselves, as in so many German cities, are elevated upon a lofty viaduct under which
are arches through which passes the traffic of the
town.

There is a remarkably fine theater building in
Hanover, where plays and operas of a superior
grade are brought out. It is a very large structure, of noble proportions, of sufficient height
only to accord well with its breadth, two stories,

I believe; which reminds me of a modern police regulation here and, I think, generally throughout Germany, that no building shall be erected higher than four stories. Across the principal façade stretches a handsome portico under which is a broad carriage approach. Nearly every day a fine band discourses the best of music for an hour or two from this portico. Twelve statues of celebrated composers adorn the balcony above. The edifice, like the railway station stands in its own grounds, which are very handsome, ornamented with statues, fountains and flowering shrubs.

Hanover is well supplied with museums. The most interesting one to me, though not the largest nor the finest, is the "Leibnitz House," an ancient structure with immense pointed roof in which are four of the eight stories of the edifice. It was built in 1652, long before the height of buildings was regulated by law.

Here are relics back to the thirteenth century, while the chair, desk and other personal effects of the celebrated philosopher, are preserved with much care.

The Kestner Museum, standing in lovely grounds, was presented to the town by Herr Hermann Kestner, grandson of Gœthe's "Lotta."

Nicolai Chapel, some parts of which date back to the twelfth century, is the oldest church in Hanover and stands in a quiet greenery and surrounded by ancient tombs, albeit in one of the busiest portions of the town. It is now used by the English colony as a place of worship.

Hanover also has its fine war monument to the fallen heroes of the vicinity. It is of Swedish granite and represents in colossal figures, a Germania crowned by two genii, and is adorned with several reliefs of trophies, while in front is a mourning figure of Hanover with two lions. It stands in a lovely parterre which in the season is a mass of brilliant bloom, while in the immediate background sway and bend the leafy branches of tall forest trees.

These trees are on the southern boundary of the *Eilenriede*, a beautiful wood extending outward from this point, and which was bequeathed to the city by two maiden sisters, with the condition that the area of the gift should never be lessened: so, as the town spreads out, whenever a part of the bequest is sold for building lots, an equally large portion must be purchased on the other side and thrown into the forest. Its name is a combination of the donors, Eile and Riede, and is a constant reminder to Hanover, of the generous old maids to whom the city owes so much.

CHAPTER XVII.

There are numerous relics of a bygone era in Hanover, especially in the "Old Town," as a certain part is called. Narrow, crooked, old streets and quaint, antique houses delight the eye of the antiquarian and give the present generation an idea of how former ones used to live.

There are some queer old graveyards too, in Hanover. In one is the tomb of a "giant," who is depicted in standing posture, full size, very tall, upon his tombstone. Opposite him is a similar tall stone whereon is graven the full length figure of a young lady popularly known as "the giant's wife."

The versatile little German governess kindly went with us to this place to act as guide. Never having been here since her childhood, she was anxious to visit it again. As an example of how tradition may be made, I will relate that on our way thither "the little one" told us that the old nurse who had charge of this family of governesses when it was merely a family of little girls, used to take them to this grave and tell them how the lady buried there had died from tight lacing, thus impressing on their youthful minds the evils of that pernicious practice. The old nurse could not read, therefore her stock of information was a mingled web of fancy and memory. To her, I believe, was also attributable the supposition that the deceased young woman was the giant's wife, and as her stone was as tall as his, she, of course was a giantess.

But we Americans are usually of rather an investigating turn of mind and not specially prone to accept without question statements leaning toward the marvelous; and thus our party on arrival upon the scene, began to view the surroundings with a "cricket's eye." We were first surprised to note that the "giant's wife," instead of reposing by the side of her husband, was laid directly opposite him on the other side of the wide path that led through the cemetery. The two tall stones stood face to face about ten feet apart. Bending down, we immediately began to spell out the worn and nearly indistinguishable, old German text upon the respective tombs. The giant's record was all straight enough; name, age, dates of birth and death given; but when we turned to the stone of the lady, we met with several incongruities. First, the giant was a hundred years older than his "wife," second, she was not a giantess at all, but a slim, little girl represented as standing. life-size, on a sort of dais or platform, which necessitated the height of her tombstone; third, she was but fifteen when she died and had never been married; and fourth, there was not the slightest allusion to any circumstance that might be construed into any supposition that she had died of tight-lacing.

The little governess was amazed. She said she had never thought of doubting the statements of her old nurse and so had continued to believe and to narrate to others the impressive story handed down by that venerable dame, who evidently possessed a vivid imagination and a fine faculty for "pointing a moral and adorning a tale."

In another old churchyard is a rather curious sight. A heavy granite tomb, seemingly as solidly built as possible, was erected many years

ago in what is termed "perpetuity," that is, a
certain sum was paid to secure a guarantee that
the grave should never be opened or disturbed
to make room for others, as is often done here.

But strange to say, a little seed fell into some
tiny crevice of the stone structure, and from that
seed has sprung a large and vigorous tree, that
expanding, has thrust aside the mighty blocks of
ponderous granite with resistless force, so that
the tomb that was to have been sealed forever,
has been opened by the hand of nature itself.
Such an incident in the romance and legend-
loving land of Germany, could not pass unnoted,
and many are the mysterious and miraculous
tales woven about this "opened grave."

In the same churchyard may be found the
grave of Charlotte Kestner, "Goethe's Lotta,"
lying by the side of her husband and other relatives.

We went also to visit the Jews' burial-place,
now closed, but dating back long ago to the time
when no Jew was permitted to reside within the
gates of Hanover. They were obliged to dwell
outside, coming in to do business but going out
at sunset. In that almost barbarous era, they
were, of course, exposed to raids and robberies
without redress, with ro protection anywhere.
Finally the monarch of that day had pressing
need of a large sum of money. This was raised
for him by the Jews without compensation, on
condition that they might be allowed a place within the walls to bury their dead. It was granted
and to this spot we now went.

Somber and grim enough it seemed with its
now never opened gates, its rank, neglected vegetation and its queer, high tombs. The little governess said that the Jews were buried standing, but
whether this is a fact or merely another instance

of the old nurse's lively imagination, I am un-
prepared to say.   I may add in this connection,
that at the present day there are no more valued
and honored citizens in Hanover, than certain
of the once despised Jewish race.

It was in Hanover that I first encountered the
unique, massive stoves of Germany.   There is
one of more or less size in each apartment of this
pension.   They are each mounted on a large
base, generally some kind of stone but sometimes solid wood heavily zincked.   The most
imposing one is in the drawing-room, being
about eight feet high.   It is composed of white
tiles built up into the form of a little temple and
ornamented over the front door with a large me-
dallion in pale gray, representing a child and a
lamb.   They tell a story in the house with much
relish, of an unsophisticated American lady
who, on calling to engage rooms, seemed much
fascinated by this structure, and finally inquired
in a melancholy tone befitting the painful reference ;

"May I ask whose monument that is?"

It really is more suggestive of an obituary
memorial than a heating-apparatus.   Some of
them are works of art in beautiful porcelain,
but most of them are built of colored tiles heavily glazed.   In many of the museums and old
palaces, one finds these stoves in very fanciful
styles representing birds, lions, bears, and other
figures ; I recall one in particular in the palace
of *Sans Souci* at Potsdam, in Frederick the
Great's favorite promenade gallery, that was in
the form of a large eagle in a surprisingly con-
voluted attitude.

Another variety of stoves of a later era is
made of iron cast in various forms ; these are interesting though not so unique as the monumen-

tal tile structures of earlier generations. There
is one standing in my present apartment, mod-
eled apparently after twin towers. The two
are connected at the base by a fire-box of good
size, having a cathedral-like door. The towers
rise to a height of seven or eight feet and at intervals are connected by what might be called
bridges going across from one to the other; in
each of these is a kettle-hole with a lid. Inves-
tigation shows that all this superstructure is
hollow and I suppose it is calculated to provide
for an extensive circulation of hot air within,
and consequent radiation from the hot metal
into the room. It is very ornamental and quite
imposing in its sable majesty. But these fanciful styles, I believe, are entirely out of date
now, as even in slow-going old Germany, are
gradually coming into use the improved and
scientific methods of heating appertaining to the
present day.

As a matter of course the semi-annual "stove-
moving" that is the horror of the rural house-
holder in our country, is not a feature in
German homes. If any change in stove matters
becomes essential, a mason must be summoned
and the entire structure pulled down and rebuilt, but this happens so seldom that the tem-
pers of families are not often unduly strained in
this respect.

I think I have omitted to mention how greatly
travelers are annoyed abroad by the continual
receipt of countless cards, circulars and letters
of business firms, on many of which postage is
due, which I, for my part, at first innocently
paid, not knowing then that I could refuse to
accept the documents. I attributed this inun-
dation so far as I was concerned, to the fact
that I had in France often put up at large hotels

from whence, doubtless, arrivals were reported to the papers. But coming into Germany, I was possessed of private addresses and in many places avoided the hotels altogether, so I could not account for still being deluged as before. On expressing my wonder one day to my hostess, I was informed that all *pension* keepers were obliged by law to send lists of the arrivals and departures of their guests to the police for publication, so that we were all "before the public," whether we pleased or not.

It is really quite surprising to an American to find how far the details of police interference extend. Though one is not, on the moment of one's arrival in Germany, seized, as in France, figuratively by the throat and commanded to yield up, at once, one's name, age, condition, intentions and so forth, yet one must by the end of a week, supply all these details to the police; and the proprietor of any place of public, nay, even also of private entertainment, must see that this is done, under penalty of fine for negligence. The purposed length of stay and intended further destination of each guest must also be reported.

Another police regulation—a very sensible one but astonishing to the American,—is that no person may take a music lesson or practice with open windows, on any instrument, under penalty of fine.

Neither can one have any festivities, lasting beyond ten p. m., even of the simplest nature, without first gaining permission of the authorities. Even in the seclusion of one's own drawing-room and surrounded by one's family in innocent merry-making, is one liable to be interrupted after that hour by the sudden appearance of a uniformed official with "orders to quit."

Nor can any person in planning a house place windows so that they overlook a neighbor's premises without that neighbor's express permission and dictation as to where and how he shall be surveyed.

Many other formalities very surprising to us who dwell in "the land of the free and the home of the brave," might be cited but these few give some idea of what it is to live under a paternal government. I used sometimes in America to think, when groaning under exorbitant transportation charges, that it would be a good thing if the government would take the railways in charge, like the postal service, and insure a uniform, cheap rate; but after knowing something of the railways here, which are in governmental hands, I have changed my mind. True, the rates are fixed and very moderate, but oh! the struggle it is to get any information out of any official. If you know all about a projected trip, he will deign to sell you a ticket for any place, but as to giving you any advice or assistance in regard to connections, facilities, or desirable routes, he has no idea or inclination. What does it matter to him? He has his salary any-way whether the road is well-patronized or not, and there is no rival line to seduce passengers by more affable and obliging treatment. In Germany, France, England and, in fact, nearly all foreign countries, such things as gratuitous time-cards, folders, and general railway literature are almost unknown.

Here again the Tourist Agencies are service-able, as a traveler can get any desired information at their offices without charge.

CHAPTER XVIII.

Leaving Hanover, I started on what the Germans call a *Rund-Reise*, this name being applied to certain trips at reduced rates on which one takes no luggage except what can be carried by hand. For the benefit of the "lone woman," I will explain that to decide on my route I went to an office, not of an "Agency," but of a private individual whose advertisement I had seen, who laid out for me a desirable route giving me a written program with all details including estimated expenses of the trip, for all of which I paid him about sixty cents. Our business was transacted in German, but if the "lone one" does not know the language, she would better take with her an interpreter to such a place, as she would not wish to misunderstand any of the items.

My first stoppage was at the ancient and most interesting town of Hildersheim on the borders of the Hartz mountains, a place that has retained many mediæval features. At a very early period, even as far back as the tenth century, this town attained great importance as a cradle of art, not only mediæval but Romanesque, and according to authorities, "one of the most attractive and characteristic features consists of its timber architecture in the German Renaissance style. The richly decorated façades executed by wood-carvers and sculptors, bear abundant testimony of the taste, the humor and the enterprise of the period."

The population is about thirty thousand and

the place is evidently quite a center of business activity. I immediately went out for a walk, following a wide, handsome street which soon led into a crooked, old-fashioned thoroughfare where, on either hand, might be seen examples of the ornamental and substantial styles of the builders of the fourteenth and fifteenth centuries.

It is difficult to describe these edifices; they are so totally unlike anything erected nowadays that a historical interest is added to the esthetic, throwing a "glamour of the past over the realities of the present."

Some one has said that "a walk through the streets of a North German town is indeed a feast of varied and permanent enjoyment for the traveler of refined taste in art." I should not make even that limitation, but declare that no one with eyes to see, could fail to be moved to admiration and to wonder.

Pursuing my way, I reached a fine mediaeval square called the *Altstaedter Markt*, which may be interpreted literally, "Old-Town Market," though there is nothing about it now suggestive of any modern market-place. It is surrounded by marvelous, antique structures. Language fails to convey an idea of their quaint and elaborate beauty, and even photographs and engravings are inadequate, as so much of the details, which are worked out in the finest fashion, is there lost.

The *Knockenhauer Amthaus* is said to be the finest timber building in Germany. It was constructed in 1529 and is described in the guide-books as a "veritable gem of timber architecture." Above the five stories of the building proper, rises the lofty gabled roof, itself containing several stories. After the quaint fashion

of the time each succeeding story projects some
one or two feet beyond the one beneath. To
quote from a popular author, "the façade is covered with figures and other ornamentation in
which painting and wood- carving vie with each
other." Scarcely a square inch of surface is
left unadorned by conceits cunningly carved in
the wood, both in high and low relief; such as
garlands, leaves, birds, beasts, human beings,
mottoes and so forth, showing an astonishing
liveliness of fancy as well as an exquisite skill
in execution.

These are alternated with panels and friezes
of paintings having a smoothness of finish suggesting enamel.

The figures are traced with a great deal of
humor, while texts in Old-German script accompanying, vary from "grave to gay, from lively to
severe." They are usually in the pithy couplet
to which I have referred before. One of these
little paintings represents a jolly-looking bur-
gher of comfortable proportions, seated at a
well-spread table upon which a huge joint and
various flagons of strong waters are extremely
prominent. Traced above this is the suggestive
legend :

> "And yet our fathers were no fools!"

Still another shows a monarch in rich robes
and surrounded by all the luxuries of the time,
with a great heap of ready coin spread out before him on a table. Just behind, however,
stands the skeleton figure of Death about to
grasp his victim. Encircling this is a motto
something to this effect:

> "Not even gold
> Can loose Death's hold!"

A detailed description of the countless ornaments and conceptions wrought out upon this structure, is necessarily impossible here, even were my stock of words sufficient for the subject. As one stands below and gazes upward on to the gradually projecting stories, where the increased height of each succeeding one is partially counteracted by its shorter lateral distance from the beholder, one views such a wealth of decoration and curious handiwork that one involuntarily wonders how long those people lived who had time thus to elaborate every inch of the outer surfaces of their buildings.

But this is only one of the astonishingly quaint, beautiful and ancient edifices in this square. The *Wedekind Haus* dating from 1598, is also most elaborately carved and painted. The descendants of the Wedekind family still occupy the building, dealing on the lower floor in colonial supplies, a business probably handed down from father to son—or daughter,—through all the generations since this old house was new.

Numerous others of unusual interest and charm might be mentioned, but pages indeed would be required for a full catalogue.

One very queer, old place in a side street, is called the House of the Emperors on account of having a row of Roman Emperors carved all along the sides.

Numerous and beautiful also are the churches of Hildesheim and the old cathedral with its wondrous bronze doors and antique candelabrum. These and other marvelous specimens of work in this metal were executed under Bishop Bernward between the years 995 and 1032. The doors date from 1015 and are adorned with sixteen curious and intricate reliefs representing the Fall and the Redemption.

The large candelabrum is unique and a model

of its era; I saw copies of it afterward in several museums in different sections.

Indeed in the time of Bernward and his immediate successors down to 1154, Hildesheim became one of the most important seats of Romanesque art in Germany. The cathedral, which was built in 1055-61 on the site of an earlier church dating from 872, is of this style, but was much changed and debased by alterations of an unsymmetrical character in the eighteenth century.

St. Michaels is called one of the finest Romanesque churches in Germany. It has a lovely location upon a beautiful hill overlooking the river Innerste, and surrounded by noble trees. From here a promenade extends along the "Ramparts," by which name is known a succession of fine, elevated parks occupying the place of the former veritable ramparts, and commanding a charming view.

Tearing myself away from this peculiarly interesting spot, I took train for Goslar, a little farther on into the fastnesses of the Hartz.

The region grows hillier and more wooded as we wind along to the foot of the Rammelsberg where is situated the quaint town which is our destination. The Rammelsberg is two thousand and forty feet above sea-level and has yielded varying quantities yearly of at least eight different minerals, a surprising variety to be found in so limited an area. It is honey-combed with shafts and galleries in every direction.

To the west of Goslar rises the Steinberg, not so lofty as the Rammelsberg but very picturesque.

The ancient town itself lying on the river Gose, is, if possible, still more charming than Hildesheim; being only about one third as large, it is more rural and the streets are diversified by frequent gardens and arbors rich in foliage and flowers.

As I left the train, a very sociably disposed *Dienstmann*, or porter, approached and, offering his services, threw my bag over his shoulder with the remark that it would much pleasanter to walk than to ride, if the "gracious lady" felt so inclined. Nothing loath, I agreed and we proceeded to thread the old-time pathways that have echoed for so many centuries to the tread of hurrying and of halting feet. My guide was exceedingly painstaking in pointing out various noteworthy and curious objects on our route, giving a brief history of each, with many original comments.

Near the station is an immense round tower, almost a ruin, though signs of habitation were evident, and sounds of hilarity issuing forth fell upon the ear. It seems that this is a part of the ancient town-fortifications, but is now used as a hotel, having an elegant, modern interior little according with its antique outside.

My *Dienstmann* piloted me to a funny little inn where I received a cordial reception; after paying requisite attention to the demands of a somewhat vigorous appetite, I retired to my room which proved to be one of the quaintest and cleanest of chambers, with shining blue floors, low, dazzlingly white walls, and heavy beams and rafters of dark, polished wood, testifying to centuries of support and shelter. There was a concert going on in the coffee-room below, and indeed all night long the sound of musical instruments and of voices uplifted in melody, floated through the air, mingling with my dreams.

There are many remaining evidences in Goslar, of its old and honorable history. Here again one sees the queer, old buildings and the wonderful workmanship before described, but it is a sleepy little place and quietly enough it lay among its cool shadows. as I walked abroad next morning to gaze further upon its beauties.

The people are cordial and friendly, as generally throughout Germany. They rarely pass one without courteous salutation, and even little children nod and smile and cry, "*Guten Tag*." It is a pretty custom and makes a stranger feel very much at home.

This fashion of salutation is very different in France and Germany than at home in America, or in England either, for that matter.

While it is carried much further in Germany than in France, one is always expected to exchange bows there with whomever one may meet in the hall, lift or drawing-room of one's abode, unless indeed there is a crowd of strangers or one is in a very large establishment, like the mammoth hotels; and even in these, one is expected to bow to his companions at table, and to bid his attendant "good morning,"and "good night," with great punctiliousness and to use much formality in making requests or thanking one for services. The French servant or tradesperson is addressed as *Monsieur*, *Madame* or *Ma'm'selle*, as the case may require, and he or she is equally courteous in response, always addressing a superior in position, in the third person. This latter form, though observed somewhat in Germany, is not so universal as in France; but in Germany a person would be considered hopelessly ill-bred who, no matter how large the table, should take or leave his seat without catching the eye of the hostess, (who always presides,) and making a profound bow as he ejaculates "*Gesegnete Mahlzeit*," which is

a German equivalent for "Good Appetite!"
New arrivals, of course, do not always know
of this usage, and the situation is sometimes a
little embarrassing. I presume we all remember
Mark Twain's comical setting forth of this
custom as he encountered it. Even in traveling,
it is usual for anyone entering or leaving a
railway-carriage, to acknowledge the presence
of others by a courteous bow.

The French and Germans too, seldom, if ever,
fail to formally present strangers to each other,
and I found the fashion of hand-shaking, which
I had supposed distinctly American, was really
particularly German.

Just across from my hotel, stands Goslar's
Rath-Haus, or Town Hall, simple but quaint,
dating from the fifteenth century. Among the
many curosities, old books, paintings, charters
and so forth, may be specially mentioned one
of a widely different nature, a *Beisskatze*,
(Biting-Cat!) a kind of cage in which shrews
used to be imprisoned.

Upon an eminence on the outskirts of the
town rises a palace, the *Kaiserhaus*, said to be
the oldest secular edifice in Germany. Its location is remarkably fine and the magnificent old
building, which was most judiciously restored
in 1878, looks down in serene dignity upon the
little world at its feet.

Within, the Imperial Hall is fifty six yards
long, seventeen wide and thirty-five feet high.
One side is almost entirely of glass, so many
and immense are the windows. Opposite
the central one, is the ancient Imperial
Throne which stood in the cathedral until 1820,
and then came into the possession of Prince
Charles of Prussia. In the chapel adjoining, is
the painted tomb of Henry III., containing
his heart, preserved at Hanover until 1884.

Somewhat distant from this castle are some venerable ruins that testify to the ancient grandeur of Goslar, around which are entwined many legends. Heine and other poets have sung many a sweet song inspired by the beauty and romance of this vicinity.

Not very far from these ruins stands the North Portal, all that is left of a once famous cathedral founded in 1039. This portal is now used as a place of worship by itself, and is indeed antique and quaint. (I know that adjective is overworked, but what is a poor scribe to do in the limitations of the English language?) A richly sculptured column stands at the entrance, surmounted by a Gorgon's head, reminiscence, it is said, of the old-time use of such heads to ward off evil influences.

In the gable over the entrance, are odd-looking colored figures of the Emperor Konrad, his wife Gesela and Saints Mathew, Simon and Jude. What living, breathing realities these old saints and martyrs seemed to the people of the earlier centuries.

Inside the Portal are several interesting relics of the ancient cathedral, among which may be noted an oblong box of brass plates, borne by four crouching figures and containing numerous circular holes. It is popularly called "Kodi's Altar," from the supposition that it was formerly a part of the shrine of that idol, but no one really knows for what it was originally designed.

That the ancient genius and skill in wood-carving are not yet extinct in this region, is proved by the existence of a most marvelous clock which is on exhibition here in the home of its maker. To visit it, I wandered down a country-like lane bordered on each side by sweet-smelling gardens and picturesque homes, until I came to a little cottage charmingly set within a bower of bloom.

Following the direction indicated by a painted hand, I entered this enchanting spot and proceeded beneath the vine-wreathed lattice-work to the open door of the dwelling. Here were gathered some half a dozen sight-seers, like myself desirious of inspecting the wonderful time-piece, though none of them from across the sea.

The maker and owner soon appeared and showed us all the curiosities of his master-piece. It was in the form of a temple and is most elaborate in detail, being all hand-work and carved with the utmost delicacy from woods of varying colors and hardness, some of which were the product of America. At the stroke of the hour, music is heard, sentinels at various points salute, soldiers in the center surrounding a figure of Christ on the cross, manipulate their arms and implements, while one lifts his spear and pierces the side of the crucified Jesus. Above, a door opens and the Twelve Apostles appear one by one, and pass before a figure of the risen Lord, each bowing his head as he comes opposite to receive the benediction of the Savior, who extends his hands in blessing.

Numerous other features, such as details for showing the seasons, the times of heavenly bodies, days of the week and month, the current year, the presenting of a birthday card at a given date and so forth, all displaying a surprising store of skill and patience in design and execution, are to be noticed.

The structure stands about eight feet high and was intended as a present to the King of

Hanover, being nearly completed when the
troublous times of 1866 arose, which ended
in his banishment; after which the "ruling
powers" would not allow the old artisan to carry
out his project, so he kept the clock himself and,
putting it on exhibition at about twelve and one
half cents a head, has made his fortune.

One characteristic of the neighborhood of
Goslar is the Farbensuempfe, ponds fed by
streams from the Rammelsberg, and yielding
the ocher dye so profitable here. Goslar was
for a long time the favorite residence of the
Saxon and Salic Emperors. Henry IV. was
born here in 1050 and the attachment of the citizens to him involved the town in his misfor-
tunes. In 1204 it was utterly destroyed by
Otho IV., but rallied for many a long year of
prosperity afterward. To-day, prosperous and
thriving in its quiet fashion, it sits among its
green hills and wooes with an irresistible charm,
the fancies of the poet and the painter.

CHAPTER XIX

And thus I kept wandering on in the beautiful June weather, each day penetrating a little farther into the mystic region of the Hartz. Never traveling at night, I had full opportunity to enjoy all the romantic scenery of this farfamed locality.

It is indeed lovely; but with this, as with so many spots of historic and legendary interest, the enchanting element is not so much the actual characteristic of the scenery about us, as it is the connection between it and the songs and stories familiar to us since our earliest recollection, and the legendary lore that has come down through so many centuries, from a credulous and impressionable people; from a time when every grove had its dryads, every stream its nixies, every cave its gnomes and every mount its ogres.

Yet this locality, while very picturesque and certain to arouse enthusiasm in the romantic breast, in actual beauty falls far below our own Green, White, Adirondack or Cumberland ranges, nor can it in any wise compare with the grandeur of our Rocky, Nevada or Coast mountains.

But there is a quaintness and a wildness, which yet is not at all like the solitude of the virgin forests and stretches of our own new land; not a real isolation but rather an arrest of development by some mysterious spell, as of the Sleeping Beauty in the Wood, which attracts and charms.

The Hartz is chiefly a mining region and con-

sists of an isolated range rising abruptly from
the plain on all sides, with heights and recesses
unattainable in former rude eras, only by the
most indefatigable.

What wonder then that those heights and recesses above, looked upon by the toilers in the
bowels of the earth below, but rarely save
through the mists of morn and eve, should be
peopled at will with ghostly multitudes, by the
teeming fancies of the mystical and poetical
German of the Middle Ages?

It seems strange to know to-day that the
highest peak is only thirty-four hundred and
fifteen feet above sea-level; but the atmosphere
is clear and the sky is lovely, Oh! so lovely ;and
there is something about the air that exhilarates
and makes one feel that the world is indeed
"very good."   What is it Goethe sings?

> "How brightly beams
>   The sun on me!
> The fields and streams
>   Smile happily.
>
> The flowers appear
>   On shrub and plain ;
> As if to hear
>   The wild bird's strain.
>
> And love and mirth
>   To all increase ;
> O, Sun and earth!
>   O, bliss and peace !'

The climate of the Hartz region is said to be
much like that of Central Norway, even the
heats of mid-summer being here agreeably tempered by the north winds of the Baltic Sea.

Many varieties of railway carriages do I encounter in this expedition; some entirely unique,
others a combination of several different styles;
altogether making such a confusion in my mind,

that I give up all idea of trying to remember
them. One, however, I specially recollect because exteriorly it had a familiar look and I
thought I had actually come across an American
car at last. To be sure, it was of a rusty brown
color, had very small windows and its outer
finish was about on a par with American freight-
cars, but it had end platforms with steps, and
doors leading from these into the end of each
car like ours. I entered, but to my disappointment found that within it was divided off into
tiny compartments as usual, though the aisle
ran between the seats lengthwise, instead of
across as ordinarily; but each compartment was
shut off from the next by a door which the conductor locked every time he passed through, so
that I could really perceive no advantage over
the common style, except the fact that the
conductor did not have to be exposed to the
weather.

Now we are in motion again. As we go on
and upward, the way becomes more winding
and we are more and more shut in by the encom-
passing hills. Oker, Harzburg, Islenburg, Wernigerode and many other beautiful hill-side towns
spread out before us, each inviting us to tarry
awhile amid its natural loveliness.

The former lies at the entrance of the wild
Okerthal, the road ascending which, affords
picturesque views of the precipitous cliffs. Il-
senburg is situated just outside the Ilsethal, one
of the finest valleys of the Hartz, presenting a
succession of remarkably striking rock and for-
est-pictures that at times are almost sublime.

The road, winding in and out and around the
most charming scenes, follows a rushing moun-
tain-brook, enlivened by a series of miniature
waterfalls, in the midst of which one sees some

surprising rock-formations. The most conspicuous, perhaps, is the Ilsenstein, a precipitous
buttress of granite, rising to a height of five
hundred feet above the valley.

Many are the foot-paths leading through all
parts of this romantic region, and pedestrians of
all grades and nations abound, from the bare-
footed peasant with shoulders bowed beneath a
heavy burden, to the fully equipped, modern
"globe-trotter" with fancy outfit and sturdy
alpenstock, for "bikes" are here at a discount.

Here and there, at the most available points,
may be seen some extensive and imposing castle.
That of Count Wernigerode, above the town of
the same name, is particularly picturesque in
its lofty situation, looking down the slopes of
the Hartz and upon the junction of two fine rivers.

Everywhere upon the most inaccessible crags,
are seen the crumbling ruins, in various degrees
of disintegration, of a ruder and more ancient
architecture, whose former possessors, once
dwelling in continual warfare among these pla-
teaus and peaks, have left little trace of their existence, other than these eloquent vestiges of
generations long since vanished.

The road now ascends still more abruptly
through the beautiful, pine-clad valley of the
Steinerne Renne, where the shadows are dense
and silent and where the dashing mountain-tor-
rent rushes downward over its stony bed,
to find its level so far away in the vale below. One becomes almost bewildered with
the constant recurrence of cascade and cliff,
of rock and rill, of sombre shade and sunny
stretch.

We are favored with delightful weather and
we hope for its continuance, for now we are
about to reach the culminating point of our ex-

pedition, the ascent of the mist-enveloped and specter-haunted Brocken.

We come at nightfall to the enchanting town of Blankenburg, which seems fairer and more charming than any before. They are so clean, these little towns, so trim and tidy, that one feels as if it were all the time some festal date and that everything was in order for the occasion.

I leave the train and am inducted into a "spick and span" little 'bus, that drives off and away, up hill and down, through smooth, twisty and narrow. but beautifully kept streets, where the old-fashioned houses seem to smile cordially upon the stranger. Finally we arrive at a queer old inn and drive right in at, apparently, the front doorway, but which proves to be a paved way, over which are bedrooms, and on the one hand, the dining-room, on the other, the office. A little farther along is a circular court under a glass roof, all within the walls of the dwelling, where the horses are unhitched and the vehicles left, while the animals themselves are led off through a rear door, to their own special quarters.

A stairway within, at one side of the front paved entrance, all decorated in gay, blooming plants and graceful vines, and overlooking the court which is also adorned with greenery, led to my apartment. This proved to be a large, old-fashioned room most comfortable and interesting, having three, instead of the usual two beds. I observed to the friendly *Ober-Kellner*, as he ushered me into my quarters, that, as I was alone, a smaller room and fewer beds would amply accommodate me, but he only replied smilingly, "*Ach! dass machts nichts*," and left me "alone with my glory."

Here the feather-bed covering reappeared,

which I had not seen for some time, and even then not quite in the present guise, for here there was literally no other covering except the sheet. In the cool, equab'e climate of this region, the funny, exaggerated cushions are by no means uncomfortable, even in summer, though exceedingly difficult to keep properly adjusted, during the ''silent midnight watches.''

I sleep well and rise next morning eager to delight my eyes with the beautiful prospect. On looking from my window, I find the street so narrow that I have to make an effort to see persons on the other side below, though I am only in the second story; but it would be very easy to converse with my neighbors on the corresponding floor across the way.

I go down and prepare for an exploration. For some time, English-speaking persons have been growing rare and rarer, and now I find that there is no one in the house, nor probably in the place, who uses my native tongue. This gives me a rather peculiar sensation and tends to foster extreme deliberation on my part, as I strive to cogitate in German.

The road past the inn-door, goes on almost perpendicularly up a hill, on the summit of which looms the lofty, ducal *Schloss*, occupied by His Grace usually only in the shooting-season. It contains numerous mementoes of the Empress Maria Theresa, in the way of books, pictures and so forth. It is a lordly building of yellowish stone and, both from its position and its architecture, is very commanding.

To reach it, one passes the stately old *Rath-Haus* into which five balls are built to commemorate the bombardment by Wallenstein, during the Thirty Years War.

I avoid the abrupt ascent and go around by

easy stages to another beautiful eminence, which I learn rejoices in the suggestive name of the Schnappenberg.

This is an almost level plateau most attractively laid out in walks and groves. I find a seat under a spreading tree and gaze off over the lovely scene. Far down below are the picturesque slopes dotted with elegant and tasteful homes, and blossoming in a riot of color. The clean, tidy, irregular streets wind in and out and echo to the steps of smiling people and the merry shouts of children.

To the north from across the valley, rises the Regenstein, a precipitous cliff two hundred and forty feet above the plain. Here may be seen the remnants of an ancient castle, standing out distinctly in the clear sunshine, its old walls sadly demolished and, indeed, little left of it except some vaults and embrasures hewn in the solid rock. As long ago as 918, this fortress was erected by Henry the Fowler, and for centuries successfully resisted the attacks of enemies, but it was finally reduced by Frederick the Great, and conquering time has done the rest.

On another side, the Ziegenkopf lifts up its bulk thickly covered with dense timber. On its very apex rises one of the present Emperor's watch-towers, a lofty, solidly built erection, which may possibly become one of the "ruins" to be noted generations hence.

Not a peak nor a cavern nor a waterfall in this vicinity, but has its store of legends and, as I drop my eyes to the little book of *Harzsagen* in my hand, I see the familiar names repeated on every page, usually in connection with a beautiful. unfortunate princess and her lover, a valiant and splendid young prince; for in the olden day, even before the "gentle Will" had

said it, it was as true as now that, "All the
world loves a lover."

There was some subtile charm about this
pretty town that made me loth to leave it, but
the Brocken unattained still loomed ahead, so I
bade adieu to my affable hosts, in my best Hanoverian German, (which, I fear however, was not
properly appreciated in this district of dialects,)
and, taking train, still set my face heavenward.

CHAPTER XX.

The next stage of my journey was made in a delightful observation-car somewhat larger than the ordinary continental carriage. It seemed more like a spacious, movable piazza, than a public conveyance. The sides, furnished with curtains adjustable at will, were entirely open except for a low wall about a yard high, in which was a gate for entrance on each side; the top formed a sort of canopy; a long seat ran across the two ends, facing each other, and two more ran back to back down the middle, on each side of a round table that was fixed in the center. There was plenty of room and every opportunity for outlook.

Our ascent was slow and gradual; now passing over slopes of verdant hue embroidered in brilliant wild flowers, now entering stretches of forest where the golden sunshine but filtered down through the close-set leaves and branches. Yet nowhere is that wild look that we see in like districts in America; everywhere there seemed to be homes, rustic and humble enough, it might be, but still places to live, while everything had an air of having been in use a long time.

The fields, the roadways, the cliffs, the ravines, were ablaze everywhere with a splendor of golden color from a vigorous shrub that seemed to toss aloft its arms in joy and beam radiantly forth upon the world, with its millions of yellow blossoms. A kindly lady, noticing my interest, told me that this plant was called *Gin-*

star; I am sorry to say that this name did not satisfy me at all; I should have expected something more suggestive from the resourceful German people.

Occasionally we come out upon a reach of level plateau where nestles some little village of red-roofed cottages. We pass a stalactite cave that has been known for centuries, and another cavern opened recently which is remarkable for the number and variety of fossil remains found within.

Presently we ascend a mill-valley with very curious rock formations, and finally quit the train at Rothehuette, for the remainder of the ascent is made by horse-carriage. The road is kept in excellent condition and for a while we roll on through a pleasant-looking country with fair, cultivated fields wherein women, old and young, and children of all sizes are toiling, rarely a man.

Beautiful shade trees relieve the landscape and frequent, tiny villages come into view, of antiquated and picturesque characteristics. The highest is Hoppe, a scattered hamlet very popuular as a resort, for all over the Brocken is to be found that modern institution, the Summer Hotel.

The contrast between the simple peasant who has probably never left his native nook upon the mountain-side, and the *blasé* "resorter," is marked and amusing. Numerous waterways intercept our path, spanned by rustic bridges. Tinkling cascades make music. Cool, green shades embosom us. The neighboring rocks assume grotesque and fanciful forms. The forest grows denser and the face of the earth is one wild conglomeration of moss-covered boulders standing at every angle. How our road was ever hewn through, must remain a mystery to the feminine mind.

Here, at one of the narrowest portions, with a stream on one hand and the tall trees springing from their rocky bed close on the other, we meet a descending carriage; consternation seizes on all; women scream and men—ejaculate forcibly. The occupants of the new carriage, being young and agile scramble out, while the men unhitch the horses and tilt the vehicle in such a way that our party is enabled to "scrooge" past, and we heartlessly leave the others to their fate as we ascend still higher.

We are now near the top. Vegetation becomes very scanty near the summit and no trees grow, so says our conductor, within one hundred and thirty feet from it.

Soon the great hotel looms up before us, black against the western sky. At one side, but detached, is a tower of mason-work from which, under favorable conditions, may be seen the domes and spires of Magdeburg, Erfurt, Gotha, Cassel, Hanover and Brunswick. A fine vista, truly, but I had in my mind's eye, the ravishing prospect beheld from about the same elevation, on Mount Hamilton, California, and this suffered in comparison; so I turned my attention to the consideration of the mental pictures evolved for us so long ago, by Goethe and others of the mighty ones in the arena of German poetry and song. Here is the "meeting-place" of the witches, on Walpurgis Night, made immortal by Goethe's vivid word painting. Here are several curious and grotesque granite formations, the Devil's Pulpit, the Witches' Altar, the Hobgoblin's Footstool. Here is the habitat of the Brocken's Spectre.

As the sun sank into his nightly bed and the pallid mists of twilight began to sweep up and

around the shoulders of the mountain, while that
peculiar silence wherein there is no chirp of
bird, no rustle of leaf, no stir of animal, became more and more impressive as the tourists
withdrew by degrees into the hostelry, I let my
fancy run backward to the time before the ma-
terialization of the "Summer Tripper," and the
"Holiday Excursionist," when here the old
Brocken lifted up its head in utter solitude.

For how many ages did storm and wind and
cloud, and all the forces of nature, hold revel
about this hoary crown?   Not strange is it, that
the untutored mountaineer, gazing upward from
below at the conflicts of the elements, should
have discerned therein the voices and the move-
ments of supernatural beings? Hardy indeed
was he who would venture to brave a closer
proximity, by clambering into these lofty areas.
But two lines of daily stages with their hilar-
ious loads of vacation parties, make short work
of sentiment, and the mystic mystery of the
spot is gone forever.

I retired to my room in pensive mood, almost
hoping that some wandering sprite of the olden
ages, might float into my vicinity, for are not
such immortal? I awoke in the morning to look
out upon an ocean of mist wherein we were shut
off from all visible connection with our mun-
dane sphere; but I had been visited by no spec-
ters, no witches, and had seen nothing of a more
startling nature than a collection of brilliantly
red matches with orange tips, which certainly
did seem allied to regions of sulphurous and
fiery character.

A little later we were driving away through
the enveloping fog, which gradually disappeared
as we descended into the valley, and I again returned to Blankenburg, from whence I resumed
my tour of this interesting country.

CHAPTER XXI.

The valley of the Bode, the grandest point in
the Hartz Mountains, is reached from Blankenburg by a daily *char-a-banc*, or picnic-wagon, to
Thale. Under the continuance of the clear
June sunshine, I entered the vehicle one day
and rode along the fair slopes and stretches lying
between the two places.

The carriage highways through this part of
the country are excellent, being hard, smooth
and, where the lay of the land permits, broad.

A smiling, peaceful scene it was, through
which we passed on this beautiful morning;
realizing on the one side, a perfect ideal of a pastoral landscape, while on the other, to the left, rises
a very remarkable series of huge, irregular
masses of sandstone, known as the "Devil's
Wall."

These do not form a plateau, but are thrust
up through the turf in broken lines; now rising singly and in thin, flat-sided, jagged forms
and again in fanciful shapes of considerable
bulk, which are named as mediæval imagination
suggested, as the "King's Chair," the "Giant's
Table," and so forth. These all spring up abruptly, penetrating the green earth which lies
smooth and unbroken on either side, so that the
whole formation has indeed the semblance of a
gigantic wall, through which some enemy has
made innumerable and irreparable breaches.

Every point is legend-haunted, of course,
while the wall itself is accounted for by the tale
that the devil, having been outwitted in certain

transactions between himself and the good bur·
ghers of Blankenburg, and being thereby convinced that they were, in modern parlance, "too
many for him," resolved to build a wall between
that special quarter of the country where he was
able to get the better of the simple folk, and
that of the proud Blankenburgians who had
presumed to overmaster his plans and had even
dared to jeer at him as "the stupid devil."

So, attended by his unholy crew, he began operations at night, and great progress was made
in the darkness. But, as the narrator quaintly
remarks, "What good was it? Whatever was
built at night, at day-break fell in pieces again
as soon as the morning sun shone thereupon;
and no matter how much and how sorely they
wearied themselves to build all firm and secure,
they found when they would continue the next
night that all their work was fallen down and
shattered." At length did the despairing devil
give over his attempt to divide "God's Kingdom" by walls and rocks, but the testimony of
his impious undertaking is yet seen in the
rent and ragged ruins which are standing to-
day, between Blankenburg and Thale.

When we reached the charming village of
Thale we found ourselves directly at the foot of
the towering entrance to the Bode-Thal, through
which plunges a roaring river guarded on either
hand by bold precipices covered with a heavy
growth of forest trees and shrubs. Midway up,
and on the top of these heights, is situated
many a comfortable inn of more or less pretentions.

The *Ross-Trappe*, a great, granite rock, here
projects bastion-like into the dale, and rises abruptly to a height of six hundred and fifty feet.
Beautiful is the view obtained from its summit.

A singular impression here in the rocky surface, resembling a gigantic hoof-print, is said to have been left by the steed, or *Ross*, of a lovely young princess who leaped across the valley at this point to escape the pursuit of an ogre who had singled her out for his victim. In her terrible spring, she lost from her head her golden crown, (for, of course, no self-respecting princess would appear without her crown,) which fell into the abyss below and is, in its turn, the central figure of many legends.

Numerous are the picturesque drives all around in this neighborhood, supplemented by footpaths leading on where vehicles may not follow, into entrancing regions of woodland and out on to the heights above.

Another "Witches Dancing-Place," more picturesque but not so weird as that of the Brocken, lies opposite the *Ross-Trappe*, than which it is two hundred and ten feet higher. The whole vicinity is indeed most interesting and, to one who enters into sympathy with the people and gathers up the folk-lore of the environment, it furnishes a wonderful store of memories.

Modern customs and conveniences, however, are by no means unknown in this charming section. Directly opposite the station, across the wide boulevard, is a splendid villa standing in an enchanting park where fountain, flower, foliage and winding way vie with each other in promoting the delight and refreshment of the visitor. This place, having the singular name of the "Ten Pound Hotel," is but one of several equally attractive though perhaps not on so magnificent a scale.

Time failed then to permit me to enjoy, as it does now to recount, all the charms of the locality, so, reluctantly turning away from the rocks

and crags and bowery nooks, I took the train
for Berlin.

The face of the country changes abruptly in
this direction, and leaving behind me the cas-
tled cliffs and rocky dells, I sped on through a
valley as level as some of our great, western
plains, arriving at my destination with nothing
more eventful than a change at Magdeburg;
which brought to mind the "Magdeburg Hemispheres," over which I puzzled in my early
school-days, little thinking I should myself ever
be within the confines of the venerable city of
their origin. The air-pump and hemispheres with
which Otto von Guericke made his first experi-
ments, are still preserved in the Royal Library
at Berlin.

CHAPTER XXII.

Berlin, the capital of Prussia and the residence of the German Emperor, is now a city of nearly seventeen hundred thousand inhabitants, including its garrison of twenty thousand soldiers.

Nature has done little for this locality in the way of the picturesque, it being simply an immense, sandy plain only one hundred and ten feet above the level of the sea. But the region is well-watered and has an intimate connection by rail with all parts of the continent, and by navigable rivers with northeast Germany and Poland, and is said to be one of the foremost seats of commerce and perhaps the greatest manufacturing town in continental Europe.

Its situation on its serpentine river, suggests the old conundrum, "Why is Berlin, of necessity, the most dissipated of cities?" Answer: "Because it is, and always will be, continually on the Spree." But the Germans craftily evade this imputation, by pronouncing the name "Spray," so that the point of the joke is lost as soon as you reach *Deutschland.* The traffic upon this river and its canals is said to be even busier than that of the Rhine.

One notes again in Berlin the lack of height in the noble edifices one sees on all sides. The royal palaces and museums, opera-house, national gallery, university, new houses of parliament, arsenal and other beautiful buildings, are all comparatively low and broad; most of them having a suggestion of the classic in their conception, though the forms of the Renaissance are also popular, while there is mainly a freedom from excessive ornamentation, that is pleasingly effective.

Berlin, I am told, is yet in a transition state. Not until after the wars of 1866, '70 and '71, and the consolidation still later of the numerous provincial governments into one comprehensive imperial authority, did the city take its most decisive strides toward becoming what it now is, one of the great capitals of the world.

The place is beautifully clean, the water and lighting systems excellent, and on the whole, while thi metropolis may, perhaps, suffer somewhat in comparison with some of the older capitals of Europe, yet it has a distinct charm of its own that will constantly increase as improvements and adornments go on.

The *Thiergarten*, which, as it translates "animal garden," I at first supposed to be a zoological inclosure, is a very extensive wooded park, really a cultivated forest, covering more than six hundred acres. It was originally a part of the Royal Preserves. The northern boundary is the River Spree, which lends itself effectively to the attractiveness of the place. Many little sheets of water dotted with tiny islets, lying in the shadows of the venerable forest trees and spanned by rustic or more ornate bridges, add infinite charm to the sylvan space.

Works of art are also scattered about through its area. Exquisite statues in white marble, of Queen Louise, by Encke, and of Frederick William III, by Drake, stand not far from each other in bowers of greenery and surrounded by graceful *jardinières* and slender trellises of flowering plants. Many other fine specimens of the plastic art might be mentioned but the beauties of these two are especially enhanced by their exquisite setting within the verdant wood. Remarkably impressive figures of Goethe in marble and of Lessing in bronze face the Koeniggraetzer Street, on the eastern limit of the park.

Cutting through the *Thiergarten* from north to south, is the broad Avenue of Victory, one of the most fashionable promenades of Berlin. In the northern extremity, in the center of beautiful "King's Place," an extensive square adorned with flowers, fountains and statuary, rises the Monument of Victory, two hundred feet in height, standing on a circular terrace approached by eight steps of granite.

This is a wonderful composition commemorating the great triumphs of 1870-71 and earlier campaigns. The massive square pedestal is adorned with exceedingly fine reliefs in bronze, each group presenting a vivid picture of some thrilling scene in German warfare. The suggestive pathos in face and attitude of many of these figures, is most appealing, and brought tears to the eyes of the writer, though an alien and a stranger. Space forbids detailed description, but one peculiar feature may be mentioned, consisting of three rows of cannon, sixty in all, captured from Danes, Austrians and French, now placed lengthwise on the great column, just above its flutings of yellowish gray sandstone. A colossal *Borussia*, or Prussia, forty-eight feet tall, surmounted by an outspread eagle in gilded bronze, crowns the monument which is truly an imposing and magnificent creation.

In "King's Place" also is situated the beautifully stately new edifice, the Hall of the Imperial Diet, which occupies an area of fourteen thousand square yards.

To the north, "King's Place" leads into

"Alsen Place" also lovely with beauties of nature and art.

At the southern extremity of the Avenue of Victory, stands the Wrangel fountain in a wide square, tree-bordered, and fitted out with comfortable seats past which an array of glittering vehicles unceasingly rolls.

Running through the *Thiergarten* from east to west and directly at right angles to the Avenue of Victory, lies the Charlottenburg road, another wide, ornamental boulevard, leading out to the suburb of same name and to the royal palace where Emperor Frederick III. spent ten weeks of his last illness. In the pleasant and extensive garden, or park as we should term it, surrounding this palace, and at some little distance from it, through shaded and quiet ways stands the widely famed mausoleum erected by Goetz. in the Doric style. Here, beneath beautiful life-size, full-length. reclining marble portrait-figures, repose the mortal remains of King Frederick William III., his lovely consort, Queen Louise, their son, Emperor William I. and his empress, Augusta. The adornments of this snowy chamber are simple and chaste in the extreme, yet marvelous in effectiveness. A soft, purplish light falls through the stained glass of a single casement above the entrance, and faintly illumines the silent figures with subdued radiance. And there they lie in unostentatious majesty, until time, regardless alike of all beauty, animate or inanimate, shall work his will upon their unresisting forms.

I dare say that most persons hearing of Berlin, picture to themselves the charms of the famous avenue, *"Unter den Linden."* I must own to sad disappointment in this historic street; many others in the city are far finer.

True, its associations are most interesting and, I presume, in an earlier day, before the era of "modern improvements," it was something to be particularly noted. To be sure, the avenue is one hundred and ninety-six feet wide, it is flanked by handsome and spacious palaces, hotels, trade-emporiums and public buildings; here are the French and Russian Embassies and other important governmental offices; but it is comparatively short, is dusty and untidy, while the two insignificant rows of scrubby little trees extending partially down its center, are poor representatives of the noble arborage in some other portions of the city.

The space between these rows of trees, intended for the pleasure of the pedestrian, instead of being neatly turfed, with cement or asphalt walks through the midst, as, for instance, in Commonwealth Avenue, Boston, is simply loose dirt, which is shuffled up in all directions by the wayfarer, to rise in clouds of dust all about.

The Brandenburg Gate, which forms the western terminus, is not at all imposing, being too low for its breadth and looking as if made from dirty putty. The lower end of the avenue is more satisfactory. Here is the masterly statue in bronze, by Rauch, of Frederick the Great, on the right of which is the plain but massive and now unoccupied palace of William I., and on the left the academy and the buildings of the University, situated in pleasant grounds shaded by a grove of fine chesnuts.

Again on the other side, the Royal Opera House, Royal Guard-house, the unpretentious palace of Emperor Frederick III., where his widow, Queen Victoria's daughter, resides, and the arsenal, follow in quick succession, forming a pleasing though by no means imposing prospect. Of all these, the arsenal is the most ornate and is one of the finest buildings in Berlin. A striking feature of this, is the adornment, if it may be properly termed such, upon the keystones of the window arches of the inner quadrangle, with sculptured heads of expiring warriors in every variety of agonized expression, depicted in the most realistic manner.

Leading off from *Unter den Linden* toward the south, is a beautiful arched passage, the *Kaiser-Gallerie*, glass roofed and richly decorated in terracotta, in the style of the Renaissance. This is one of the busiest and handsomest arcades in Europe, I am told, though not the largest. The display of goods is similar to that along the colonnades of the *Rue de Rivoli*, in Paris, and the locality has the further advantage of being entirely protected from the weather.

Berlin has many handsome and massive stone bridges which are really works of art in more ways than one, being ornamented with fine statues and groups in bronze and marble, both of mythologic and historic subjects, all wrought and finished in a highly artistic style.

Over one of these, the *Schloss Bruecke*, we cross to the eastern prolongation of the ''Linden,'' and find on the left a lovely, spacious square of nearly fifty thousand square yards. Large shade trees here form a beautiful grove branching over emerald turf and brilliant flowers. In the center is a fine statue of Frederick William III. This place is called the *Lustgarten*, and was originally the pleasure garden of the Royal Palace, which fronts it on the south across the avenue. The square is inclosed on the east and north by the former cathedral and the Old Museum; in front of the steps of the latter, is a curiosity in the shape of a ponderous granite basin said to be twenty-two feet in diameter and seventy-five tons in weight, having been hewn from a solid block of ten times the weight. As I looked at it, half a dozen small *Deutscher* laddies with little bare feet and well-ventilated garments, were trying to scramble inside of the huge hollow.

The Royal Palace, official residence of the reigning sovereign, is located upon an island in the midst of the city, formed by a division of the Spree into two arms at this point which is reached from the west, as noted before, by the *Schloss-Bruecke*, while, going eastward, one passes over Emperor William's Bridge to the Boerse, or exchange; this, by the way, was the first modern building of Berlin executed in stone instead of brick. The palace is huge and impressive in a solid, severe style, with nothing particularly remarkable either in point of age or architecture. The oldest part was erected by Elector Frederick II., in 1443-51. His various successors have added or altered and pulled down, until the time of Frederick, the first king of Prussia, who desired to replace the irregular pile by a uniform structure of imposing proportions. This project, however has never been completely carried out, and from 1716 to about 1845, comparatively trifling changes were made.

From that time to the present, exterior and interior alike have been undergoing a gradual process of renovation. Connected with this palace is a ghostly apparition known as the *Weisse Frau*, or "White Lady," whose appearance in the castle occasionally, exactly at the midnight hour, is reckoned to be always a harbinger of death to some member of the House of Hohenzollern.

Fronting the principal façade of the Royal Palace, is the colossal bronze figure of William I., recently unveiled, the accessories of which are yet unfinished. When complete, with its semi-circle of statuesque adjuncts abutting on the river below, it will suggest the decoration and general effect, though on a smaller scale, of the *Place de la Concorde* in Paris.

In the line of antique structures, Berlin is rather deficient, those it does possess not being particularly remarkable or ancient.

In the Kloster Street is a gymnasium founded in 1514, containing some chambers of an old monastery dating from fourteen hundred and seventy-four, that are still in a fair state of preservation.

St. Nicholas Church is, I believe, the oldest sacred edifice in Berlin, although as it now stands it has many later additions to the original building. The square blocks of granite forming the bases of the two towers, date from the beginning of the thirteenth, the choir from the fourteenth, and the nave from the fifteenth century. Marien Church, built at the end of the thirteenth, and restored in the fourteenth century, is noteworthy as being the second parish-church of Old Berlin. Its peculiar Gothic spire, however, was added in 1790. In front of the principal entrance is the expiatory cross for the murder of the Provost of Bernau in the beginning of the fourteenth century.

There are a large number of fine sacred structures dating all along from the year 1840 to the present day; one, the most modern and splendid of all, is the Memorial Church to Emperor William I. It was in one of these modern churches that I listened to what my program styled (in German letters) a *Geistliche Konzert,* which I blunderingly translated as a "ghostly concert," forgetting for the moment that *geistliche* is "spiritual" and " spiritual" is "sacred;" but it was truly enjoyable, whatever it might be called.

The old cathedral has been pulled down and on its site a splendid new one is building. They have a queer fashion here of entirely inclosing any building in process of erection, with great walls as high as the main parts of the contemplated structure, inside of which only the workmen are admitted, and which completely hide all operations from the outside public. At the corner of King street and the "Long Bridge," abutting on the river and just west of the statue of the Great Elector, is such an enclosure, and I passed it many a time with curious eyes; through chance crevices, or some occasionally swinging door, now and then I could get a glimpse of outlines of rare beauty and of decorations wrought out in fine stone and marble. Often did I inquire what this edifice might be, but strange to say, no one could tell me. Finally one day I resolved not to be baffled and, as I came to the spot in my daily walk, I turned into the large semi-circular area about the old Elector and, pacing back and forth for about half an hour, I accosted every pedestrian who came along. Among these was one couple. a lady and gentleman who evidently were tourists like myself; they were sauntering along, Bædaker in hand, and gazing here and there after the fashion of strangers in a strange land. They could give me no information but we got into a pleasant chat during which I was much puzzled to place the nationality of my interlocutors. I had never heard English spoken in quite their peculiar style. They certainly were not German nor

French nor Scandinavian,—what were they?
Could it be possible that they were English? I
had met many English persons, but never
any who spoke thus; still, I had not then been
to England, and possibly,—no, it was impossible;
no cultivated English tongue could ever twist
its own mother-speech into such accents. It
was only by the closest attention that I was
able to understand. They were very friendly and
had evidently seen much of the world. Finally,
as I was about to turn away, the gentleman said :
    "You are not English, I think?"
    "No," I replied, "American."
    "Ah—h!" rejoined the gentleman, with a
pleasant smile, "Yes, thy speech bewrayeth
thee."
    "Well!" I mentally exclaimed, "Thy speech
bewrayeth thee, too; unfortunately not quite
enough, however, to satisfy me; I wish I could
know your country."
    But before I had opportunity to voice my de-
sire, he went on :
    "Yes, I noticed you spoke differently from us;
we are from Edinburg; but you speak well, very
well indeed; we could understand you perfectly.
Very pleased we met you; hope we shall see you
again."
    And with mutual bows and compliments, we
separated, each marveling at the speech of the
other.
    But I had not found out about the new build-
ing. Of the twenty or more passers by of whom
I inquired, three, though native Germans, were
strangers to the city; two besides the Scotch
tourist and his wife, were foreigners; six seemed
to be just ordinary citizens, male and female;
one was a porter; another a soldier; one a
baker's boy; and the rest were children, boys

and girls of varying ages. Every one had essentially the same answer:

"*Ach! Dass kann ich nicht sagen, meine Dame,*" which, being interpreted, declared that nobody knew. Imagine such a state of things in an American community. My national, investigating spirit was subdued; I gave it up. When you go there, O, solitary sister, do you straightway betake yourself to that quarter and find out for me the desire of my soul. The shrouding timbers may then have been torn away and the structure within be known unto men and women, in free and open exhibition.

Not very far from the Royal Opera House and the ' Linden" lies Schiller Place, an extensive area wherein are found several noble buildings; of these, the French Church, the New Church and the Schiller Theater, are considered the finest architectural group in Berlin. In front of the Theater's principal entrance, stands a fine figure of Schiller and the whole area is lovely with trees and flowers. This group is particularly beautiful by moonlight; though, in making this statement, I resemble Walter Scott, if it be true, as declared, that he had never seen "fair Melrose" at night, when he wrote that to view it "aright" one must,

"Go visit it by pale moonlight,"

yet he spake truly, for all that, and so do I.

While I find this city very pleasing, I have one fault to find with the Berliners and with Germans in general, so far as I have observed over here, and that is that they do not, like the French, throw open their pleasant little parks and gardens, as a rule, to the public, nor do they provide so many resting-places for the wayfaring man, woman or child. True, the public is permitted to walk through and sometimes a seat will be observed, but usually a high, iron railing divides off the pleasant and shady, leafy retreats. and often there is no entrance allowed into the interiors at all, even for a stroll, as in *Leipziger Platz*; of course, there are exceptions; noticeably here, the *Thiergarten*, Wilhelm and Alexander Places and a few others. In French gardens there are very few railings, and those are usually about some bed of delicate plants, or the like, while seats are everywhere.

Very odd names may be noted upon the various signs and placards of a German city, particularly so if lifted over bodily into their equivalent English. Fancy accosting anyone by the name of Mr. Nodding-goose, Mr. Big-head, Mr. Sweet-and-good, Mr. Gas-pipe, or a polished gentleman as Mr. Blood-sausage.

Some of the streets also have odd names when translated, as Bone-hewer, Big-berry, Young-fellow or Invalid Street, Forsaken Way, Wedding Place, and so forth; there is in Germany, too, a queer fashion of naming a thoroughfare by a phrase, as "To the Station" Street, "Behind the Catholic Church" Street, "On the Island" Street. and the like. One day I was startled to notice "Holy Ghost" Street, but soon saw this was only meant as short for "Holy Ghost Church" Street. I am told that here in Prussia, the national Government regulates municipal affairs in many departments. While the city may nominate, it cannot confirm its choice for mayor, the government does that; it also names all streets and public squares and no change can be made in any nomenclature without governmental assent

Berlin is not chary in her recognition of public men. In every square or locality of any importance, may be seen statues of more or less pretentions, to the memory of some general, philosopher, scientist, poet or otherwise famous personage.

The art-collections of Berlin are comparatively inferior in importance, consisting largely of casts and copies and comprising few masterpieces or originals of worth, though I believe the Pergamenian sculptures acquired in 1879, and one or two other collections purchased since, are really valuable.

Though I cannot expect even to allude to the major part of Berlin's characteristics, I will mention in closing, the circular Belle-Alliance Place into which three great avenues converge and which is laid out as a garden, in the center of which rises the fine "Column of Peace," placed here in 1840 to commemorate the peace of 1815. Four marble groups representing the four principal powers that participated in the decisive struggle, surround the column, which is crowned with a "Victory," by Rauch. On the south side of the Place, a flight of steps ascends from the street and is adorned by allegorical figures in white marble. Opposite the top of the stairway and leading to the river, is Halle Gate, a monumental portal decorated with figures of the four seasons.

Berlin is remarkably well supplied with facilities for intramural transportation, though I saw but one electric line, and that running away out from the heart of the city, as seems to be the custom in large towns abroad. The conductors and drivers of the trams and 'buses, wear a very pretty uniform of light fawn-color, set off with leaf-green collars and ornaments; this is varied on hot days by "continuations" of white duck, which somehow they manage to keep in very fresh condition. The uniform of the foresters, or, as we would call them, the park-police, is also very tasteful, consisting of rather wide trousers, a double-breasted, somewhat full-skirted coat and a wide-rimmed, quite high-crowned hat, all of a soft gray-green relieved with cords and frogs of a slightly deeper tinge, and a feather of the same in the hat. As for policeman in general, and soldiers, their costumes are glittering and varied beyond description and show to good advantage on the almost universally fine physique of the North German citizen.

These large cities abroad are usually well supplied with postal facilities of various sorts, but Berlin, I am informed, has, in addition to more ordinary conveniences, a system of Pneumatic Tubes for the rapid transmission of telegrams, letters and postal cards from one part to another of the city, including Charlottenburg. The places for deposit and delivery, are called Pneumatic Post-Offices, and letters or packets must not exceed a certain size and weight.

Postage on letters is about seven, and on cards about five cents.

CHAPTER XXIII.

A hasty visit to Potsdam accompanied by a "lone sister" whom I encountered at my *pension*, (which, by the way, is kept by a *von*, the lowest rank of German nobility,) could not, of course, serve to gain a very thorough knowledge of this great suburb of Berlin, but so far as it went, it was very interesting.

The weather was charming; the distance about half an hour's ride; and, as I had never yet been in a third class carriage, we concluded to take this grade and found it to be very like a large street-car in style and finish. The compartment-walls reached only about three-fourths of the distance between floor and ceiling, and each compartment opened into the next without any intervening doors, though each had doors on each side for entrance and exit, as usual. The seats and floors were bare, the former of varnished slats, as in a tram, and all was clean and comfortable, the rate being very cheap, about twenty-five cents for the round trip.

Potsdam, though a suburb, has fifty-five thousand inhabitants and a garrison of seven thousand soldiers. It is situated on a large island in the Havel, which island abounds in lakes and wooded hills.

The town first came into prominence in the time of the "Great Elector," who did much for the place, founding here his park and garden; its later importance arose a hundred years after, under Frederick the Great, whose favorite residence was at Potsdam.

One enters the main town over the Long Bridge, a remarkably handsome, finely decorated structure, that leads directly to the Royal Palace. so called; though, as there are several other Royal Palaces here, within walking distance of each other, it strikes me that the definite article is rather misapplied.

After leaving the bridge, we pass an old linden, much bepropped and protected, under which, it is said, petitioners used to station themselves to attract the notice of Frederick the Great.

The spacious pleasure-garden to the south of the palace, is inclosed in two rows of columns surmounted by a series of statues, groups and the like. This palace was erected in 1670. but re-constructed in 1750 by Frederick the Great. whose rooms here are preserved in good condition. There is much to be seen that is very interesting, but I must be brief and will allude to but one or two features.

In the apartments of Frederick William I, are a few pictures of his majesty's own painting under peculiar circumstances, that is, while suffering from an attack of the gout. The library of the palace is separated from the bedroom of Frederick the Great, only by a massive silver balustrade. Adjoining the library is a cabinet with double doors, from which a dining-table could be let down by means of a trap-door, and where the king might dine with his friends, at will, without danger of being spied upon by his attendants.

The town contains many fine public buildings, both sacred and secular, and the streets seem mostly wide and pleasant. Here also is a Brandenburg Gate, more effective than the one in Berlin.

We have time to visit but one church and we select the *Friedenkirche*, an edifice in the early Christian Basilica style, completed in 1850, containing the burial vaults of Frederick William IV. and his queen, Elizabeth, also of the Emperor Frederick III.

The church stands apart from the busy highway and is surrounded with much verdure and bowery greenery. We enter at a little side door and, treading over the velvety turf of a shaded inclosure, we step around a side wall and come into a quadrangle shut in by arcades, where we are confronted by the bell-tower, one hundred and thirty feet high. Still farther on beyond the cloisters, we enter an *atrium* or "paradise" containing Rauch's Group of Moses and a copy of Thorwaldsen's Risen Christ. Then turning, we pass into the interior of the basilica, the roof of which is supported by sixteen Ionic columns in black marble. Some fine sculptures are within, and the recumbent figure of Emperor Frederick III., is especially good.

The marble forms lie on immovable and they all seem to be indeed very far from any vital interest; we do not quite understand why Frederick III. is placed here by the side of his uncle, and so remote from his father and mother. Frederick the Great and Frederick William I., his father, are buried in the Garrison Church.

We do not tarry long but step out from the cool silence again into the "garish light of day," and return to the green bowers and highway road, passing the "Great Fountain" which later on is seen in full play, mounting to a height of one hundred and thirty feet.

We reach a broad flight of steps sixty feet high, intersected by six terraces, in the top one of which are buried the grayhounds of Frederick

the Great. Crossing the last terrace, we come
to the entrance of the Palace of *Sans Souci*, the
favorite and almost constant residence of this
monarch.

His rooms are preserved unaltered and contain
many interesting relics of the erratic yet illustrious sovereign and of his famous contempor-
aries. In a room once occupied for some weeks
by Voltaire, are some very odd and rather ugly
wood-carvings and embroideries. Room after
room are we conducted through, which have all
been used for the varied needs of life by the
great king, but now "empty, swept and garnished." We are shown his spinet, flute,
music, books, bed, the clock that he always
wound and that stopped—as clocks of illustrious
beings seem to have a way of doing,—at the
moment of its owner's death, the chair in which
he died and the like. How is it, I wonder, that
so many of the world's celebrities of ancient
date, died in chairs, instead of comfortably in
their beds?

One room which impressed me most, was a
long gallery, one side of which was glass, looking out upon the park, and where the king used
to pace up and down in his later years, accompanied by his greyhounds. I could seem to see
the irascible old man, in the grotesque dress of
the period, traveling to and fro, chafing impo-
tently at the infirmities that set to his activities
a limit which even he could not overstep.

It makes history seem very real to visit these
places, yet it is but a melancholy satisfaction,
after all, giving one the feeling that every one
is dead and gone, and causing one to reflect in
the words of the Psalmist: "How shall thy servant stand before Thee, O, Lord?" and "What
is man that Thou art mindful of him?"

The extensive domain about is very pleasant,
diversified by hill and dale, by pool and fountain.   Some laborers were cutting grass near by
in the broad meadows, and the air was fragrant
with perfume.

Several other royal residences are within convenient distance, by way of lovely avenues
through the imperial acres.   We pass the famous
mill which the old owner refused to sell to Frederick the Great, to that testy monarch's ineffable disgust, but the stubborn man's heirs were
more tractable and it is now royal property. We
next visit the Orangery, a comparatively modern
structure in Florentine style, completed in 1856.
The *Charlottenhof*, transformed, it is said, from
a plain country-house to an Italian villa, contains many memorials of Alexander von Hum-
boldt.

All these palaces are crowded with luxuries
and curious articles of "bigotry and virtue,"
too numerous to name, though I will mention a
chair of steel and silver, made by Peter the
Great.   To the west of the Park of *Sans Souci*,
rises the summer residence of the present emperor, the palace of *Friedrichskron*, founded by
Frederick the Great in 1763, at the end of the
Seven Years War, and completed by him in 1769,
at a cost of about two and a quarter million
dollars.   Among its beautiful and elegant apartments is conspicuous the modern "Shell Room,"
a vast chamber inlaid with shells, minerals and
precious stones, in a most wonderful and tasteful fashion.   These objects, we are told, are mementoes of the visit of William II. (who, by the
way, is styled the "wandering emperor,") to
northern Europe.   The chamber was seven years
in construction.

We were weary now, physically and mentally,

and resolved to do no more sight-seeing. As we strolled along the fine, winding highway, beneath large forest trees, we espied a placard at the beginning of a woodland path, which placard bore the legend "To the Dragon's Cafe." This was tempting, so we turned aside and scrambled up the little hill until we came to a fanciful pavilion, above the cornices of which fiery dragons were snorting defiance to the world at large.

In spite of their ferocious appearance, we ventured near and, seating ourselves at a little table under a leafy tree, were promptly served with coffee in a dragon pot, and bread and butter upon dragon plates. This with tips to the waiter, cost us about twelve and one half cents each, which to the American mind was somewhat surprising. The coffee not quenching my thirst, I asked for ice-water; not to be had; then for an ordinary, plain, everyday drink of water; not to be had either; nothing but *selzer*, which somehow did not seem to "fill a long felt want." But refreshed and restored, we resumed our walk and, as we strolled along the avenue, which had now re-entered the park, there was a sudden reverberation of wheels, a clatter of hoofs, a gleam of scarlet and gold, and lo! an imperial carriage dashed by. This being royal domain, no other would be allowed to traverse it, so we had the spectacle for what it was worth. We then trudged on reflecting, perhaps, that "the rich can ride in chaises," but we—could catch a tram, which we did, and in due time, arrived safely in Berlin.

CHAPTER XXIV

The next week I went on to Dresden, a monotonous trip of about three hours by express, which would have been very dull but for the delightful weather and the pleasant look of the fields and groves in the summer sunshine. The effect was marred for me, however, as it had been so often during my travels on the continent, by the sight of poor, exhausted looking women toiling with such a hopeless appearance at all sorts of heavy labors incident to the tilling of the soil; and at the same time having charge of infants of the tenderest age, which are sometimes strapped to the mother's shoulders, sometimes swaddled up in a bundle upon the grass, and sometimes, when the little feet have become more ambitious, are tied to trees or posts in the vicinity, with long bands that permit some degree of locomotion. And at other times I saw in the beautiful grounds of enchanting estates, feeble, old women who were past their time of usefulness in the fields, bowed down upon hands and knees and crawling about the turf to pick up, one by one, the leaves and twigs that might be scattered there. I have been told that, for this service, they each receive six or seven cents a day; this may be an error, I did not verify it.

Women drag wagons and bear burdens of all descriptions, young children clinging to their gowns; older ones assist. I was fain to ask: "Where are the men?" Many, of course, have gone to be soldiers, but the question was answered in another way, by a spectacle I saw one day upon the street.

To a heavy cart laden with lumber of all kinds, old stoves, boxes, barrels and so forth, a middle aged woman was *harnessed with a dog*. Both were straining every muscle to move the vehicle, while behind, coolly lounging along, occasionally spurring up the ''beasts'' with harsh commands, pipe in mouth and hands in pockets, was the ''lord and master'' of the outfit. I suppose they were thankful he did not get into the cart and ride.

What enchantment of nature or beauty of art can compensate for such a state of things? In France, while women bear, as is just, their full share of the responsibilities of life, I saw no such degradation, and though I do not know the status of woman in French law, I do know that dog-labor is forbidden.

Fair Germany, so beautiful and so endowed, why permittest thou these things so to be?

Still the wheels turn tirelessly onward and soon we enter the lovely suburbs of Dresden and note the grand sweep of the River Elbe as, spanned by three fine stone bridges, it curves in front of the fair city.

Here, as in Berlin and some other German cities, the traveler is handed a metal ticket as he passes through the station-gate, and with this ticket he secures a cab of corresponding number. These vehicles are of two kinds, called first and second class. The latter is cheaper and roomier; the drivers wear yellow hat-bands and collars, instead of white as in the first class; the latter are supposed to be better fitted up, as a rule, than the second class, but in reality there is no very striking difference in the appointments of the two classes.

Dresden, as we all know, is noted for its magnificent picture gallery, which now ranks with the Louvre, the Pitti and the Uffizzi, and there are probably few travelers who do not make it the first objective point of their sight-seeing. Abler pens than mine have set forth its treasures, and I will make no attempt to follow in their lead. But what a privilege it is to have these wondrous creations close at hand, where one may retire at will to marvel and to admire, or to be led in spirit, either backward to the eventful scenes of bygone eras, to the days of romance and chivalry, or up and away through the realms of imagination, to those elevated regions of thought and hope, to which we all strive to attain, in our best and noblest moments.

Dresden's collection is fitly housed, the edifice containing it being considered one of the finest examples of modern architecture. The picture-gallery occupies the first and second floors of the Museum, and the Museum forms the north west wing of the *Zwinger*, which is a splendid structure that one really must see to obtain any adequate idea of its magnificence. It owes its existence to the splendor loving "Augustus the Strong," and, to quote a popular writer, "as Augustus the Strong bore some resemblance to Louis XIV., so the erection of the *Zwinger* recalls the palatial edifices built about that period as monuments befitting the glorious reign of the *Grand Monarque* of France." It consists of seven pavilions connected by a gallery of one story, inclosing a court one hundred and twenty-eight yards long, and one hundred and seventeen wide, but only a small portion of the original design has been completed.

According to Baedeker, the present site of

the Museum was to have been occupied by a huge portal which was to lead to an elevated plateau flanked by two long palaces; these edifices were to have been connected by galleries, whence flights of steps would have descended to the Elbe. But the magnificent plan, conceived in 1711, and carried out until 1722, was never fully executed; and the Museum, now forming a part of the group, was built there in 1847-54.

Nor do the *Zwinger* and the Museum stand alone in their beauty. A grand old pile, the Roman Catholic Court-Church, rises diagonally across from the *Zwinger*, in a remarkably spacious square, and is truly an imposing and majestic structure; the parapets and entrances are adorned with seventy colossal statues of saints; the tower is two hundred and eighty feet high.

Opposite on the northeast stands the Court-Theater, a magnificent *Renaissance* building, covering an area of fifty-five hundred and fifty square yards. It is so richly ornamented with paintings, with medallions, with figures in stone and bronze, that, like the *Zwinger*, it must be seen to be realized.

A handsome guard-house with vestibule upborne by six Ionic columns, is also in this square. All these edifices being detached, their full beauty and dignity are manifest to the beholder; across on the southern side, is the Royal Palace, the proportions of which are not so evident as it does not stand out by itself. Not far from this is a fine elevated terrace, that, lined with beautiful villas and handsome public buildings, and interspersed with great trees and lovely plats of plants and flowers, stretches away off toward the east along the margin of the Elbe. This was originally laid out as a private pleasure-garden, by Count Bruehl, and is approached from the *Schloss-Platz*, or Castle square, by a broad flight of steps adorned with gilded groups in sandstone, of Morning, Noon, Evening and Night.

The new Bohemian Station in Dresden, unfinished at the present writing, though completed enough for traffic, is I think, the finest that I have ever seen.

Dresden has no lack of American visitors and students, and is, perhaps, as well known by people of other lands, as any foreign city in the world. The wife and daughters of one of our ex-consuls were at my *pension*. There was also a Dane lady, one French, one English, and one Russian; the hostess was German and all the others were United States Americans. Oddly enough, we were a family of women, our hostess being the kindest and most genial of old maids, with no masculine belongings, and her patrons also, at this particular epoch, all unattended by gentlemen.

My windows overlooked a pleasant little park, where I would hear children frolicking at all hours of the day, and singing airs as familiar to me as to them, such as any group of American children might sing, "Lightly Row," "The House is Haunted," "Baby Bye," and sometimes what we call "My Country." Odd about this last air, that so many nations claim it as national music. Of course, these little folks sing in German, but, as I cannot distinguish any words at this distance, the effect is quite "homey."

One thing I particularly approve about these German towns, is the clear and distinct labeling and numbering of streets and roads.

There is very little possibility of a stranger losing his way if he can read the placards that are placed at frequent intervals all along the routes at every turn and corner, high enough to be out of the reach of marauding hands,—though such would be sternly dealt with here,—and placed solidly against some background where wind or storm cannot disturb them. In addition to the name of the street, on every corner building are painted the numbers contained in that side of the block, with an arrow showing which way they run; and though Germans do no not invariably, as we do, place odd and even numbers on opposite sides of the streets, yet under this system no one can fail to locate any desired spot, with very little effort.

Dresden has a fine system of both horse and electric trams, but I saw none of the 'buses that have been so numerous in many other places.

Desiring to visit the *Albertinum*, I entered a tram one day and when paying my fare, I explained to the conductor that I was a stranger and requested him to tell me when I had reached my destination. A nice-looking old gentleman sitting next me, asked me if I were a foreigner; on my answering that I was from the United States, he was interested at once.

"Oh! the United States," he said; "I have always wanted to see that great and wonderful country; do you know Denver?"

I replied that I had visited there; whereupon he went on to tell about a son he had in some college there, who had evidently filled his old father's mind with admiration for the home of his son.

"You must go to visit him;" I suggested.

"No, I am too old," he rejoined, "I am seventy years old,"—he did not seem sixty,—"and I have been one of the King's Huntsmen for fifty years; much would I delight to get a shot at some of the grand and wonderful game in that far, far west."

His son, he said, was thirty-five years of age and had just married a lady of twenty, what did I think of that?

I replied that they had probably suited themselves, and he assented with a smiling "*Ja, ja, ja*;" but suddenly pointing outside, exclaimed, "The King, the King!"

I turned hastily and beheld a plain, single carriage wherein was seated a kindly looking old gentleman who bowed pleasantly right and left, but who was without the least insignia or appurtenance of exalted rank and with no attendant except his driver.

My old gentleman remarked that the king was always like that, simple and unostentatious in the extreme. About this time the old huntsman took his departure, after giving me most minute instructions for finding my way. I was sorry to lose him, he was so friendly.

I visited the palace of this same King Albert of Saxony, the next day and saw his portrait in regal attire, looking down in dignity from the stately hall, but seeming even so, the same kindly-natured being.

The palace is not specially noteworthy with the exception of its treasure-room called the "Green Vaults," which are splendid beyond description. Here is a most remarkable display of curiosities, jewels, trinkets, plate, gold and silver smith's work of the sixteenth and seventeenth centuries, enamels, ivory carvings and crystal cuttings, said to be one of the most valuable collections in existence.

I noticed in this palace, as I had done previously in Potsdam, Versailles, Berlin, in fact, in most of the ancient palaces, great mirrors composed of many panes, or pieces, not larger than a medium-sized window-pane; at first, I could

not imagine why they had been so divided, but
learned later it was because they were made before the invention of the process for making
large sheets of glass. The effects in reflection from these numerous divisions, are very
odd.

Fourteen miles from Dresden, lies Meissen, an
ancient Saxon town most picturesquely situated
at the point where the rivers Triebisch and
Meisse flow into the Elbe. In lofty prominence,
one hundred and sixty feet above the town, towers the rocky Schlossberg, to attain the summit of
which, one follows a winding, steep and narrow
way, paved with square, flat stones.

A charming view is had from the top, before
one crosses the massive bridge leading from one
battlement to another, and enters the high walls
that form part of the defences of the citadel.
Here upon a spacious plateau, stands a gray
old cathedral, and the vaulted castle, Albrechtsburg.

But the chief interest at Meissen is the Royal
Porcelain Factory, where is manufactured what
is popularly known as "Dresden China." The
art of making this, it seems, was actually discovered in a chamber of the Albrechtsburg,
where the chemist Boettger had his laboratory
and where the porcelain was made for a year,
until 1710, when the present works just below
the Schlossberg, in the Triebischthal, were established, since when the process has been
carried on there. There is an interesting painting in the old laboratory in the Schlossberg,
representing Boettger at work, and explaining
his process of making the china, to Augustus
the Strong. The porcelain as first made was
of a soft, "crushed-strawberry" color, but
it is now wrought out in most delicate blue and

white, ornamented, of course, in various styles. We were taken all over the Factory and found it marvelously interesting, our guide explaining everything in the most painstaking manner. At Sevres, visitors are not allowed in the workrooms.

CHAPTER XXV.

Rising boldly from adjacent steeps and over-looking the winding waters of the Elbe, looms the Bastei, the finest point in Saxon Switzerland, ten hundred and thirty feet above sea-level.

Taking train at Dresden, one passes over a route growing more and more picturesque, as it follows the course of the sinuous river.

In the genial, but not oppressive sunshine that is so characteristic of the summer season here, our party set forth to view the beauties of this romantic region.

Arriving opposite the little village of Wehlen, we quitted the train and walked past the few small houses clustered about the station, and down a winding path to the river, where we found a not over large, but rather unwieldly row-boat, the owner of which consented to take us across.

Two or three persons from other points had already assembled here and just before me in stepping into the boat, was a stubby, impassive-looking fellow of middle age, in rustic garb, while already sitting in the boat was another man, somewhat older, short, fat and "roly-poly," with a jolly, red face and an expression "childlike and bland."

As these two spied each other, they rushed ecstatically together at the risk of upsetting the boat, clasped each other in the most fervent of embraces, kissing one another over and over on both cheeks and ejaculating euthusiastically:

"*Ach Himmel!*"

"*Du lieber Mann!*"

"*Mein bester Freund!*" and so on repeatedly until at last they subsided into their seats, still clasping hands and beaming upon each other delightedly. We looked on with amused interest, striving to fancy the closest of American male relatives going through such a scene even in private. Not that we condemned the spirit; indeed, we considered it rather refreshing and infinitely preferable to the bored and *blasé* demeanor affected by many of our exponents of good form; still, it might be well to take account of stage-setting and audience, before fully giving way to one's emotions.

By this time we had all found places, and soon moved slowly across the stream.

Arriving safely, my companions scattered their several ways, and I wandered through the delightfully quaint little village, on past an ancient church where, turning, one follows a good wide path that ascends gradually but constantly as one proceeds. It winds along through a narrow ravine, thickly wooded, and almost immediately there is no trace of human occupation and one seems to be in the very depths of some "forest primeval."

The path gradually contracts and soon the way becomes but a mere defile between great, towering buttresses of gray rock, which stand out in solid masses of such substantial and regular continuity, that they seem to have been reared by giant hands under the leadership of some mighty master-mason.

Though the trees have now removed themselves to the top of these lofty battlements, for there is no room for them in the gorge, yet the air is cool and the light shaded, for these reach down to the wayfarer, from above into the abyss, between hundreds of feet of solid rock.

Though it seems so isolated, yet it is not lonely, for merry parties are continually coming and going upon this marvelous, meandering way. A company of children under charge of two or three adults, passes on singing; it disappears around a turn of the mighty chasm, and the voices come back echoing and re-echoing from the granite walls.

Still upward and onward; here and there a vine trails downward from far above, or some aspiring moss stretches up from the foot of the prolonged precipice, and embroiders the gray surface of the rocky ramparts in traceries of living green. A little rill flows out now and then, and a daring blossom thrusts forth its dainty head at occasional intervals.

Up and up and up; still tower the rocks on high, growing more grotesque and tremendous; but we are coming to the top and finally we emerge from the defile, into an extensive pine wood through which we clamber still upward. And now we come to level ground and discover a tiny, woodland restaurant, *Der Steinerne Tisch*, or "The Stony Table," with inviting attractions for refreshment; but we are too near the aim of our exertions to stop here, so we press on, and at length we reach the highest peak of this huge precipice called the Bastei.

There is a fine inn on the summit of the cliffs, and the whispering forest creeps up close to its walls. Between the main façade of the inn and the brink of the crags, are exceedingly wide verandas, railed in for safety's sake, and here was found a motley company of pleasure-seekers, eating, drinking, chatting cosily, or listening to the music provided for its entertainment.

Finding a seat close to the edge of the platform, I look down on the wonderful panorama spread out below.

North, south, east and west, the eye sweeps in voiceless admiration. Far down in the green and peaceful valley, the Elbe rolls its placid waters, six hundred and forty-five feet beneath, bearing upon its bosom many a little craft of pleasure or traffic and curving gracefully from point to point until lost amid the wooded ravines and stony steeps at either hand. Tiny hamlets dot its borders, country roads and fertile fields lie all along its stretches, until the mighty bastions of rugged rock tower up beyond, seeming to say: "Thus far and no farther."

We are told that from this pinnacle one overlooks the whole of Saxon Switzerland, and we are willing to believe it as we gaze abroad.

And now, having feasted bodily and spiritual eye to the full, a more ignoble, perhaps, but not less useful organ asserts its claims to recognition, so I summon a *"Kellner,"* and demand some slight internal refreshment.

"And what will the gracious lady be pleased to desire?" is the polite inquiry of that functionary.

The "gracious lady" intimates a longing for chocolate and cake.

They appear; the first is tempting; the second—interesting but unrecognizable. I appeal to the waiter: "What is this?"

"Cake, gracious lady."

"What makes it so dark?"

"It is the flour, gracious lady."

"But why is it so dry and queer?"

"It is its age, gracious lady."

"Its age! I don't want aged cake; bring me some fresh, please?"

"But perhaps the gracious lady does not know that we make it only once a year and it is not now the season."

I am aghast. Cake a year old! How do they ever manage to keep it in any wise, for that time, and why do they wish to do so? For it is not a rich fruit cake with wines and spices to preserve it.

But I have exposed my ignorance, doubtless, by my horrified expression, for the servant goes on to explain that this cake is a specialty in this region; that it is prepared from a recipe handed down from time immemorial and is, by some method which I really did not comprehend, subjected to a sort of "curing" process; perhaps on the principle applied in treating certain celebrated cheeses, that must lie for a year or so in special caves under peculiar conditions, to acquire their distinctive qualities. At all events, the waiter prevailed upon me to taste the cake and, to my amazement, I found it to be very good indeed. I regret that I neglected to ask its name, so I can only refer to it, on occasion, as the "aged cake."

One has a choice of a variety of routes on the Bastei, and, in descending, I took the shortest and most precipitous, that leading to Rathen.

After going down the first descent from the hotel, one passes over a massive, mid-air bridge constructed in 1851, that connects the various summits of the rocky pinnacles that here rise hundreds of feet from the valley.

Most astonishing and diverse are the views one obtains from this bridge, as one is alternately completely shut in by the huge turrets of ragged rock, or gazes off into space and down into the abysses at either hand; that on the right revealing the smiling valley, that on the

left, great masses of rock clothed in hardy
woodland growth of varied green.

High up on these grim walls that rise so far
above one's head, is set many a tablet commemorative of some honored citizen or eventful occasion of the vicinity.

Shortly after leaving the bridge, the path
broadens and a space of perhaps fifteen feet in
width is reached. Here, at the extreme verge
of the precipice, looms a mighty boulder, so
vast that one's mind fails to take in a computa-
tion of its solid contents.

Apparently poised and ready for a plunge, it
is in reality perfectly firm, and its base is beautified by neatly kept beds of blooming plants
and flowering vines; for this boulder has been
converted into a monument to some sweet singer
dear to the Saxon heart, and his name and fame
are set forth in graven letters far above.

Then again the path contracts between the
stern stone walls and, growing steeper and
steeper, is at length merged into one long staircase of stony steps, to cut which must have cost
almost inconceivable time and labor, and which
is so narrow that one's out-stretched hands may
easily touch the rocks at either side, nearly all
the way. Occasionally there will come a short,
comparatively level stretch, where trees spring
up and mosses and ferns abound, then more
steps and again down, down, down.

This, though very tiring, is exceedingly rapid
traveling, and presently a lovely, green, sloping
meadow is reached, around the edge of which
the path leads on, until soon it descends again
steeply and a few more steps appear; then a
paved way which finally leads down into the
pretty, rustic village of Rathen, with a ruined
castle overlooking the cottages and lanes.

The railway station is on the opposite side and, as I am about to embark in a little row-boat to reach that point, I glance up the stream and perceive a small steamer coming down, and find that I can return to Dresden by water.

So I board the trim vessel and, finding a quiet and sheltered nook on the rear deck, I compose my weary limbs in a comfortable position and watch the lovely panorama unroll itself behind us, as we make our way back to the city; stopping with shrill "toot" and much churning up of the current, now on one side of the river, now on the other, at the neat villages scattered all along the shores.

Some of the towns are of considerable consequence, as Pirna, with its fourteen thousand inhabitants, its old fortress and its quarries of sandstones; or Koenigstein, not so extensive in population, but possessing a still more important fortress imposingly situated eight hundred and fifteen feet above the Elbe.

This great pile was originally a castle, down to 1401; then a monastery, then again fortified in 1540. Its well is six hundred and twenty feet deep and contains sixty-five feet of water. We are told that the treasures and archives of Saxony, are deposited in this fortress in time of war, but at present it is used as a state-prison. But most of the landing-places are merely rural hamlets or the summer homes of urban denizens.

Not far from Koenigstein and rising some one hundred and fifty feet higher, appears the Lilienstein of tragic memory. At the base of this huge crag in 1756, fourteen thousand Saxon soldiers were surrounded by Prussians under Frederick the Great, and compelled to surrender on account of hunger. But nature smiles on as ever, and fair and peaceful glints the landscape in the summer sunset.

It is a much longer distance back by water than by rail, and evening tints and shadows begin to creep athwart the scene, ere we come to the long rows of fine villas that mark the approach to Dresden. The noble contours of the city's impressive architecture and the graceful spans of its artistic bridges, are thrown distinctly against the deepening sky as we glide into port, and find ourselves at our journey's end.

CHAPTER XXVI.

From Dresden to Leipsic is but a short journey, only two and one quarter hours by express. The train winds along through a very pretty country on leaving Dresden, keeping for some time at the base of the Loessnitz Hills, which are "with verdure clad" and dotted with many fine villas and country homes.

I did not stop long enough in Leipsic to gain much of an idea of its characteristics. It is, of course, well known as the center of Germany's book trade, a position it has held for over a hundred years. Statistics show there are more than a hundred printing offices and about six hundred and fifty publishers, and book-establishments in this city of three hundred and fifty six thousand inhabitants, while publishers in other parts of Germany have, almost without exception, emporiums of their books at Leipsic, whence they are sent out over all the world.

Leipsic is also the seat of the supreme law-courts of the German empire, while its facilities for the study of music and other special lines, are taken advantage of by hundreds of foreign students. The city is not so handsome, to my thinking, as many another in this region, but it has of course, its fine and interesting features.

The name is said to have been at first *Lipzk*, or "the town of lime trees." It is mentioned first in history in the eleventh century and was soon after fortified. These fortifications are now changed, as in so many other old-world

towns, into pleasant promenades beyond which
lie the inner suburbs, which in turn are inclosed
by the outer suburbs.

The New Theater is a handsome building;
the Museum opposite is chiefly noted for its collection of modern pictures; the *Augusteum* is
the seat of the University founded in 1408 and
now attended by more than three thousand students. These edifices, with the post-office, surround the spacious *Augustus Platz* where is also
a fine, monumental fountain.

Goethe was a student here in 1767-8. Auer-
bach's *Keller* on Grimmaische street, is celebrated as the scene of a part of *Faust*; it contains
some curious mural paintings representing, we
are told, the tradition on which the play is
based.

In Goethe street is an obelisk celebrating the
completion of the Leipsic and Dresden railway,
which was opened in 1837 and was the first of
any importance in Germany. Of course, as an
old University center, Leipsic has numberless
relics of celebrated men.

Poets, philosophers, musicians, painters and
others are commemorated by tablet and token, by
monumental brass and stone.

The *Rosenthal* and the Connewitz Woods are
both pleasant sylvan retreats beautified by skill
and taste. Two miles southeast of Leipsic, is
Napoleonstein, a wooded height from which Napoleon watched the progress of the battle of
Leipsic in 1814. It lasted, as history tells us,
four days, and is the most prolonged and san-
guinary on record. Many relics have naturally
been found about here and are preserved with
great care. The only building on which bullet-
marks are still visible, is the *château* at Doelitz,
two miles west of the obelisk.

Leaving Leipsic by the Thuringian railway, I found myself passing through an exceedingly picturesque district.

We change cars at Corbetha, near which three celebrated battles were fought in the years agone, in the first of which, Lueten, Gustavus Adolphus, king of Sweden, was mortally wounded. At Rossbach, Frederick the Great gained a signal victory in 1757; and in 1815 a fierce engagement took place between the allied Russians and Prussians against the French. How every foot of these ancient lands has been dyed over and over, throughout the centuries, in the bright tide of human blood. Even so in our own land, no doubt, but the red chieftains and warriors of those bygone ages there, had no poet, no historian, and so their bravery and valor, their struggles and conquests, are all unwritten and unsung and we know them not.

All is smiling and peaceful here now as we run along in the valley of the Saale. amidst many spots of quaint and historical interest; the country gradually becomes more broken and we see vineyards all about on the hill-sides, while from frequent castle and cathedral, turret and pinnacle spring aloft toward the clear, blue sky.

A pleasant lady now joins me in my compartment where I have been for some time alone. Seeing I have English literature, she is interested and we get into conversation. She is familiar with this part of the country and kindly calls my attention to many a point that otherwise might have escaped my notice. The dusky evening begins to gather as we wind in and out of the hills and along by the rippling river. We have left the Saale and are now on the banks of the Ilm. Suddenly we are abreast of two striking ruins so near that they are startlingly distinct in the shadowy light. They are not of the soft gray hue that is usually the result of the wear and tear of ages, but of a light yellowish tint, something like the cream-colored brick of our central states.

They stand facing each other across a narrow gulch and are not perched, as is general, upon some dizzy height, but stand on two moderately high elevations that slope gently down to the valley. Cruel rents and jagged breaches are in their dismantled walls, evincing the desperate struggles through which they have passed.

My companion says that it was an ancient custom of certain tribal enemies, to rear castles thus near each other on the edges of a ravine, and then to fight across until one or the other party was conquered or exterminated, when the vanquisher took possession of his victim's property. The slopes seemed so soft in their contours and the green grass so velvety and tender, that those grim objects looming up in the dim light had a weird and peculiar effect.

Weimar is reached only in time for supper and bed, but the next morning I start out with renewed vigor. Very lovely indeed looked the old town which has so many literary associations, the master spirits among which are Goethe and Schiller.

The houses of each of these two distinguished writers and "world-poets," are kept as far as possible in the condition in which they were left by their distinguished occupants.

Schiller's home is modest and unpretending, consisting of a few rooms in the upper story of a medium-sized house in Schiller Street. They are plainly furnished and contain many personal and family mementoes. Schiller's life in Weimar was brief as compared with Goethe's, and the former had neither the time nor the opportunity to gather about him such treasures as Goethe accumulated in his long and varied existence.

It seemed strange to look out at the windows and reflect that I was gazing upon the same scene that Schiller had viewed day after day; to sit at the desk and in the chair where he wrote his wondrous lines; to go down the narrow stairs which he must have trodden so many innumerable times back and forth. It made me sorrowful for, speaking from his immortal works, he had ever before seemed a living presence to me, and now I realized that he was dead and that the places that knew him were empty forever.

I did not feel the same sensation of sadness in Goethe's house. Perhaps it is because the place is so very different, so much more extensive, and fitted up so much more in the style of a public museum, that the idea of personality is lost in a measure, and one feels rather as if merely viewing another of the numerous art and curio collections that so abound abroad.

Goethe was a wide traveler, a most cultivated and many-sided character. He lived in Weimar fifty-six years, during forty of which this house, presented to him by Duke Karl August, was the dwelling of the great poet. A spacious staircase with wide ante-rooms, designed by Goethe and profusely decorated with statues and cartoons, leads to the reception-rooms. To the left is the Juno Room; then follow the Urbino Room; the *Deckenzimmer*, which with the adjoining chamber, forms a suite; the Bust Room; the Garden Room, besides the more usual living-rooms.

In these apartments, arranged and classified by Goethe's own hand, are his wonderful accumulations of portraits, antique gems, medals, orders, rings, copies of and original valuable manuscripts, paintings, sketches and drawings, besides a large number of Goethe's own handiwork, medallions, gifts from countries, cities, corporations and friends from all parts of the world, including one from the United States, which consists only of a small circular disc of some kind of wood, on which was imprinted the name of some newspaper and the date, 1846; (I am sorry that I omitted to take a note of the inscription, and find that I can not recall it;) vases, cups, drinking horns, rare china, coins, plaques, minerals, precious stones, statuettes, sculptures, the piano on which young Mendelssohn played, and so forth, including, I verily believe, every variety of objects that can be collected, except living specimens.

One is first dazzled, then dazed by the variety, value and beauty of this astonishing array, and it is rather a relief to come at last to the back of the house where, overlooking an old-fashioned garden, are Goethe's simple study and bedroom.

These two are furnished in the sparest and plainest fashion, the bedroom containing nothing but a single-bed, a bare wooden wash-stand and a large arm-chair by no means luxurious, in which he died. The floor is bare, the room narrow and contracted, with but one small window, yet it is just as he left it.

From these close confines, that mighty genius which had moved the world with its wondrous power, went out into the mystic beyond; leaving in passing, no feeblest trace or impress upon the material objects that had served its earthly needs so long.

Oh! the mystery of spirit, which, while here in mortal guise, can sway the whole round globe; and yet, departing, freed from fleshly housings, can send back no slightest manifestation thereafter, through all the ages of the circling spheres.

There is no one left to inherit Goethe's fame and treasures; they are accredited to the state; the family is extinct.

Passing out from all these mementoes of a vanished existence, I come again into the warm sunshine and roam about where fancy beckons. Of course Weimar has its *Schloss*, and I come upon it quite accidentally, in passing through a queer and crooked street which takes me round many a turn and corner.

Suddenly it broadens out and upon the opposite side stretches away a beautiful domain of emerald turf and majestic trees, while a massive and stately edifice rears itself in the midst of the cool shades. Noticing a seat at hand by the door of a shop, I take possession of the same and, looking across, enjoy and admire.

Young Germany, in the guise of a toddler of about eighteen months, comes out of the shop and welcomes me rapturously. I return the small man's expansive smiles and shake the chubby, little paw, somewhat begrimed, that he insists on offering. Not content with this, he ambles back into the house and returns with his mother, performing all that is essential in the way of introduction, by renewed smiles, many gestures and several ''gee-gees'' and ''da-das,'' a sort of infantile Volapuek. The mother also proves friendly and is much pleased to learn that I am admiring the view. And then rested and cheered, I go on to the many other interesting spots that I must not attempt now to chronicle, merely referring to the *Stadt Kirche*, with its parsonage near by occupied by Herder for so many years, and to a fine, bronze statue of him, standing in front of the church and bearing on the pedestal his favorite motto, "*Licht, Liebe, Leben,*" (Light, Love, Life.)

There are numerous monuments in Weimar to its celebrated men, as Karl August, Wieland and others, but the most imposing of all, is that erected to Goethe and Schiller in front of the Theater, where the colossal figures in bronze of the two poet-friends, are represented standing side by side, with clasped hands.

CHAPTER XXVII

Without having half exhausted the interests of Weimar, I continue through the hills and dales and beside the numerous water-courses of this picturesque region.

The weather is still delightful; in fact, I am charmed with the summer climate of the continent, so far as I have experienced it. The sun shines out clear and genial but not oppressive; our excessive heat is unknown and in the warmest days it is cool in the shade. Another most remarkable thing is the scarcity of flies and insects. I have not yet seen a screen in use, though I did notice two windows in Potsdam that had screens at hand, also one later in a hotel in Holland, but they are almost unknown. Doors and windows stand wide open; night after night I read or write by gas, oil, electricity or candle as the case may be, before open windows, and yet never a fly or a moth disturbs me then, nor during my highly prized morning nap. This could not be done with us at home in mid-summer, nor indeed at any time from April to October. The nights are cool and refreshing and I have never yet been inconvenienced by the heat, though the "natives" frequently complain because it is so "awfully hot."

Not far from Weimar we come to Erfurt, a quaint old town near which is a salt mine with a shaft thirteen hundred feet deep.

The train now approaches the north slope of the Thuringian forest. The hills grow more towering and on nearly every height is a castle,

either in ruins or "brought down to date" for
modern use.   About five miles from Erfurt, are
three isolated hills called the *Drei Gleichen*,
which might be freely translated as "three of a
kind;" they are each topped by a castle; one of
these, the Wachsenburg, is in good preservation,
the other two are beautiful in their decay.

Skirting the Seeberg, we come in view of
Gotha, a busy mercantile place, beyond which a
fine outlook is obtained on to the Thuringian
mountains.

Now we follow the course of the river Hoersel.
A long, jagged and precipitous range rises on
the right, called the Hoerselberg.   This attains
a height of fifteen hundred and seventy-five
feet and extends nearly to Eisenach.   Tradition
locates here the grotto of Venus, into which that
goddess lured the knight Tanhaeuser.

Soon we see against the horizon the towers
of Eisenach, a town of twenty-one thousand inhabitants and commonly called the finest point
in the Thuringian forest.   Five hundred and
sixty-five feet above the city looms the great fortified castle of the Wartburg, situated on a mount
of the same name.   Founded in 1070, it has
passed through numerous startling vicissitudes,
but in the last half century has been restored
to its original grandeur and ranks as one of the
best   Romanesque   secular   buildings   now
existing.   A   grand   retrospect   of   the
frowning old fortress, is had as the train follows the Hoersel to its junction with the Werra.
The ruins of Castle Brandenburg are seen on
the left and then an envious tunnel shuts off our
view.

We next find ourselves in the valley of the
Fulda.   Fine streams are numerous and the
country is undulating but with few prominent

elevations. At Hersfeld is pointed out to us a Benedictine Abbey founded in 769, once of great importance but now used as a school-house. The abbey church was destroyed in 1761, but its ruins are majestic in their beauty.

This section of the country was occupied at a very early date.

The town of Fulda owes its origin to an abbey founded in 754, while its little church of St. Michael, was consecrated in 822.

Many ruins all about in vale and on height, give picturesque evidence of time's tireless energies.

The train descends the valley of the Kinzig. In this river is an island whereon are the remains of an imperial palace erected before the year 1170. Here the emperor Frederick Barbarossa held a Diet in eleven hundred and eighty, to pronounce the deposition of Duke Henry the Lion of Saxony. Beyond this point the country is level. We reach Hanau, noted, among other things, as the birth-place of Jacob and Wilhelm Grimm. We cross and recross the mighty river Main and find ourselves in low-lying Frankfort.

Flat indeed it seems to eyes for some time accustomed to the diversified scenery farther east, of the Hartz Mountains, of the Saxon peaks and pinnacles, and to the pleasing heights and wooded slopes of the Thuringian and the Black forests. Not an eminence is to be noted as one's eyes sweep about, and the horizon is unbroken except for the uprising towers and turrets, of which Frankfort has its full quota.

Ages ago, we are told, a vast expanse of water rolled over this plain, "filling the space from the Alps and the Jura to the Taunus and Hundsrueck mountains," and connected by a narrow sea-arm to the German Ocean. But now we see no rolling waters except the magnificent Main, which adds so much to the attractiveness and importance of the city.

Frankfort ambitiously dates itself back to the first century when, it is claimed, the Romans built a castle on the present "Cathedral Hill," so called, though why "hill," I am unable to divine.

This Roman military post fell before the conquering German tribes of the third century, who themselves were conquered centuries after, by the Franks.

The place is first mentioned as *Franco-furt*, "the ford of the Franks' country,"—in a document dated 790; and three years afterward, Charlemange came here with his whole court and remained eight months. I came across a little German poem the other day, written long ago by August Kopisch, which gives the traditional discovery of "the Franks' ford." Perhaps my "lone sister" may be interested in a translation :—

The best of all his heroes in Saxony lay dead,
Thence Carolus Magnus, Kaiser, in dire disaster
    fled.

"On to the Main, my soldiers, a ford we there must
    find,—
But woe,—the mist lies forward, the foe crowds
    close behind!"

Then Carolus sank down praying on knee beside his
    spear,
When lo! the mist divided, while forth there
    sprang a deer;

She led her young in safety through to the other
    side,
And thus by God's own favor the Franks the ford
    espied

Then forward all pressed over, as Israel through
      the sea,
The Saxons, mist-enveloped, no ford beyond could
      see.

Then struck the Kaiser Carol upon the sand his
      spear,
And vowed, "It shall forever be called the Frank's
      ford here."

But later back he came there with mighty warrior-
      band,
By which he then had conquered the lovely Saxon
      land.

But yonder on the river now shines a city proud,
With noble sons and daughters, with wealth and
      fame endowed.

And there has many a Kaiser been crowned with
      Carol's crown,
And on his throne be-jeweled, in splendor sat him
      down.

There oxen whole are roasted, there wine in foun-
      tains flows,
There gifts for every poor man the horn of plenty
      strows.

The chief lord to the Kaiser lifts cup in Roemer's
      hall;
With Kaiser-portraits covered gleams forth each
      glittering wall.

With Kaiser-portraits covered o'er every inch of
      space,
No later ruler's picture could find there now a
      place.

Thus Germany's first Kaiser name for the city
      found,
And Germany's last Kaiser was in this city
      crowned.

Stirring and vivid have been the fortunes of
the ancient city; fierce and tireless the war-
fares waged by opposing powers, for supremacy
within its borders: hard indeed is it to realize

its vicissitudes of the past, as one walks through the handsome city of to-day.

There are a few traces yet existing of the later day fortifications of the town. One of these is the Eschenheimer tower, a noble specimen of mediæval, defensive architecture. This tower has its tradition as follows:—

Hans Winkelsee, a poacher, fired at a municipal gamekeeper and, after an imprisonment of nine months in this tower, was to be executed. He claimed to have fired only to frighten the keeper and not with intent to kill, as otherwise he certainly would have hit him.

In order to show his unerring markmanship, he offered to shoot nine bullets in nine shots into the weather-vane of the tower; as he succeeded, his life was spared and he was set at liberty.

Frankfort has a fine cathedral but, though it occupies the site of a succession of previous sacred edifices running back to the ninth century, the present building is very modern, having been erected between the years 1869 and 1880, the structure immediately preceding having been destroyed by fire. There is a very peculiar mortuary memorial in the inclosed yard of this cathedral. It consists of a most realistic representation of the crucifixion, with life-sized figures and all the accompanying dreadful and agonizing details. These are wrought out in stone and are made still more conspicuous by being raised upon an eminence of some two or three feet, which forms the base of the singular monument erected to himself by some one whose name is duly inscribed on a tablet below, but which has entirely escaped me in the horror excited by the grewsomeness of his taste in art. The cathedral was shown to me by a very pleasant young man who, to his honor be it recorded, not only did not expect a tip, but actually declined it when offered. And to my great and increasing surprise, the same thing occurred here in another church, that of St. Leonard's, and this episode was quite a refreshing incident in my experience.

The churches of Germany are not so universally accessible to visitors as in France, though I believe the Roman Catholic ones are always open.

I have seen here none of that ceremonious and pompous display at funerals which is so common in France, and am told that it finds no favor in Germany. The Germans, however, have one odd custom on such occasions, and that is the heading of the funeral train by a woman whom they style the *Toten-Frau*, or "Death-Woman," whose office it is to prepare the body for the grave, and then clad in black, with long streamers from her sable cap, and with as many of the funeral garlands as she can carry, to march in front of the procession,—which is not made up, as with us, of a line of carriages, but simply an open hearse having canopy but no sides,—followed by men walking in couples. With the exception of the *Toten-Frau*, no woman takes part in German obsequies, so far as I have been able to ascertain.

Frankfort has many modern public buildings of a noble and majestic order of architecture; especially may be noted the New Exchange, the General Post-Office, and the Grand Opera House. The Central Railway Station is a magnificent and artistic edifice costing, I am told, the sum of thirty-five million marks, or more than eight million dollars.

There are also some remaining specimens of

the beautiful timber architecture of the middle ages, of which the *Roemer*, or city-hall, is a remarkably handsome and interesting example, with decorations of marvelous variety and finish. The great festal-hall within, alluded to in the poem, is truly a splendid chamber.

Goethe was born in Frankfort and his birthplace, a substantial structure of three stories, having dormer windows and a pointed gable having two stories more, has been thoroughly restored and is carefully preserved by the Frankforters.

One especially odd building stands at the corner of the Eschenheimer street; it is call *Zum Kaiser Karl*, or "The Emperor Charles," from the fact that Charles VII. lived in a house on the same site in 1742-3 and -4. The present edifice is not at all modern. The outside is adorned with allegorical figures representing pride, laziness, envy, avarice, intemperance, voluptuousness, and anger; also the virtues of charity, husbandry, valour, love, industry and honesty; further supplemented by illustrations of the domestic labors of the days of the week. The heads of these figures are particularly grotesque, and from this fact the house is called the *Fratzeneck*, or "grimaces-corner."

The streets of Frankfort, however, though usually well built, are not so pleasing as in many other places. The location is unfavorable to picturesque vistas, and as a rule there is too little variety in architecture. One of the finest and most important avenues is called the Zeil.

Like most German towns, Frankfort has a delightful wooded park and numerous monuments to public men and events. The Gutenburg memorial commemorative of the invention of printing, is perhaps the most imposing of the latter.

The year 1866, diastrous to the fortuncs of so many German provinces, terminated the independence of Frankfort and led to its annexation to Prussia. It evidently has no reason to regret its change of dynasty, and keeps on the even tenor of its way, a busy and prosperous city.

CHAPTER XXVIII

A run of two or three hours from Frankfort, through scenery gradually changing from a monotonous level to diversified heights of rare beauty, brings the traveler to that famous old town apostrophized so long ago by the German poet as:

> "Old Heidelberg, thou beauty,
> With many honors crowned,
> Along the Rhine or Neckar,
> No town like thee is found."

The location is indeed charming; the little city lies at the foot of the lofty elevation from which the place takes its name, and upon the margin of the fine river Neckar which winds gently through this fertile valley.

The objective point of interest to the sight-seer here, is the massive old castle towering aloft in ruined majesty upon the precipitous well-wooded hill called the Jettenbuehl. Diverse have been the fortunes of the old pile, since Rudolph I. built the most ancient part in 1204. In the Thirty Years War, the old structure suffered so much that it was rendered absolutely uninhabitable; it was restored and fortified anew in 1649, only to be repeatedly blown up and pulled down by the French in the Orleans War, as fast as the breaches were repaired. After this war, the castle was again in a measure restored, when in 1764 it was struck by lightning and the whole interior fell a sacrifice to the flames. Since then no further restorations have been attempted, but from 1830, the greatest care has been exercised to preserve the ruins from further decay.

The easiest and quickest way to ascend the mountain, is by funicular railway, though it is rather trying to susceptible nerves, the grade being so remarkably steep and the line passing through so many tunnels of inky darkness.

On this hill there once stood an upper and a lower castle. That which is known to-day as "The Castle," is the lower structure and stands upon quite an extensive plateau about half way up the great hill. After this one had been completed, the upper castle, which was the o'der, was used as an arsenal and powder magazine till it was struck by lightning in 1537; the explosion was so terrible that not only the upper castle was almost entirely demolished, but the lower one and the town were seriously damaged. After this, the upper citadel remained forsaken until 1853, when a *Molkenkuhr*, or "Whey-Cure," was established at this point, the name of which has entirely superseded that of the "Old Castle," by which the place had been always known.

From the top is seen a most splendid view; the castle ruins are particularly picturesque and have a certain desolate grandeur that is very impressive. At times the old pile is artificially illuminated and the effect from below is weirdly beautiful.

In the cellars of the lower castle lies the far-famed Heidelberg Tun of which school children learn with wonder. It is about twenty-four feet high and thirty-three feet long and its capacity is fifty thousand, nine hundred and twenty gallons. Lying in front of it is a small tun—so called—noted for its artistic construction, being held together without hoops. Near by is a statuette representing the dwarf, Clemens Perkeo, court fool of Karl Philipp, which dwarf, tradition states, drank daily from fifteen to eighteen bottles of strong wine. On the tenth of November, 1753, the great tun was filled for the first time, and, later on, twice again. Since the great fire at the castle, it has remained empty. There was a pump fitted to it, that passed up into the banquet room, thus rendering the tun's contents easily accessible.

The vault where it lies was probably constructed for holding it, as no other one in the castle is lofty enough to accommodate it.

A staircase leads up one side of the tun and down the other, and we tourists ascended and decended the same, dancing an extempore fandango on the top of the tremendous cask.

Another cask called the lesser Heidelberg Tun, is in another vault and holds twenty thousand gallons.

Turning from things spiritous to things spiritual, we visit some of the churches of Heidelberg, which are ancient but in good preservation. The Holy Ghost Church, built in 1400, was long the scene of a bitter religious strife. The reformation was begun here in 1546, by preaching the gospel and administering the sacrament in both forms; the Electoral House having turned Roman Catholic, the possession of the church was hotly contested. In 1705 it was divided by a wall, the choir having been assigned to the Romanists and the nave to the Protestants. Then the Elector told the Protestants if they would resign their claim, he would build them a new church; they refused and the Elector, to use the vernacular, "got mad" and took forcible possession of the church, pulling down the wall. The Protestants appealed to the Diet and the wall was rebuilt. In 1886 it was pulled down again only to be put up once more in 1893

I am moved to wonder if, in all this time, they ever gave any consideration to the text: "Behold how pleasant a thing it is for brethren to dwell together in unity." Probably they did, but each one was convinced that it applied not to himself, but to "the other fellow."

In St. Peter's Church is the tombstone of Olympia Fulvia Morata, "the most learned woman of the sixteenth century, who was warmly devoted to religion." Near this church is the old university founded in 1386 by Ruprecht the Red; this institution has flourished or declined according to the fortunes of the town. At one time its possessions on the left bank of the Rhine, were confiscated by the French, and the university was reduced to such poverty that it could not pay its professors for years. But better days dawned and in 1886 it celebrated its five-hundredth jubilee.

Heidelberg College is situated on the opposite side of the river. This institution offers special advantages for acquiring modern languages.

In the High street is an ancient structure which escaped destruction by the French when they devastated the town in 1693. This is called the *Ritterhaus*, (the House of the Knight,) and is now used as a hotel. It was built in 1592 by a French emigrant, and is in the style of the French renaissance. On the summit of the façade is the bust of a knight, and the busts of four Frankish kings adorn the fourth story. Between the windows of the third story are the busts of the builder and his wife, with their arms and the inscription in Latin: "Except the

Lord bless the house, the labor of the builder is vain." Between the windows of the next lower story are the busts of the builder's two children.

As this edifice is very narrow and there is no more place for likenesses, it is well that the builder's family was no more extensive.

A handsome bridge decorated with sculptures leads from the Steingasse across to Neuenheim, a suburb of Heidelberg.

Lovely indeed is the view from this bridge; especially so as I saw it in the last rays of a vanishing sun on a mid-summer evening, just as the rising moon began to show its reflected splendor on the other hand. Toward the west the lingering glow of the sunset was tinting river and low-lying cloudlet, while in the east the silver gleams of the moonlight showed stronger and stronger, pouring over the dark bulk of the lofty hill and throwing out in clear relief the dismantled walls, the shattered buttresses and the gaping window-spaces of the ruined castle.

It was a romantic and enchanting scene, and I wondered not at the enthusiasm of the bard previously quoted, nor that he should declare in closing,—

> "And oh! if thorns crowd thickly
> And life grows bleak and pale,
> I'll spur my steed right quickly
> And ride to Neckardale."

CHAPTER XXIX.

From Heidelberg I took a brief trip into Switzerland, going first to Lucerne *via* Basle, that great busy junction of so many lines, with its handsome, modern station more like those of America in its appointments, than most others abroad, having many conveniences and privileges which are, alas, all extra. Almost every one changes trains at Basle, which by the way, the Germans call "Bah-zle" and the French "Bahl," thus making much confusion and perplexity for unsophisticated foreigners, as both languages are heard interchangeably through most portions of Switzerland.

We passed through Freiburg, noting its great cathedral outlined against the summer sky. We soon began to perceive *en route* that we were really indeed entering the marvelous land of the Alps, for towering hills began to push out into view, threatening to bar our way as we wound along the most level portions of the vale, skirting streams and frequently, to my extreme dissatisfaction, dashing through exceedingly long tunnels.

The weather was enchanting, the scene constantly increased in beauty, and, when finally a succession of lakes suddenly stretched out before us, with the white-tipped mountains shining in the distance, no one in the compartment could repress an ejaculation of delight, and by the time we reached Lucerne, we were almost speechless with admiration.

Lucerne the lovely! Gifted indeed far beyond usual endowment, must be the pen or brush that could even in faint degree, fitly set forth its beauties. The gleaming waters of the river Reuss, so strangely green, rushing on in irresistable current surpassingly swift, through their rock-bound banks; the majestic slopes that, tree-studded and diversified by quaint towers and ramparts, by stately villas and modest cottages, rise abruptly to the feet of greater heights above; the gigantic Rigi on the left, the stupendous Pilatus on the right; while beyond and between spring still loftier eminences, snow-crowned and sun-kissed, or wreathed in misty veils, far on high; and over all, blue and beautiful, the radiant immensity of exhilarant atmosphere losing itself in the infinity of ethereal space.

Such phrases do but sketch in barest outline the salient features of the ravishing loveliness bursting upon the beholder in this enrapturing region, yet give no true conception of the wondrous whole. For the first time I admit that my native land, though it may equal, cannot excel this peerless picture, and that over the great round earth one could scarcely find a scene so fair.

Yet, why is this? Are there not mountains otherwhere? And lakes and streams and islets fair? And charm of sun and shade and sky? Not here alone has history's page been written over and folded back; not here alone do ancient spire and tower antique rise side by side with palace new and modern cot; nor only here the gay, light-hearted, brilliant throngs, meeting, separating, shifting back and forth, like the glittering atoms of some huge kaleidoscope. How is it then that over all there seems to lie some mystic glamour so filling one's vision that one rests content to gaze, beatified as never before? Perhaps it is the blending in one broad sweep of the eyes, of all these features in their loveliness of varied charm, that so delights and enchants.

From all parts of the civilized world, come summer visitors to this beautiful spot, and many indeed are the sons and daughters of our own fair country gathered here. To all such indeed, were it a work of supererogation to dwell upon the attractions, either natural or artistic, of Lucerne; the pictures upon memory's tablets are fairer far than can be evoked by words of mine. But to her "the lone sister," who has been my inspiration in these desultory lines, and whose migrations are yet in the future, may be given perchance even in these inadequate jottings, some slight meed of pleasure or information.

The history of Lucerne dates back to 735, when was founded the convent of St Leodegar. Thrilling and momentous have been the events that gradually evolved this fine and picturesque modern city from the primitive little assemblage of fishermen's huts, once clustering about the convent walls on the banks of the river Reuss.

This magnificent river, to whose rapid flow and deep green tint I have already alluded, runs directly through the wealthy and fashionable portion of the place, from the Lake of Four Cantons along the banks of which the city spreads out continuing lines. The shores of the stream are built up with solid masonry, forming a broad and elegant promenade, or quay on both sides, protected by iron railings and set out in lovely chestnut trees. All along this boulevard is a succession of handsome structures of most varied architecture, broad and low, as is the custom in this part of the world.

The fine railway station of cream-colored stone, with noble vestibule and imposing cupola, all spacious and well-lighted and almost spotlessly clean, first attracts one's attention, then the wonderful panorama of lake and mountain, stream and sky, ruin, rampart, cottage, villa, promenade and people, flashes upon one's gaze.

I have spoken at different times of the many grand stations in various places on the continent, and again of how unfavorably they compare with our own, and I will pause here to explain this seeming discrepancy. In general, so far as concerns artistic design, elegant spaciousness, tasteful decoration, beautiful grounds and almost absolute cleanliness, the stations abroad far surpass our own; but in practical details, in convenience and comfort, in accessibility and completeness of all things necessary for the information and speeding of the average traveler, ours are far ahead. Many things that we in America take as a matter of course, such as toilet conveniences, drinking water, and so forth, may be had here, it is true, but not without money and without price, as with us.

Close to the station in Lucerne, is the fine *Seebruecke*, or Lake-Bridge, fifty-two feet wide and five hundred feet long, built of stone at great expense some eighteen years ago. But still more charming to one who likes to muse over relics of a by-gone age, are two quaint old bridges that have stood stretching across this rushing current for hundreds of years.

One of these, the *Kapellbruecke*, crossing the river diagonally, is a curious structure dating from 1333, and is built entirely of wood, which is sound and strong to-day. It is perhaps eight feet wide and is approached by a few wooden steps. The sides are inclosed to a height of

possibly three feet, and queer wooden posts at
regular intervals on each side, support a pointed
roof that covers the entire structure. In the
triangular spaces formed by the peak of the roof
and the junction of its sides with each pair of
opposing posts, are fitted smooth boards upon
which is painted a succession of historical pictures, queer and interesting in the extreme.

Here are depicted the heroic deeds and sufferings of the old Switzers and their patron saints,
Leodegar and Maurice, from the most primitive
times down to the mediæval period. Under each
picture is inscribed one or more of those rhym-
ing couplets in which the German of the Middle
Ages so delighted to express himself, as I
have had occasion to note before; and while the
Switzer is not a German, yet there is enough
similarity between the German language and his
own to imbue him with much the same shade of
thought and expression. The colors in the pictures are dimmed and the script nearly effaced;
one must go on step by step, with eyes raised and
head thrown back, in order to see them at all.

Nearly half way across in the midst of this
bridge, stands an old octagonal tower. The
municipal treasure was stored here in the long
ago and the tower was also used as a governmental prison; it is said to have contained a
torture chamber. Some authors state that this
tower was a light-house in the time of the Romans, but it is more commonly believed to have
formed a part of the fortifications that surrounded Lucerne in the thirteenth century.

The other old bridge, called the *Spreuer* or
Muehlenbruecke, is a century younger than the
first one. This also has paintings in the roof,
old and dim but more decipherable than those
first described. This series was painted in the

sixteenth century by Casper Meglinger, and represents the Dance of Death.

How this old town has changed since first these bridges spanned the rapid river. How the Lucerners themselves have changed in custom, in attire, in deed and in thought. Fancy the stern, almost savage citizen of the Middle Ages, stalking across here in his coat of mail, armed with battle-ax or two handed sword; or possibly astride his war charger also in armor, with spurs jangling and accoutrements clashing. No provision was made for the passage of a carriage, and great, no doubt, would have been his amazement had such a conveyance been even suggested to him. But they are all gone, though the bridges remain, still echoing to the tread of busy feet as in centuries past.

Every means for the enjoyment and entertainment of visitors seems to have been supplied by nature and skill in this region. A landscape of infinite variety, mountain, forest, vale, meadow, lake and stream, a bracing yet genial atmosphere, sun and shade in pleasing contrast, lovely drives and devious foot-paths leading through bosky dells and leafy glens at every hand; while train, steamer, gondola and skiff glide back and forth, ready to convey to greater distances, through scenes of equal beauty.

Should skies prove unkind or should, at times, even the worship of lovely nature become too great a strain, one may turn for change and recreation to the fine library and reading-room, to the great museum, to the interesting churches, to the vast cathedral with its daily sacred concert, to the many theaters, exhibitions and so forth, or to the mediæval remnants of another day and generation.

A singular feature in the landscape at Lu-

cerne, is the Musegg, an irregular line of gray
ramparts on the heights above the town, where
nine old watch towers rise up at intervals, their
antique architecture and the uncertainty hanging over their exact origin and purpose, combin-
ing to invest all with a peculiar, romantic
interest.

On an eminence to the west of the city, above
the dwellings dotting the slope and the woods
in the background, may be seen a commodious
edifice with a slender and elegant turret.   This
is the famous Goetsch, whereon is a summer
hotel and pleasure-garden.   One reaches this
point easiest by a miniature funicular railway,
five hundred and ninety-one feet long, of which
the motive power is water.   The gradient is
fifty-three yards in one hundred.

Although the Goetsch is only a hill in this
land of mountains, yet it commands a surprisingly fine view of the picturesque city on the
Reuss at its feet, and of the lake as far back as
the huge bulk of the Rigi and of the Burgen-
stock; above which the Alps of the Unterwalden,
with the snowy dome of mighty Titlis conspicuously visible, pierce the southern sky.   A skilful arrangement of great mirrors in the large
reception *salon* of the Goetsch, overlooking the
view, duplicates the wonderful prospect with a
bewildering effect of vastness.

With such a wealth of material on every side,
from which one must cull but a few specimens
to represent the magnificent whole, one becomes
confused in trying to make a, in any wise, satisfactory selection, wavering here and there between this point and that, and possibly at last
leaves unnoted some most characteristic feature
or scene.

Fain would I dwell on the historic interest

and esthetic details of the great *Hof-Kirche*, on the imposing architecture of the Post and Telegraph Office, the impressive style of the *Kurhaus*, or the graceful outlines of the Government Building, the Museum, the Town Hall and so forth, and above all, on their harmonious relation to each other and to their environment in general; but all these triumphs of the builder's art, while adding as they do to the diversified charm of this entrancing spot, are yet so cast into insignificance by the grandeur and beauty of their natural setting, that one passes them with a cursory glance as the eyes rove onward from the fair fields and forests sloping upward from the gleaming waters, to the majestic masses of emerald declivity or somber crag or snowy peak, shouldering against the blue empyrean.

Among all these beauties there are a few of special, local interest, which one should not fail to visit; one of these is the romantic nook containing the famous "Lion of Lucerne."

This monument sculptured by Ahorn in 1821, from the solid rock, after a model by Thorwaldsen,—which model, by the way, is to be seen in a little curio-shop across the road,—commemorates the desperate struggle of the Swiss guards before the Tuileries, under the onslaught of the Jacobins, August 10, 1792. After a most heroic resistance, two battalions were overpowered by the revolutionists, and on the second and third of September, the remainder also fell at their post.

A winding way leads on through wide cheerful streets and leafy avenues, up a gentle ascent to a secluded dell where, in the shade of noble trees, behind a miniature sheet of water, rises a perpendicular rock sixty feet in height. In the midst of a great recess hollowed out from these granite walls, prone upon a shield and spear and battle-axe, lies a wounded lion of gigantic proportions, defending even in death the charge intrusted to him. Graven above, is the brief legend: *"Helvetiorum fidei ac virtute,"* and below, the names of the officers with the date of the tragic event. There is a dignity and repose about this majestic composition, that seems to proclaim the ineffable though intangible recompense of brave deeds nobly done, even unto death.

With a gravity engendered by the contemplation of this artistic memorial with its multitudinous suggestions as to man's mighty possibilities in his highest exaltation of moral and physical courage, one turns to follow the little path that goes meandering on.

Almost at once, one's reflections are transferred from the achievements of art and the powers of man, to the mysteries of the universe; for within a few yards one comes upon an unique spectacle called "The Glacier Garden." Here is a very interesting natural phenomenon consisting of nine "pot-holes,"—so named,—of an ancient glacier. They were discovered by accident in 1872, when excavating for the foundations of a building. The largest of these holes is twenty-six feet in diameter and thirty-one feet deep. They are supposed to have been hollowed out in pre-historic times, by the action of the glacier then extending through this district. The water that found its way through the fissures of the ice, imparted a rotary motion to the stones also finding their way down through the crevices, and in course of time these stones, grinding around upon the rock beneath, formed these circular "pot-holes," in which the stones were left as the glacier receded. There are many wonderful objects, natural and manufactured, in this garden, but this exposition of the stupendous forces of nature, silent, slow, but irresistible, working away from the dim ages of the past, is most curious and remarkable.

The summer evening was well advanced when I left this interesting spot and retraced my steps over the pleasant route along which I had come.

The streets lay picturesque and peaceful in the luminous twilight, the way growing brighter and more brilliant as I neared the broad quay, where the electric lights were flashing and quivering through the tremulous foliage of the stately chesnuts rustling in the cool, lake breeze.

From out the elegant gardens of the splendid hostelries, fair with perfumed leaf and vivid blossom, rolled forth most witching strains of jocund melody, while on the quay joyous groups, assembled from every clime, kept step in concord with the pulsing cadences.

Beyond the low parapet, the lake was rippling and sparkling in the rays of the mellow moon riding afar in the illimitable sky; the snow-capped peaks were gleaming on high in a beauty of heavenly purity, while, dotted with glittering points from cotter's candle or luxury's lamp, the shadows lay heavy on the hillsides below.

Gay gondolas were gliding hither and yon, their colored lanterns making stars of fire, that glowed again from the bosom of the waters.

My path lay onward across the handsome *Seebruecke*, down along the riverside, beneath whispering trees and past plashing fountains, to a quiet inn, from the windows of which, as I sank to slumber, my eyes looked out upon the rugged bulk of grim Pilatus standing stern sentinel immovable forever, above the magic beauty and bewildering charm of lake-laved Lucerne.

CHAPTER XXX.

Chief among the many delightful excursions possible from the romantic city of Lucerne, is, perhaps, a tour of the lovely sheet of water commonly known as Lake Lucerne, otherwise the Lake of Four Cantons, or the *Vierwaldstaetter See.*

Indissolubly associated with this vicinity and recalled at once by its name, is the history, traditional or otherwise, of William Tell, whose heroic deeds gleam forth so brilliantly from this marvelous setting, in the radiance of Schiller's immortal genius.

It was a charming day in mid-summer that I stepped aboard the elegant little steamer that daily makes the round of this grandly picturesque lake, and settled myself for a period of uninterrupted inspection of this renowned "treasure-house of natural beauties."

The attractive little vessel was filled with a happy, animated throng, and accents of diverse nationalities fell upon the ear as we steamed away from the wide quay.

At the very outset one is entranced by the aspect of the little harbor itself, with its gardens, its villas and its ancient towers lying back on, and rising from the verdant slopes, and climbing the steeper sides of the great hills and promontories that intervene between the bery-line waters of the broad bay and the huge mountains in the farther distance.

As we glide out into the lake, the view continually changes and, as one grand and dazzling peak falls back or presents to us a new angle of observation, we get glimpses of other still more stupendous elevations; while across the gleaming tide, transiently visible above a depression in the high outline of the nearer crags, the monarchs of the Bernese Oberland, Lauterhorn, Wetterhorn, Schreckerhorn and the peerless Jungfrau etched sharply above in icy splendor, move for a brief moment into our field of vision.

The small isle of Alstad with tiny châlet peeping forth from shades of living green, lies almost in our path as we round the Meggerhorn and enter the Kreuzrichter where we find ourselves in the spacious expanse formed by the meeting of the lake's four great arms; each of which, having its own fair quota of matchless landscape, reaches off in the distance. Kussnacht to the north to where the narrow, wooded isthmus divides from Lake Zug; Alpnacht to the south flowing on past the base of gigantic Pilatus; behind us to the west, the shining stretch over which we have come; while eastward, Weggis spreads out before us until some slight change in our direction, brings us abreast of a range of mighty precipices that seem to bar our progress completely. But the little boat is undismayed and skilfully feels its way along the threatening shores, and lo! a silvery channel opens out again and we wind on amid untellable delights.

The area of Lake Lucerne is about forty-four square miles; its surface is fourteen hundred and thirty-two feet above sea-level; its greatest length, from Lucerne to Fluelen, twenty-three and one half miles and greatest width a little more than two and one half.

While partial freezing has taken place at irregular intervals, the congealing of its entire

expanse is unrecorded either by history or tradition. The banks of the lake display a remarkable diversity of character. Some anony-
mous writer has said:—"Here the boundary is the
broad end of an Alpine valley; yonder it is a
steep precipice rising from the very margin of
the waters; elsewhere it is an expanse of grassy
meadow-land affording pasturage to numerous
herds of sleek cattle, and planted with row upon
row of thriving fruit-trees. At the point where
the larger valleys open, the eye penetrates to the
mountain heights some of which are carpeted
with rich pastures and dotted with *châlets*,
while others appear rocky and barren, and yet
others loftiest of all, display their spotless ves-
ture of eternal snow."

But it matters not what phase of prospect is
presented; for whether bounded by mighty
bluffs and cragged cliffs close at hand, or stretching back into the woodland shades and smiling
loveliness of pastoral scenes, or rising aloft in
dizzy heights of unapproachable grandeur, it
entrances the imagination and dominates the
soul by alternating sublimity and romance,
magnificence and unutterable charm.

All along, sheltered from rough winds, embowered in groves and vines, and almost within
stone's throw of one another, nestle quaint little villages, picturesque and cheerful; while
scattered everywhere from the water's edge to
dizzying heights, rise villas, cottages, *pensions*,
restaurants, hotels and so forth, in often apparently inaccessible locations.

And now we go on under the shadow of the
huge Rigi and its mighty neighbors standing together in everlasting majesty. A bright ray of
sunshine picks out and glows back from a lofty
crag of vivid red, that towers far above the

small village of Vitznau charmingly set out against a background of somber green.

As in a dream of delight we go on and on and on. Again the waters narrow before us as we approach two great precipices which leave us no visible means of egress; but another dextrous shift of our wise little vessel, and we pass between the opposing promontories called *Die Nasen*, (The Noses,) which are separated here by a distance of less than a thousand yards.

After this we reach Gersau with its bulky mountain rearing its proud crest above, and make our way out again from the little port so shut in by rocky walls, past the romantic chapel Klindlmord, that has for uncounted years lifted its quaint turret here to the changeful sky.

And now so stupendous a spectacle bursts upon the vision, that the average mind sinks down aghast, realizing that nothing but the sublimity of genius should venture to portray the sublimity of nature. Here in one mighty panorama, opens one of the grandest of Alpine landscapes, disclosing the wondrous eminences of the Schwytz, with the frightful steeps and naked summit of the Mythen towering in the background. Here as before, on every hand rise wooded height and rugged rock, with cot and villa, *châlet* and *pension*, dotted all abroad on shady slope or sunny elevation, until far above, imposing pinnacles and frowning crags loom inaccessible; and over all and pervading all with its mingled charm of sun and sea and sky and shore, the radiant, indefinable atmosphere of summer Switzerland.

Each picture presenting itself as our craft turns and winds through the sea-green waves, seems fairer, grander, more sublime than aught before. The soul aches with a pervading pain of dumb and awful admiration.

Now we round a seemingly impassable barrier
and turn into a quiet little harbor where a curving pier stretches out into the still waters. There
is no village here in view, only an antique and
venerable inn call the Trieb, whose high-peaked
roof, projecting stories and exterior decorations
are all along the lines of the wonderful timber
architecture of central Germany. This old edifice is largely identified with the actual and
legendary history of these shores. It rests
partly on piers in the lake, and partly on the
solid rock of the bank, and stands embosomed
in forest trees and decked with velvet moss, under the overhanging bastions of the eternal
hills; the soft, natural grays of its roof and
walls, blending harmoniously into the dull
greens and browns of its umbrageous nest.

Around the next headland not far from here,
we note a pyramidal rock rising abruptly from
the lake; divided but by an exceedingly narrow
channel from the perpendicular cliff behind. Of
a whitish tint, it stands out distinctly above
the heaving waves and presents to the beholder
its unchanging face, upon which is graven an
inscription in honor of Schiller. A fitting monument, in its immutability amid the billowy
waters foaming about its everlasting base, to the
great poet whose undying verse has so perpetu-
ated the glories of Switzerland and her band of
heroes.

Still passing from one romantic and interesting point to another, still crossing and re-cross-
ing the crystal sea as one or another of the tiny
villages presents itself on either side, we reach
Brunnen situated in the midst of verdure, with
pretty promenades and public grounds, and consecrated by its souvenirs of the Rise of the
Swiss Confederation; and now we enter upon

the last branch of the lake, a beautiful basin
shut in by rocky banks and stupendous mountains.

On the right, high above, stretched beneath
the walls of still loftier overhanging crags, lies
the Ruetli, a steep meadow surrounded by
stately trees. This is the most sacred spot in
Switzerland and celebrated in song and story,
for here on November seventh, 1307, Fuerst of
Uri, Stauffacher of Schwytz and Anderhalden of
Unterwald, each backed by a few devoted adher-
ents, formed a league in the name of their cantons, against the despotic rule of Austria. Schiller makes thrilling use of the dramatic elements
of this episode in his great work. The Ruetli is
regarded as a national place of pilgrimage and
every year is visited by processions of schools
and societies of all descriptions. Peaceful and
secluded it looks, far above our heads, accessi-
bly only by a rocky pathway through the
tangled groves.

The view from this point onward seems to increase, if possible, in beauty and grandeur. On
the left appear the granite heights of Ober-and
Nieder-Bauenstock, and yet these are almost
dwarfed by the imposing immensity of massive
Urirothstock rising like some vast citadel from
the lake below to the clouds above, where its
snowy summit towers impregnable. Still we
make our way over the clear waters that reflect
so vividly the picturesque hamlets and blooming
terraces coming into view wherever the stony
walls recede enough to grant a few acres of foot-
hold. We leave Sisikon and Bauen and Isleton
behind us, reaching Tellsplatte, the spot where
Tell is said to have escaped from the tyrant's
boat. The chapel bearing Tell's name stands
close to the water's edge and is visited every

year by the country people in solemn proces-
sional. How the present vanishes and the
intervening centuries roll away from one's consciousness, as one gazes upon the diminutive
temple with its unpretending walls and modest
spire hidden from view by rocks and twining
shrubbery, except at the water-front, from which
its few steps ascend immediately into the plain
little portico. Above rises magnificent Axen-
fluh flanked by sky-piercing Urirothstock, while
straight before us, the pyramid of jagged Bris-
tenstock lifts up its lofty brow. Beautiful Seelisberg and mighty Fronalpstock greet us anew
from the other side, looking down from the re-
moter distance; while all about and everywhere
are new vistas of enchantment, until at last we
reach Fluelen where the boat pauses for an hour
or so before starting on its homeward journey.

There is a wonderful carriage-road, wide and
hard, from Weggis to Fluelen, which is thought
by many to surpass in variety and grandeur of
natural scenery, any other highway in the
world. Lying along the lake and following its
changeful and meandering contour, it winds on,
now skirting sunny meadows, now penetrating
leafy shades or rounding giddy precipices, now
drilled in archways through solid rock. It is
divided into four sections, the first of which
stretches along through a delightful series of
green pastures, beautiful groves and charming
lake aspects; the second and third are more romantic, commanding the banks of the Weggis
and Brunnen basins, and presenting witching
glimpses of the Rigi, the Urmiberg, the Mythen,
the Seelisberg and many others; while the last
section is the celebrated Axenstrasse, leading
along the east shore from Brunnen to Fluelen,
and forming a part of a system of mountain

highways constructed by the Swiss government many years ago.

The St. Gothard railway is also visible at times along these shores but disappears into the depths of every huge hill. All along here, picturesqueness again rises to grandeur and beauty to sublimity, and once more words fail to convey an idea of the ravishing scene. The limpid lake with its emerald tinge; the varying green of groves and gardens fair in the distance; rocks strangely grotesque rising far above; dimly lighted tunnels with openings here and there through which renewed glimpses are caught of mountain and lake and wonderful views of the distant Alps; while every place is replete with souvenirs of the ancient heroes of Switzerland.

From Fluelen one may return to Lucerne by railway, if preferring a change of route. Of this privilege I now availed myself, plunging into fresh beauties as well as looking on former ones from another equally bewildering point of view.

Snowy summits, awful abysses, emerald slopes, ragged rocks, sparkling waters, luxuriant meadows, barren crags, fertile valleys, gay watering-places, woodland heights, handsome stations, trim terraces, picturesque *châlets*, cosy farm houses, elegant villas, wonderful bridges and inky tunnels are all whirled about through my mind in inextricable confusion, as I step from the train and seek the seclusion of my modest inn.

CHAPTER XXXI.

To the ascending of mountains by railway in this era of marvelous engineering and enterprise, there is no end; but it is not so very long ago, in fact I believe but forty years, since the system that has made this variety of excursion feasible and safe, was provided to the world. To the United States, records say, belongs the honor of having given birth to the man whose peculiar genius "evolved from his inner consciousness," this unique method that has proved so adaptable in scaling tremendous heights.

It was in 1858 that Sylvester Marsh, of Littleton, New Hampshire, received a charter to practically apply his ingenious mechanism to the ascent of Mount Washington. That road was finished in 1869, that of the Rigi in 1871, and since then their name is legion both in our own country and abroad.

Though both in America and in the old world, there are peaks more lofty and mountains more stupendous than the Rigi yet this has a distinctive charm in its wonderful situation between three lakes,—rising abruptly from their very margins,—and the incomparable scenery, of which its own magnificent loveliness is but a fragmentary portion; and it has the additional advantage of being accessible from either side, so that the necessity of doubling back to any great extent upon one's route is avoided, and in one trip is combined a surprising variety of outlook.

There are a number of footways up the Rigi; from every steamboat landing as well as from every St. Gothard railway station in the vicinity, is a well-defined path, each of which is thronged with hardy and ambitious pedestrians pressing onward to the heights above. There are also three railway routes, of which the Vitznau-Rigi is the oldest and perhaps the most comprehensive.

The skies were fair and the waters sparkling as we left Lucerne on the small vessel that plies between that city and Vitznau.

After a run of less than an hour we arrived, and disembarking, crossed the picture-like little *Platz* to the railway station. Here we found our observation car arranged with nicely tilted seats inclined in just the requisite degree to keep us on a level up the great slope, and our ungainly locomotive, ponderous and panting, all ready to begin the powerful push that was to send us steadily on our way heavenward for thousands of feet. As is customary in such ascents, but one car was given to each engine.

Contrary to our previous mountain experience, we find every pound of luggage must be weighed and paid for. And I may mention here that a lady traveling alone in Switzerland is at much disadvantage regarding her hand-luggage, for porters are not allowed, even by paying a gate fee, to enter the trains, and, the carriages being set up on high wheels and en'ered from the end platforms, like ours in America, it is impossible for her to avoid lifting and handling her *impedimenta* herself. She must either receive her property from the porter at the outer steps and lug it into the car, or else through the window from the inside; and in either case must heave them herself up into the high receptacles over-

head, as the cars are too small and the available
space too contracted to admit of their being
placed elsewhere. Many foreigners, noting the
difference between Swiss cars and the ordinary
continental carriage, fancy that the former are
like American cars; they do resemble the latter
somewhat on the outside, being entered from the
ends and set up on high trucks, though they
lack utterly the finish of our railway coaches;
but the Swiss car is much smaller than ours,
and the interior is very different. True the
passage runs lengthwise instead of across the
carriage, but it is very narrow and, instead of
running through the middle and dividing the
car in halves, it is nearer one side than the
other, leaving on the one hand, space for a row
of small, single seats, and on the other, a row of
double ones; and, while the carriage is not
divided off into closed compartments, it is
divided by breast high partitions between each
set of opposing seats, though there are no doors
within; the whole arrangement is close and inconvenient, though a vast improvement on the
compulsory confinement system in other parts
of Europe.

The car that we enter to-day, however,
specially adapted to mountain travel. is exactly
like a large, open street-car, with three exceptions; first, its "up-tiltedness;" second, gates
at the two ends of every two opposite rows of
seats or benches that run quite across the car
from side to side; and third, a small compartment in the rear, wherein our luggage, reduced
to the smallest possible compass, is stowed away.

We are an animated and expectant party from
almost all quarters of the globe; diverse and
polyglot are the accents that greet the ear. Let
not my "lone sister" be dismayed; she will

probably hear her native tongue; if not she has only to show her ticket and point to her luggage, and a railway porter will take her in charge with safety. But lest she may picture in her "mind's eye" something akin to the trim-uniformed train men of our lines, I will say that the continental porter wears the unmistakable garb of a laboring man, and either upon his cap or upon a chain about his neck, he bears a huge metal number, which it is well to take cognizance of, for future recollection in case anything goes wrong. However, they are usually very civil and anxious to please; the fee must be paid by the traveler as, though the porters are licensed they are not recompensed by the railway.

In our motley throng. cycling costumes mainly more serviceable than elegant prevail, though no wheels are in evidence; several tourists are supplied with sturdy but unmanageable *alpenstocks*, that stick out in all directions and get into everybody's way.

We are soon in motion, beginning to ascend almost from the very verge of the waters, and at once leaving behind us the charming village lying so snugly in its cosy nooks and angles against the mountain side.

Rushing upward through chesnut groves, we dash into a murky tunnel, then over a wildly romantic bridge of skilful but terrifying construction, and pause for a moment at Freibergen Station, thirty-three hundred feet above sea level. From this point on, the scene is all one bewildering vision of beauty unutterable. The lake drops away from us like a falling mirror; gazing downward at our left, we see its glittering surface sinking lower and lower, as we mount the dizzy elevations between which and the shining depths below, nothing whatever is visible to indicate that we are otherwise than poised without support in this realm of light and radiance through which we are speeding.

A glance toward our right scarcely reassures us, for here close at hand, less than an arm's length from the side of the car, impregnable battlements of everlasting rock tower straight upward, upon the perpendicular surfaces of which, no slightest foot-hold or hand-clutch were possible even in the direst emergency. But the incomparable grandeur and splendor of our position serves to engulf all thoughts of mortal risk, and we breathe into our very souls a spirit of magic enchantment.

Now the outlook changes; mountains begin to show their crests around within our range of view; we swerve away from the dizzy verge as the crowding crags fall back, while our eyes, but this moment gazing abroad into apparently illimitable space, now rest on emerald slope and wide plateau, with terrace on terrace of vivid bloom and verdure reaching back to the confines of a park-like forest. Here is situated the far-famed sanitarium of Rigi-Kaltbad, adjacent to which are some of the loveliest views from the Rigi. At this point another mountain-route meets our line and some of our passengers leave us, disappearing round the curves that lead to the great hotels in that direction. We who remain, continue in our upward course through rocky cuttings, over frightful trestles round giddy precipices, through bosky shades, up and up and ever up, until after an interval, as we come to the fine Hotel Staffel, there all at once opens before us the immense prospect of the wondrous hill-country of northeast Switzerland, lovely, magnificent, infinite.

Still onward, higher and higher, toward the summit far above; while advancing, receding, ever changing but ever entrancing, appear and vanish the contrasting beauties of the marvelous outlook.

Vista after vista opens out, falls back and fades beneath us, until at last we find ourselves at the summit, where, a little below the rounded grassy top, stands the imposing Hotel Rigi-Kulm.

Now verily do the limitations of language press sore upon us as we look abroad on the overpowering grandeur of the prospect. What words indeed can depict with justice, a landscape more than two hundred miles in diameter? Here the undulating, ever varied hill-country toward the north; yonder the Black Forest and the Vosges Mountains stretching onward; in the middle ground, lake after lake in limpid loveliness reflecting back fair heaven and wooded height; while far away to the southward, glittering in snowy splendor, sublime and unsullied as in creation's dawn, rises range after range of towering pinnacles, silent, majestic, immovable save by the same almighty force that placed them there in awful magnitude, eternal, "rock-ribbed and ancient as the sun."

River courses wind beneath us, and meandering roads, like lengths of ribbon as they wander away; fair meadow-lands stretch onward and white towns and villages shine forth from leafy recesses; while on the Rigi itself and forming a part of its mighty bulk, are rock and ridge, declivity and dale, fertile plain and barren crag, bowery dell, gleaming cascade, mountain rill, rich pastures and picturesque structures, all enveloped in one bewitching haze of ineffable loveliness.

It is impossible to drink one's fill of the glor-

ious scene, and we turn aside exhausted yet un-
satisfied. But as our eyes drop from all this
splendor of natural beauty and fall at last to
things at hand and lying literally at our feet,
we begin to note what a diversified little world
it is here immediately about us, on the small,
irregular plateau.

First and foremost is the great hotel with its
spacious verandas, glittering windows and wide
corridors. A little removed from this are two
or three other roomy edifices for accommodating
the "overflow" in the busy season. Around a
little bluff where the path turns to reach the
extreme summit, stands a Post-Office, diminutive indeed but complete in all modern requirements, including telegraph, telephone and supplies of stationery and picture postal-cards.
Just below the hotel and reached by a long flight
of steps, is the neat little station of the railway
terminus.

Following the path to the upper plateau, we
suddenly find ourselves in the midst of a miniature, open-air bazar, for a dozen or more knick-
nack venders have taken up their stand under
spreading, cream-colored umbrellas,—for there
are no trees at this height,—which shelter themselves and their collections. Here trinkets of all
descriptions pertaining to the Alpine region, are
to be found at not exorbitant prices, pictures,
curios, geological and floral specimens and so
forth, while interested purchasers are gathered
about in shifting groups.

For the first time the widely famed *Edelweiss*
comes under our observation, being offered for
sale in profusion with Alpine roses, so called.
There is no chaffering and the dealers are re-
spectful and quiet.

Men, women and children of confusingly diverse sorts and conditions, wander hither and yon, or stand entranced, rapt in the glorious prospect abroad.

A group of Alpine singers, male and female, in picturesque, peasant costumes, have made the ascent on foot from some one of the neighboring hamlets, and are now refreshing themselves with beer and black bread in the clear sunshine, occasionally bursting into fragments of song, or the melodious, far reaching *jodel* of the Swiss mountaineer.

All this busy exhibition of life on a small scale, seems so very strange up here on the open mountain-top, under the near, blue sky amid the grandeur of the Alps, and brings us down at once from the boundless realms of imagination and of infinite space, to human associations and human interests. And so, inspecting the curious wares and motley groups, we while away a little time before withdrawing into the huge caravansary for food and repose.

One does not find such unvarying exorbitant charges throughout the country at places of resort in Europe, as we have at home.

True, one can spend any amount of money if one feels no special limitation, but there is at the same time, at all these resorts a scale of prices suited to travelers of moderate means, providing sufficient and satisfactory service and entertainment at comparatively small outlay. Our foreign brothers seem to recognize the fact that every one, even among travelers, is not a Crœsus, and to look out for the accommodation of such, also. I must confess, however, if they know that one is an American, it is very hard for them to realize that one is not necessarily, a millionaire, so ingrained is it into the consciousness of other peoples, that "all Americans are rich."

In descending the Rigi, we followed the Arth-Goldau route, which branches off from the Rigi-Kulm section at Rigi-Staffel, a short distance below.

Another panorama of indescribable grandeur and not less impressive and imposing than that seen from the other side, is spread out before us as we gradually go down through magnificent Alpine pastures and shadowy fir groves, to our first halting-place below the junction. This is the Rigi-Klosterli, the most sheltered place on the mountain. Here are two grand hotels, several less pretentious inns and a picturesque old pilgrimage-chapel; also a Capuchin hospice, a somewhat peculiar institution, being a sort of conventual hostelry devoted to the entertainment of travelers. We are told that this point is most popular with persons desiring to make a prolonged stay upon the mountain.

Off again and down, down through scenery of wildly romantic character, from the midst of which we command an extensive view of the Schwytz and the Eastern Alps.

Now we hug the rocky side of a deep ravine, the abysmal depths of which our vision cannot penetrate; now we cross marvelous bridges and horrifying trestles and plunge into long tunnels, still winding ever down and down and down.

By degrees the landscape loses its expansive sweep; we begin to be shut in again by the nearer hills, and the pleasant valley of the Arth becomes prominent as, studded with fertile farms, flourishing fruit-trees and rustic dwellings, it stretches beyond the important station of Goldau, where the mountain railway terminates on this side.

One might remain weeks upon the Rigi without exhausting its countless resources and astonishing variety of land and water scapes.

The Rigi-Kulm, five thousand, nine hundred and five feet above the sea, is the highest point. The Rigi-Scheidegg—for all these various points are but different pinnacles of the one vast mountain,—is five thousand, four hundred and six feet in elevation. At this spot is a "view-tower," one hundred feet high, where one might pass hours observing the magnificent prospect and "paying one's tribute to the majesty of the universe." Here too is an "Alpine-Garden," or experiment station, where trials are made in the cultivation of Alpine fodder-plants and forest trees.

The Rigi-Hochfluh is five thousand, five hundred and eighty-four feet high. This is the most southern summit of the mountain and is perhaps the most fantastic in character. This ascent, which can only be made on foot, leads past grotesque formations and through a fir forest, up a steep and stony defile, where only by an iron ladder fixed into the solid rock, can one mount to the bold and barren summit.

One feature through all this region, especially striking to an American coming from a land whose mountains are sparsely settled, if at all, and where an air of bleak desolation pervades the upper heights, is the number and contiguity of villages, hamlets, *châlets*, villas and farm-houses everywhere visible in all directions, high and low, over the mountains; so that the sweet, familiar sounds of rural domestic life, the laugh of children, the low of cattle, the bleat of lambs, the shrill clarion of chanticleers, fall continually upon the ear, and all the peaceful avocations of life are seen to go on amid a lofty environment unsurpassed in beauty and sublimity.

The Rigi itself, though so rich in its infinite variety of scene, is yet but one of the countless stately and mighty monarchs that lift their proud and beautiful heads above the shining waters at their feet. Gazing at them as a whole, they form a circling chain of such matchless loveliness and majesty so far beyond the flights of the imagination, that the reverent spirit is inevitably lifted above the cloud-capped peaks, beyond the radiant atmosphere, "up through nature to nature's God.

CHAPTER XXXII.

With comparatively but a glimpse and a taste
of the delights of Switzerland, I tore myself
away from the enrapturing locality of the *Vier-
waldstœtter See*, taking the St. Gothard line at
Goldau.

This is a very important railway junction and
a bustling town, reminding me in a way of some
of the new "cities" of our far west, where a
large amount of business is transacted sometimes, before the necessary buildings and facilities for properly carrying it on, are much more
than in embryo. Carpenters, masons, diggers
and hewers were at work all about, and we had
to step over and around many obstructions and
across many unprotected tracks,—a state of
things very unusual abroad,—in passing from
one railway station to another.

Goldau is the place where, in 1806, a tremendous landslip fell from off the Rossberg, burying
in its débris nearly five hundred persons with all
their belongings.

As our train moves off, our way lies through
a wild confusion of rocky fragments and over-
turned strata, which have lain here ever since
their descent into the valley, all undisturbed except so far as needful to construct the railways
now lying through the area.

Some one has said that the St. Gothard railway is the great international highway
between north and south, a commercial route
comparable to the Suez Canal or the Straits
of Gibralter. The impressionable traveler

will not be content with only this point of
view, for it is also a highway of most remarkable and magnificent spectacles, both of natural
scenery and of engineering achievements.

My way lies but a short distance over this
route, but even in this brief stretch, dark tunnels and deep cuttings continually alternate with
open reaches affording successive vistas of great
heights beyond, of mighty chasms spanned by
marvelous trestles and bridges, and of all possible variations in prospect, from simple beauty
up to awful grandeur.

Between Goldau and Walchwyl we find yellow circulars distributed profusely about our
seats.   Taking one up I translate as follows:

WARNING! WARNING! WARNING!

"The Iron Columns of the in-construction-un-
dertaken St. Andrienbridge between Walchwyl
and Goldau, come so near to the Wagons of the
through-riding Trains to stand, that by only
some Forth-out-bowing of the Over-body out of
the Wagon Windows upon the Lakeside, Dam-
ages infallibly are.   The Travelers become on
that account, stringently therefore warned
against themselves from so questionable Places
in anyhow-which-wise, lakewards to the Wagon
Windows forth-out-to-lean.

"The Direction of the Gothard-Road."

Glancing farther down I find the warning repeated in Italian, in French and finally in
English, with a somewhat freer rendering than
mine given above.   I wonder if every train in
every direction has every seat in every compartment of every carriage, filled with these slips
every day; and if so, what the printer's bill of
the "Direction" amounts to in the course of a
few centuries.   However, it is kind of the di-

rectors to strive to prevent us from "forth-out-bowing,"and we all keep our "Over-bodies" very erect as we speed over the great bridge.

As I am now bound for Zurich, I change lines at Zug, a romantic looking town beautifully situated on its mountain-inclosed lake of the same name, and known from its quaint towers and ancient fortifications as the "Nuremburg of Switzerland." A long ridge of considerable elevation called the Zugerberg, is a noticeable feature of the place, affording an exceedingly varied and pleasant opportunity for excursions either on foot or *en voiture*, as the French say. By the way, one never knows in this region, whether one will be accosted in French or in German, which rather serves to keep the not over-proficient linguist in a "tenter-hooky"condition as he strives to have immediately available an assortment of pertinent phrases in both languages. We have gone back to French money also, to my great confusion, as I have for so many weeks, in my struggle with *marks* and *pfennige*, put behind me all thoughts of *francs* and *centimes*. The functionaries will take your German gold and give you change in French silver but, as a rule, the silver and copper of Germany are refused. Occasionally I find an amiable *Dienstmann* or *porteur*,—you never know which he is going to style himself,—who does not object to German change, so I go about with two purses, one French, the other German, and adapt the "nationality," so to speak, of my disbursements to the requirements of him who serves me.

Our train is crowded, for now is the height of the season and this is a most popular route. The scenery is lovely and had we not just come from the very heart of enchantment ineffable,

these cliffs and slopes were inexpressibly bewitching. We rush through some tremendous
tunnels, one in particular, of more than eighteen
thousand feet in length. As the carriages are
unlighted and we have no warning to close our
windows, we find ourselves every now and then
suddenly in the midst of inky darkness and sulphurous smoke that can find no outlet. Very
soon "Zurich's fair waters" open out before us,
the fine city lying upon the lake and the river
Limmat, and bounded on the west by the river
Sihl.

To properly appreciate this place, one should
see it before Lucerne, otherwise Zurich suffers
in comparison. But it is a very beautiful and
particularly interesting city, extremely ancient
in origin. It is at this point that so many relics
of the pre-historic "Lake-Dwellers" of Switzerland, and have been found; the *Helmhaus*, an
antiquarian museum, contains one of the finest
collections extant, it is said, of the old pile
structures excavated from the lake. But as
there are traces of Roman occupation here, some
authorities maintain that Zurich was founded
by that people, it having been the Celts who
lived on the pile-structures in the water. Be
that as it may, it is now a flourishing, handsome,
modern town, containing, with its nine suburban
districts, about seventy-five thousand inhabitants living, as my hand-book informs me, "in
fifty-two hundred and seventy-six houses and
forming sixteen thousand, one hundred and
ninety seven families."

It is a leading city both commercially and
politically and has numerous manufactures for
soap, silk, cotton, paper, machinery and so forth.
It is solidly built in a great variety of architecture.

Churches, cathedrals, museums, asylums, institutes, theaters, hospitals, picture-galleries, schools. colleges, monuments, bridges and squares abound; and the beauty of its broad, smooth streets, its blooming gardens, leafy terraces, charming nooks and secluded courts, its fountains, ponds, river-shores and lake-fronts, its "up-to-date" and tastefully ornamental, as well as its antique and venerable structures, is very striking.

One peculiarity in the very center of the town, is a quiet, elevated place called the *Lindenhof*, from which all the bustle and turmoil of a large city seems to rush away, instead of concentrating. It is studded with lime trees and offers an extensive view, unobstructed and undisturbed. This spot was the property of the Imperial Governors of Zurich and was the original Roman stronghold, or "First Quarter," of the town. Many coins and inscriptions of very ancient times have been found here.

Then there is the "old town," little changed for many generations, with queer, zig-zagged ways and antique edifices. One, in the narrow, crooked street, *Auf Dorf*, is pointed out as the former residence of a famous civic official, Hans Waldmann, who "had to die on the scaffold on account of his 'overbearance' and insolence toward his fellow-citizens whose idol he had been and who had promoted him to the high post of burgomeister." Another of the numberless instances of the Swiss hatred for and defiance of oppression in any form.

Delightful excursions are to be taken in every direction, surpassed only by those nearer Lucerne. A miniature railway having a rolling-stock of four engines and ten cars, leads up the Uetliberg, a hill to the north of the city. This

line is nearly thirty thousand feet in length,
with a gradient of seven per cent, so there is
nothing very marvelous about this excursion in
this land of tremendous heights, but the view
of the vari d landscape beneath, with the distant Alps rising in mysterious beauty far beyond,
is very charming.

Prices in Zurich seem quite cheap, especially
when one recalls what it costs to spend a few
days at any of our popular resorts in the United
States. One can hire a carriage for fifty cents
an hour, or six hours for two dollars and a half;
or to be driven from one point to another not exceeding a quarter of an hour in time, for sixteen
cents. Tramway rates in the city, two cents;
from or into the suburbs, four cents. Row-
boats for one or two persons, ten cents
an hour, sail-boat, twenty cents. At the theater a single seat in a large front box, eighty cents,
which is the highest price anywhere in the house.
A messenger with or without a load of less than
thirty-three pounds in the city, four cents; with
that weight or more, with or without a cart,
eight cents. A man and cart moving furniture
or cleaning house or carpets, twelve cents an
hour, or one dollar a day, and so on.

In going about Zurich, one notes at occasional
intervals, very odd specimens of rock, or "boulders," set up, as inquiry develops, as ornamental
curiosities. Some are dark blue, others red,
still others variegated, and all of most erratic
conformation. They do not appertain, we are
told, to the spots wherein they rest, but have
been discovered at points in the vicinity of Zurich and have been brought at great expenditure
of force and money, into the city and deposited—
to quote a popular phrase,—"where they will do
the most good."

The Grand Central Railway Station of Zurich is magnificent and the remarkably spacious square in which it stands is a marvel of urban beauty and artistic adornment.

With a "longing, lingering look behind," at the thriving city with its flowing river and gray-green lake at its feet, and its verdure-clad background reaching into snowy heights above, I watched it all fade in the distance and merge little by little into the less striking region about Basle, toward which converging point of multitudinous lines, I again sped. Here changing trains and resuming German money and German language, I journeyed on via Offenburg and Appemweier to Heidelberg, and thence by way of Mainz and Kastel to Wiesbaden.

CHAPTER XXXIII

Mainz is a fine city of ancient origin and modern improvements, and very fair was it to look upon as it lay spread out before me in the warm sunshine. I paused not, however, to enjoy its beauties nor its glories, making only a short halt between trains.

The Rhine here is broad and splendid. It is from this point that the "Rhine-journey" is usually begun, passengers for train or boat to the north, being taken by carriage through the town and across its beautiful bridge to Kastel opposite.

Thus far my way lay, so I entered the waiting vehicle with five other travelers. Three of these were a family party, father, mother and son, English, who were in great perplexity concerning their luggage, about which they conversed volubly in the language of their country.

It was impossible for me to remain ignorant of their grievances unless I had been suddenly stricken deaf, but of course, it was all none of my affair. Finally the conductor appeared demanding tickets, and there was another overflowing torrent of speech turned in his direction, as all tried to explain at once, but the conductor

> "————shook his flaxen head
> and smilingly answered:——"

"Nix-fer-stay." Then they said it all over again, with that calm and indomitable assurance which all English seem to have, that if they only speak distinctly and forcibly enough in their native tongue, every foreigner will surely understand.

But it was of no avail; the conductor "had no English," and the party "had no German." At last as the English began for the fourth time to rehearse their "tale of woe," I ventured, seeing no one else was likely to come to their relief, to say a few words in German to the conductor. At this the English party turned to me and poured forth the story once more, as if I had not been able to hear the relation the other four times; but I listened gravely and did what I could to elucidate matters, enough so that finally the conductor ejaculated, "*Ja, ja, ganz recht,*" slammed the door and we rolled away.

Then the English party added for me a few personal details, saying that they had traveled in India, in Egypt and nearly all over the globe, this being their third trip through Germany. "And you do not speak German?" I inquired, rather superfluously, it must be admitted. "Oh, no?" they returned complacently, "We do not speak any language but our own; we can always make ourselves understood in English." I was sorely beset with a desire to laugh, but managed, I trust, to keep my countenance as impassive as the faces of the fifth and sixth occupants of the conveyance, who had not moved a muscle during all this confabulation.

Reaching Kastel, I took train for Wiesbaden, which lies inland, principally in a broad and smiling plain bounded far away on the one hand by the river Rhine, and encircled otherwise by the southern declivities of the Taunus Mountains. Off in the distance, the peaks of the Odenwald and the Donnersberg are silhouetted against the horizon. The woodland slopes that rise gently away from the main town, are threaded by picturesque and leafy avenues whose umbrageous nooks are studded with stately mansion and ornate cottage.

Records show that Wiesbaden was first known as Mattiacum, and the graver citizens of this now fashionable watering place, are fond of mentioning that Pliny himself stated, *"Sunt et Mattiaci fontes calidi."* These "hot springs" of volcanic origin, are certainly in evidence to-day and to them the city owes its distinctive prosperity. About some of the principal ones, the ground is warm at all times and even in winter no snow can remain there. Most of the great hotels have their own boiling mineral springs, and the facilities for laving in and imbibing the curative waters are innumerable.

It is a pretty town; its gay and cheerful appearance somewhat suggestive of Lucerne, but without the superb setting of that gem of pleasure-places. As in Lucerne, the attractions of the old and the new are inseparably blended. Traces of old Roman occupation, such as the ancient "Wall of the Heathen," numerous votive stones, massive antique baths excavated from far below the present surface, tiles with the stamp of the Legion, coins and various other relics, are to be noted within stone's throw of, if not actually contiguous to pleasant modern parks and promenades, gay gardens, fine churches, theaters, ornamental villas and the like; and in addition, all the concomitants, architectural or otherwise, incidental to a popular "cure;" such as palatial bath-houses, splendid drinking-halls, or "pump-rooms" and so forth, with every *fin de siècle* convenience and improvement.

The one defect in natural beauty, is the lack, within the immediate area of the city, of lake or river; hence artificial ponds and fountains are

much more numerous here than in Lucerne, as
there Nature herself has wrought on so mighty
a scale, that man's efforts seem puny and in-
effective; but here he has had wider scope and
the beautiful adornments of square and *Platz*
and of the spacious grounds of the various
Kurhausen throughout the place, are indeed
diverse and enchanting.

Everywhere also as in Lucerne, one meets a
brilliant, light-hearted throng, but here there is
a very large supplement of the aged and infirm,
"the lame, the halt," and I do not know but
"the blind," also, who flock here with canes and
crutches and in rolling-chairs, to obtain the
benefit of these healing waters.

The city in some respects also reminds me of
some of our thriving American towns, as improvements seem to be continually under way;
new tramways are in progress, though there are
many previous lines; old buildings are in de-
molition and new ones in building, so that there
is an air of pleasing activity to be noted
throughout the streets, though there is none of
the rush and clangor of a large commercial
center.

Wiesbaden is now a city of sixty thousand or
more inhabitants. Much of its development is
said to be due to the late Emperor William I.,
who made this his favorite bathing-place for
many years and never failed to show special
favor to the town.

Of the many splendid and picturesque edifices
of Wiesbaden, I will say little. One of the most
conspicuous is the great synagogue standing
upon steep Michaelsberg. It is of noble, orien-
tal style, wrought out in light-gray sandstone
decorated with arabesques. With its Moorish
spires, its domes and huge cupola, it is a grand

and impressive structure. In the *Markt Platz*
stands the new Town-Hall, a peculiarly shaped,
seven-sided building, of variegated sandstone,
seeming to be in composition, a blending of Renaissance and Gothic features. Many balcon-
ies and galleries give variety to the façades. A
standard-bearer of chased copper decorates the
main front. In the upper field of the middle gable
is the civic coat-of-arms borne by allegorical figures. In the window medallions are busts of
the emperors William I. and Frederick III.
Adorning the central balcony are colossal statues
of Justice, Power, Diligence and Benevolence.
Various other details abound, of fitting and interesting decoration. The whole effect is picturesque without lacking in dignity.

Passing along Wilhelm and Taunus streets,
we come to the entrance of the Nerothal where
we find a fine bronze monument in honor of
Wiesbaden's sons who fell in the campaigns of
1870-71, against the French.

All about here are verdant vineyards and, beyond and above, the well-wooded heights of the
Neroberg, accessible by cog-wheel railway.
Reaching the top one finds a wide, elevated, undulating plain pleasingly diversified
by grove and garden, and quaint as well as
elegant detached structures. A few steps
brings one to the Nero Temple, a small pavilion
of white marble with rounded dome supported
by slender columns upon a circular platform.
From here one has a lovely view; but, going on,
one comes to one of the finest hotels in the
vicinity, eight hundred feet above the plain,
with an observatory of odd construction seventy
feet higher, from which is seen a vast, unobstructed prospect over a marvelous expanse of
landscape. One's gaze roves abroad over a

wide emerald plain, through the far distance of which the silvery waters of the Rhine, spanned by the graceful bridge at Mainz, gleam in their winding course. Wiesbaden is at one's feet, and the whole immense sea of Taunus' green foliage stretches north and north east, wafting afar its balmy odors. Outlined against the sky are the proud summits of the Wurzel, Platte, Feldberg, Alt-koenig, besides Melibokus and Donnerberg: between them lie verdant and shadowy valleys inhabited by all manner of game. To quote an enthusiastic visitor, "Forest and fountain seem to do their utmost to give back health to suffering mankind."

Still strolling onward, one reaches the spot where, 'midst forest green and sylvan shade, lies Wiesbaden's "city of the dead."

Gazing upon its peaceful loveliness, one recalls the words of an ancient minnesinger who so long ago felt that

> "Here beneath these leafy shadows,
>   With the soft breeze roving past,
> And the songsters' mellow warbling,
>   It were sweet to lie at last."

Here, as elsewhere over all the "wide, wide world," has grieving affection striven to render immortal the memory of its vanished ones; but among the many artistic tributes are two of such rare beauty, that possibly a brief description may be of interest.

The one, representing a small chapel, is hewn from pure white marble. The sad figure of mourning Love stands at the threshold, and to her the door is opened by a little Angel of Peace. To the left of the door stands a youth with a wreath of poppy leaves and an inverted torch. There is a simple and classic beauty about the whole conception, that is very affecting.

The other, just beyond, known as the "Grecian Chapel," is entirely diverse in type. It is in the form of a Greek cross and is richly adorned without and within, while above its green embowerment, rise five golden cupolas into the clear light of heaven. This sepultary edifice was reared to the memory of the wife of the Duke of Nassau, the lovely princess Elizabeth Michaelowna, who died in the flower of her youth. A flight of broad, marble steps leads to the interior, where the light filters in through splendidly ornate, stained windows and falls in countless, prismatic hues over the polished marble walls, whereon are hung many a rare painting of themes sacred and sublime. In the center of the beautiful rotunda, under the gentle light of the cupola, lies the lovely sculptured figure of the fair princess. Rich curtains draped far above fall in folds of artistic grace, shielding but not hiding the pure young beauty here so delicately, so touchingly represented. Faith, Hope, Charity and Immortality stand at the four corners of the sarcophagus, keeping silent guard forever.

In this chapel, the Russian community of Wiesbaden holds its religious services.

With so much beauty of art and nature on all sides, one would fain linger discovering new delights at every step, but the shades of night are gathering and, though there is no darkness in this electricity-illumined spot, yet tired feet and eyes petition for respite even from the pursuit of beauty, and I return to my hotel, which, by the way, is somewhat different in arrangement from any that I have seen before.

There is a large, imposing entrance-portal, or

vestibule, that opens directly from the street on the same level, and extends inward about fifty feet; up two or three steps at one side, open the great dining and breakfast-rooms; from the other, a large, square hall, from which access is had to the elevator, the porter's lodge and the like.   The rear wall of the vestibule is of glass, with a wide opening in the middle, admitting to a central court gay with flowers and trees. Here meals are served *al fresco*.   But the peculiarity is that around this court, which is inclosed by the inner walls of the hotel, are a number of doors with steps and sometimes little porches before them, and these lead into complete apartments or *suites*, so that the occupants have a private entrance of their own, opening only into their own quarters and through which no guests of the hotel pass, except themselves. These families may take their meals in the dining-room, or in the court under their windows, or have them sent in, or go outside for them, as they prefer.   It struck me as a happy mingling of the advantages of public and domestic living.

I did a little shopping in Wiesbaden, and found to my surprise, when the saleswoman put the wares before me, that I had asked for embroidery-needles instead of pins.   In the laugh that we had together over my blunder, I discovered that she spoke English, so I made no more errors.

Speaking of shopping, reminds me that while I was in Hanover, a German lady told me that it was not "good form" to leave any store which one had entered, without purchasing something. Visitors are not expected to inspect goods unless desiring to buy, and, if the stock fails to contain the article desired, one must purchase something to recompense the dealer for showing his wares. "Opening Days" are unknown and "one's room is better than one's company" unless one buys goods whether wanted or not. Naturally, the raids of the genus "shopper" are sternly discountenanced. It was quite different in Paris, where the salespeople give a visitor every facility to look about.

On the whole goods are not expensive and are made for service. Gloves, millinery and silks, though dearer than in France, are much less so than in America. Rates for tailoring and needle work in general, are lower than in France; though to my surprise, I found them moderate there, outside the large, fashionable emporiums so well known on both sides of the water.

Here, as in most foreign countries, American shoes are found at the head,—not meaning that they take the place of hats,—the German shoe especially being "fearfully and wonderfully made." I am reminded of a little incident that occurred as I was walking to church one morning. I was not quite sure as to the way and, as I crossed a street, I met a pleasant-looking lady of whom I inquired.

She replied in English, adding:

"You are American, are you not?"

"Oh!" I replied, somewhat chagrined, "is it possible my German is so faulty that you can even tell whether I am American or English?"

"Not that at all;" she answered, "it is your feet. I noticed as you held you skirts out of the dust, that you were wearing American shoes, and as you are a stranger and a foreigner, I decided that you were from America."

I felt quite relieved and went on my way rejoicing, though I marveled at the keenness of her observation.

I think I have remarked before that I like

Germans the best of any foreigners that I have
encountered. As a rule, they are very friendly
and "level-headed," and occasionally they show
such delicious and unexpected simplicity. As
for instance; one day at dinner in my *pension*, the
conversation turned upon the subject of divorce
and the greater facility,—which unfortunately
is too true,—with which it may be obtained in
America, and especially in Chicago, than in
Europe. The report as to how far South Dakota
had out-stripped the older community, in this
special line, had evidently not yet penetrated
into dreamy old Germany. At any rate, our
hostess, a traveled and cultured lady, remarked
in perfect good faith :

"Why, is it not dreadful? I was reading to-
day in a paper, how it is over there in Chicago.
There is a place right in the post office, where
you can go and get divorce-papers while you are
waiting for your mail."

Her shocked expression, with her implicit reli-
ance on a newspaper squib, were too much for
one having a keen sense of the ludicrous, and in
spite of my efforts, I "ha-ha-ed" right out,
almost before the words had left her lips. It
was some time before she could comprehend why
I laughed, and I fancy she even yet believes it was
principally due to the reprehensible folly of
"those dreadful Americans," for the other
Americans at the table laughed too, though it
was I who disgracefully led the van.

It was while at this *pension* that I learned that
visitors are not desired in German schools, and
only admitted after much use of "red tape."
Expressing a desire to see something of the
practical educational system of Germany, I was
informed that it would be necessary to make
application to the authorities for a permit, which

might not be granted for several months, if at all. A case was instanced of a gentleman from Kansas, who, being a professional pedagogue of repute in his own country, applied on his arrival in Hanover, for such a permit; he made a long stay there, followed some branch of study, made himself familiar with the city and busied himself in various ways, but finally was obiged to return to America to take up his professional duties; and not until he had been gone three months, did his governmental permission to visit the schools of Hanover, arrive at his foreign address. Old-world citizens are continually complaining because the Americans are "always in such a hurry." Not wishing to remain indefinitely in any place, I decided to make no application of any kind to the authorities.

CHAPTER XXXIV.

By way of variety, instead of going back to Kastel for the "Rhine-Journey," which is the usual route, I took a steam tram at Wiesbaden and went over to Biebrich-Bahnhof, a short distance below Kastel on the river. For several weeks now I have seen nothing of my luggage excepting two small "grips," as my *Rund-Reise* ticket, taken at Hanover, allows nothing free but what can be taken into one's compartment; so I expressed my heavy pieces to London to be stored there until my arrival. I might better have left a large part of it in America.

It is really amusing to see what an amount of "traps" under the guise of hand-luggage is brought into the compartment by the average traveler, to avoid paying excess charges; as it all is transported in any case, I do not see why it could not as well be stowed in the luggage-van, out of the passenger's way; it would weigh no more there than in the compartment, certainly. Probably, however, the baggage coaches are so small that such a course would necessitate putting on an extra one, and that would entail much additional weight. And here let me once more sound a warning to the "lone one." True, I had been warned myself before sailing, and thought had I reduced my "things" to the smallest livable compass, but here I have been existing for weeks, in two "grips," and shall have to continue so to do, for some time more. But there was one point that I did not realize and which I emphasize for the benefit of my solitary sister; namely, the slight degree of variation in temperature over here, from day to day. One does not appear in flannels and furs in the morning and in frillls and fans before night, or *vice- versa*, as so often with us; and I have never yet, even in the crowded cities, experienced any of what the average American would call "truly torrid" weather, though the native on this side may be complaining of the "beastly heat." This state of things naturally renders the wardrobe question less complicated, fewer changes being required. Since winter has really taken its leave, the atmosphere has been mostly genial and delightful. To be sure, I can only speak regarding the parts I have visited.

It was charming indeed to-day as we ran along in the open country and through two or three trim and quaint little hamlets, before reaching our destination at the boat-landing of Biebrich, a small village that has sprung up around *Schloss Biebrich*, the property of the Duke of Nassau. If one prefers, one may leave the train at Mosbach and walk thence to this same point, through the lovely grounds of this castle, and past its interesting antiquity; though, being a little less than two hundred years old, it is considered rather modern in these regions.

A goodly multitude of expectant humanity of assorted nationalities, awaited the coming of our steamer from Mainz-Kastel, which cities we could see distinctly on opposite banks of the Rhine, as we looked up the stream. Finally the "German Emperor" came puffing sedately down the river with much dignity, though, being but a boat, he—or "she"—did not ignore the manifest desire of the populace, but swerved gracefully toward us with several discordant shrieks little creditable to her—or "his"—majesty. Quite a number of persons had already taken passage from the "twin cities" above, and we hastened to swell the throng.

The Rhine steamers are of good size, not so large as the Hudson River floating palaces, but pleasant and well-equipped. It seemed queer to have first and second class even here. I believe the second classers must not go to the salon-deck, but their quarters, from what I could see as I passed up the companion-way, seemed clean and attractive.

And now I am really abroad upon the famous river around whose very name there lingers so much of romance and poetry. It is a gay scene; tug-boats, passenger-boats, freight-boats, pleasure-boats, of nearly every size and type, are passing to and fro and all is life and animation. The sun shines brilliantly, the fields are smiling, pennons gracefully flutter, the wavelets foam and sparkle about our steamer, reflecting all the colors of the rainbow, and happy hearts make holiday with laughter and song.

Countless little tables are set about and lively groups gather around with various *kucken* and other edibles, washed down by the light beers and wines of the country. The American tourist, distinctive by his unconquerable *penchant* for "ice-water" though he may also swallow much stronger beverages, is on hand and appears to oscillate between two extremes, the wildly rapturous and the loftily disparaging. I, wishing to avoid either, do not parade my nationality but sit quietly in as German a seeming as I can command.

But I soon lose all thoughts of self as the lovely pictures on either side gradually unroll before me. A little hand-book I have picked

up, declares that "the Rhine is the most interesting river in the world," and I do not know
but the author has struck the key-note of its
peculiar charm.   There are longer rivers; there
are grander rivers; there are rivers whose shores
spread out in sublimer landscapes; but what
other river has the legends, the traditions, the
myths and mysteries, as well as the splendidly
authentic record of bravery and chivalry through
hundreds of years, handed down from generation to generation, that cluster along this meandering stream which first transmitted to Germany the culture of the Romans?

Story and verse, epic and lyric, from time
unreckoned have rendered immortal its fascina-
tions and its renown; while frowning castle and
crumbling ruin give visible attestation to its
present and its former importance.   There is a
charm about it all, that is well nigh untellable;
and one begins to comprehend the emotions of
that aged German sire who so long ago in appo-
site verse, adjured his son to "go not to the
Rhine," lest he "never come back any more."

For the water smiles up at the mountains so blue,
    And the mountains smile back to the stream,
And the lassies and lads are so friendly and true,
    That thy soul shall in Paradise seem.

Entranced by the smiles and bewitched by the wine,
    Ecstatic its vineyards thou'lt roam,
And singing forever, "The Rhine, O, the Rhine!"
    Thou'lt never come back to thy home.

We are fairly under way and, leaving Castle
Biebrich embowered in its leafy nook behind us,
our boat winds along amidst the islands that so
numerously intersperse this stretch of the river,
and nears Niederwalluf, at which point the
famous "Rhine-Wine-District" begins.   The

slopes are dotted with elegant villas and picturesque cottages, with castle or ruin on every height; while in all the green intervales and reaching back upon the fertile declivities, twine the verdant tendrils and droop the purple clusters devoted to the worship of Bacchus.

On the right appears Elfeld, which, in contrast to all the misty romance of this interesting locality, claims to have possessed as long ago as 1465, that very practical and matter-of-fact machine, a printing-press. A handsome Gothic watch-tower reared in 1330, looks down calmly upon us as we pass beneath its portals and move on, approaching first one side and then the other of the sinuous stream whose delightful shores lie so near at either hand and stretch back into vistas of enchantment.

The vineyards of the "Rhinegau" are getting more numerous. Yonder lies Hattenheim with its giant pipe; beyond, the vines of Steinberg and Marcobrunn; near at hand, the gray walls of the monastery Eberbach; and everywhere creeping close to the borders of the river, are the cheerful little villages that give pleasing vivacity to the beauteous scene.

And now rises a fair incline that undulates in gently sloping terraces to a considerable height, on the top of which appears an extensive but simply designed edifice. This is the world-renowned *Schloss Johannisberg* where is produced the precious wine of that name. This, with adjacent grounds, is the property of Prince Metternich, and comprises a vineyard of many acres. Some one has enthusiastically called it the "Pearl of the Rhinegau;" in consideration of the wine it produces, I should think "ruby" the better term, but there!—what do I know about it? "Johannisberger" may be pearl-colored for aught I can testify, for I have not yet, in spite of my now lengthy sojourn in the land of the grape and vine, learned to imbibe their liquid products with any more gusto than when I left my native land.

Still on we glide. On either side of the river, running mostly parallel to its shores, stretches a railroad track; occasionally we note a train rushing along, sometimes on the one hand, sometimes on the other, frequently on both at once, all far out-stripping our own rate of speed; but as we watch them plunge into the black tunnels under every hill, we are glad that we may float down the stream in the free air and sunshine.

More and more fascinating grows the scene. Now rise into view the towers and gables of fair Rudesheim, nestled with its numerous hotels and pleasant wine-gardens at the foot of the great Niederwald, a dark forest above whose oaken branches and shadowy crown of foliage looms far up on the summit of the mountain, the pride of the nation, that great master-piece of commemorative art, "*Die Wacht am Rhein.*"

It is a grand and beautifully impressive object visible for miles around from vale and river. One may leave the boat here and take a cog-wheel railway up through vineyards and groves to the top of the mountain, and thus inspect closely this noble creation.

The figure of Germania, a woman richly garbed, with flowing robes and corsage of mail, stands boldly forth before the imperial throne. Her left hand grasps a mighty sword wreathed in laurel, her right holds proudly aloft the august, jeweled crown of Germany.

The figure is thirty-six feet high and is the design of Professor J. Schilling of Dresden. The bronze casting was done in Munich and consists partly of metal of conquered cannon, a fact adding to the significance of the memorial. The masonry beneath the monument is mighty and solid, being circular in form. From the grand boulevard below, a wide flight of many steps, broad and imposing, rises to the base of this foundation and terminates at a spacious platform. Leading from one side of this, a narrower flight passes around the great bulk of the structure and up to another extensive platform in the rear, which is on a level with the substructure. All exposed verges are carefully railed in. Upon the substructure stands the pedestal of the monument. At the front, on a small pedestal of its own, is a noble group representing the rivers Rhine and Moselle. On the right upon the main pedestal and above the river-group, stands the haughty figure of War, stern and defiant; on the corresponding left, the graceful form of Peace, prosperous and serene.

Between these two, in the main façade, is a magnificent high-relief of *"Die Wacht am Rhein,"* with portrait figures of the late Emperor William I. and many of the princes and officers instrumental in the reconstruction of the German Empire; the lofty and commanding form of Bismarck standing out almost as haughty and defiant as the figure of War itself, while below is graven in letters of unusual size, the full text of the stirring poem from which the memorial takes its name.

On the right and left faces respectively, are fine reliefs, "The Departure" and "The Home-coming." The foundation-stone was laid by the old Emperor William, and the monument was unvailed in his presence and that of an enthusiastic multitude in 1883. Since then it has been a place of pilgrimage for the whole German nation.

And who can wonder?   Even the bosom of an
alien pulses more quickly, gazing at the majestic object rising a b o v e the lovely scene
spread out far below; and when to all this
beauty of art and nature, is added the consciousness that here, from away back into dim ages,
one's forefathers struggled even unto the death,
to defend and prosper the "Fatherland," how
one's heart must swell.   From so long a time it
is that German right and German might
have stood here supreme in spite of foreign foes.
The old bridge at Drusus speaks of Roman invasion; still are standing at Ingelheim the pillars
of Charlemagne's imperial palace; and have not
these blue mountains looked down through all
the centuries upon the tremendous warfare of
German knights, who "put not lance in rest"
until the enemy was driven from the borders
and no marauder dared again to venture upon
the sacred soil?

And now beneath these same blue mountains,
upon this arena of a heroic past, moves the busy
and joyous pageant of modern life with its incessant activity, its gayety, its elegance.   Barge
and row-boat, yacht and steamer, glide along
the stream; trains dash back and forth and in
and out of those stupendous tunnels; thousands
of persons on business and pleasure bent, pass
to and fro; luxury, invention and speculation
have wrought miracles innumerable; and to-day,
above all, immutable in beauty and majesty,
stands this glorious monument, typifying sub-
limely forever the thought of a united "Fatherland."   And ever joining the past to the present,
the silver Rhine flows on.

We rouse from our musings and return to
Rudesheim where we re-embark upon the rolling
stream.

A little above Rudesheim, on the opposite bank, is Rochusberg with its interesting chapel on the mountain, where is annually celebrated in August the festival of St. Roch. Gœthe, who has given us a vivid description of this festivity, presented the little chapel, during his sojourn in the vicinity, an altar-piece which is carefully preserved and cherished.

A little further down the stream is the old ruin Kloppburg, thought to be of Roman origin, and noted as one of the many places where the unfortunate Henry IV. was detained by his unfilial sons in 1105.

The country flattens out somewhat here and, looking to the left, we note the spires and turrets of a considerable city becoming visible just where an arm of the river branches off to the westward. What a thrill runs over one on learning that this is "Bingen, fair Bingen on the Rhine." How the tide of recollection rolls backward and we see ourselves in the old-time school-room where, once a week, are held the "literary exercises" of the various classes; see the agitated maiden, whose trembling hand can scarcely hold the "Fifth Reader" from which she voices in nearly inaudible accents her favorite selection, as ubiquitous in that day as the "Curfew shall not ring to-night," of a later era.

Who does not recall the opening lines?

> "A soldier of the legion lay dying at Algiers,
> There was lack of woman's nursing, there was
> dearth of woman's tears."

Or perchance it is a sturdy youth, whose graces of elocution are entirely dormant, if at all existent, who, in shaky, uncertain *basso*, proceeds to declaim with few pauses and no inflections, the same perennial poem; but whichever, or whoever it is, each invariably declares in lugubrious tones,

"For I was born in 'Bin-jun', fair 'Bin-jun' on the
    Rhine."

Fair indeed it is to-day; and beautiful beyond telling, the green shores and hurrying waters that here race so merrily onward with ripple and swirl of contrary currents, carrying us on swiftly until we pass below the ancient city, and come abreast of a tiny island, principally a rock of quartz, separated by a deep channel from the main shore.

And now what do we see, tall, attenuated, antiquated, with slim, battlemented turrets and narrow slits, rising grim and ghost-like from the very bosom of the waters?   Do you

"———think of the Bishop of Bingen
    And his mouse-tower on the Rhine?"

For that is what it is.   And now I am consumed with curiosity to know why "mouse" tower.   My ignorance is dispelled by a reference to the wise little book in my hand, whose terse elucidation I will give for the benefit of some "lone sister" who, like myself, may never before have learned what it all means.   Thus the book:

"The Mouse-Tower, properly Mus-Tower, muserie-gunnery; cf. musket; a tower built for levying toll by Archbishop Hatto, as is told by a popular legend."   Short and to the point. We shall not forget it.

Prior to the year 1832, this portion of the river was considered very perilous. as great volumes of water were forced through an exceedingly narrow channel; but at that date the operations and improvements upon the stream were completed and the roaring river was subdued below the danger-point.

Just below the tower, on the right, lie the ruins Ehrenfels, built in the thirteenth century, also for the levying of toll on passing boats, in that period when so emphatically might meant right.

Mountain and vineyard, grove and hamlet, appear and fall behind. Again on the left rises a steep rock nearly three hundred feet high, on the summit of which sits the mediæval castle Rheinstein, known to have been in existence in the thirteenth century. It was restored in 1829 and is the property of Prince George of Prussia. Now is seen a continuous succession of high, bold precipices rent by great ravines and yawning chasms. Here stands the Falkenberg with thrilling history; centuries ago a Roman castle, later a robber's stronghold and once destroyed by Rudolph of Hapsburg.

Yonder upon that huge rock wall, eight hundred feet above the river, looms the magnificently restored Castle Sooneck, the property of the Emperor and his brothers, its modern impregnability contrasting strangely with the ancient ruins so close at hand.

Bolder and loftier grow the shores. The vineyards are now behind us. Castle after castle bristling with defences, towers upward on the crags, or ruined and dismantled displays its crumbling buttresses and fallen arches decked with moss and climbing plants.

Scant space here have the little villages to crowd in between the river's margin and the rugged cliffs behind. On the left again is the recently rebuilt Castle Heimburg, or Hoheneck, rising from the fragments of a Roman castle wholly destroyed in 1689. To the right the ruin Nollingen, of the eleventh century, looking down over its "Devil's Ladder;" a steep incline of sharp-notched, rocky up-thrusts apparently insurmountable, yet over which a daring and impetuous knight of an ancient day is said to have forced his "noble steed" to gain his "beauteous bride." Whether she too was brave and dared to ride down with him again, "deponent," alas, "sayeth not." Opposite rises a huge, round tower, almost all that is left of Castle Furstenburg, taken by Lewis the Bavarian in 1321, and finally demolished in 1609.

The line of elevation descends for a space to a lower height. Here in a narrow area, crowding against the overhanging declivities, is the quaint town of Bacharach, whose well-preserved city-walls connect with the ruined Castle Stahlick on the rocks above.

On the other side of the river, the town of Kaub, with considerable remains of ancient fortifications; this spot has a more modern interest as the place through which Blucher passed on New Year's eve, 1813-14. Above here, old Castle Gutenfels, destroyed by Napoleon in 1805. In the center of the stream at this point, is another huge rock upon which stands the *Pfalz*, a vaster and more imposing, but not so romantic a structure as the "Mouse-Tower," reared for the same purpose, the levying of toll in the days of mediæval oppression.

I cannot name all these mighty castles and majestic ruins, but which shall I ignore? Not beautiful Schoenberg with its three ivy-mantled towers rising so picturesquely on yonder wooded height; nor the "ancient, free and imperial town," Oberwahl, with its antique defenses;; nor yet Ochsenthurm stately in mediæval masonry.

O, fair and thrilling picture! O, crumbling castles and ruins gray, and frowning crag and rolling river! Higher and closer rise the mountains. Deeper and narrower grows the stream and the near rocks cast shadows. The flowing waters roll on and sweep around an eminence huge and high, far above the river. Steep and ragged is its front, and cruel the reefs that show their jagged teeth beneath the crystal waves; but aloft the sunlight glitters and the grass grows green in dappled dells. Do you hear the Loerlei singing?

> A maiden of loveliest seeming
> Afar on those heights so fair,
> With golden ornaments gleaming,
> Is combing her golden hair.

Sha'l she lure us on till the grinning rocks shall dash us to our doom? Oh! Heine, how your measures weird and thrilling, and how the "witchery of the Rhine-land," do "work like madness in the brain." Rouse up, O, Sense; put away the glamour of song and music and legendary lore; look out with vision unclouded and say what, in verity, you now behold. A narrow turn in a beautiful stream and a lofty bluff, 'tis true; but modern science has widened the channel and the bluff is not more than five hundred feet in height; not so high as the Sooneck some distance back. And have you not also looked upon the ice-topped Alps of Switzerland and the white ruggedness of the Rocky Moutains that thrust themselves against high heaven?

But should one then bring out one's measuring-line and say: "This height is so many feet lower than that; this rock is but one-third as vast as another; I have seen wider streams and summer skies?"

Not so: let us rather yield again to the spell
of ancient days, of tradition and of poesy, and
float on enchanted, in a haze of dreamy delight.
So we turn again to the lovely scene.

Yonder is St. Goar where dwelt the venerable
hermit thirteen hundred years ago. Farther on,
perched on a prominent height, the ruins of the
so-called "Cat," a fortress of the Katzenelbogen
(cat's elbow!) family and torn down in 1806;
and just below, another crumbling pile said to
to be in a military sense, (which I do not comprehend,) "at the mercy of the cat," therefore
with fit though rather grim humor, called "The
Mouse."

How closely crowd the castellated ruins along
each bank. Yonder appear two bulky elevations looking out from their height, upon the
winding river that curves gracefully here around
the base of the mountain. Each is crowned with
a fortress that long rose up impregnable, and is
divided from the other only by a deep, narrow
chasm called "The battle ditch."

Here, ages ago, tradition tells, there dwelt two
brothers in these two castles on these twin mountains, in splendor of pomp and power, each with
his numerous retinue. But in the course of
time, instead of inclining to

> "Each his friendly aid afford,
> And feel his brother's care,"

they sought only war and strife, and so fought
unceasingly across the narrow ravine, whose
depths have hidden many a ghastly victim and
echoed many a dying groan. But their warfare
is accomplished; centuries since, the last armed
watchman left these battlements, the last mailed
warrior abandoned these ramparts; the mighty
walls are weakened; chaotic fragments fill the

spacious inclosures and modern warfare laughs
their defenses to scorn. But still the old bul-
warks stand gazing off over this great theater
of time's infinite changes, and still the smiling
Rhine rolls on.

With a wide sweep the river turns eastward
and then again as far west. Fair Bornhofen
lies near with its cloister to which, even in this
prosaic age, flock crowds of pilgrims every year,
to pray before the hallowed shrine where sits
enthroned a Holy Mary of wondrous, miracle-
working grace. Soon bold Marxburg lifts into
view, the only castle on the Rhine that has never
been destroyed, though dating beyond 1100.

But now a most unique edifice appears on the
left, at some distance from the shore, for here
again the hills have receded somewhat and are
less precipitous. This, like the other antique
structures, is of heavy masonry, but is low and
broad and seems little but a massive, flat roof
resting upon many open arches. A flight of
steps about half the height of the building,leads
to a rather stately portal rising perhaps five or
six feet above the main front.

A kindly neighbor here informs me that
this is "The King's chair;" is eighteen feet
high within and has eight stone seats. one for
the emperor, seven for the electors. Here the
emperors were elected down to the fifteenth century,and in 1330 it was decided that "the pope's
approval was not necessary to confirm a choice."
All this is truly quaint and old-timey.

Across on the right, just before the river Lahn
empties into the Rhine, stands the very ancient
town of Oberlahnstein; and above on yon steep
rock, Castle Lahneck, once the property of the
Knights-Templars, and the scene of many an heroic conflict and defiant death in the centuries

agone. It was finally dismantled by the French
in 1688, but is now private property, having
been restored in 1860.

Now haughty Stolzenfels, constructed in the
thirteenth century rears up its great, pentagonal
tower on the left, nearly five hundred feet above
the Rhine. It is a stately stronghold, splendidly restored, and contains, we are told, every
elegance and many rich collections. How wonderful must be the view from off its pinnacles,
down over verdant groves to fair Capellan at its
feet, and off eastward where the tortuous Lahn
reaches away toward Ems.

More marvelous still the changes it has wit-
nessed in the status of mankind, both subjec-
tively and objectively, through all this wide
expanse, aye, through all the world abroad;
while northward ever the rippling Rhine runs on.

Some distance along to the left, we see the
suburban villas of a populous city and soon
beautiful Coblenz spreads out into view, magnificently situated at the junction of the Moselle
with the Rhine. Three fine bridges, the first
since we left Biebrich, cross the main riverbe-
tween here and Stolzenfels. In the Moselle in
1864, were found the remains of a Roman
bridge; to-day a handsome solid structure of
stone leads across this river just above its mouth.
We note the quaint old Castor Church which,
with its Gothic towers, has stood here for more
than a thousand years.

A strong fort with garrison of fifty one hundred soldiers, commands the city and all the immediate vicinity; while opposite the mouth of
the Moselle, the great fortress Ehrenbreitstein,
inaccessible on three sides, frowns down from
its height of over three hundred feet. Never
but twice in all the centuries of its existence,

has this fortress succumbed, and both times only through hunger. What tragedies of resistance and endurance that brief phrase implies. What scenes of agony and horror have been enacted within and before these invincible barriers which to-day look so tranquilly down upon the fertile plains stretching off so far below; for here lies the lovely Ehrenbreitstein valley, whereof it truly seems that its "ways are ways of pleasantness and all" its "paths are peace."

In this fair district Goethe abode in 1774, with Basedow and Lavater; and still as then and in ages past, the restless Rhine sweeps on.

Two large and leafy islands almost intercept us at this point, but we carefully feel our way along in the channel, and our gaze, so long restricted by lofty cliff and peak, now roves freely over arable field and grassy meadow, while anew the clustering villages crowd close to the water's edge. But yet a little farther, and once more arise the heights crowned as before with castle and watch-tower, rampart and ruin.

O, wondrous Rhine! What pen shall fitly trace the glorious history of its borders? Here is Engers, where Cæsar is said to have crossed the river. There are the ruins of Sayn, one of the most ancient strongholds upon the Rhine; and Andernach, with its walls of Roman origin and beautiful remains of tower and rampart, that resisted even the gunpowder of the French in 1688.

On yonder high and craggy rock, are the extensive ruins of Hammerstein, once strongly fortified and one of the places of refuge for the sorely beset Henry IV., but finally demolished in 1660 by that warlike prelate, the Bishop of Cologne. Over on the left, above its verdure-crested hill, rises Burg Rheineck, rebuilt in 1832 upon the ruins of the old fortress that, dating from the eleventh century, had again and again been leveled and re-reared by opposing hosts. On the other side again, stately New Ahrenfels, erected above the ruins of an ancient robber-castle, looms up proudly in all the bravery of *fin de siècle* façade and tower.

Thus on and on we glide adown the broadening stream. Citadel, castle, cloister and convent, ancient and modern, ruined and restored, ever rising before and sinking behind us. Each has its own thrilling record, each its baptism of fire and blood, from away back into the shadows of antiquity. How impossible to realize the conditions through which primitive man has struggled up into the comparative peace and civilization of the present; yet through all, nature smiles serenely and still with ceaseless flow the limpid Rhine moves on.

The pleasant and popular village Remagen,—the Roman Rigomagus,—now comes into view to the left in the valley of the Ahr. At a little distance beyond, in abrupt contrast to stern castles and ancient ruins, appears a beautiful modern church of Gothic architecture, built in 1859 upon a slate rock, and dedicated to St. Apollonaris. This is another celebrated resort for pilgrims; the head of the saint is preserved within and works, so say the faithful, many miracles.

A little further on, a rounded arch of quaint design, all that is left of some antique edifice, stands out conspicuously on the left, three hundred and forty-four feet above the river. Tradition calls this "Roland's Arch," though who Roland was, save that he may have been one of Charlemagne's paladins, and why he had an arch, there are few to-day who know and still fewer who care. The view from this ruin is considered the most incomparably beautiful of the whole Rhine.

But what is this that towers aloft so high across our very path and seems to loom in grandeur up to the steps of heaven itself? 'Tis thy grim steeps, Oh! Drachenfels, and, set thereon, the remnants of that mighty pile which ancient dragon and mediæval engine could scarce overthrow. And now, just below that ruined magnificence, there rises, grand and massive, a new Drachenburg, in haughty defiance to modern energies. What now the monster housing here within thy secret caverns, and where the "horny Siegfried" that shall rise to lay the ravener low? Impassive in its solid majesty it rears itself above, while far below we round its base and seek the current that shall bear us on.

There on the right, volcanic Siebengebirge, and yonder to the left, the ancient fortifications of Godesberg, rent and dismantled, lift up their peaks and pinnacles. And now the hills fall back once more; the railways veer farther inland and across the country we see wide, straight highways stretching from point to point, lined by beautiful trees. We are approaching Bonn, well known to all the world. It was a flourishing town in the days of Constantine the Great, and so it is to-day. Opposite the city, the river Sieg with many islands, flows into the Rhine from the east, and an extensive forest stretches along its banks.

The Rhine still broadens and now makes another sweep to the east and then winds again to the north. The shores on either side are here flat and little varied, but studded thickly with thriving villages and lovely farm districts. Fair and unobstructed lies the level prospect to the clear horizon. We seem to have emerged from the dread domain of "grim-visaged War," into the smiling plains of Peace; from the narrow confines of mediæval environment again into the complex and diversified atmosphere of modern existence with range illimitable.

Suburban villas and pleasure-gardens begin to appear; soon long lines of streets and avenues with compact rows of massive buildings and a sea of roofs pierced by spire and cupola; above all of which, in sublime dignity, rises the ineffable beauty of the great cathedral.

Making our way to the docks and stopping just above the two bridges, one a pontoon, we disembark at Cologne and our voyage is over. Yet ever welling from its snowy source in the distant Swiss-Alps, and hurrying along to its destination in the far North Sea, the beautiful Rhine flows on.

The brief glimpses one may obtain in a continuous journey from the German frontier across Holland to a near seaport, are not sufficient to afford any great knowledge or wide comprehension of this country and its people. Still one may lay up a store of pleasing recollections even in this short transit, as I find after bidding farewell one morning to the lovely and interesting country of Germany, taking train again at Cologne and speeding away over level areas growing continually lower and more watery as we approach Holland. It rains gently and the whole outlook is indeed aqueous and monotonous.

But the little stations at which we pause are so trim, the more considerable towns so thriving, and everywhere the people are so kindly and cordial, that one is loth to leave them behind. They all smile and ejaculate *"Guten Tag"* or *"Glueckliche Reise,"* if they chance to catch one's eye. On this journey I note again the foreign rendering of the "news and gum fiends" of our own land. At each station newsdealers pass along outside the train,—the doors of which open out on and are at an exact level with the station platforms,—and carry or push before them light racks on which are displayed a small assortment of newspapers, rarely any other reading matter. Refreshment venders have neat little tables, often with canopy to shield from sun and rain, and resting on trucks that are easily wheeled along. These tables are tastefully set out with fruit, little cakes, various sausages, beer, wine and so forth, and are often adorned with flowers. One rarely meets a sandwich on the continent. Everything about the tables, cutlery, glass and the like, is spotless and shining. Passengers looking out, can readily make their wants known and be served by the white-aproned, white-capped attendant, either through the wide-open door, or the lowered glass upper-half; but if not desiring anything, are not annoyed in any way by solicitations, or by having diverse wares dumped upon their knees by the passing peddler. Sometimes a youth or maid runs along with either a pitcher of hot *café-au-lait* or *bouillon* which are very refreshing and cost about two cents a cup.

By and by we cross the frontier; a civil-appearing officer looks into our compartment and takes our word for it that we have nothing dutiable in our bags. A little placard in English informs us that the Custom-House officers may allow the passengers to "Keep"–with a capital K,– "their places if the latter should prove to have any difficulty in descending." This is kind and humane, surely,and though I, personally, do not "prove to have any difficulty in descending," I still do not leave my place,as my heavy luggage has all gone on ahead. So we roll onward into the domain of the Dutch.

How flat it all is; not an elevation to be noted in all one's range of vision. I have never seen anything just like it. I have been on the great plains of Iowa and Kansas, but there, there was no water in the landscape; the one was all a great expanse of waving corn, the other,—it then being early winter,—a boundless area of gray, wind-swept waste. I have also seen the marshy lowlands of southern Alabama and Louisiana, where there was no lack of water, but there the effect was of being in a great hollow below the surrounding surface; in a sort of huge bowl as it were, of which the sea-wall of the gulf in one direction, and the higher, solid ground of the remaining circumference, constituted the rim, so to speak. But here to-day, it seems as if we were running along on a mere crust, cut in all directions by the canals, and liable at any moment to give way and plunge us into the bottomless deep. How strange to think we are actually beholding the "dykes and ditches" of which we have heard from our veriest childhood. This reclaimed land, it is said, is remarkably fertile. Vegetation looks extremely flourishing, and graceful trees with feathery foliage are especially noticeable.

Strange, outlandish names begin to appear on the signs and placards that meet one's eyes, while funny little villages and quaint rural scenes come into view, all on a dead level, with nothing more striking in the way of elevation, than the huge wind-mills that slowly move their heavy pinions. Queer, little, square-built boys and girls, with thick, stiff garments, odd head-coverings and wooden shoes, occasionally look up at us from the highways, and we get glimpses of short, thick-set men and women at work about their hay-ricks and low cots, behind screens of luxuriant, but mainly dwarfed greenery. But the chief characteristic of the scene, is water, water; not in winding rivers or picturesque lakes, but in the straight, seemingly endless canals that stretch off monotonously in all directions.

I am not sorry when we come to our destination, the little town of Vlissingen, where I step out wondering, among the Dutch folk.

For the first time in my wanderings, I find

myself unable to speak, after a fashion, the language of the country; but alas, I "have no Dutch," so fall back on English. The first official I accost does not speak this tongue, but evidently recognizes the sound, as he disappears and returns with some one who does speak it.

I mention my desire for a cab; am told there are none there at present but that I can "take a boat," or can hire a guide and walk. Finding the distance short, I elect to do the latter, and my guide, who I find speaks German, slings my bag over his shoulder and off we start.

The rain has ceased and the sun shines warmly. The flat, green fields stretch off to the right, the level, glittering sea to the left, for here we are, eight hours straight and steady sailing, from the English coast, and no land is visible upon the horizon. The main city lies beyond the railway station and past these meadows.

We strike into a wide, paved path stretching, like the canals, straight onward, and fringed at intervals by small shade trees, under which are occasional seats, whereon here and there sit ladies reading. A wagon-road lies on one side of the path, a canal on the other. We see a casual cow off in the fields and we meet one or two phlegmatic-looking pedestrians, but a spell of silence seems to lie upon panorama and people. My guide seems to be infected by it, for he vouchsafes only a *"Ja, gnaedige Frau,"* or *"Nein, gnaedige Frau,"*to my attempts to extract information, so finally I too yield to the taciturn spirit and we walk mutely on.

Reaching my hotel, my man recovers enough of speech to voice a desire for sixty cents. I mention to my hostess, who speaks English, my surprise that he should be familiar with United States money; whereupon she explains that "cents" is also Dutch money, though one cent Dutch is worth only two-fifths of one cent United States, so I disburse German coin to the required amount, which the lady exchanges for the current coin of the kingdom, and my guide meanders slowly and silently away.

And now begins anew a struggle with a foreign currency this time of *florins, gulden and cents*, but thanks to the decimal system so prevalent on the continent, one soon acquires the new names and proceeds as before.

My hostess I regret to learn, is French instead of Dutch, and so not typical, either in manner or habitation, of this odd people.

She leads me through a roomy hall, up a spacious staircase, into a remarkably cheerful room, large, well-equipped, with a broad, double glass-door in the middle of the front, overlooking another canal immediately before the house, separated from it only by a wide, paved road. More canals reach hither and thither everywhere, with intensely green banks and bearing all sorts of queer-shaped boats; and still farther beyond the canals, the sparkling, open water of the great harbor.

Retiring to an inviting couch, the first double bed that I have seen except in museums, since I left home, I soon succumb to the assaults of the "sandman" and drift into dreamland.

Vlissingen is a flourishing town of some seventeen thousand inhabitants, a well-known port and bathing resort.

My place I find is somewhat in the suburbs, but "trams" and boats are near at hand so I soon start out "to see what I can see."

At one extremity of the town a fine promenade called the "North Sea Boulevard," one and one quarter miles long, commands a boundless sea-

view over the broad sands white as snow.   Here
is situated the "Grand Hotel of Baths," crowded
with resorters.   The long line of bathing-ma-
chines on wheels, drawn up out of the tide after
bathing hours and resembling nothing so much
as a row of United States "prairie schooners,"
looks rather odd, as if the population was about to
emigrate overland.   Back of the wide stretch of
snowy sand, is the high dyke or levee, along the
the broad top of which I walk, gazing off first
on one side over the silver sea, then off on the
other across the flat, flat landscape and the quaint
little city spread out in rows along the verdant
banks of the intersecting canals.

Everything in the far distance inland, seems to
dip down into the sea, so monotonously does the
unvarying flatness of the level land, meet the
misty horizon.   Compact, ancient, trim little
houses, closely set together, line the narrow
streets that follow the banks and quays along
the "ditches," while masts and ship-riggings
appear in surprising contiguity to roofs and
chimneys.

Descending from the sea-wall, I find my way
along cityward in the lower areas, crossing innumerable bridges, passing motley groups of
peasants, and sailors of apparently all nations,
and meeting many a wholesome-looking Dutch
serving-maid, in her work-a-day costume of neat,
close, white cap and tidy, short-sleeved, ankle-
lengthed, blue linen gown; bearing on her
shoulders a peculiar wooden yoke, from which
depend long hooks which help sustain the two
pails of water she seemes to be always carrying.
Another novel spectacle to the foreigner, is the
little dog-team often met with, trotting along the
quays.   Sometimes there are as many as six or
eight dogs to one cart; they usually travel on

very harmoniously and obediently, but occasionally a diversion arises. It was my fortune to witness a decided difference in opinion between some of these sturdy and efficient servants, as I strolled along.

On the opposite side of the quay a team of six canines was dogfully doing its duty, hauling a large cart of milk-cans and attending strictly to business, while the driver, a dumpy little old woman in wooden shoes and a singular cap, walked calmly at the side. In front of a large edifice with high steps, another dog-team had paused evidently for rest, and its various members were lying on the pavement lolling their tongues while their mistress sat on the steps gossiping.

As the first team drew near, the other dogs pricked up their ears, growled derisively, and apparently threw insulting remarks at the approaching ones. These, before so complacent, began to grow restive, to toss their heads and to utter low rumbles of remonstrance. Still came the jeers and floutings thicker and faster, from the more fortunate beasts resting in the cool shade, toward their unlucky fellow-creatures still sweating in the harness, until mortal dog could stand no more and there was a wild rush of the industrious team, pell mell, upon their recumbent taunters. These sprang to the combat, and for a few minutes the landscape was obscured by a wild storm of flying cans, carts, milk, butter and green groceries, mingled with tufts of hair, broken straps, madly waving tails and glittering teeth, while all sorts of dog-profanity and Dutch peasant objurgations, resounded upon the air, as the excited mistresses strove to quell the tumultuous conflict.

With a hearty laugh, I left them to their fate and went on my way.

CHAPTER XXXVI.

There is little pretense of artistic effect, architectural or otherwise about the streets of Vlissingen, though there is an ancient church or two, an interesting museum of antiquities, and along the Quay Bellamy are some fine buildings rising behind the tree-shaded promenade on either side; and a few modest specimens of memorial art meet one unexpectedly, as a barrier of but a few feet high completely obstructs one's outlook, such an absence is there within the city of any vantage-ground from which to overlook the scene. I feel a strange sort of helplessness as I walk along, caused I suppose, by my ignorance of the language and by the before mentioned sensation that I cannot conquer, of the instability of what should be solid earth, but what may be, and but for the Hollanders' indefatigable exertions would be, a rolling waste of wide waters.

Thus I go meditatively on, making devious turns as fancy beckons, when I am suddenly brought to a standstill against a blank wall. I look about finding no egress except behind me, and seeing nobody of whom to inquire, except two or three stolid individuals in appearance hopelessly Dutch. I naturally retrace my steps a few paces, but where to go? Across this canal or along that one? On which side is the sea, for it is not visible at this "depth" wherein I stand? Where is the sun? Ah, its vanishing rays are gleaming yonder, that must be seaward; so I proceed in the opposite direction, wondering who of these foreign-looking beings can understand the speech of the alien wanderer. I accost one; alas, "no English, no French, no German;" I pass on; by and by I try again, same result. Still going, I cross a bridge that seems familiar; I am encouraged; but which way to turn? Now I see approaching a man in naval uniform, the style of his "get-up" showing him to be an officer. Owing to the daily plying of steamers between Holland and England, I feel sure that a naval officer must know English, so I again make inquiries. My surmise proves correct and I am politely informed to my astonishment that I am almost at the very door of my hotel, it being only around the next corner and along the next canal, though invisible from our point of view. So I am again housed in safety.

As the sun pours into my chamber next morning, I am dazzled by the glorious radiance of his beams reflected from the shining waters stretching off from almost directly beneath my window. Rising to shut out the too great brilliance, I hear a sort of high, attenuated melody that excites my curiosity; so I look forth and behold a detachment of Dutch soldiers keeping step to the odd music and marching sedately past wearing tall, quaint caps and grave uniforms of somber blue. They do not look as if they were much exhilarated by any prospective "pomp and circumstance of war;" and no wonder, poor fellows; for what an unceasing conflict have they, the Hollanders, had with nature and with man, to preserve their identity as a country and as a nation. At this time great preparations are making for the coming coronation of their young queen, who attains her majority the next year. Among other things is a great, glittering, golden coach, in which she is to ride on that important day. All of these proposed details come to pass later, in successful splendor, as her youthful majesty assumes the reins of her kingdom.

I go out afterward into the radiant atmosphere which yet has no corresponding warmth in it, and take train for Middlebourg, having previously been "coached" by my hostess as to price of ticket and so forth. So I hold out my exact fare to the conductor, but to my dismay he asks me something in Dutch; I do not understand, of course, and inquire successively, "Do you speak English?" "*Sprechen Sie Deutsch?*" and "*Parlez-vous Français?*" but receive in answer only a smiling and apologetic shake of the head. Here a kindly Dutch lady across the aisle notes our perplexity and comes to the rescue in English. She discovers that the conductor wishes to know if I would like a return ticket which is somewhat cheaper. I take advantage of the opportunity and this being settled, thanks to the courteous Dutchwoman, I turn my attention to the watery, windmilly view.

Much of the time we run along between continuous green lanes that, hedged in, shut off any outlook. On the other side, I suppose, are more "ditches."

Arriving at Middlebourg, I find a provincial fair or "kermess" in progress, which is interesting beyond telling. This takes place annually I learn, at this season and continues ten days. To this on certain days of the week, repair the peasants and "peasantesses" in full regalia of their national costumes, which are picturesque in the extreme. They are very diverse, though I am told each province has its distinctive style that is handed down, cut, colors and texture, from generation to generation.

The women are much handsomer than the men, having beautiful, clear, white complexions and noble, intelligent faces. They all wear the close, white coif, which reveals a little of the hair on the forehead but comes down snugly about the ears. A few have frills falling over the neck or standing away from the face. Each is adorned by strange metal ornaments, whether brass or gold I did not ascertain, which are fastened apparently into the very head itself, at the temples, close to the eyes, over which the ornaments dangle or wave, according to their configuration. Some are like flags, others spirals and still others like beads. So far as I observed, the arms were invariably bare and the skirts in no case hid the feet. The colors of the costumes are very modest and tasteful, usually a dark rich brown, plum or wine colored main garment, with delicate blue, lavender or green accessories and with vests or chemisettes of heavily-wrought, snowy lawn or cambric. They wear numerous adornments in the line of necklaces, brooches and chains, and the fingers of many are loaded with rings. It looks particularly odd to see tiny tots of four and five years, tricked out in these antique and elaborate costumes.

The men's garb is not so picturesque. Dark, short jackets, knee-breeches, long hose, low buckled shoes and close-fitting head gear, a sort of compromise between hat and cap, are the chief features of every costume, with little attempt at decoration.

Middlebourg is the capital of Zealand and, according to statistics, has nearly nineteen thousand inhabitants. Some of its promenades are beautiful, though of course, all on a dead level, and its architecture is nobly quaint and remarkable.

The City Hall, situated in the center of the town, is a magnificent and uniquely imposing structure, built by Charles the Bold in 1468. More remote from the busier parts of the city, is an ancient abbey, dating from the twelfth century. To reach this, one follows an angling, narrow way seeming scarcely wide enough for two carts to pass each other, but surprisingly clean, with queer little houses standing close to the pavement; so close indeed that the passer-by may get glimpses of occasional exquisite interiors, some of the rooms being paved and lined up the sides to various heights, with lovely blue and white tiles, while copper, brass and pewter gleam out of unexpected corners, all burnished to a painful degree, and the shining windows are gay with colored blooms.

This street leads into a sort of wide ornamental area still inclosed by the little houses, but across which, filling in the opposite side, is a queer, old Dutch manor-house of 1590, wonderfully and astonishingly ornate. Off at the right, an arch through the solid mason-work of the encircling houses, leads into an extensive court paved with brick. Here too an unbroken wall of buildings, but of a heavier, loftier order, surrounds the place, and is so high that a nearly perpetual twilight pervades the scene. A ponderous erection in the center is designed, I presume, for a decorative fountain, though no water is visible. The great tower of the abbey looms up at one hand. Perfect silence reigns. It is the very abode of peace, or is it death? Not a footfall echoes but my own as I cross the court and pass through a corresponding arch in the opposite wall, coming out on the other side of the abbey, which looks grim and forbidding. I do not enter, but go on down a pleasant street and soon find myself on the way to the station, along an avenue of some pretentions and importance, architecturally and commercially, and shaded by handsome trees.

The quaint wares of the Dutch country are set forth attractively in great profusion, and the quainter people throng the thoroughfares, passing placidly along. I am unable to resist the novel displays at every hand and finally pause at an entrancing window to wonder and to admire. The proprietor comes out to welcome me and proves to be a very attractive young man of fair skin and large, candid, blue eyes. He speaks English perfectly and is most cordial and polite to the foreigner, giving much courteous and acceptable information. I indulge in a few modest purchases and learn that his name is "Mynheer F. B. Den Boer," which truly is deliciously "Dutchy."

Then I go on to the station and soon find myself once more in Vlissingen.

Unfortunately I can not tarry in this singularly interesting country, so, London being the next stage of my journey, I inquire next day as to means of transportation to the docks. Again I am told to my amusement that I can "take a boat," this seeming to be as matter of course a proceeding here, as elsewhere to take a "tram." However, I start out piloted by a friendly German porter; crossing the road, we go a few steps along the canal and lo, here is the point of embarkation.

A bustling little steam-launch puffs up and, for the almost infinitessimal sum of ten cents Dutch, or four cents United States, the porter, my bags and myself are conveyed over the smooth, dark waters of the canal, to the other side of the town, where is the slip of the "Zealand Steamship Company."

Though I found transportation rates so exceedingly small, my expenses otherwise in Holland did not show that prices here are particularly low, and I am told that living in this country is really very expensive, very much more so than in France or Germany.

But now I must bid it all good-bye, so turning my back upon the low-lying shores, I board the waiting vessel and soon we steam out of the harbor, with the prow of the good ship ''Duitschland'' set forward toward the ''white cliffs of Albion.''

CHAPTER XXXVII.

My lone sister, we have journeyed long in
spirit together.   The record is lengthy, yet the
half is not told.   Far enough away, indeed, am
I still from my "ain countree," and

> "Many a day
> Must roll away"·

ere again I set foot upon my native shores.

How I returned across the tossing channel, on
to rare old England with its lovely lakes and
scented hedge-rows : how I wandered thence into
stern Scotland, through its tangled glens, its
heathery slopes, its mountain and its moors, past
Stirling bold, up to ' 'Edinboro' Town;'' thence
across to gray Glasgow and out once more upon
the mighty main, is yet unuttered and unwritten.

I would not exhaust your interest nor hold
you till your eye be strained and your ear
weary.   Shall we here wave adieus and drift
apart as

> "Fair laughs the morn and soft the zephyr blows;
> While proudly riding o'er the azure realm,
> In gallant trim the gilded vessel goes?"

As for the rest, shall it be written hereafter?
Who can tell?

Take up the tale for yourself, dear sister, and
bring it to your own conclusion ; thus will you
be more fully edified and entertained ; thus will
you lay up for yourself stores of refreshing recollections for that season when you sit solitary,

'Between the dark and the daylight,
When the night is beginning to lower.''

Thus may you prosper ; and in whatever journey you may undertake, above all in the wide,
devious and but once traveled journey of life,
both now and forever may God be with you.

FINIS.

**** The author would explain that wherever quotations
from foreign poems, placards, inscriptions and so forth, have
been given with quotation marks, the translation so used is the
author's own.****